Gangsters of Shanghai

An International Mystery Thriller

A novel by Gerry O'Sullivan

Rosetta No. 3 A/C Pty Ltd
PO Box 318
Darlinghurst NSW 1300
Australia

Editor 1st edition: Jim Parsons
Editor 2nd edition: Claude Lambert, Damien Peters

Cover Design (ebook): Josh Murtha
Cover Design (print): Fahimah Badrulhisham

Print layout by eBooks By Barb for booknook.biz

ISBN: [978-0-9874517-2-9]

A CIP catalogue record for this book is available from
the National Library of Australia

Dedicated to my wife Yumi and my daughter Sophia

Table of Contents

Part One

–

The Bridge of the Nine Turnings

Shanghai – 1927

Chapter 1

THE SEVERED HEAD OF A young man had been squeezed into a bamboo birdcage and hoisted on a pole above the Nantao market place. It swayed gently in the early spring breeze. When I saw it, I learned the true nature of Shanghai.

But I should have recognised it for what it was, an omen. I didn't know it then, as I stared at its leering grimace, but before the afternoon was out I would face death myself.

I took a deep breath, ignoring the fear clawing at my gut, and tried to remain calm and unruffled like the people walking by, most of them hardly glancing at the horror of it. 'You're a long way from Ireland now, Mikie Gallagher,' I thought to myself.

An hour earlier I had taken a rickshaw from the International Settlement down through the French Concession and passed through an ancient arched gateway to enter the Old City.

I'd briskly stepped through the gate to Nantao and entered the China of a hundred years ago, excited to return. This precinct continually drew me back because it was the only part of Shanghai that looked like real China. The country of dragons and curved temple roofs and kerbside calligraphers, unblighted by neon lights, opium fumes, automobiles and the blare of jazz.

Perhaps Nantao reminded me of the pictures I had seen in the Burleighs' Chinese Room. I thought then of their grand home, of that eerie Chinese room and their love of all things oriental. Seven years since I last saw her alive, a chasm in my life seven years wide.

China had been Fiona's dream not mine. Yet after that last day I had made it my dream too, and I hoped that if Fiona's spirit watched over me, she would see that I had taken on the country and made a man of myself here, a man worthy of Fiona Burleigh.

In the heart of the Old City was the four-hundred-year-old Yu Gardens, a Chinese delight with a rockery, temple, ponds, towers and pavilions. The Lotus Pool, crossed by a zigzag bridge, was known as 'the Bridge of the

Nine Turnings.' Markets, teahouses and street hawker stalls surrounded the garden area.

My destination was the Gardens. I liked to sit by the pond and think about China, and I would daydream that Fiona would appear from nowhere and just come sit beside me on the bench.

Since arriving in Shanghai, I'd spent many hours checking both the French and International Settlement phone books, shipping lists, as well as customs arrivals records since 1920. I looked for her name everywhere, even becoming an obsessive reader of the mosquito press for their gossip, party photographs and reports of love affairs, engagements and marriages. But I never saw any mention of her. I had to content myself with my dreams and memories.

Nantao was the original city and had once been surrounded by a high stone wall. Although most of the wall had disappeared over time, the district had kept its sense of separateness from the cosmopolitan, neon-lit Shanghai, inundated with the latest fashions and entertainments of the west.

Few foreigners ventured into Nantao, apart from a very small number of White Russian refugees who had fallen as low as the poorest Chinese peasant.

Now, transfixed by that vile sight of that bloody, severed head, I stood in the thoroughfare and let the crowd mill around me. I squeezed my eyes to blink the sight away and pressed on.

What was it that drew me into such an alien place on the one day of precious leave that I had? I could have been above at the police canteen on Gordon Road drinking a few bottles of stout and getting vital tips from the older constables. God knows I needed all the help I could get on the most dangerous police beat in the world. I'd only been in the thick of it with the newly-formed Emergency Unit for about eight months, the opportunity to leave day-to-day policing having come as a complete surprise to me, especially as an untested twenty-three-year-old.

The canteen at Gordon Road Depot of the Shanghai Municipal Police was a pleasant enough room, with a billiard table, dartboard, card table, a nice hot coal fireplace and a gramophone perpetually wound up to play John McCormack and Caruso. McCormack provided a nice sentimental touch of Ireland here on the opposite side of the world.

Shanghai was in a virtual state of war and for a young constable of the Shanghai Municipal Police Emergency Unit, it was sixteen-hour days of stop-and-search patrols and constant tension. Our nerves were shredded in no time. The next Chinaman you stopped could pull a gun on you in a flash. You could have a bullet between the eyes as quick as you'd get an insect bite.

Yesterday afternoon, patrolling down Nanking Road past the swanky department stores with John Everett, a young constable from Berkshire, the two of us leading a mixed patrol of Chinese and Sikh constables, I suddenly stopped dead, my heart jumping out of my chest.

It was a four-foot square picture of Fiona, her eyes lowered and her lips pouting at me from the wall. I stood there, frozen. I stared at the picture in shock and excitement. Was she still alive?

'Bloody hell, Gallagher, it's only a film poster,' laughed Everett. 'Get a grip on yourself.'

It took a few seconds for his words to sink in. I looked again. It was a publicity poster for a new Hollywood release, '*Mantrap*' starring Clara Bow. Miss Bow bore a most uncanny likeness to Fiona. The same heart-shaped face, high cheekbones, pouting lips, and wavy hair. Those deep soulful eyes, penetrating and longing, asking a question that couldn't be answered.

That night, in my narrow single bed in the unmarried men's quarters at Gordon Road Police Depot I dreamed of Fiona and the day she showed me the Chinese Room at Burleigh Castle.

'Wouldn't it be great if you took me to China one day,' she said. 'I would really like that, Michael.'

It was the last conversation I ever had with her before she died. And here I am, still a griffin, trying to figure out a country that scholars couldn't understand after a lifetime of study. But I had this idea that, if I could somehow understand China, it could help me understand Fiona and what she was thinking on that last day.

As soon as I walked inside the Nantao archway, I was immersed in an alien world—unfamiliar yet powerfully compelling to me. Mothers held babies that looked used up, eyes like saucers in their heads. Bursts of conversation in Shanghai dialect, every sentence like a shouted argument.

Skinny, ragged children crowded round me, even children of five or six, shouting, 'Cigarette, mister.' Voices hissed at me, 'Smoke, sir?' 'You want my sister? Very young and clean.'

I felt a tugging at my trousers leg. I looked down to see a toothless old creature smiling at me grotesquely with two stumps of legs covered in putrid sores—smiling and waving a begging bowl towards me. Repulsed, I pulled back from this horrid sight, and hurried along through the crush of people.

'Fuck off' was my response to all. English speaker or no, the sentiment cut through.

If I were seen handing coins to one person, in the space of a second, twenty people would surround me with hands out for more.

Every aspect of life was displayed on the narrow streets. Mothers cooked for families on charcoal heaters, and men received a shave and haircut as they squatted on child-sized kerbside stools. Old men wearing reading glasses on the end of their noses painted letters of Chinese calligraphy for illiterate coolies from the countryside. From open shop-houses came the click, click, click of abacus beads. A poverty-stricken intellectual chalked his biography on the pavement.

I saw a newspaper pasted to a wall, and a group gathered around, pushing and shoving to read it. A headline stated in large bold print: '*City under siege.*'

Street-side butchers beheaded chickens, trails of ash from their cigarettes floating down onto the meat. Entire refugee families sat kerbside, slurping bowls of noodle soup. A wind-up gramophone shrieked out the discordant wails of Peking opera, while across the street another gramophone drowned it out with an Al Jolson song.

A well-dressed Chinese man, wearing a snazzy tailored suit, stepped in front of me and hawked a glob of phlegm in my direction. Only a quick step to the side prevented it from landing on me. 'Get out of China, you child killer,' he sneered, before turning and swiftly moving off through the crowds. I stared after him, wondering if I should give him a bloody good thrashing, but in seconds he was swallowed up in the Nantao crowds.

The narrow space widened and fed into a central square. The crush of bodies was intense and I remembered to check my wallet.

I pressed on towards Yu Gardens. There was a commotion in the middle of the square and I saw that a young man wearing a student's black silk robe stood on a wooden box, making a speech to the crowd. Several of his colleagues distributed leaflets. Someone thrust a leaflet in my hand and I glanced at the paper, taking in the poor quality ink on cheap paper. The headline, in large, thick characters, said in both Chinese and English: *China for the Chinese – Throw out the Foreigner.*

I felt the press of bodies as a line of khaki-uniformed Chinese policemen, carrying tall bamboo poles, barged through the crowd. The young man jumped off his soapbox and struggled through the sea of bodies, but in a few moments he and his colleagues were caught and soon had their hands trussed like the legs of the live chickens for sale at the nearby stall.

Within minutes the police had pushed and manhandled the crowd to create an open circle in the middle of the square. The trussed-up students were brought to the centre and made to kneel. Then, through the crowd came another policeman, a tall, muscular man with a shaved head. In a moment he had stripped off his tunic and shirt and stood bare-chested. One of his comrades handed him a long, broad, evil-looking sword. He flexed his muscles like a circus strongman about to do a trick. He turned in a circle surveying his audience—haughty and defiant.

I pushed my way to the front of the crowd, flipped open my brown leather wallet, and addressed the Chinese policeman directly, speaking in my Gordon Road classroom Shanghainese.

'*Stop! I order you to stop. I am from the Shanghai Municipal Police and I demand that you stop at once.*'

The policeman held the sword up to his eye, and peered along the blade —a slow, careful examination.

'*Fuck off, you foreign pig,*' he said, '*you have no power here. Fuck off back to the Settlement where your badge might mean something... for now.*'

I folded my arms and looked him in the eye.

'*You cannot summarily execute someone without due process. The Municipal Council will not stand for it.*'

Clenching his sword in his fist, he punched my face, the sword handle acting as a knuckle-duster. I reeled back and would have fallen except for the crush of bodies behind me. His companion pointed his long-barrelled revolver in my face, his finger whitened as he squeezed the trigger.

'*Watch the show, foreigner. This is for you.*'

Two policemen gripped my arms and pulled me to a standing position.

Then, a small, slim, raggedly-dressed Chinese man of indeterminate age was suddenly standing beside me. He spoke to the policeman rapidly in Shanghai dialect, almost too fast for me to follow. '*Leave the foreigner with me. He is soft in the head. I will carry him home. Let me make a fare. Please, brother, let me eat today.*'

The policemen pushed me towards the ragged man. He gripped my arm and said, '*Come away now,*' as if speaking to a young child. But I had to look.

In a matter-of-fact businesslike way, the big, bare-chested policeman with the sword stepped from student to student and, with a smooth, lazy movement, sliced off the head of each man, one by one.

'*Ayah!*' cried the audience, half in fear and half in admiration of the showmanship of the executioner.

In just a few seconds, four bodies had slumped on the ground, and four heads rolled on the cobblestone like footballs, blood gushing. It was ghastly but I couldn't look away. Each head still bore the expression of its owner at the moment of death: surprise, horror, defiance, fear.

The other policemen stepped forward with sharpened bamboo poles. They speared the points into the open wounds of each neck, leaned on the poles, to apply pressure and wedge the poles securely into the severed heads. Then, they hoisted the polls aloft and marched onward through the crowd with a chant of '*Death to the communists.*' Drops of blood flecked them like the first hint of rain. They appeared to take delight in the splashes of crimson appearing on their khaki uniforms.

I pushed through the bodies to the nearby laneway and vomited bile into the smelly drain.

'*I take you home,*' said the raggedly-dressed man. I recognised him then; he had been my rickshaw coolie on the journey to Nantao.

'*What's your name, boy?*' I asked him in Shanghainese as I mounted the rickshaw and he stooped to raise the handles.

'Wang,' he grunted, and didn't speak another word for the rest of the journey.

Chapter 2

THE RICKSHAW COOLIE JOGGED ALONG at a cracking pace and in a short time we were through the archway from Nantao and into Frenchtown. The pleasant cobblestone streets were clean and orderly, nicely shaded by plane trees; the aroma of fresh baked croissants came from the brightly lit patisseries. Smartly uniformed gendarmes marshalled traffic. The red-painted window frames and doors enlivened the pretty grey stone buildings. The rickshaw coolie stopped to let a green-coloured tram, its bell clanging cheerfully, turn from a side street. A movement caught my eye. I turned to look towards the kerb. A live fashion model posed in a shop window as she displayed the latest style from Paris. She was a Chinese girl, tall, beautiful and elegant, her face frozen in haughty disdain. As the rickshaw pressed on, I twisted my head, staring at the model, transfixed by her beauty and yearning to touch her. But, as always, that weighing scale inside my head began its measurement, judging and comparing the model to my incomparable, irreplaceable lost love.

As soon as we moved north of Avenue Edward VII we had crossed from the French Concession to the International Settlement. Rickshaws and cyclists darted in and out between American sports cars and French sedans, while stately green trams rattled along their track lines, bells ringing 'ding-dong' to clear the way.

Banners ablaze with Chinese characters hung from shop front awnings. The bright lights of department stores, cafés, cinemas and restaurants competed for the attention of pedestrians on the densely packed kerbside.

I saw a couple of lost English tourists—very few of them left now due to the crisis—stopping at the street corner, squinting at the street sign, unfurling a tourist map, their confused faces an invitation to be robbed or gulled by a conman.

Pretty young *modeng* girls wearing cloche hats, coats and carrying handbags from London and Paris promenaded along the kerbside, walking confidently, stopping occasionally to examine the shop windows. I stared at them all, dreaming of the possibilities. Older women in black silk pyjamas minced along with small baby steps, their bound feet encased in baby-sized slippers.

I felt my spirits soar. There was something about Shanghai; it was simply *alive*. The most alive city in the world, I reckoned. Crowded, insane, hot, dirty, corrupt, a cesspool of illness and poverty. And yet... glamorous, sophisticated, worldly. Jazz clubs, casinos, movie stars, opium dens, and, oh, the women.

The sun had set and in a few minutes it was dark. My favourite time was after sundown when the International Settlement was lit by a million neon signs. Red, green, blue and orange lights pulsed, casting a multi-coloured glow over the streets. When it rained, the colours were reflected in the puddles. It was an electric city, throbbing with colour, sound, move-ment and sex. Anything seemed possible now.

Shanghai was the place to be, it was so *hai pai*. The term meant something cool, hip or fashionable. The literal translation was 'Shanghai Style' which said it all. Peking intellectuals had used it as a criticism of Shanghai—criticism of Shanghai's admiration of money and western culture, all that was crass and new, the jazz, the sex, the movies. But in true Shanghai style, the locals had embraced the term *hai pai* and turned it into a compliment. Shanghailanders would say, 'I love your hat; it's so *hai pai*!'

No matter there was an army camped outside the city, or teams of saboteurs and assassins inside it. No matter that in Nantao children died in the streets while severed heads floated overhead in birdcages; Shanghai was simply buzzing. If you wanted to drink, shop, fornicate, gamble, or stare at visiting Hollywood movie stars, then Shanghai was the place for it. Every day—until recently, anyway—the Shanghai papers carried breathless reports of the visits of the likes of Douglas Fairbanks, Mary Pickford and Charlie Chaplin. Since arriving in Shanghai I had never felt so alive, ever.

* * *

The events of the day had a strange effect on me. I felt restless and agitated, tired but unable to sit still. I found it impossible to forget—the image of that execution never far from my mind. And the model in the window... Christ, she was beautiful. The day's brutality, but also the display of sexual allure, created a strange and unsettling compulsion to break the rules. A longing—for something.

I drank a few bottles of stout in the canteen, remaining silent while conversation flowed around me. All the talk was of the emergency facing the city.

A Scottish sergeant, a red whiskey-nosed man with greying hair, a former merchant sailor, had been in St Petersburg in 1917 and had stories that would set the hairs rising on the back of your neck.

'I'm tellin' yez, God's own truth, I saw them take Imperial Naval officers off the ships and nail their gold epaulettes into their shoulders. You wouldn't do it to a dog.'

'Unless you were Chinese, of course,' laughed one of the canteen wags. 'And you'd have the dog fried with noodles and sour sauce!'

Everyone at the table roared with exaggerated laughter. In truth, we were as nervous as anybody else in the city. A gun and a uniform didn't give you immunity from revolution.

I finished my drink and bid the group good night. But I didn't go to my room. I left the depot and flagged a rickshaw and went to Bubbling Well Road. I paid off the coolie near a row of bright, loud, neon-lit nightclubs. Walking along the street, I saw young women from a dozen nations walking up and down, their walk exaggeratedly sexual. 'Hello, handsome', 'Hey there, Joe Brooks', 'Which hotel you stay?'

A woman stepped in front of me, aggressively blocking my path. She was older than me, European. Blonde and blue-eyed, quite tall. Pretty face, heavily made up, the cosmetics almost hiding her tiredness.

'Come to my room for a drink,' she said in Russian-accented English.

'All right then,' I replied. We linked arms and she led me to a narrow side street off Bubbling Well Road. Entering a dark doorway, we walked up an unlit, narrow stairwell, the ancient steps creaking under our feet. After climbing two flights of stairs we entered a small, dark apartment. She turned a switch and a side lamp came on. The room was small and clean, but didn't contain much in the way of comfort other than an old couch and a cracked glass-topped coffee table.

A curtained doorway led to what I presumed was a bedroom.

She slipped off her jacket, revealing a slinky, body-hugging silk dress of a vivid cobalt blue colour. Her figure was slim and full-breasted.

She held out her hand and said, 'Five American dollars. You can do anything.'

Just then, I could hear my father's voice, as clearly as if he were in the room. 'Women of easy virtue,' he intoned in a voice laden with condemnation.

I fumbled in my pockets and found the requisite money. My hands trembled as I counted out the dollar notes. Feeling fear as much as excitement, I thought, well, I have to start somewhere. Time to grow up, boy.

She took the money and walked to an old sideboard. As she slipped the money in the drawer, a framed photograph on the wall caught my eye. It was a family portrait, and showed a man wearing a Russian imperial navy uniform, heavy with gold braid, and the four gold hoops of a captain on his sleeve. Beside him, his wife, a handsome elegant woman, in a white dress with an extravagantly wide white hat, and three pretty young girls, in their early and mid teens, wearing white party dresses with ribbons in their ringleted hair. Clearly, the youngest of the three girls was my companion of the night.

Oh God, can I do this, I asked myself. An aristocratic girl reduced to selling herself. I thought again of Fiona.

There was a sudden motion as the curtain was swished aside. A man stood there in the bedroom doorway. He was a big man, well developed and strong-looking. He wore a careworn suit, black pinstripe, glossy with age, a narrow stringy tie knotted in a grimy collar. His hair was cropped short, scars from an old wound visible through the stubble. In his hand he held a sharp, evil-looking flick knife, pointed towards me, the blade held strong and steady, menacing.

'Give me your wallet, pretty boy,' he growled. A Russian accent.

'I can't do that,' I replied, keeping my voice even and slow.

She turned to him and snapped, 'Stop it, Alexei! He's a paying customer.'

'I will fucking cut you, boy.'

'You've made a mistake. You don't know who I am,' I said slowly and calmly.

He stepped forward, waving the knife towards me, its point glinting in the lamplight. A smell of vodka hung heavy in the air.

'Think you can take me, pretty boy? I rode with the Tsar's Cossacks.'

'You don't know who I am,' I said again.

He came nearer, sweeping the knife in a wild motion.

I bent my knees slightly, my feet pressing into the ground. I shifted my body into the basic '*Defendu*' stance.

He swung the knife again; I stepped aside, allowing his motion to carry him past me. I grabbed his arm with both hands, and simultaneously drove a kick into his knee. As he stumbled, I jerked his arm, causing him to drop the knife. He collapsed on his knees like a man at prayer. I drove an elbow into his face, controlling the blow so as not to drive his nose cartilage into his brain and kill him. He collapsed backwards, moaning as he held his face in his hands.

'I told you,' I said, as I picked up the knife, folded it and dropped it in my pocket.

The woman stood aside impassively, observing. Watching me now, she stared defiantly, arms folded.

'I will not refund you,' she said sharply.

'Keep it!' I said and turned abruptly, almost stumbling, and walked rapidly towards the entrance.

As I hurried down the dark stairwell, I heard a lock closing behind me. When I reached Bubbling Well Road I dropped the knife through the grille of a storm water drain.

I felt my whole body shake. Jesus, that's twice in one day to be nearly killed. What kind of city was this? What was I thinking to land myself in this cauldron?

Ireland – 1917–1919

Chapter 3

June 1917

WHEN I WAS THIRTEEN MY father, Sergeant James Francis Gallagher of the Royal Irish Constabulary, took me up to Burleigh Castle. He was responding to a report telephoned in to the police barracks of poaching on the estate, and he took me up there on the bar of his big black RIC issue bicycle. It was a lovely early summer day, not a cloud in the blue sky.

Located a mile from the town of Kilmallock in County Limerick, the castle was the seat of the Burleigh family, and it was the finest and most impressive ancestral castle in the whole county. It had been a 16th century castle, had been built on and added to many times, each wing showing the architecture of a different era. In the summer time, an orchestra was heard to play in the castle's ballroom, and cars drove down from Dublin, crammed with smartly-dressed people to attend the goings-on. In the wintertime, scarlet-jacketed horsemen rode out from the castle and hunted the fox, packs of hounds baying for the poor creature's blood.

Standing at the kitchen door, Father spoke to Lord Burleigh's head gamekeeper, recording the details of the poaching case in his black police notebook. He wrote slowly and meticulously, as always; even the most casual note was always penned in the most elaborate copperplate hand-writing.

I checked to ensure that Father was fully occupied. If he spotted me sneaking off he would give me some tedious but character-improving chore, like oiling his bicycle.

'And what time was that, Mister Ryan?' I heard him ask the gamekeeper in his deep cadence, the same voice he used to deliver his pronouncements to me.

Father's back was turned away from me so I wandered round to the kitchen garden and as I stepped through the green wood gate I came close to colliding with a pretty girl of about my age, wearing a sky-blue dress and shiny black patent leather shoes.

'My dog's caught in a snare!' she gasped at me, her face ashen with fear.

'Show me where,' I said.

She pointed in the general direction of the meadow beyond the gardens. I sprinted as fast as I could, heading towards the sound of the dog's howling. At the far end of the field, near the ditch there was movement. A little brown and white dog thrashed and struggled for air, his neck caught tight in a wire snare, looped round his neck like a hangman's noose. Such a snare was intended to catch rabbits but could be deadly for a little dog or cat. I kneeled beside him and hooked my fingers under the wire. Holding it tight, I sawed through with my pocketknife. The snare was cut and the dog free. He collapsed where he was, panting and gasping for breath, his whole body heaving.

I felt much the same myself. I lay back on the ground and then the girl was standing over me. She was extraordinarily pretty. Her hair was blonde but she had dark brown eyes.

'What's your name?' she demanded, imperiously.

'I'm Michael Gallagher,' I replied. 'Who are you?'

'Don't be silly,' she said. 'Everyone knows who I am. I'm Fiona Burleigh. I'm Lord Burleigh's daughter.'

I stared at her with my mouth open.

'Close your mouth. You'll catch flies. Do you want to come back and play here with me?'

'Y-yes,' I replied uncertainly, for I had never in my life talked to such an apparition.

* * *

Two days later, I walked slowly up the long, lonely driveway, and found Fiona in the kitchen garden. She came running towards me, the little dog held in her arms. 'Look, look, Brownie,' she cried excitedly, 'it's our knight in shining armour.' She held the dog close to me and his little pink tongue began licking my face excitedly.

'Thank you for what you did,' she said.

'You're welcome, miss,' I replied.

'Don't call me "miss"; you're my guest.'

I looked into her dark brown eyes as she smiled.

'What should I call you?'

'Call me Fiona, you silly boy.'

'Yes, miss.'

She raised her eyes in exasperation.

'Yes, Fiona.'

We played in the formal gardens and around the farmyard and stables, and as we played games through the long summer afternoon, into the bright evening, I forgot that she was a daughter of a peer.

The garden and farm provided an endless range of hiding spots, places to explore, and ladders to climb. Dusty lofts and hay barns became the decks of pirate ships, castle battlements and secret hideouts. Fiona was a strong girl and, despite the pastel dresses she wore, she enjoyed the same games of adventure and imagination that I did. We became buccaneers, African explorers, knights-in-armour, and Robin Hood and Maid Marion. The summer evening stretched out endlessly as we played until we were exhausted, Fiona's little dog 'Brownie' following us everywhere, barking and panting with excitement.

* * *

After the first day, I visited as often as I could get away from Father. One evening, towards the end of summer, when there was a sense of finality in the air, we walked through a field below the castle. The field was dotted with well-fed, contented milking cows lazily chewing the cud and watching us as we walked by. I stopped by a gap in the hedgerow and stared at Burleigh Castle, fine and regal in the afternoon sun. Fiona said, 'Would you like to see the castle?'

I felt my face blush and I shook my head.

'Don't be silly; everyone wants to see the castle. Come on,' she said, as she took my hand and pulled me towards the front door.

The building was large and square and imposing. Fiona pushed open the main door, dark timber bound with metal strips. As the door opened, there stood a middle-aged, grey-haired gentleman with a severe expression. It must be Lord Burleigh, I thought, and felt my face blush hot.

'Good evening, Miss Fiona.'

'Good evening, Porter,' replied Fiona. She turned to me. 'That's Porter the butler.'

I stammered a greeting to him and felt Fiona pulling my hand impatiently.

The floor was a polished, chocolate mahogany timber as was the stairway that rose up from the end of the long hallway.

Fiona turned and spoke to Porter. 'We will use the drawing room.'

'Very good, Miss Fiona.'

Porter walked down the hallway, his gleaming leather shoes clicking smartly on the timber floor. He opened a door and we stepped inside. The room had a sunny bay window looking onto a garden with a riot of vivid flowers and shrubs. It was warm and comfortably furnished with a variety of soft couches, armchairs, and rugs. The walls displayed a mixture of English landscapes and what I much later recognised as Buddhist artefacts.

I walked around the room, taking note of its casual elegance. The walls were a soft white, and contrasted beautifully with the chocolate mahogany floor. Vases of cut flowers were placed around the room.

'Sit down, silly,' said Fiona.

I sat, my body sinking into the soft couch.

My eye was drawn to a painting on the wall. It was large, about four feet square, in a very narrow black frame, and the picture itself was almost all white space. With a few lines of black ink, the artist had drawn simple brushstrokes to represent a young woman wearing a long robe, standing by a lake and holding a parasol. In the background was a weeping willow tree, its leaves trailing into the water, and in the far distance, a mountain peak was enveloped in summer haze. It was exquisitely beautiful.

'Wait here,' said Fiona. 'I want to show you the book my aunt sent from London.' She ran to the drawing room door, opened it and went through to the hallway.

My mouth tightened, an unexpected rush of jealousy overwhelming me. I knew I wanted this. When I'm a man I will live in Fiona's world, I thought.

Fiona bustled in with a heavy gilt-edged book in her arms. 'What's up with you? You look like you have seen a ghost.'

She followed my gaze and saw that I was staring at the painting.

'Oh yes, that's China. Beautiful, isn't it? My grandfather brought it back. My family is very interested in China. I long to see it one day.'

* * *

Over the next days and weeks we explored great big dark rambling rooms, the library, a portrait gallery, and attics that held all sorts of strange and wonderful objects.

One day in the main hall we really did encounter Lord Peter Burleigh,

Fiona's father. He was a tall, thin man who wore a tweed suit and carried an air of professorial distraction. He wore a yellow silk cravat. A folded copy of the *Irish Times* stuck out from under his arm. 'The Protestant paper', my father called it. His Lordship waved to us distractedly with his pipe.

He stopped and peered at us through his reading glasses.

'Hello, there,' he said. 'And whom do we have here, then?'

'This is my friend Michael Gallagher, Daddy.'

'Oh, Gallagher. Your father is the sergeant?'

'Yes, sir, that's right.'

'Oh, grand fellow, Sergeant Gallagher. And do you want to be a policeman, too?'

'No, sir. I want to be a gentleman.'

His Lordship laughed gently. 'Well, jolly good show, young Gallagher. If you work out how to do it, you must tell me how it's done.' Then, with a distracted wave of the newspaper, he padded down the hallway.

Summer 1919

During the summer holidays Fiona and I were inseparable. Then, come September, she would take the train to Dublin and catch the boat from Kingstown to make her way to her boarding school in England. I missed her when she was gone and, by the time she came back during the following summer holiday, I was so shy with her that it took several hours of awkward silence and gazing at my shoes before I found my voice again.

The Fiona that returned from school during the summers of 1918 and 1919 was a strange creature, increasingly sophisticated and glamorous. She didn't come home at Christmas or Easter, spending those breaks with her aunt in London. Fiona's mother had died when she was only two years old and Lord Burleigh, Fiona explained, wanted her to spend time with her nearest adult female relatives in the absence of a loving mother.

When she spoke of her time in England she described alien things— lacrosse, hockey, omnibuses and taxicabs. There were descriptions of afternoon teas and pantomimes and experiments with lipstick and powder.

Nevertheless, once she had settled at home and I had found my voice with her, we fell again into that easy friendship that had started in 1917. As soon as she had put on an old summer dress and sandals and tied up her hair, she was my playmate again. We resumed our games of pirates, explorers and damsels in distress.

Now we were almost fifteen and our games were played with less enthusiasm. Instead, we experienced moments of awkward eye contact and hands that accidently brushed against each other, causing what felt like electric shocks.

She gave me a portrait photograph of herself taken at the school. In the picture the sun shone through her pinned-up hair as she stared wistfully into the distance, her eyes turned away from the photographer and his device. I kept the picture under my pillow and would fall asleep staring at it, a soft kiss placed on its smooth surface before my eyes grew too heavy to continue my vigil.

In my heart I knew I loved her, but she was the daughter of Lord Burleigh; I was the village sergeant's son. I was certain I would marry her, despite the unbridgeable gap between us. It was clear that I needed to find a way to bridge that gap.

For guidance, I looked at my books full of heroic derring-do. My task was difficult but clear. I needed to become a famous explorer, or soldier— an empire man. I would win a great battle, discover a lost continent, or find a diamond mine. I would receive great awards. I dreamed of the possibilities. General Sir Michael Gallagher VC. Lord Gallagher of Kilmallock.

Then, as Fiona's equal, I would speak to Lord Burleigh. The butler would call me 'Sir.' Lord Burleigh would greet me in the drawing room, shake my hand, and offer me a drink and say, 'Welcome to the family, old chap. Jolly good work you did in the Transvaal.' I would modestly deflect his praise, declare my love for his daughter, and ask for her hand in marriage. He, of course, would say yes with hearty congratulations and remark, 'Thought you'd never get around to it.'

Shanghai – 1924–1927

Chapter 4

I'D COME OUT FROM IRELAND in 1924, aged twenty, looking for an adventure—and something more. Something that I could not even define.

By 1923, Dublin was a bleak, grey city, run by bleak grey men. All bowed down before the strangling grip of the moralising Catholic clergy. There wasn't much to do unless you counted belting down endless pints of Guinness. And I had done enough of that.

I had a yearning, a longing, for something—a different life. Something was missing, that I could almost taste, but couldn't name. I knew that my yearning was caught up with Fiona's death, and my father's, and all that had happened to my family, my country and myself.

There wasn't much excitement in Dublin. Working as a sales clerk at Brown Thomas Department Store in Grafton Street didn't satisfy me. It was a job arranged by my uncle; I had no choice in the matter. I resented touching the forelock to the wealthy customers, and I'd quickly become bored and yearned for something more. I wasn't so old that I didn't occasionally flick through my old schoolboy collection of adventure books. G. A. Henty was my favourite; '*Under Drake's Flag*' and '*With Clive in India*' were my bedside companions.

I'd often gone to the dances at the Banbay Hall in Parnell Square. It was a venue for country people. A big hall, with a stage for the band, and seats around the perimeter. Girls sat on one side, boys and young men on the other. When the band started, it took an age for the first couples to appear on the floor. It was a brave man who'd take that long walk across the polished floor to the girls to ask somebody to dance, almost certainly get refused, and then walk, shamefaced, back to his lair among the drunken young men he arrived with.

The girls, from the country, were there to meet a man who would marry them and save them from a job in the new Free State's Civil Service, and take them back to a nice farm down the country, just like the one they came from. The girls prized their purity to an extreme; I gave up on them and took refuge in the drink.

I often thought of the ambitions I'd had when Fiona was alive. Becoming the great empire man, winning medals, becoming one of the toffs. Perhaps it was worth pursuing even now. It was either that or become suffocated in a country run by priests, marry some red-faced country girl and spend my life bowing and scraping to customers at Brown Thomas.

I knew there had to be more to life than working five and a half days a week, a half-day off on Saturday, a few pints and a dance on Saturday night, and Mass on Sunday.

Dublin 15 April 1923

It was a pleasant spring day, and I walked along Grafton Street, a ham sandwich in greaseproof paper bulging in my jacket pocket and a flask of sweet, milky tea in my hand. I was heading towards St Stephen's Green with nothing in mind other than some lunch and enjoying the sun.

As I walked by the Shelbourne Hotel, about to cross the road to the park, I saw a member of the Civic Guard walking towards me, a man with sergeant's stripes on his sleeve. It still felt slightly strange to see the dark blue uniform, when I had spent my life surrounded by the RIC bottle green.

'Well, hello there, stranger,' said the policeman.

I stopped and looked at him, confused for a moment by the peak of his cap pulled low over his brow.

'Dan! Is it yourself?' I replied happily as I shook his hand vigorously.

'How're you, Michael? You look more like your father.'

It was a pleasure to see Dan Ryan, a Corkman who had been a constable in my father's station up to my departure from County Limerick in 1920.

We chatted for a few minutes and, seeing my packed lunch, he suggested that he would sit with me for a short while and we chatted about the old days, mainly the happier times before The Troubles began.

As we chatted a question began to form itself in my mind.

'Dan, I hate to talk about that last day, but do you mind if I ask you something?'

'A sure, go ahead, Michael.'

'Well, you know that I was close to Miss Burleigh. Do you have any idea what really happened to her?'

He sucked air through his teeth, a habit I remembered from the times when my father asked him a difficult question.

'Well now...' he said, and hesitated. 'The thing is...' he said tugging at his sleeve.

'Anything at all, Dan?' I asked.

He heard the pleading note in my voice, sighed and continued. 'We never found a body, of course. I'm sorry to speak of such an indelicate subject now, Michael, but there's no getting around it.'

'It's all right. Go on.'

'Well, the castle was burned to the ground and, in that kind of fire, it isn't really too surprising that there was no body found. I wouldn't put too much store in that.'

'Is it possible that she lived, Dan?'

'Well now,' he said, sucking through his teeth again. 'Sure, if she were alive, wouldn't you be the first to know it? If she's not in those ashes, where is she?'

'I know it's strange, but I just find it so hard to imagine her dead.'

'I know you were fond of her, but don't set yourself for any false hope now, Michael.'

'How would I find out?'

'Find out?' he replied, struggling to mask the sheer incredulity in his voice.

'Well, there's nothing that will give you a definite answer short of a fortune-teller. I don't mean to speak lightly of it,' he said when he saw me draw back at the mention of the fortune-teller.

He turned his gaze upwards, eyes watching the woolly white clouds scuttling fast across a light blue sky.

'Look, I'll tell you what, Michael, I will enquire if there is any recent evidence has turned up that will lay the matter to rest for you once and for all. I'll make sure to drop you a line.'

'That would be grand, Dan, thanks very much.'

I shook his hand, gave him my address, and watched as he walked towards the top of Grafton Street.

* * *

A week later I received a note in the letterbox from Dan Ryan. There was much in the way of opening salutation and wishes for my good health and talk of meeting again, and a closing salutation. But there was only one line I was interested in:

> *'I'm sorry to say Michael that my enquiries up at Phoenix Park were fruitless. There was no information at all. I am certain the young lady has departed this life, God be good to her.'*

29 April 1923

I approached the enquiry desk of Dublin City Library. The figure behind the desk was a formidable woman, of medium height, but stoutly built; her grey hair was tied in a tight bun, and gold-chained pince-nez spectacles were perched on the end of her nose. She wore a small Irish tricolour pin on the lapel of her tweed jacket.

She looked at me, as I approached, her gaze without warmth.

'Yes?' she said without any polite flourishes of conversation.

'Begging your pardon, madam, I'm wondering if you would have a copy of *Burke's Peerage?*'

'*Burke's Peerage?*' she asked in tones of surprised indignation. 'We don't get any call for that sort of book here.'

Her expression couldn't have been more indignant had I requested one of the infamous Mister Joyce's publications.

'Yes, madam, I am doing some research.'

She sighed heavily. 'Very well. Wait over there.' She pointed towards a large reading table with a low-lying green reading lamp suspended over it.

I took a seat, skimming a copy of the *Irish Times* from the table as I waited. Finally, after a long wait, she walked slowly towards my table and dropped a large, thick, leather-bound book heavily on the table, causing a noise that made other library patrons stare in my direction.

'There you are,' she said loudly. 'There's your book of English aristocrats. I hope you find your friends there.'

As soon as she left me, I scanned the index until I found a page marked 'Burleigh.'

---

18 Belgrave Square
London

13 May 1923
23 Ashfield Road
Ranelagh
Dublin

Dear Mr. Gallagher,

I read your letter of the 6ᵗʰ inst with a great deal of distress.

You enquire if I have heard from my late niece Miss Fiona Burleigh, late of Kilmallock County, Limerick and daughter of my brother Lord Peter Burleigh.

As you would be well aware, my niece perished in during the tragic period your people describe as 'The Troubles.'

I find it extraordinary and distressing that you should speculate that she might be alive and somehow abroad in the world.

Your letter was particularly shocking, as I understand your own father perished in the same incident.

My advice to you, Mister Gallagher, is to put such fancies out of your head. Carry on with your life and please do not bother my family again.

Sincerely,

The Honourable Hilda Talbot-Holland

Working at Brown Thomas, I had become close to an older man, Charlie Watkins, the uniformed doorman. I think he felt sorry for me and realised I was feeling lost. Charlie was a bit of a character, a Dubliner from the Liberties who had spent more than half his life in the British Army.

Retired with the rank of sergeant after twenty-five years in the Duke of Wellington's Regiment, Charlie regaled me with stories of India and Egypt, Singapore, and the Malay states. Fights, adventures, marches, battles. The Pyramids, desert sands, jungles, strange exotic fruits. He described the parades at Buckingham Palace, voyages to the east. All the sensations of the tropics, curry, and beer on hot steamy nights. And the camaraderie. That most of all. Men you would die for because they were closer than family.

He filled my head with his tales of the empire. His eyes would close in fond memory as he described the coffee-coloured girls, long shining hair a black waterfall, skin as smooth as silk. As he drank the black pints of stout he would close his eyes, and with a sigh that was half contentment half yearning, quote his favourite lines from Kipling.

The British Army didn't appeal to me after the troubles of '19 to '21, but Charlie showed me an ad in *The Times* of London for men wanted to serve in the Shanghai Municipal Police. I was excited; a paid passage to China was irresistible to me given my last conversation with Fiona. I wrote to Pooks and, after a busy few weeks of bureaucratic detail, I was stepping off a ship on the Shanghai Bund.

After the standard square-bashing, police training and language instruc-tion at the Gordon Road Depot I became a beat cop, a walloper, pounding the pavement through the Shanghai International Settlement. 'The most dangerous police beat in the world' is what they told us.

The streets of Shanghai were a shock after a life spent in rural Ireland and Dublin. Every moment on the street presented me with alien sights. The rickshaw coolies, wizened ageless men, barefoot and bare-chested. Their stringy muscles glistened with sweat as they jogged along, pulling fat Western men in suits who reclined like kings on the passenger seats.

White Russian bodyguards, ex-Tsarist soldiers, accompanied the *Taipans;* kidnapping was a constant danger for the rich. They were frequently snatched off the streets and bundled into triads' cars and ransoms were paid quickly, to prevent bloody fingers arriving in the letterbox.

Despite the tension and the danger of the streets, I found it intoxicating to wear the uniform of a constable of the Shanghai Municipal Police. As an SMP man, servants were available to me for all domestic duties; I needed only ring a bell and help was at hand. This was a rather enthralling facility, especially for new recruits from the British and Irish working classes who in some cases had been servants themselves. I heard many describe it as 'heaven.' But it was all part of the process of becoming empire men. It created an illusion of wealth and power. The SMP did not pay well—our standing joke was that it was 'a champagne lifestyle on a lemonade budget.'

Notwithstanding our lack of policing experience, we were immediately put in charge of the Chinese and Sikh constables, some of whom already had years on the beat and knew a lot more than we did. Nevertheless, we were required to demonstrate the superiority of the white man. The official SMP manual told us that we were the 'brain and supervising power' of the force. The Chinese constable was, we were told, shifty, lazy, untrustworthy, and in need of strong guidance.

* * *

Although we enjoyed our jokes about a champagne lifestyle on a lemonade budget, there was a great deal of truth in it. It was very frustrating and, for me, the initial exhilaration was quickly wearing thin. By the time we had paid mess bills, cleaning and laundry bills and so on, we hardly had two shillings to rub together. It wasn't much, considering we put our lives on the line for the people every day.

I walked the streets of the Settlement watching the beautiful girls and gazing longingly into the nightclubs and bars, feeling embarrassed that in most of those establishments I didn't have the price of a drink. No wonder the older men drank their nights away in the police canteens, where beer was available at cost price.

I thought back to my ambitions of riches and fame and my longing to enter the world that I had tasted through my time with Fiona. I saw the extraordinary wealth on display in Shanghai, shoulder-to-shoulder with the most extreme poverty; I became more determined than ever to somehow get rich. But how? My boyhood fantasy about becoming a daring and much-rewarded empire man faded to dust in the daily realities of Shanghai.

I found myself making up for the lack of money in other ways, playing the big man, snapping at servants and native constables. I came to my senses one day after upbraiding a Sikh constable for some minor infraction. He mumbled something under his breath.

I shouted at him, 'What did you say, Constable?'

He remained silent. I shouted again.

He hung his head and said, 'I'm old enough to be your father, sir.'

I felt ashamed then, thinking of my own father who, despite the power of his uniform, was respectful to all men.

I muttered an apology to the Sikh and after that I stopped shouting at servants and native constables.

* * *

But policing Shanghai wasn't entirely without benefit for me. I'd been caught up in the May 30 incident of '25 outside Louza Station where that fool of an inspector had panicked and given the order to fire into a protest march. Twenty dead Chinamen on the street and things became very dangerous, the situation quickly turning into a major riot. Nobody had a clue how to handle it, including the senior officers. They lost their heads as much as anybody else. But I did well personally, if I may so myself. Ignoring the panicked orders of the very rattled inspector, I threw myself into the mob and saved the life of a Chinese constable who was about to be ripped apart by the angry mob.

Chapter 5

Shanghai 10 October 1925

THERE WAS A BIRTHDAY PARTY one Saturday night in the police canteen at Gordon Road for an Irish sergeant, Pat Sweeney, from Galway. He was a popular man, very generous and well liked. He was even nice to the Chinese and the Sikh constables under our command. He also got on well with the Japanese members who had been part of the SMP since 1916 when the first of them had transferred from the Tokyo Police.

The bash had been organised by the Irish Social Committee and no trouble or expense had been spared. A special collection had been taken up and the committee had pulled out all the stops in terms of food and drink. They'd gotten the depot servants to take care of the catering and the buffet table was straining under the weight of the food. No local stuff, just the kind of thing we knew from home.

Any Irishman who wasn't on duty was there, plus a fair scattering of the Scots, and several English and a couple of Americans.

It wasn't an officers' do but an affair for the rankers, constables, sergeants and senior sergeants. The men ate and drank their fill and there was much hearty backslapping, joke telling, banter and the hurling backward and forward of good-natured insults. Several men wore their civilian suits but the vast majority were in uniform; however, as the night wore on, collars were unbuttoned, jackets opened, ties unknotted, and boots slipped off. The scene began to resemble a Dublin pub on a Saturday night. The gramophone grinding away at top volume, playing all the favourites from home, completed the illusion.

Suddenly the door opened and a tall, crisply-uniformed man wearing the silver pips of an inspector stepped smartly into the room. Bloody hell, I thought, surely not an officer's inspection at a time like this?

Several others had the same thought as I saw men hurriedly sit up and begin buttoning shirt collars, tightening ties and pulling their jackets on.

The inspector, a dark-haired, handsome man of about thirty-five, waved his arms magisterially and said in a broad working-class Dublin accent,

'You're all right, lads. Sure I'm only here to see if there's a drink going at all.' This was greeted with laughter and an immediate relaxation of tension.

Someone handed him a bottle of stout and said, 'There you are, Jack, get that into you.'

I turned to the man beside me, Pat McGrath, a fellow Limerick man, and said, 'Who's the inspector?'

He replied, 'Ah, that's Jack Dell, sure everyone knows Jack.'

'He doesn't stand on formality, does he?'

'Ah God, no! Jack's a very good officer, but he doesn't go in for all the saluting and boot stomping that most officers like.'

'Where is he based?' I asked.

'He's here at Gordon Road, but you probably wouldn't bump into him. He's with that new crowd that Superintendent Fairlight is putting together.'

As the night wore on and men began to look more bleary-eyed and dishevelled, someone turned off the gramophone, creating a sudden silence. 'Time for a song,' someone else shouted.

Men were called upon to give a song and, in the time-honoured way of the Irish, no matter how good a singer you were, you had to feign shyness and be practically begged to stand up and sing. As the evening progressed, many men sang and people joined in with choruses. We were treated to a whole range of songs, some funny, some sad, some bawdy and some nostalgic.

I felt a warm glow of intoxication and familiarity. Much and all as I was intrigued by the exotic swirl of life on the streets of Shanghai, there were moments when a simple taste of home was more refreshing than the coolest spring water.

'What about Jack!' someone cried. A chant went up. 'Jack! Jack! Jack!'

The inspector stood and said, 'All right, lads. I'll give ye a song.'

I noticed that he didn't go in for any of the false modesty of the other singers.

He didn't need any begging. He left his seat and walked up to the mantelpiece, the focal point in the room. All other singers had simply stood up by their seat.

Even though I'd seen him put away several bottles of beer, his uniform remained immaculate, not a button undone or a glossy hair on his head out of place.

Jack leaned one arm on the mantelpiece, and placed his other hand elegantly in his tunic pocket. He stood, still and silent, his eyes moving around the room. His presence had the effect of silencing the room. There was an air to him, a way of getting men's focus, a way he had of being taken seriously by all.

When he had everyone's complete attention he cleared his throat and said, 'Here's a nice one that ye all know.'

His chest expanded, and he began to sing. In a crystal clear tenor voice, perfect and sweet, he began to sing '*Macushla*'.

Jack's melodious and powerful voice filled the room; the song of sweet, melancholic loss reverberated around the walls of the canteen.

I listened intently to the words—a story of death and loss and heartbreak, of a young man whose love had died.

My mind was filled with pictures of my dear Fiona, my lost girl, the one I would never see again. The alcohol, the nostalgia, the sheer Irishness of the evening, and the sad plaintive song got to me, and I felt my eyes water.

Jack's voice rose, strong and vibrant and sweet, the young man in the song desperate now.

I blinked back my tears, furtively glancing around the room to see if anyone noticed. As I focused again on Jack, he briefly made eye contact with me; I bit my lip to control myself.

His tenor voice reached the climax, soaring, soaring majestically, pleading, heartbroken, shattered, a man who'll never love again.

Then, his voice fell back, gentle now: the song faded away.

Jack stopped and the room was silent. There wasn't a man in the room who wasn't touched by his performance. Then, the room erupted in applause and cheers and whistles, and cries of 'Good man, Jack. Give us another one.'

'A sure ye don't want to hear me banging on all night,' he said to the room at large as he walked back to his seat. 'There's plenty grand singers here.'

Other singers went up, but nobody could match that performance. I could hardly concentrate on the party now for the memories of Fiona were so raw. If I had been alone I would have cried like a baby. But I couldn't let the men see me like that.

A bit later and the party was beginning to wind down. Some of the men had gone back to their rooms, and one or two heavy drinkers had fallen asleep on the old padded couches. The gramophone was back on but playing arias from various operas.

I saw Jack stand up and tug at his jacket, straightening it even though it remained as uncreased as if it had just come from the tailors. As he walked to the door, I felt compelled to speak to him. Nobody had moved me so much in years.

'Inspector Dell,' I said, suddenly shy. 'That was a grand song.'

He shook my hand vigorously.

'Ah sure 'twas only a bit of entertainment for the masses,' he said with a grin.

'Ah no, sir, that was another standard entirely.'

'No need for "sir" here in the canteen. Just call me Jack. And what's your name?'

'Gallagher, eh, Jack, Michael Gallagher. From County Limerick.'

'Ah, yes,' he replied, 'weren't you the chap at the Louza Station riot? Saved the Chinese constable from the mob?'

'That's right, sir, but it was nothing really. Any man here would have done the same.'

'I don't know about that,' he said glancing around the room, his eyebrow raised quizzically. 'I must mention you to Mister Fairlight.'

'Jack, that was a grand night—and that song of yours—I haven't heard anything like it in years.'

'Ah I understand,' he replied with a smile of recognition, ''tis hard to be away from home. Or is it that it made you think of someone?'

'That's right, Jack. There was a girl…'

He slapped my shoulder. 'Good man. Glad to hear you aren't stuck here in the canteen every night like a lot of these fellas. They couldn't find Nanking Road without a map and a torch. Anyway, grand talking to you, Michael. Sure I'll see you around.'

With that, he marched smartly to the door, as sharp as if he was on the parade ground outside.

I walked to a corner of the room and sat in a battered old leather armchair, my body sinking into its half sprung embrace. I sipped my whiskey, the taste of peat and smoke on my lips.

11 November 1925

The weather had turned autumnal and we had already marked the change of season by changing from our light, summer khaki uniform to the thicker, winter, dark blue serge rig. Yesterday I'd come back from patrol to

Bubbling Well Road Station where I'd been assigned for patrol duties. I was handed a note by the station sergeant. It was a hand-written request, on police notepaper, for me to contact Superintendent Fairlight. I telephoned him, made an appointment, and the next day was back to Gordon Road Depot for special training.

Chapter 6

THE MURMUR OF MALE VOICES in the lecture room lowered to a quiet hum and then came to a stop as we saw that Superintendent Fairlight stood at the lectern. His penetrating blue eyes scanned the room and his glance brought final pockets of conversation to a sudden stop. He was an Englishman of medium height and slim build, with grey hair and spectacles. His hair was neatly trimmed and his eyes sparkled with energy. His appearance was deceptively mild, the glasses reminiscent more of one's family doctor than a cop.

'With your help, I intend to smash the gangsters of Shanghai.'

A ripple of movement ran through the room as men sat up straight and leaned forward, listening intently.

I noted his uniform was smart and well pressed, medal ribbons making a colourful splash on his chest. As I observed him I recalled the stories I'd heard. The fact was that Fairlight could kill with his bare hands. An ex-marine and Shanghai beat cop, in 1907 on a lone street patrol he'd taken a bad beating from a gang of thugs. After recovering from his near-fatal wounds he had dedicated twenty years to martial arts training under Japanese and Chinese masters and had black belts in *karate* and *ju-jitsu*. In addition, he was an outstanding boxer and street scrapper and had been a bayonet-fighting champion in the Marines.

'Gentlemen,' he continued, 'every day this force fights gangsters, terrorists, kidnappers, armed robbers, Chinese warlords, gun-runners, opium smugglers, triads, communist spies, strikers, and the drunks, lunatics, and off-duty soldiers and sailors from a dozen countries.'

At the mention of the drunks and soldiers, there was a ripple of laughter in the room and men nodded in recognition of the facts. He paused for a moment until there was silence again.

'The Shanghai Municipal Police come under more gunfire in a week than the Chicago police do in a month, even with their Mister Capone to contend with.'

A hand was raised in the middle of the room

'Yes, Constable?' said Fairlight.

'Begging your pardon, sir, but the triads are better armed than we are. Our revolvers are from the last century. We might as well be spitting at the gangsters as shooting at them.'

'Good point, Constable. Your Webley revolver is a museum piece. It is heavy, slow, and awkward and, as you say, doesn't pack a punch. Today, you will be issued with the Colt .45 Automatic. There isn't a finer weapon in Shanghai.'

After a short silence, broken only by the hiss of a struggling radiator, a hum of excitement ran through the audience. When they had settled, Fairlight went on.

'This, gentlemen, is the Emergency Unit. The purpose of this new unit is to engage in all non-routine police duties. I emphasise *non-routine*. Your training will make you a better gunfighter than the gunmen. I have devised a training course, gentlemen, with two main components. One is called *"Shoot to Live"* and you are to be my first students. I will make you the finest gunmen in Shanghai, maybe in the world. I have constructed a building that I call Mystery House.

'You will go through the narrow, dark, rubbish-strewn, claustrophobic corridors of Mystery House, winded and tired, lungs heaving, hands shaking, from having just run a fast and difficult obstacle course timed by stopwatch. When you get inside Mystery House you will find we have set up moving targets—they will move, you will shoot them. Human hands direct the targets, and these people will return fire, shooting blank rounds at you. It will feel exactly as if your target is returning fire. It will be a highly realistic reproduction of a real-life shootout. This drill will be repeated again and again until you develop the reflexes of a cat.'

The silence was broken by an excited murmur that ran through his audience like a fever. Suddenly we had hope. We would no longer be easy targets.

'God bless you, sir!' came a shout in a thick Scottish accent.

'Thank you, gentlemen. The second component I have named *"Defendu"* and it is my amalgamation of the best of martial arts from East and West. It combines *karate* and *ju-jitsu*, boxing, and unarmed combat as devised by the Royal Marines. Learn *"Defendu"* and you will fear no man. I guarantee that you'll be able to handle yourself better than the toughest street thug.'

By this time, the excitement in the room was higher than ever. Men could hardly sit still in their seats. It was like the last day of school five minutes before the final bell rang.

He held up his hands like an orchestra conductor. 'Bear with me for a moment, gentlemen. The other aspect of your job will be riot control. You will also be experts in close contact fighting with baton and shield. You will work in teams to break up riots. When an alarm rings you will turn out, fully kitted for emergency response, in less than three minutes. The unit will be on alert twenty-four hours per day, seven days a week, for 365 days of the year.'

He paused for a moment. I felt thrilled. Could this be my chance to make my mark? What would my father have made of this? I'd write to Dan Ryan about this, he'd understand.

'You are about to undergo a tough course. Not all of you will make it through. I will think no less of a man who does his best but doesn't make the grade. I *will* think less of a man who *could* make it but refuses to give his all. If this is not to your taste, then I suggest that you withdraw immediately. Ordinary policing is tough enough and I will not disparage any man who wishes to depart now.'

As he slowly looked around the room there was an electrified silence. But nobody left.

* * *

That night I dreamed of Fiona again. I woke in a sweat, her name on my lips. I spent the rest of the night remembering, sleep unable to claim me.

Chapter 7

A HOT STEAM BATH OF a day brought sweat dripping down my back. The emergency bell rang and a cry of 'Bank robbery on Nanking Road' echoed through the building. Our convoy took off at high speed from the Gordon Road Depot—three scarlet 'Red Maria' armoured trucks and six Big Chief motorcycles and sidecars, purchased from the NYPD. Each sidecar was mounted with a Thompson sub-machine gun, or 'Chicago typewriter' as the American press had dubbed them.

I sat huddled with the other men in one of the Red Marias. We were bunched together shoulder to shoulder; the space seemed tighter because of the bulletproof vests and helmets we wore. The vests were made of overlapping bands of silver clock-spring metal, covered in a khaki canvas cloth; they were reputed to stop any bullet apart from a Mauser. *Please, God, don't let them have Mausers.* The Emergency Unit man's prayer.

For the thousandth time, I reached to check my pistol. You could always tell an Emergency Unit man from a regular cop by the position of his gun. Regular SMP men carried theirs on their hip but Mister Fairlight considered this an invitation for the gun to be snatched by a criminal during a hand-to-hand struggle. Like all Emergency Unit men, the holster was positioned to the front-left of our belts. I remembered Fairlight's words to us during training: 'In the future, you will cross-draw your weapon from the left side, with your right hand. This change alone, gentlemen, could save your life before you fire a shot. There is no worse tragedy than a policeman being shot with his own weapon seized during a struggle.'

The air in the truck reeked of nervous sweat and every man looked grim. Some made jokes to gloss over their nerves, but nobody laughed. My pulse pounded in my ears. A trickle of sweat ran down from under my helmet into my eyes. The man next to me said something and I didn't reply. My mouth was too dry. I imagined what the gunfight would be like. Would I get shot, wind up dead before I had a chance to live? Or would it be a bullet in the spine, leaving a shell of a man to be spoon-fed in some nursing home? I squeezed the butt of my pistol.

Our Red Maria stopped with a jarring of brakes, the doors crashed open, and we tumbled out, equipment jangling like medieval knights. We dived for cover in any available spot—doorways, in the gutter, under the truck, anywhere on the ground. The air was peppered with bullets, pinging off the wall. An elderly lady clutched a straw grocery bag to her bony chest. She was almost doubled in two, as she trotted across the street, heading for an open door in a house opposite. Her progress was slow, her bound feet taking mincing, child-sized steps. A young man stood inside the doorway, urging her forward: '*lai, lai, lai*.' Jack Dell shouted, his Dublin accent broad and familiar, 'Someone get that fucking grandmother off the street.' I was near her, squashed down in the gutter, and almost stood up but hesitated, my courage deserting me. The old lady took a few steps forward, crumpled over, and dropped to the ground, the grocery bag still clutched tightly to her chest.

* * *

When the shooting was all over, we cordoned off the area, pushing the onlookers back out of the crime scene whilst the wallopers from Bubbling Well Station interviewed witnesses. I was euphoric, floating on air. I could have hugged and kissed every living person on the street. I'd done it. I'd been through a firefight with the unit and lived to tell the tale. God, I'd murder a beer.

The young man who'd been in the doorway pushed his way through the cordon and ran to where the old woman lay on the ground. He bent down and touched her body, then began to wail mournfully.

Jack Dell went to him and put his arm around the young man's shoulders, leading him gently back to the kerb. I moved closer, curious to see how Jack handled the young man. I heard Jack whisper softly and his hand emerged from his jacket clutching a bundle of banknotes which he slipped inside the young man's shirt, and then he pushed him away, saying, in Shanghainese, as if sending an infant off to bed, '*Off with you now*.'

Jack saw me looking in his direction. He came over to me and said, 'Better not say anything about that, Michael. I have a reputation to keep up.'

Chapter 8

19 February 1927

JACK DELL CALLED ME INTO the Duty Inspector's office, his expression serious and concerned. He said, 'I noticed that you're a bit quiet these days.' I told him about the executions I'd seen during my walk through Nantao

51

two weeks before, and my near-disastrous and stupid intervention, and he said that he understood. I didn't mention the Russians. I wouldn't take a chance on it. A lot of the senior SMP men were very puritanical.

'Shanghai is a very tough place, Michael. It's not for the faint-hearted. If you can't stick it out, you should consider if you really want to stay here.'

'No, Jack, I want to make a go of it. Anyway, where would I go?'

'Well, it's a big world, Michael. But if you really want to get on here, you have to… to accept it for what it is.'

'I'll try, Jack, but it's a hard place.'

'So why did you come to Shanghai, anyway?'

'I suppose I was searching for something… I lost a girl once and… I don't know.'

'I know that feeling. But what keeps you here? You could resign. We're not the French Foreign Legion, you know.'

I hesitated for a moment, feeling my face blush with the embarrassment of what I was about to say. 'I thought I might find her again in Shanghai…'

Jack laughed heartily, sparing me the compulsion to reprise my grief. He leaned back in his chair propping his feet on the desk. I couldn't help but notice that his non-regulation black leather brogues were polished to a high sheen and looked expensive.

'Or someone like her, anyway! Damn it all, Michael, I didn't know you were such a cake eater! And there was I thinking you were an altar boy. Sure if you like the women, Shanghai is the place for it.'

I wasn't sure how to reply. How could I explain to a decorated senior police officer, a man of action and results, that I was pursuing a dream, a boy's fancy, the spirit of a dead girl?

'There's not much to be had on a policeman's wage,' I muttered in reply to his enthusiasm.

In a flash, he'd taken his feet off the desk, the chair's legs hitting the floorboards with a loud bang. He sat forward, eyes shining.

'Ah, sure you never know your luck. What you need is someone to keep an eye out for you. There's a lot of Irish lads in the force and I was helped a lot when I came out in 1918.'

'You were lucky to miss all the trouble at home.'

'I was, right enough. Good luck seems to follow me. I joined the army in 1915, but was never posted to the Western Front. I was in Palestine.'

'That must have been interesting.'

Jack reached into his jacket and pulled out a silver cigarette holder. He opened it with a practiced flick of his wrist and held the box towards me, a line of cigarettes neatly displayed inside.

'Have a gasper, why don't you?'

I held up my hand in blocking gesture. 'Ah, no, thanks, Jack, I never got the taste for them.'

He flipped the box closed after taking one for himself.

'Anyway, where was I?' He paused again, to light the cigarette, cracking a match on his desktop and flicking its remains accurately into a sand bucket in the corner. He inhaled and blew a cloud of smoke with a satisfied sigh.

'Palestine was hard enough, but not a patch on the Western Front. In fact, that's what put me on to the joys of the East. One day, I had what a religious man might call a "Road to Damascus." I was sitting in a café in the old Arab quarter of Jerusalem, smoking a hubble-bubble, with some black-eyed Arab girl tending to me. Jasus, she was beautiful. Those dark eyes.'

He paused to smoke his cigarette again. I leaned forward, fascinated by his story.

'So, anyway,' he went on, 'I thought: this beats the hell out of sellin' fruit at me mother's stall in the Coombe, with the rain lashin' down and you keeping the wet off with a hessian sack. And so I never went back home. Haven't been back since. You know Kipling's line about "hearing the East a-callin'?" I met Lawrence of Arabia once in a bar in Cairo. Got drunk with him; he didn't care about rank at all. Now he was a gas man. He had the Eastern bug pretty bad.'

I remained silent, again picturing the head in the birdcage. There was a moment of silence before Jack stood up, signalling that our meeting was reaching its conclusion.

'Look, Michael, you're a good lad. My door here is always open, if you need any advice or anything at all.'

'Thanks very much, Jack. That's jolly decent of you.'

'Ah sure, no bother at all. Do you know the Blue Lady nightclub? I often go there for a tipple. Look me up when you're in the mood for a chat. 'Tis an odd sort of place. No police go there, which is why I like it.'

'I will, I will, thanks very much, Jack.'

He shook my hand then. It was like being gripped by a bear and I suddenly felt safer than I had in a long time. There was a certain quality to Jack. He could make people feel like he was in their corner.

Jack was, I would say, about twelve years older than me. He leaned his tall, solid frame back against a battered metal filing cabinet and ran his fingers through his thick, dark hair. You're a handsome boyo, I thought— bet the local ladies love those eyes. The 'black Irish' as they used to say. He had an easy, informal manner, and despite being an inspector, didn't make you feel like he was above you. I found his North Dublin accent comforting to hear in a strange place so far from home. He was there with a ready joke and a commiseration rather than a condemnation if you got it wrong. Maybe it was his war experience, but he reminded me in some ways of Charlie Watkins, the old soldier who took me under his wing at Brown Thomas.

We stopped by the office door and Jack reached for the doorknob and then drew back, his face thoughtful, as if he had come to a decision.

'I could do with a bit of help with a job, right now. It takes a man capable of discretion. Can I trust you, Michael?'

'Of course you can, Jack.'

'Good. It's very hush-hush. It's a job that requires complete discretion. Need you to drive a car for me. Off the books, so to speak. We're taking some big cheese to a secret meeting. I need a good man—what do you say?'

'All right, Jack. You need a chauffeur, I'll do it.' I felt my face flush hot with a mixture of pleasure and shyness to be singled out for something special by such a man.

'Good man, Michael. Change into civvies and meet me downstairs in half an hour. We'll be using a private car. It's a dark green Durant. Make sure you've got your bean shooter.' He patted his pistol holster.

Chapter 9

I FOLLOWED JACK'S INSTRUCTIONS AND, half an hour later, I was in at the wheel of a dark green Durant, heading towards the city centre with Jack beside me.

'We're to pick up an important passenger and take him to a discreet meeting. That's all I know at the moment.'

I navigated the car through bedlam and shortly we pulled up at the front of the Shanghai Municipal Council building. A man came to the side window and spoke to Jack.

'Pull around to the back exit,' he said. 'Your man will be waiting there.'

Jack nudged me in the ribs. 'You heard the man.'

I drove around, hearing the tyres crunch on the gravel of the rear driveway. I pulled up near an arched doorway and we saw a man in hat and overcoat standing in the shadows. His collar was up and his hat pulled low. He got into the back seat and I heard an American voice say:

'Rue Wagner in Frenchtown, please, boys. Make sure we don't have a tail on us.'

As we drove on, our mysterious passenger took off his hat and opened his overcoat. To my surprise it was Mister Sterling DeVere of the Shanghai Municipal Council.

DeVere was a skeletal, grey-haired man, his thin neck emerging from a loose collar and bow tie. His thinness gave him the look of a martyr facing the lions in the colosseum. 'Say, fellas, I'm going to a top-secret meeting. Shanghai is on the brink of destruction and I am going to save it if I can. You're going to hear some highly confidential material but it is never to be repeated.'

'Yes, sir' from Jack and I.

* * *

We drove through the Settlement, across Avenue Edward VII and into

Frenchtown. Rue Wagner was a narrow, wealthy street off the Avenue Foch—a very nice street with expensive four-storey houses displaying lacy ironwork balconies. It looked for all the world like a street in Paris.

I parked the car at the kerb in front of number twenty-six. The house was as picturesque as the others but its elegance was marred by a covering of sandbags, rolls of barbed wire and groups of men lounging around behind the sandbags brandishing a variety of Mausers, rifles, pistols and sub-machine guns.

There was something disturbing about seeing the paraphernalia of war in such a pretty street. It was menacing to see hard-faced men with guns behind those sandbags, while young women in governess's uniforms strolled by pushing prams. I felt an unease I hadn't felt since 1920. The madness of guerrilla war. I had somehow placed myself back in the midst of what I most dreaded.

An unusually tall Chinese man, with a shaved head glistening in the sunlight, his jacket straining over the bulk of his muscular body, walked to our car. He stopped, taking his time, sucked deeply on his cigarette, hollowing his cheeks. He leaned down and said, speaking through the side window: 'Yes, who are you?'

Mister DeVere spoke. 'I have an appointment with Mister Lu.' The man looked at him, and then at us and, with a jerk of his head towards the front entrance to the house, said, 'You go in.'

Two men wearing black overcoats, with long-barrel Mausers with wooden stocks slung across their backs, pulled the barrier open to allow us to drive inside. Once we had pulled the car into the driveway, a slim, neat, bespectacled Chinese man wearing a dark pinstripe suit came to meet us.

'I am Jason Lau, Mister Lu's comprador. Mister DeVere, you are so very welcome. Won't you please come inside? Your men are welcome to join you.' He spoke English with a cultured Cantonese accent—most of the compradors to the rich were from that region.

Mister Lau led us through the house, which was richly and tastefully appointed, but marred by the sight of rough-looking men lounging around, most smoking and many cleaning their Mausers. Their alert eyes followed us as we walked the length of the corridor. Despite the opulence of the house, I was reminded of the Emergency Unit depot. It had the same sweaty, rough, male smell, mingled with the scent of gun oil.

Lu, I read in the mosquito press, had three wives and each one had a separate floor of the house for herself and her retinue of maids.

The comprador walked with us to the top of the house. We stopped in a golden-wallpapered corridor and waited for a moment. A door opened and we were ushered inside. As we entered the room, Lau shut the door behind us, but remained in the corridor.

* * *

We had been brought to a bright, comfortable drawing room. Several armchairs and couches had been arranged in a wide circle, and a coffee table stood in the centre, laden with silver pots of tea and a delicate English tea set.

Seated side by side in armchairs were two men. The first man, tall and thin, with a big bony face and the most extraordinary large, protruding ears, was Lu Sun Yu, otherwise known as 'Big Ears Lu.' He was well known as Shanghai's most generous philanthropist but also as its most powerful gangster, controlling the city's prostitution rings, gambling, loan sharking, opium dens, kidnapping and protection rackets. Lu sat in a gilded Louis XIV chair, stately and still.

The second man, older than Lu, was small and portly with the oily, fat, pockmarked face of a toad. He was Fan Xian Dun, better known as 'Pockmarked Fan.' Fan Xian Dun was both the Head of Chinese Detectives of the French Police and, at the same time, the boss of the Green Gang, operating Frenchtown and Shanghai's largest opium smuggling business.

There were many in the French police who claimed that it led to a more smoothly run administration, with less violent crime, and they frequently expressed puzzlement at the reluctance of the British and Americans to come to a similar arrangement in the International Settlement.

An oil painting, a portrait of Lu in the robes of an ancient mandarin, dominated the room. The artist had painted the eyes so that they were looking directly at us no matter where we stood.

Jack and I stood by the wall of the room nearest to the door, while a group of Chinese gangsters took up corresponding positions near the window. The bodyguards' eyes locked with ours and we spent half a minute staring each other down. DeVere sat and tea was served.

Lu flicked his hand to dust crumbs from his silk robe. His movements were regal, slow and stately, every flick deliberate and considered.

'Shanghai faces a bloodbath, Mister DeVere. Are you aware of the danger?' Lu's English was very good, considering his humble background and lack of education. I'd read in the papers that, as he rose in importance and wealth, he refined himself, employing a tutor to teach him to 'speak English like a gentleman.' His voice had a deep, gravelly quality.

DeVere hunched his body forward in supplication. 'Sir, that is why I'm here. As I'm sure you are aware, the forces of Sun Chuanfang are already fleeing. The KMT forces are now camped outside of the city. I fear that the Communist unions will organise a coup and will take over greater Shanghai, and from there launch attacks into the Shanghai International Settlement and French Concession. Our days may be numbered.'

'And how may I be of assistance?' asked Mister Lu.

'We are asking for your help in dealing with this crisis. We appeal to your patriotism as a good Chinese citizen.'

'Are you not aware of the rumours? They call me a triad boss.'

'Mister Lu, I believe that you are an upstanding citizen and a model for your countrymen. It is my honour, and pleasure, sir, to appeal to your good nature in the salvation of this city that we both love.'

Lu reclined, his eyes cast towards the ceiling. There was a long silence. He slowly sat forward, his body alert now.

'The Communists will take over greater Shanghai exactly as you fear. They will fight the Nationalist army and then they will seize the entire city.'

I listened to the conversation with rising incredulity. I flicked a glance in Jack's direction. His face was serene with perhaps a hint of amusement.

DeVere cleared his throat and put down his teacup. 'The Special Branch believes that the Communists see the KMT as an army of liberation.'

'That is a lie!' Lu said with a chopping motion of his big, bony hand. 'If you believe that, then Shanghai is truly doomed.'

DeVere nodded gravely and said in a forlorn voice, 'Can you help us?'

Lu said, 'First of all, I require your government to provide me with five thousand rifles for my patriots.'

DeVere nodded his head and said, 'I believe my people would be amenable to this request.'

Lu enunciated very slowly and deliberately, like a man reading a prepared speech: 'Mister DeVere, I will ask you to do something that the Shanghai Municipal Council has consistently refused to do. The Council has never allowed any Chinese force to cross its borders. I require that my men travel by car and truck through the International Settlements without hindrance. If both Councils can accede to my requests, then, gentlemen, I will save Shanghai for you.'

My stomach felt nauseated.

I stood deadpan, the good cop. I glanced at Jack, raising my eyebrows in silent query: '*What do you think of that?*' Jack winked, his eyes now twinkling with amusement.

There was a tense silence in the room for several minutes. Then DeVere said, 'Mister Lu, you have yourself a deal, sir. Let's shake hands as gentlemen.'

I clenched my jaw shut. I wanted to shout my outrage. How dare they? A bunch of thieves and murderers slicing up the city like a birthday cake. And Jack, damn him, as amused as if he was at a Bubbling Well Road cabaret show.

DeVere stood, bid his co-conspirators goodbye, turned to where Jack and I stood and said, 'Thanks, gentlemen, and now if you wouldn't mind running me back to the office.'

The drive back was uneventful. In the car he leaned forward from the back seat and said, 'Of course, gentlemen, I need to rely on your absolute discretion in this matter. You are sworn to complete secrecy.'

Chapter 10

North China Daily News March 21 1927
Revolution in Shanghai! State of Emergency Declared

The communist leader Zhou Enlai with five hundred men from the Chinese Communist Party launched a coup in Greater Shanghai early this morning. Armed with only 150 guns, and supplemented with knives, axes, cleavers and crowbars, the rabble successfully took over Greater Shanghai, seizing post offices, police stations and other Chinese government facilities.

Nearly all foreigners who live in Greater Shanghai, and many Chinese of the more respectable classes, have fled to the International Settlement and French Concession where a state of emergency was declared. Barricades now seal all roads leading to the International Settlement from Greater Shanghai. Shanghai Municipal Police, Shanghai Volunteer Corps, British Army, US Marines, and various other military forces from Europe are manning the checkpoints.

Twenty thousand troops have arrived from Europe, the USA and Japan, and forty-five naval battleships are docked, but ready for action, on the Whampoo River.

The International Settlement and French Concession are closed for business. Many shops are boarded up and those who are not engaged in emergency work have stayed in the safety of their homes.

22 March 1927

I WAS ON DUTY WITH a group of Emergency Unit men at the checkpoint between the Great Western Road and the far western end of Bubbling Well Road. Two of our Red Marias were parked crossways blocking the street.

A line of Chinese refugees, desperate to escape the communists, queued up on the far side of the gates. Men, women and children, many carrying their life's possessions, waited to go through. Soldiers, Shanghai Volunteer

Corps and SMP men searched and screened them as they went through the gates in groups of two or three. It was excruciatingly slow and the crush of people was building up to an explosive venting.

A plain-clothes Special Branch detective controlled the screening. Some refugees were ordered back. Families were separated; in some cases, parents were allowed in but children not. Often, couples were split, with one turned away and one allowed in. It was inexplicable. An eight-year-old boy howled his distress and fear as he was separated from his mother.

The crowd became aggressive and began to crush against the gate. As people tried to climb the gate, we threw them back into the crowd. One young man, wearing grey slacks and a white shirt, got through and began to run for it.

A British Army officer calmly raised his revolver and, carefully taking aim, fired a single shot. The young man fell, his white shirt turning crimson. I watched his young life slip away, horrified but silent, my protest swallowed in my dry throat. A uniform, I realised, can control its wearer as much as it intimidates the people around him.

The officer marched smartly back to the barrier, the heels of his riding boots clicking on the concrete. 'Keep the gate closed for half an hour, chaps,' he said. 'That'll remind 'em who's boss.'

Just then, the roar of a powerful engine and the honking of a car klaxon silenced the babble of protesting voices. Quickly, bodies scattered in all directions. Tearing along at top speed was a big, gleaming car coming from the Western Roads towards the International Settlement. It was a dark-blue luxury model, big and expensive and, without question, must have been carrying one of the Settlement's rich *Taipans*.

'Open the barrier and let the car through. Pull back the Red Marias,' shouted the army officer. Two SMP constables pulled back the barrier and the car accelerated through, almost knocking a constable as it jerked forward, its powerful engine growling like a lion.

The car slowed for a moment as it waited for the Red Marias to move apart. As the car passed me, I had a side view of it. It was driven by a uni-formed chauffeur and carried one back-seat passenger. Through the slightly smoky tinted window I saw the profile of a young woman wearing a scarf and sunglasses. For a second she glanced in my direction.

I saw the face of Fiona Burleigh. Then the powerful engine took the car speeding off down Bubbling Well Road, heading east.

I stared after the car, too confused to read the numberplate. I screwed up my eyes and wiped the sweat off my brow. My hands shook. Was it her? She was wearing a scarf, sunglasses; it could be any rich young woman. Stupid! Stupid!

My legs felt weak and I slid to the kerb, sitting like a Nantao beggar.

In a moment the army officer was standing by my side.

'You'd better get up,' he said sharply. 'Doesn't do to have the natives see us look weak.'

I wearily pulled myself to my feet. 'Right, sir. Would you have any idea who owns that car?'

'No idea, old chap, but you can be sure it's someone rich. Take some water, why don't you? Can't have you keeling over in front of the Chinks.'

Ireland – 1920

Chapter 11

24 June 1920

FIONA AND I WERE IN the attic at Burleigh Castle. We were looking through dusty old photographs of members of Fiona's extended family—various groups of men, some in morning suits, other groups in cricket whites, and some in nineteenth-century military uniforms. Under a pile of dusty, cobwebbed leather-bound albums we found a framed photograph of a young man in army uniform, his lean youthful face partly concealed behind a thick, waxed moustache. I wiped the film of dust away with my sleeve. The picture showed the young officer standing in a flat open area, on dusty ground with a tall, multi-storied pagoda in the background. Each tier of the pagoda had corner roof points that curved upwards like the swirl on my father's copperplate lettering.

'Oh, that's him! My grandfather in China that I told you about,' Fiona gasped excitedly. 'China, doesn't it look magnificent?! So mysterious, so romantic.'

Then, she put her hands on my shoulder and kissed my lips. Her full lips feather light on mine. We gazed in each other's eyes for a moment. I felt shocked and pleased and embarrassed all at the same time. I was the man. I should have kissed her.

But surely this meant that she loved me? After a moment of silence, she smiled and said, 'Would you like to see the Chinese Room?'

'The Chinese Room? What is that?'

'You'll see. But you must be careful. It is a private family room, very secret.'

'All right,' I said.

Taking me by the hand, she led the way and we tiptoed softly downstairs to the library.

It was a large, rectangular room, with bookshelves full of dusty, leather-bound volumes covering every available wall space. Fiona led me to the wall at the end of the room furthest from the door. She reached behind the bookshelf to fumble with something and then it moved silently on hinges—a secret door to a secret room. The hairs stood on my neck.

We stepped through. The floor was covered with lustrous black tiles that glistened like a liquid mirror. The walls were painted blood red. Hanging on the walls was a series of framed paper scrolls covered in light, delicate paintings showing trees, birds and strangely-shaped buildings with roofs that curved up at the corners like the building in her grandfather's photograph. There were a few pieces of black, heavy, glazed furniture placed at intervals around the walls.

'Is this the Chinese Room?' I asked, immediately feeling stupid at the irrelevancy of my question.

'My grandfather made this room for all the things he brought from Peking. He went there in 1860. There was a war, you know. The English and French. We beat the Chinese and sacked the city of Peking. When the soldiers went to the Emperor's summer palace, my grandfather found many Chinese antiques and eventually brought them back here. It changed his fortune, he believed. He was just a poor man, a junior lieutenant in the Army. But he rose very high in the world. He lived in China for many years and so did my father for a while. China holds a special place in this family. That's why I wanted to show the room to you.'

She took my hand and gazed into my eyes.

'Wouldn't it be great if you took me to China one day?' she said. 'I would really like that, Michael.'

An uneasy fear came over me. It was an eerie premonition of danger that I wasn't able to put in words. 'I don't know, Fiona,' I said. 'My father might need me here.'

'We shall see what the *Book of Secrets* has to say about us,' she replied in her most formidable, *will not take no for an answer* voice.

Fiona led me to the far wall of the room to a black double-door cabinet. Dark red characters of an entirely alien style were carved into the wood. She put her hands on the brass doorknobs and opened the two doors, pulling them outward. Inside was a black timber box of great age. It was about the size of a shoebox or a little larger. She removed the box and brought it to a table placed beside the black cabinet. Fiona carried the box with great gentleness and I knew, from the way she held it, that it was very important. It made me think of the way the priest held up the host at Mass.

'What is it?' I asked.

'This is the *Book of Secrets*,' she told me, 'also known as the *I-Ching*. My grandfather brought it from Peking. The Chinese believe that the *Book of Secrets* can tell you anything you want to know.'

Then Fiona took my hand in hers and said, 'Would you like to find out about you and me?'

'Yes,' I replied, trying to sound offhand. I couldn't name the fear, but there was just something about the contents of this box. The priests had always warned about the dangers of fortune telling.

I watched Fiona open the box. She removed various items. There were six coins, unusually shaped. They were round, made of brass, small, about the size of an English penny, but with unusual square holes punched in the middle.

Then she removed a book bound in red leather, but so old it looked more brown than red. Rolled up beside the book was an ancient parchment with yellowed, wrinkled paper. I watched as she unrolled the parchment, which was covered in a series of strange symbols.

Fiona placed the coins in my cupped hands and said, 'Throw them so that they land in a row.'

I shook the coins in my cupped hands and threw them like a gambler throwing dice. The coins landed in such a way that they formed an approximately straight line. Fiona studied the pattern for a few more minutes and I realised that she was searching among the patterns on the parchment to find one that matched the order created by the thrown coins. After several minutes, she pointed at a particular pattern of six lines.

I noticed that each group of lines had a lightly pencilled number written beside it, as if someone more recently had very lightly written numbers in English on the much older manuscript. Fiona's finger touched the number thirty-six. Then she picked up the leather-bound book and opened what I assumed was a corresponding page.

'This is the translation my grandfather had done by a Chinese scholar in Cambridge,' she said.

She studied the page for a few moments and then again to read aloud.

"Life takes the scholarly man across the bridge of nine turnings
The stream bubbles over the rocks, then the flow is dammed
The mind of the poet is filled with thoughts of life and love
His learning may sit heavily upon his shoulders
When two lovers are united, both hearts beating as one
They break the very rocks of the mountain itself

And when young lovers grasp the most secret corner of their hearts
Their whispers are sweeter than the plum, more refreshing than the stream.'"

When she stopped reading, she paused for moment, thinking.

'Don't you see, Michael? There, the *Book of Secrets* tells us everything. We are going to China together.'

She took my hands in hers and gazed into my eyes. I didn't know what to say to her, but I knew in my heart that I loved her. I simply didn't have the ability to express my racing thoughts and feelings.

After a moment's thought, Fiona released my hand, her face an expression of disappointment. 'Oh well, it's just some silly old parlour trick, I suppose.' And then she frowned. 'You must never tell anybody we were in here, Michael. Only Father is allowed in here,' she said.

'No, I won't, I promise.'

That was the last time that Fiona and I played together.

Shanghai – 1927

Chapter 12

LU'S PREDICTION WAS WRONG. BY March 22, the combined forces of the KMT and Zhou's communists controlled Greater Shanghai. Peace reigned. Red flags flew from every building. Meanwhile, the Shanghai International Settlement remained sealed off. 'Island Shanghai' was the name people gave to the International Settlement and the French Concession—twin islands of order in an ocean of chaos.

* * *

Although the events in Shanghai were dramatic and powerful I could barely concentrate on what was happening. My life was made up of stop-and-search patrols, interspersed with the swallowing of half-chewed sandwiches, swigging bottles of tepid water and falling into bed exhausted.

I couldn't sleep. The face of Fiona Burleigh peering through a tinted car window haunted me. Were it not for the crisis in the city I should have gone entirely mad.

* * *

On March twenty-sixth, a KMT gunboat docked at the Bund in the International Settlement. Apart from the crew, it carried one passenger. That was Chiang Kai-Shek. The head of the SMP Special Branch, John Higgins from County Cork, gave Chiang an official pass, which allowed him into the International Settlement and to come and go as he pleased. It was the talk of the Shanghai Municipal Police for days. The gossip in the police canteens speculated endlessly on what business the Special Branch had with the head of the KMT. I remained silent. After witnessing the meeting at Lu's house I sensed with a rising dread what was coming.

12 April 1927

At five a.m. I heard the boat's foghorn ring out from the river in a mournful wail that lasted for a full two minutes. I didn't know it right then, but all over greater Shanghai, an assortment of thugs, organised by Lu, stirred. Members of the Green Gang, plain-clothes members of the KMT and any corner boy who could be roped in put on white armbands marked 'Labour' and went about dealing butchery. Lu's men had simple orders: kill anyone who was armed but not wearing a white armband. Lu's strike on the communists became known as 'the White Terror.'

* * *

After five days of working sixteen-hour shifts on the boundary, mercifully I had a few hours off. I changed out of uniform and, in my best suit, I decided to spend a bit of time promenading along Nanking Road. Inside 'Island Shanghai', life continued almost normally. I just wanted to clear my head and forget the brutality for a few hours. I fancied the idea of an outdoor café on Nanking Road, sipping a coffee, reading a newspaper and looking at the pretty girls. I would read nothing more serious than Hollywood gossip. I'd finally come to accept that the apparition of Fiona had been a fancy of the mind, brought on by fear and exhaustion.

I stood by the kerb on Nanking Road, watching a green tram approach from about a hundred yards away. As it came nearer, I stepped onto the roadway, jogged to the middle, and jumped onto the moving platform, feeling light-hearted at last.

Pushing my way through the passengers, I went inside and scanned for a seat. The tram was full to overflowing, hardly a square inch available. I pushed and elbowed until I was secure in the middle of the crush. I held on to an overhead bar and the tram trundled along the busy street. The babble of conversation was loud and boisterous. Clearly I wasn't the only one trying to forget the bloodbath.

Then the tram came to a dead stop. Commuters, impatient with the unexpected delay, muttered curses. I peered over the shoulders of my fellow travellers and saw a black SMP police car parked lengthways on the tram tracks.

Shortly, two SMP Chinese constables and a foreign sergeant came on board. I realised that I knew him. He saw me looking, and he nodded.

'Afternoon, Gallagher, day off, have you?' I nodded in greeting as his name came back to me. Sergeant Fisher, from London. We'd chatted a few times above at Gordon Road.

Fisher, I saw, had in his hand a head-and-shoulders photograph that he was comparing to faces in the crowd.

A young woman wearing small round glasses, short and thin, her hair tied back in a ponytail, stared intensely at a textbook. The policemen stood in front of her. She continued to read.

'All right, Miss, come along with us.' Her face blanched with fear. In a few seconds, the constables had gripped her arms and hustled her through the crowd.

Once the police had reached the street, two men stepped from the kerb to join them. They looked like typical Green Gang scum—fedoras and glossy two-tone shoes, and wearing the dreaded white armbands. Their dead eyes assessed the young woman, their minds already gutting and filleting her.

A sour taste rose at the back of my throat as I realised that the SMP were handing the young woman over to the Green Gang trigger men.

I examined the faces of my fellow passengers, mostly Chinese, some Europeans. What was I looking for? I don't know. Some sign, some light of intelligence, a connection. What? Some sign of shared outrage?

A small, elderly Chinese man smiled towards me and said, 'We live in terrible times. Nothing you can do, young man.'

I pushed my way through the passengers and exited the tram. Sergeant Fisher stood with a group of uniformed constables, including the two who had picked up the girl.

'Gallagher, how are you?' he said, sounding friendly enough.

'Are you handing that girl over to the Green Gang?' I demanded, my voice quivering with rage.

'As far as I know, they're representatives of the KMT,' Fisher replied.

'You know they'll shoot her as soon as they cross the line into China-town?'

'I'm only following orders from the Municipal Council, as you well know,' he replied.

A traffic jam was building up caused by the stopped tram.

Then Fisher called, 'Let the tram go!'

The police car was moved off the tracks and Fisher said to me, 'Why don't you get back on the tram like a good lad? Don't be interfering with a colleague doing his job.'

I walked away from the tram and the policemen; my fists clenched hard, my jaw locked tight, as I suppressed a scream of frustrated rage. I walked back in the direction I came, not wanting to see what was going on behind me.

* * *

Next morning I was back on duty. We were given an address of a boarding house on Museum Road, told to arrest every occupant and hand him or her over to the KMT.

Early in the morning the Red Marias pulled up in front of the house. The team, wearing body armour and armed with Thompson sub-machine guns, smashed open the door and stormed through the house, kicking open doors upstairs and down.

I ran to the top of the house to an attic room. I kicked open the door, which flew apart like matchwood. I stormed into the tiny room, so small that only the single bed fitted its confines. Sitting up in the bed was a young Chinese couple, both undressed. In their naked state, they looked small, skinny and vulnerable, like schoolchildren. He was a handsome young man, his face grimacing in determination, while his eyes betrayed his fear. She was young and pretty; her hands clutched at the sheets as she tried to cover herself. She began to cry as the young man put his arms around her. I felt ashamed when I saw their raw fear and vulnerability.

I realised that I knew the girl; she was a waitress at the Café Paris on the Avenue Joffre.

I heard the thunder of running boots on the stairs behind me. Other constables would be in the room in seconds.

'Listen to me,' I said, speaking Shanghainese, in a very soft voice. I pointed towards the skylight window. '*Go up there. Make it faster than you've ever been in your life. If you get caught and betray me, I will fucking shoot you personally. Do you understand?*'

They jumped out of bed, naked, and used a chair to hoist themselves through the skylight.

I went outside and stood blocking the two Emergency Unit men about to enter the room.

'It's all clear,' I said. 'No bloody Chinks in this part of the house.'

The two men tramped back down the stairs. I stayed on the landing for a moment. I had a disturbing thought then. What if one of those communist kids remained at liberty only to kill a policeman?

* * *

I found sleep next to impossible. It was unseasonably hot for April; it felt more like June or July. I lay in bed in my room at the Depot, watching the blades of the ceiling fan slowly turning in the moonlight. I counted the slow revolutions. The linen sheets stuck to my body, wet with my sweat. It was dark but I could hear a confused mosquito buzzing, trapped behind the net curtain of the window. I heard booted footsteps marching down the corridor.

I sat up and poured myself cold Chinese tea from the pot on my bedside locker. I had found it a strange drink at first but was quickly gaining a taste for the clear, refreshing quality of it, not swamped in milk and sugar like back home.

I looked around the Spartan room provided for unmarried constables of the Shanghai Municipal Police. It was felt that 'living-in' was a guard against the temptations of Blood Alley, in the absence of the restraining influences of home life. The room was nothing much—a bed, wardrobe, locker, table, chair, and a reading lamp. I lay down again on the bed, feeling the sweaty map of my body imprinted on the sheet. My mind went over my experiences of the past few weeks—the stop-and-search patrols, the refugees and the arrests, the madness of the streets, the noise, confusion, aggression, shouted curses in half a dozen languages. I thought of the looks of hate and fear, the calls of the prostitutes, the screams of the legless beggars and the severed head of the young man in the birdcage.

My stomach churned with acid. I turned on my side and faced the wall. I closed my eyes but I knew there was no sleep to be had this night. My best hope was that exhaustion would eventually carry me off to some peace. I pictured the Singsong girls of Blood Alley; their flashing eyes and cheeky scarlet-lipped smiles burned themselves into my mind's eye. Beautiful girls, heavily made-up, silk cheongsams split to the thigh, cruising the streets like sharks.

* * *

Sunday morning and a few hours off for the Catholics on the force. There were quite a few of us between the Irish and the Scots, and the SMP was quite keen on religious observation by its members.

The Cathedral in Frenchtown. The altar bell rang as the French priest held up the chalice and spoke the familiar words in Latin. The church was dark and cold, a bit of Gothic Europe in the tropical East, and my linen suit was not able to prevent the chill from touching my skin.

I sat up, back against the pew, feeling the hardness press into my spine. I cast my eyes to the stained glass windows depicting scenes of saints passively offering themselves to heathens for sacrifice. Their martyred faces were uncannily similar to the beheaded students in Nantao.

More words in Latin, sounds of bells, and the smell of the incense, which I had hated since the day of my mother's funeral. It made me think of grey November days and black soil, muttered words at a graveside.

I got up then, incense in my nostrils, feeling utterly sick of it all, and walked briskly to the big heavy oak doors. My leather shoes made sharp clipping sounds on the Church tiles. Glares from the Europeans in the congregation. I'd had enough of martyrs and blood and offering it up for the souls in purgatory. I wasn't coming back.

I walked through the oak doors and heard them slam loudly behind me. The rays of sun beamed through the grimy clouds. The unseasonably early humid air wrapped itself to my cold limbs. I squinted my eyes, looked around me—cars honking, cyclists tinkling their bells, shouts, arguments, old men hawking their phlegm on the pavement. I breathed a sigh of relief: every spit, every shout, every cloud of exhaust fumes was like a breath of freedom to me.

19 April 1927

Two days after the raid on the boarding house—two more days of cooperation with lawless butchery—I left the depot very early, wearing a civilian suit and hat. I was determined to find a way to remove myself from cooperation with wholesale illegal executions.

I flagged a rickshaw and had the coolie take me to Nantao. Evidence of the White Terror was everywhere. Here and there, bodies lay unattended in pools of blood on the kerb. Shoppers picked up their feet daintily to keep their shoes clean. I swallowed hard to keep down the acid as I saw a scrawny dog lap up a pool of blood gathered around the body of a dead man wearing a tram conductor's uniform.

I stopped the rickshaw coolie in a narrow street, by the door of a small shop. I dismounted and paid him off. I pushed open the door to the herbalist's shop. A bell tinkled as the door closed behind me. I was overcome with the dark, musty smells of the Chinese herbs.

In front of me was an aged wood counter and, behind, a series of small wooden drawers, from floor to ceiling, which held the strange powders, roots, dried twigs and animal parts which made up the ingredients of the darkly bitter herbs.

Behind the counter stood an old Chinese man. He was small but perfectly proportioned, his body supple and athletic despite his great age. Kindly eyes peered through round spectacles. A Western shirt and bow tie displayed itself over the half-unbuttoned white coat, the universal doctor's uniform.

'Constable Gallagher,' he said. 'What a pleasant surprise.'

'Good morning, Doctor Peng.'

'Do you have a health problem you wish to discuss with me?'

'In a way, I do, Doctor. Do you remember when I assisted you after you were attacked by a pickpocket at Hongkew market?'

'Of course I do; you were noble and kind to a distressed old man.'

'You said that if there was anything you could do to help.'

'You need only name it.'

I looked around the shop, carefully checking that nobody was present.

'We are quite alone,' he said.

I stepped closer to the counter and explained what I needed.

I waited patiently while he gathered together a mix of dried twigs, leaves, roots, mushrooms, and strange twisted objects that I could only imagine the source of. He wrapped them in brown paper and thrust the package into my hands.

'Boil this up, and let it simmer for half an hour. Drink the water.'

Later, in my room at Gordon Road I used the hot plate to boil up the concoction in my teapot. The smell was foul. I threw open the window to dissipate the pungent fumes.

I poured the water from the teapot and watched a thick black sludge drain into my cup. I put it to my lips and nearly gagged. The bitter, musty, earthy foulness of it turned my stomach. I forced it down, nearly retching from the bitter after-taste. I lay down on my bed and waited.

Within half an hour I was pale, shivering, vomiting and running a fever. The SMP doctor diagnosed severe food poisoning and wrote a certificate excusing me from duty for two weeks. After I had seen the police doctor, I went back to my little room and hardly emerged for the full two weeks granted to me on the certificate.

Chapter 13

1 May 1927

NIGHT-TIME, THE STREETS FULL OF life. Food hawkers cried out and rang bells advertising their dishes, clouds of steam arising from cauldrons of soup heated by charcoal. I walked past a man selling fruit and vegetables from an ancient wooden cart. He had unrecognisable fruit nestled between exotic greenery. My mouth salivated, but I walked on. I couldn't buy fruit on the street because we'd been warned to be obsessively careful about street food. Living in Shanghai exposed both natives and foreigners alike to smallpox, cholera, typhoid fever and tuberculosis. The very water was a threat to life. Shanghai and its water were so foul that the rich had their laundry shipped weekly to Kobe.

Through windows came the clatter of mah jong tiles. Rickshaw coolies yelled for custom and mopped the sweat off their brows.

On every second street corner lounged triad gangsters. Red Gang or Green Gang, I wasn't sure, but they signalled their gang allegiance by the way they held their cigarettes, wary shark-eyes scanning the street from under the brims of their fedora hats. Coiled energy, ready to pull a knife or a gun at the first hint of danger or excitement.

The pungent smell of fish hit me as I passed an open-air fishmonger's stall. Portly Indian tailors stood in the doorways of their shops and offered to make suits: 'Better than Savile Row, sir, in four hours!' Children scampered between the feet of their families.

I rounded the corner into a street full of nightclubs and cocktail bars. Garish neon signs pulsed, shouting out their messages: Joe's Tavern! The 'Frisco! Mumms! Cold beer!

Ancient Chinese Mandarins in their long, black silk robes rubbed shoulders with American businessmen in pinstriped suits and sharp hats. Commercial travellers checked the rates in the windows of the Armenian currency dealers. French soldiers, ebony-coloured Africans, Indochinese and Moroccans, from the barracks in Frenchtown, negotiated with Singsong girls. The girls indicated with pantomimed hand gestures and shrieks of laughter that the black soldiers' large manhood would attract a supplementary fee.

Japanese girls in silk kimonos clipped along on their wooden clogs leaving a blurred image in the mind of a slash of red lipstick on white-powdered faces.

* * *

Then I was standing at the door of 'The Blue Lady.'

My jaw clenched with anger and disgust when I remembered the way DeVere and those gangsters sat around and carved up the city for themselves while kids died in the gutter. I thought of my father, and the day I had to walk back to Nellie Woods grocer because I'd been given a shilling too much change. What fools we were.

The doorman was a big Chinese man, a solid muscular slab with cropped hair and a thin moustache. He blocked the door with a beefy arm. I stopped and looked him in the eye.

'*Shanghai Municipal Police. I am here to see Mister Dell.*' He smiled and slowly opened the door and gestured for me to enter.

I walked into a gloomy corridor and vaguely heard music and voices as if very far away. I continued down the corridor and pushed my way through a heavy velvet curtain. The room inside was very softly lit, and the predominant colours were dark red and blue. There were people seated at tables around the room and also on deep, soft couches around the walls. There was a heavy rich smell in the air that I could not identify. Italian opera played from a scratchy Victrola. Things seemed to move slowly, as if the room was under water, and the atmosphere was strange, morbid rather than celebratory—definitely not a typical nightclub.

A young Chinese woman wearing a deep blue cheongsam appeared.

'Yes, sir, how can I help you?'

Then I heard a voice. 'Michael, Michael! Up here!'

I followed the sound and saw Jack sitting at a corner booth. I was relieved to see him. His tie was loosened and his jacket off. He looked relaxed but there was something alert about him even now, like a tiger taking the sun. Two young women sat with him. I walked over.

'Michael, young fella. Take the weight off. I thought I'd see you by and by. Have a drink.'

I sat and one of the young women poured me a tall glass of beer from an iced jug. I drank deeply and began to relax a little.

As my eyes adjusted to the gloom I could see that the women were Chinese, very beautiful in a heavily made-up kind of way, and young—perhaps seventeen or eighteen. They sat on either side of Jack and both leaned snugly against his broad body.

'All right, young fella. Tell Uncle Jack. Let's hear it.'

I drank again and wondered where to start.

'Jack, my father was an RIC Sergeant. He believed in law and order. But the things I've seen in this city…'

''Tis a rough place all right. What's on your mind?'

'I keep thinking about the meeting between DeVere and Big Ears Lu. If the most important man in the city government can make a deal with its biggest gangster, then the whole place is a cesspit.'

'That's a good description.' He grinned wolfishly.

'And then, we were expected to hand a bunch of school kids over to the bloody KMT. I don't know, Jack. Why are we doing our jobs at all?' As I said this I felt a weight lift from my shoulders. It was such a relief to voice my doubts.

Jack sat back with a sigh, placing a meaty hand on the upper thigh of each girl. He closed his eyes for a moment.

'Michael, didya ever hear the one about the chap who went home and brought back a wife from dear old Blighty?'

'No, Jack, I didn't hear it.'

'Well, anyway, this chap he worked in a bank or insurance company, or some such. Anyway, he was a *box wallah*. So his five-year long leave comes up and he decides to go back to Blighty to get himself a respectable wife, as expected by the *Taipans* and just the ticket for his career prospects. He finds the right girl, talks to Dad, proposes, marries, honeymoons, and takes her by ship back to Shanghai.'

I nodded for him to continue.

'The ship docks on the Bund late in the evening. They arrive at the house late at night with all the servants in bed and the house in darkness. Not wanting to wake anyone, they enter the house silently and go straight to bed.

'In the morning, he gets up at the crack of dawn and goes off to the stables to get in his morning ride before the office. The missy sleeps late, tired out from travelling.'

'I'm with you so far.'

'Well, anyway, the Number One Boy enters the master's bedroom and sees an attractive young woman sleeping there. He wakes her up and says, "You go now, amah clean room." Naturally the young lady protests; she is, after all, the lady of the house. So the Number One Boy hands her five dollars and says, "Master always say give five dollar for lady take taxi home!"'

He shouted with laughter, his heavy hands slapping his thigh.

'D'ya see, Michael?'

'Very funny, Jack, but what's your point?'

'It shows the way life is run in this city.'

'So, Jack, how *is* this city run?'

'Let me tell you about who runs this city. The public school boys. I got to know them in the war. They are all talk about the old school chums, and the regimental tie, and the huntin' and the shootin' and the fishin', you know.' Jack said this in a tone of cruel mimicry of the English public-school accent. He went on: 'But you know what they care about? Do you?'

I shook my head.

'They are here to wring every last drop out of the Chinese. Children in Shanghai are left to die on the streets or get bought and sold like cattle. The West's been pushing opium on the Chinese for a hundred years. And all so they could pay for their tea from India.' As he mentioned tea, he held his hand out, little finger extended daintily, in mimicry of polite tea drinking.

'So what's that got to do with us?' I asked.

'It's dog-eat-dog here and it's too big a mess for anyone to change it. Michael, do you know what well-informed people call the Municipal Council? A band of unconvicted crooks, that's what! This whole city is run on corruption. Do you know that the best hotels in this town have opium on room service?'

'Then how do you get on in a mess like this?'

'Michael, there's a couple of Irish lads, along with myself. Did you ever hear the old Irish song *"Ye ramblin' boys of pleasure"*? You must've sung it in the pub a few times, as we all did. Well, that's the name of our little club. We are the *ramblin' boys of pleasure*. We just take a bit of *cumshaw* from the opium dens and brothels. We give 'em a quick phone call before a raid and they pay generously for it. Dropping a dime, as the Yanks call it. 'Tis harmless stuff. Sure if we close them, they open up the next day a couple of yards down the street.'

He clinked his glass with mine.

'*Slainte*! Welcome to *the ramblin' boys of pleasure.*'

'Jack, I'll be honest with you. I've never said this to anyone before, but I've thought of it since I was a boy. I want to be rich. I want to live in the world that the toffs live in. There are certain girls… well, a man would have to be rich to enter their world.'

'Good man, yourself,' he replied with a broad smile.

'But what would we do if we were caught? You and I have no connections at all. We're working class boys.'

He sat forward, his eyes intense.

'Michael, do you *really* want to make something of yourself? No peeler on the beat ever got rich.'

'I do, Jack. I want it.'

'Look, young fella, the current king of the social scene in Shanghai is Sir Victor Sassoon—and he's a Persian Jew. So don't you worry about the old school tie.'

'It's very tempting.'

'Michael, what do you like—cards, booze, girls, horses?—You can afford it all. We all can.'

As Jack reeled off the benefits of his proposal, I felt excitement rise within me. Greed made my pulse race and I sat straighter in my seat.

Jack smiled grimly. 'This is a city in chaos. It's the busiest trading port in the world. The place is awash in money. The West runs Shanghai and it functions well enough from day to day. But warlords run the rest of the country.'

He picked up his beer and drank deeply, his Adam's apple bobbing with each swallow. He sighed noisily as he put his glass down, carefully positioning it so that it landed exactly on its original condensation ring.

He spoke again. 'The city itself is really three cities in one, as you know: the French sector; the International, run by the British and the Yanks; and the rest, Greater Shanghai, run by the Chinese. Different law in each area. Different police. Nobody can even figure out who controls the Outside Roads area. The triads run prostitution, opium, and smuggling. Every second building in the city houses a brothel, a nightclub, a bar or an opium den. It's awash with refugees from every civil war and revolution in the world. Anyone can turn up without a passport or visa. There's a dozen foreign armies and navies based here. There's three or four different currencies in use. It's chaos.'

'You make chaos sound like a benefit, Jack.'

'I do indeed, Michael. In chaos, a man has a chance to make good for himself. You are a working-class boy, as am I. How would we get on at home? I'd be running a fruit stall. You'd be a peeler on the beat like your old man. Here we have servants, cars, and money to be made. The chaos, Michael, is like Europe in the Middle Ages. We can be knights on horse-back. We fight for what we can get, and we make something of ourselves. We don't bow down to our betters. We fight like men, take what we can, and devil take the hindmost. Shanghai is the place to make it.'

'That sounds grand, Jack. But Mister Fairlight would kill us if he found out anything. He is straight as a die.'

His jaw tightened. 'Ah, Jaysus, Michael, would you take the broom handle out of your arse and cop on to yourself? There's a wonderful saying I picked up from the Chinks.' He closed his eyes for a moment in recollection and recited in excellent Shanghainese, '*The Mountain is high and the Emperor is far away.*'

'But what about the oath we took?'

'Fuck the oath, Michael. Did you learn anything from the White Terror?'

'We're still cops, aren't we?'

Jack's face darkened.

'Listen here to me now, Michael; let me make one thing clear. We are all good cops. Any one of the *ramblin' boys* would lay down his life in defence of a decent citizen—no matter who they are—foreign, oriental, anything. But I refuse to go storming into an opium den with a gun in my hand, putting my life on the line, just 'cause some crazy, bible-thumping, sex-starved Missus Grundy of a Christian missionary thinks that someone, somewhere, might be enjoying themselves.'

He reached forward and shook my hand firmly. 'You are one of *the ramblin' boys of pleasure* now. Don't let us down and we won't let you down.'

I felt alert, excited, thinking of the possibilities.

'Let Uncle Jack advise you and all will be well. Now, in the meantime you can take a weight off my hands.' At a signal from Jack, one of the girls moved to my side.

She put her arms around me, kissed me, and I felt her tongue flutter between my lips. I squeezed my arms around her, feeling her slim delicate body through the silk cheongsam. Hungrily, I returned her kisses. In the background, I heard Jack say, 'Plenty rooms upstairs, young fella.'

The girl stood and took my hand, pulled me up from my seat and guided me away from the table. I began to follow her. My eyes devoured her body through the silk dress. A thought began to form in my mind and I stopped, turned, and faced Jack. 'This will cost something…'

'All on the house, young fella,' he said with an imperious wave of his hand.

The girl pulled me by the hand as if leading her pet poodle. She walked towards a dark narrow stairway and began to climb. I followed, still holding her hand. We walked down a long corridor and came to a doorway.

The girl knocked and an old Chinese woman in an amah's black pants and jacket immediately opened the door. They exchanged words in rapid Shanghai dialect. The old woman laughed lasciviously, a hacking wheezy cough, as she stood back and gestured for us to enter. As we stepped inside, she closed the door and left us alone.

The room was plain, having nothing more than a bed and a washbasin. The plainness of it was disguised somewhat, because the only light came from a pleasantly glowing red-shaded side lamp.

With a brisk, efficient movement the girl removed her cheongsam and stood before me, naked and perfect. I reached for her like a starving man. With a laugh she pushed me back onto the bed. She made a shushing sound as if calming a baby. Slowly, she began to untie my laces, undo my buttons, and, piece by piece, remove my clothing.

Finally, I lay naked and suddenly ashamed of my virginity, and my Catholic scruples.

'What's your name?' I whispered.

'May,' she replied with a giggle as she started to cover my body in soft kisses.

Afterwards, I lay on my back staring at the shadows on the ceiling. The girl slept softly, curled up like a cat.

This time I didn't hear my father's voice at all. Soon I slept deeply.

Chapter 14

North China Daily News June 1 1927
Philanthropist awarded The Order of the Brilliant Jade

Eminent businessman, community leader and philanthropist Mister Lu Sun Yu, resident of the French Concession, has been awarded The Order of the Brilliant Jade. Generalissimo Chiang Kai Shek of the Nationalist Government presented the award. Along with Mister Lu, the same award was presented to Mister John Higgins, a native of County Cork and head of the Shanghai Municipal Police Special Branch. The award was based on their efforts in calming the situation and restoring order during the recent troubles caused by Communist agitators.

In addition to this award, Mister Lu has been appointed to the position of Chief of the Bureau of Opium Suppression. During the presentation ceremony the Generalissimo said: 'There is not a citizen of Shanghai who has displayed a greater concern for the scourge of opium among the working classes of the Chinese citizenry.'

The Generalissimo also noted in his speech that Mister Lu is one of the greatest contributors to charity in Shanghai and is a member of the French Municipal Council, president of several banks, and the founder and director of a middle-school for poor but deserving Chinese children.

3 June 1927

THE WHITE TERROR FINALLY CONCLUDED with thousands of communists, trade unionists, left wing students and intellectuals executed. With a sigh of relief, I read that the State of Emergency was suspended. I'd taken to reading every English-language newspaper from cover to cover and now I read all the coverage of Chiang Kai-Shek's takeover of Greater Shanghai.

The newspapers boldly stated that the West considered Chiang a man to be trusted. The gates of the International Settlement and the French

Concession were opened. I watched workers remove the sandbags and barriers. Normal traffic resumed. KMT soldiers and their police force, called the Public Safety Bureau, kept order in Greater Shanghai. For the first time, as a sign of the friendship between Chiang and the West, Chinese were allowed into the public parks of the International Settlement.

I was patrolling the Bund with a stop-and-search patrol as the hated sign 'No dogs or Chinese allowed' was ripped down and trampled by grinning municipal workers. I was relieved to see it go. I'd found the sign offensive in the extreme and it had made me think of the worst excesses of British rule in Ireland.

Rivers of booze flowed, the jazz was loud, and the girls plied their trade.

Foreign residents finally began to sleep easily in their beds. Shanghai was saved. But they forgot that it wasn't their troops who saved Shanghai from Communism; it was the gunmen of Big Ears Lu.

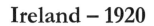

Ireland – 1920

Chapter 15

The Times – July 1st 1920
Great Houses of Ireland under threat from arsonists

The Irish Republican Army continues to unleash a wave of terror on the law-abiding citizens of Ireland. As if the armed hold-up of banks and post offices, and the assassination of policemen and government officials wasn't enough, the 'shinners' have now taken to burning the great houses of the old Anglo-Irish Aristocracy.

Heads of households of the finest families, with the most distinguished histories, are sending their wives and children away to the mainland for their own safety. These brave men, many of whom recently spilled their blood on the Western Front, sit awake at night, shotguns at the ready, waiting for the 'shinners' to slink from the bushes to do their worst.

Many of the finest houses have already been torched by the so-called 'freedom fighters.' What good does it do, we ask, to burn a house that has stood as a monument to the community for two hundred years or more and is furnished with the finest collections of art, china, furniture and libraries of immeasurable value?

The problem is exacerbated by the fact that the Royal Irish Constabulary is stretched to breaking point by a combination of resignations under intimidation, assassinations of constables, and incidents all over the counties. The Chief Constable of the RIC, from his post at Dublin Castle, told this correspondent that 'the situation is growing increasingly tense in all parts of the country, but particularly, the south-west region.'

20 August 1920

I WAS EATING THE MIDDAY dinner in the kitchen with my father. Bacon and cabbage, the standard fare for the Irish working classes. I ate silently and slowly, feeling very uneasy, my mind consumed with the morning's events.

About mid-morning, I'd stood by the main door of the station, watching as my father brought in a well-known character from the town.

Mister Galvan wore a smart tweed jacket with leather patches on the elbows, jodhpurs and glistening riding boots. His ensemble was topped off with a bowler hat. He was a well-known sporting man who attended every race meeting, card game, dance and boxing match in the country. A constant gambler, he was often drunk but mostly polite and rarely disorderly. He'd won and lost more than most had earned in a lifetime, was fond of the whiskey and was prone to getting in fights when he was down on his luck.

He was picked up after a fight in Maloney's pub. My father gripped him by the right arm, and ushered him towards the cells. Mister Galvan took his left hand out of his britches pocket and I saw something fall to the ground.

'Wait, Sergeant, wait, there's a pound in it for you if you'll oblige me and let me go home.'

Quickly I darted forward and my hand closed around the crumpled pound note.

Father glared at his captive, his jaw tight and his eyes blazing. 'Bribery of a police officer is extremely serious, Mister Galvan.'

Galvan remained silent, his mouth open but no words coming. Father turned his gaze towards me.

'I'm sorry you had to hear that sordidness. Remember, a policeman who takes a bribe loses his very soul. Remember that, always,' he said as he pushed Mister Galvan towards the cells. I ran to the door as I observed Mister Galvan's face redden and his mouth open in voiceless protest at the indignation of being both detained and robbed in the same moment.

Now, as I sat at the table, I was almost faint with excitement and fear. Should I hand over the pound note and lose it, and expose myself as a thief? Or should I say nothing but have the theft of a pound on my conscience? I longed to buy a gift for Fiona. Father would disown me if he knew. Stealing is a mortal sin. How many times did I hear the priest say it from the polished mahogany pulpit? His voice raised in outraged indignation that anybody in this parish would *dare* to break a commandment. After the way Jesus Christ suffered for *your* sins, you dare to defy the Son of God in *this way*? I was going to hell. What was it like, hell? Could you get used to it, or would the fires get hotter and hotter so that you were always in agony?

The kitchen door flew open, banging against the wall.

It was one of the RIC Constables, Dan Ryan, a young Corkman who was always very kind to me. His face was flushed and his eyes wide with fear.

'Sergeant!' he shouted. 'The Shinners are coming!'

'All right, Constable Ryan, thank you,' my father replied.

My father turned to me, calm and unflappable.

'Listen here, boy; this is the time for following instructions. Go up to your room and crawl under the bed. Now, go. Don't come out for Jesus Christ himself. Only me. Now! Go!'

I ran up the stairs to my room and dived under the bed. The hand of fear squeezed my guts. The dust and fluff from the linoleum floor made me cough and sneeze. I heard the voices of men shouting downstairs. Commands, heavy boot steps running, smashing glass, and the slamming noise of the opening and closing of doors.

Then, the sound of the truck, pulling up on the main street. And the sound of gunfire. Sporadic bursts, loud and flat, each one terrifying. There was rifle fire coming from the street and the Auxiliary Unit inside the barracks responded with a heavy mix of rifle fire, shotgun blasts, and machine gun bursts. Bullets shattered the window of my bedroom; shards of glass covered the floor. A chunk of plaster fell from the ceiling, sending up a cloud of white dust. I thought of petrol bombs, a common IRA weapon. If the Shinners set fire to the station, I would never get out alive.

I imagined the flames then. The flames of a petrol bomb to take me to the flames of hell.

I heard the sound of the truck starting up and quickly driving away. The gunfire petered out.

The door opened. I saw the bottle green legs and black boots of my father.

'Alright, lad, you can come out now.'

I crawled on my elbows from under the bed. There was a streak of white dust across the left shoulder of his uniform.

'Did you shoot any of them, Father?' I asked in my bravest voice.

He shook his head. 'I'm no killer of men, Michael. Ah, what man would want to kill his own neighbours, cut a man down in cold blood?'

'By the time I was standing, he had already left the room.

* * *

The heavily armed Auxiliary Unit together with the regular RIC Constables took off at top speed in their two lorries in pursuit of the IRA Flying Column.

About half an hour passed and, suddenly, one of the lorries used by the Auxiliaries pulled up in front of the barracks. Major Flyte, commander of the unit, came bounding in to the day room. Despite the day's activities, he looked immaculate in his glistening riding boots, tailored khaki uniform and leather bandoliers.

'Sergeant Gallagher, I need you,' he shouted briskly, a voice straight from the square at Sandhurst.

'Yes, Major?'

'I've just been given an urgent message from Burleigh Castle. Burleigh's gamekeeper stopped us at the Mount Coote crossroads. The family's been given an hour to get out before the building is torched by the Shinners. But his Lordship is refusing to go. Told 'em to go to hell. He needs all the help he can get to defend the place. We haven't a moment to spare. Most of my men are still off in the other lorry. We split up at the crossroads of Bruree. But there's you and me, Sergeant Gallagher, and my driver; we'll go up there now and make a show of force. With a bit of luck that'll be enough to frighten them off.'

'Very well, Major. I'll come with you. Of course any prisoners will be placed under arrest. Is that understood?'

Father said to me, 'Don't move under any circumstances until I come back.'

I heard the truck take off and the gears crash and grind as it struggled to gain speed. I felt utterly alone, as I locked and barred the doors and windows of the barracks. Father had released Mister Galvan before they left. There wasn't another living soul in the barracks.

It began to get dark slowly, the way it does in Ireland in the summertime. Hours went by with no sign of anybody. I picked up and discarded several books, flicking through the pages but unable to concentrate. Finally, off in the distance I heard the faint sounds of gunfire. The sound rose and fell and lasted for a long time. I felt terrified. Time went by, eventually the sound of gunfire died down. And still nobody appeared.

I noticed an orange glow above the trees. It was like the glow of sunset but coming from the wrong direction. I could see smoke rising. Burleigh Castle was on fire.

I pulled on my leather sandals, ran down the stairs, and grabbed my father's big, black police-issue bike. I mounted the bike and pedalled through the twilight.

I arrived at the gates of the castle. Two British army lorries were parked near the main gate. Several regular British soldiers stood around, in their tin helmets and battle-dress. In the middle of the group, the parish priest Father O'Brien stood. He was a tall, very thin, almost gaunt man with large soulful eyes and a receding hairline.

I tried to veer around him and he reached for me, grabbed me by the front of the shirt and pulled me off the bicycle.

'Come here to me, boy. Over by the wall now.'

I stumbled off the bike and walked with him towards the wall.

'I have some terrible news,' he said. 'There was a battle up at the Castle. The Shinners, they're after killing your father, and everyone in the castle. They're all dead, Michael, God rest their souls.'

The priest's strong hands held me by the arms. I struggled free. I dodged around him and ran through the gates towards the castle, up the long, tree-lined avenue that I had only ever walked up during daytime.

There was a glow of bright light. I ran faster and faster. I came to the end of the driveway and stopped dead.

In front of me were smoke-blackened walls, shattered windows, and a building without a roof.

British soldiers stood around cradling their weapons in their arms. A line of human bodies under blankets lay along by the rose bed.

A soldier inhaled deeply on his cigarette, his cheeks hollowing. He blew out a cloud of blue smoke and in the same breath remarked to his companion, 'Fuck me, mate, they're torched beyond recognition.'

Slowly I walked towards them. A pair of legs in the scorched remnants of bottle green RIC trousers stuck out from under a blanket. I felt strong hands grip my shoulders; it was the priest.

'Your father is with God now. I'm very sorry, Michael.'

'Who else?' I demanded.

'It's your father and also Lord Burleigh. Miss Fiona Burleigh's body has not yet been recovered.'

'Where's Major Flyte? Is he all right?'

'They're recalled to Limerick City. Terrible trouble there; the Lord Mayor's been shot. Their truck left just now. Major Flyte asked me to say that he was sorry about your father.'

Then, I was falling.

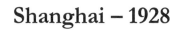

Shanghai – 1928

Chapter 16

I WAS OUTSIDE THE DEL MONTE nightclub queuing to get in. I'd gone out alone for the night, as I didn't fancy another night in the police canteen talking rugby and horse racing and listening to McCormack on the gramophone. I didn't come half-way round the world for that.

A big black Packard pulled up at the front of the club. Five hoodlums emerged from the car, eyes swivelling, hands on their bulky pockets. They strode inside the club, ignoring the queue, and within a few minutes they re-emerged and stood forming a protective cordon by the door. 'Now this is interesting,' I thought, and pressed back into the shadows. One of the thugs raised his hand in signal and three more cars drove fast towards the club.

When the convoy of cars pulled up, I saw that the first and last of the three cars, also Packards, were bristling with gunmen, and in the middle of the convoy was a bulletproof black Dusenberg. It was a big, powerful ocean liner of a car with an impressively long bonnet and wide running boards. The uniformed chauffeur got out, a big solid man, cropped hair, typical of the ex-Tsarist soldiers working as hired muscle in Shanghai. The chauffeur opened the rear passenger door, and out stepped Big Ears Lu. On his arm was a heavily made-up young Russian woman, dripping with jewels. I'd read that he had a penchant for blonde, blue-eyed women.

The queue stood back to allow the great man to enter. As he passed me by, he stopped for a second, looked in my eyes and nodded in greeting. I tensed, hoping he wouldn't speak to me. Did he remember me from the meeting?

Then, as the doormen held open the red doors, he and his girl walked inside. When I entered the club a couple of minutes after, one of Lu's men brushed past me and I felt a note slipped into my hand. I went to the men's room, locked myself in a cubicle and read it. It simply said:

Please take tea with Mister Lu tomorrow morning at eight,
in the teahouse by the Bridge of the Nine Turnings.

I sat there in the toilet cubicle re-reading the note. What could Lu want with me? Unease spread out from my guts. Lu was a snake; his bite was poison. Why would I have anything to do with him? What if I was seen and how would it look to be consorting with him?

But the main thing was fear. I was scared of Lu. Yet there was something about his power. This was not a man to take refusal kindly, and I knew I didn't have the guts to refuse Lu Sun Yu. I felt compelled to see him.

* * *

I took a rickshaw to Yu Gardens. I stood by the Bridge of the Nine Turnings. From the teahouse there was the babble of loud conversation in harsh Shanghainese, the song of birds in bamboo cages, the loud clipping of mah jong tiles on wooden tables. All the sounds mingled with the barks of laughter and argument, and impatient shouts for service.

'*Why am I here?*' the voice in my head kept repeating. In truth, I was afraid to offend the most powerful and dangerous man in Shanghai. But I was curious too. What does he want with little Mikie Gallagher from Kilmallock?

Here was a man who sat in his lair and whispered his commands. In response, armies moved, men lived, men died, some were elevated to great fortune, and those fallen from grace died with their head garrotted from their shoulders.

The teahouse was open to the elements; bamboo blinds had been rolled up to let in the morning sun. The corners of the green-tiled roof curved upward, dragon faces snarling at the world.

Chinese men, mainly elderly, and for the most part wearing traditional mandarin robes, sat grouped around tables, loudly slurped tea, and daintily picked up morsels of yum cha with long ivory chopsticks.

Through the packed room, waiters in black silk jackets glided like ballet dancers, skilfully pouring aromatic Chinese tea and delivering trays of dim sum.

My stomach growled; my senses activated by the food smells. It had been six a.m. when I left my room—too early for breakfast and, besides, I was too scared to eat.

I felt inside my jacket and gripped the police pistol. My hand was slick with the sweat of fear. With my other hand, I wiped my brow with a handkerchief. I wondered if the whole of Yu Gardens could hear my pounding heart.

Seated at a spacious corner table was Big Ears Lu. He wore a long Chinese robe that looked expensively tailored. He sat alone, holding his *North China Daily News* in one hand while he picked up his cup and blew on its surface to cool his tea. Such an ordinary gesture from one so monstrous, I thought. It seemed as if there was an invisible field around Big Ears Lu, as if he was in a different room to everyone else. The noise and babble of the room did not affect his corner. No one spoke to him or made eye contact and one waiter seemed dedicated to Big Ears Lu's table.

Using a *Defendu* technique, I softened my knees and allowed my feet to feel the ground beneath me. I concentrated on my out breaths until I felt my racing heartbeat slowly come down. With a final deep breath, I stepped forward onto the zigzag bridge.

I reached the teahouse. A waiter shouted at me in Shanghainese and I barged past him, saying in Shanghainese, '*I have an appointment.*' I cut through the melee of moving bodies until I was in front of Big Ears Lu's table.

He glanced at me briefly and resumed reading his paper. Big Ears Lu sipped his tea and slowly put the delicate china cup on the table. After a long pause, he looked at me, made a hand gesture as if swatting a fly. 'Sit down,' he said.

I sat and after a moment he looked up from his newspaper and said, 'Allow me to choose tea for you.' He whispered a command to a waiter and shortly a cup was placed in front of me. The waiter, using a teapot with an extremely long spout, poured the tea while standing several steps from the table. A thin jet of amber tea poured almost horizontally from the pot to my cup, a distance of three or four feet, as precise as a circus trick.

Lu nodded his approval. 'We call that stretching the tea. It cools it down.' I took a sip and found that it was dark, smoky and strangely appealing.

'I have a task that you might carry out for me,' Lu said. 'I will, of course, pay you well.'

'But why me, sir?'

'I remember when you came to my house with Mister DeVere,' he replied.

'That was a long time ago, sir.'

'Have you heard of *Mien Shiang*—the Chinese art of face reading? I like to judge a man by how his face reads. I believe you are reliable.'

'Thank you, sir.' I felt strangely pleased to be complimented by the gangster.

As I sipped my tea, Lu continued. 'In order for your task to make sense, it is necessary to tell you something of my history.'

I nodded that I was listening. As he began to speak I watched him carefully, observing his tall, thin frame, his granite-hard face with the enormous handle-like ears. Rather than make Lu look ridiculous, the ears accentuated his Sphinx-like face. His long silk gown complemented his face, and as he sat back and crossed his legs, his hem rose up to display red silk socks and elegant polished leather European shoes.

'As a result of my help to the International Settlement and the French Concession against the Communists, I have been awarded The Order of the Brilliant Jade by the Generalissimo himself. It is also my pleasure to contribute to many of the charities in this city of many unfortunates. I am happy to help, because I know poverty well. Do you know poverty, Mister Gallagher?'

'To some extent,' I replied, picking my words carefully. 'I come from Ireland, which is a poor country.'

'Good, good,' Lu said. 'I was born in Pudong to a life of crippling poverty. As an infant, hunger was my companion. I was orphaned in my infancy and raised by a grandmother, who also died when I was a child. I could neither read nor write. One of my earliest childhood memories is of my baby sister—sold, in order to put food on the table.'

I shook my head, trying to imagine what it must be like for someone to sell a child.

Just then a man who had been seated at a nearby table rose and approached us, his shoulders hunched in an attitude of supplication. He carried a sheaf of papers and, with an apologetic bow, he placed them on the table. I realised then that the men seated at the neighbouring table were part of Lu's retinue.

Lu grunted impatiently, snapped his fingers, and an expensive fountain pen was instantly placed in his hand. He leaned forward, scanned the paper, and then in an awkward, child-like scrawl, he appended his signature to the paper. He wrote slowly and clumsily, his lips parted in concentration. When he had finished, he grunted another order, and the man took the papers away with another apologetic bow.

Lu looked me in the eye as if daring me to comment on his obvious illiteracy.

'You were saying, sir,' I said softly, anxious to move on from the tension of the moment.

'Ah yes. At the age of fifteen I came across the river for the first time. A stupid, poor, starving boy with my eyes weeping pus from infection; I had never even learned to read or write. But I had something, Mister Gallagher. I had *puèdìng*—the will to live. I started out as an assistant to a fruit seller. I wasn't paid; only given one yuan a month to wash in the public baths and have a haircut and be presentable for the fruit stall's customers. My pay was food and a bed.'

There was something about the way Lu spoke, steel in his voice. I felt a power in him. This was a man who could thrive no matter what disaster was thrown at him.

He sipped his tea, gathering his thoughts. I took a moment also to sip the dark smoky hot liquid.

'That must have been very difficult, sir,' I said.

'Where could a boy like me go from there? The Green Gang gave me my home. They became my brothers, my father, and my mother. For a time I became lost in gambling and opium. It was my brotherhood that pulled me out of that abyss. I worked hard and had the help of generous men. I rose up until I find myself where you see me today, Mister Gallagher. I enjoy wealth, privilege and connections.'

He sipped his tea again. I became aware of the chirping of the birds in their cages. Just then one bird panicked and began to thrash against its cage, its wings battering hysterically. Its master reached inside the cage and soothed the bird.

Another Chinese man approached the table. He was elderly and upright, dressed in the ancient silk robes of a Mandarin scholar. He cleared his throat softly.

Lu turned towards the old man and spoke gently: '*Good morning, uncle. May I offer you tea?*'

'*Oh no,*' replied the old man, '*I have no wish to disturb your important work. I merely wanted to thank you for your wonderful donation to the museum. Many precious artworks have been saved, thanks to your great kindnesses.*'

'*It is nothing, uncle,*' Lu said.

He turned back to me as the old man walked away. 'I like to help my people.'

'I understand, sir,' I replied, wondering what direction this conversation could possibly take.

'But there is a great sadness in my heart. Not a night goes by that I do not dream of my baby sister. To whom was my sister sold? Did she become a slave? A servant? Did she replace a dead daughter in some grieving mother's arms? I vowed that I would never rest until I found her.'

'That must have been terrible, sir.'

'You too have lost someone, Mister Gallagher. I see sadness in your eyes.'

I stiffened, feeling exposed. This powerful and evil man could read my story, as if it were printed on my face like a newspaper headline.

For a moment I wondered if I should tell him about Fiona. Perhaps he could help me?

'If my sister is alive, and she is found, it is well known that I will pay a great reward. Many women of my sister's age have approached my people with stories of various plausibility. My agents have been able to debunk all claims. However, a month ago, a woman came to us with a story that appears to be entirely genuine. Should I take her into my heart, as my long-lost sister? I want to, of course, but Lu Sun Yu will not be fooled. It cannot be allowed.'

I sipped my tea slowly, allowing small drops to trickle down my throat, wondering how this could involve me. What did he want from me?

'What I wish you to do, Mister Gallagher, is to investigate this young woman and establish the truth.' He leaned forward, his dark eyes blazing intensely.

I cleared my throat and spoke, feeling my throat tightening.

'You realise, Mister Lu, that I am not a detective?'

'I am aware of it. Nevertheless, you caught my eye when you came with Mister DeVere.'

'I am not sure I am the right man for the job, sir. There are perhaps private detectives. Or the French, perhaps Mister Fan and his colleagues in the *gendarme*…' My voice trailed off as I saw the shining, fanatical determination in Lu's eyes.

'I have made enquiries and I have been told that you are a reliable man, a rare thing in this city of ours. Show some compassion for me, Mister Gallagher. Find my sister—or tell me the truth. I will pay you in American dollars, the equivalent of three years of your salary.'

I inhaled sharply. Even with my not inconsiderable income from the *ramblin' boys*, three years' salary was a substantial sum of money for what could surely be but a few days' work.

He reached into a briefcase by his side and extracted a large manila envelope. 'This is her file, Mister Gallagher. Please study it, do your research and report back to me here. You will find me here, or you may telephone my comprador Mister Lau.'

He gazed at me, his eyes hypnotic. Refusal was impossible.

'What if I find that she is not genuine, Mister Lu?'

'Bring her to me and she will be taken care of.'

'What do you mean?'

'Shanghai is a jungle, Mister Gallagher. I thought you would know that by now. If she is a fraud she will be dealt with. All you have to do is bring her to me.'

'Very well, Mister Lu, I will try, but I cannot guarantee a definite result.'

He offered me his hand and we shook. 'All I ask is that you do your best. Now please excuse me; I have business to attend to.'

Chapter 17

I STEPPED OUT OF THE shower at Gordon Road gymnasium and headed towards my locker, a white towel draped around my wet body. I saw a slim, handsome young Chinese man dressed in an elegant light-grey suit, with gleaming two-tone shoes, walking towards the exit of the dressing rooms. He was small and slight, but had the coiled energy of the martial arts devotee, his body muscular and powerful, his movements suggesting a man who could spring into action as fast as a panther. There was something familiar about him.

'Hey!' I shouted. 'Hold up there; I want to talk to you.'

The young man stopped and stared.

'I know you, but I don't know from where,' I said.

He smiled and nodded. 'You likee trip Nantao?' in the Pidgin English of Chinese servants.

I slapped my forehead. 'You're the rickshaw coolie who got me out of that jam. How the hell did you wind up here?'

He reached into his jacket, pulled out his wallet, and flipped it, revealing a Shanghai Municipal Police badge. 'Chinese Police Co'stable 366, CPC Wang,' he said. 'Freddie Wang.'

'Why were you pulling a rickshaw?' I asked.

'Lot communist activity 'mong coolie,' he said. 'You wan' know more?' he said with an obsequious bow.

'All right,' I said, feeling intrigued.

'You eat chow big time me tonight?'

I agreed to join him, feeling curious about this mysterious young man. Like most westerners in Shanghai, I considered Chinese food to be slop eaten only by the natives, who knew no better and couldn't afford a decent joint of lamb. But I'd give it a try for once.

That evening, Freddie Wang, wearing a different but equally elegant suit, picked me up at our agreed meeting point, the main entrance to Central Station.

'Let's get a rickshaw,' I said.

'No! Walk good,' he replied and began to move briskly. I followed and we stepped along in silence.

We walked to the Bund, turned south towards Frenchtown and into the old Chinese City of Nantao. When we came through the gates and reached the market I glanced upward to where the birdcage had hung that day.

'Nantao safe now,' said Freddie, reading my thoughts.

We walked through the narrow, ancient streets until we reached a small and gloomy Chinese restaurant.

Freddie ushered me inside. A bell jangled as the door swung closed behind me. I was immediately enveloped in a smog of garlic and oil, steam, heat, dampness and a babble of harshly spoken Chinese. Groups of Chinese, all men, sat at round tables, chopsticks flashing in the air, as they reached forward, like seagulls ducking for a morsel, dipping their chopsticks into big steaming bowls of food. I watched for a moment and saw strings of thick yellow noodles, coiled and glistening with fat, oily and slippery. My stomach turned over. I grabbed Freddie by the arm.

'I can't eat here,' I said.

'Too Chinese for you?'

'Yes,' I replied. He laughed, but without humour.

'Aw right, *gwailo*, I take you tourist place.'

He led me back to the street and we walked for several minutes until we reached a large, clean, glaringly bright Chinese restaurant with, I was relieved to see, several European diners, and a menu displayed on the door in English.

We went inside and were taken to a table, whereupon Freddie handed me a menu.

'Please choose anything you want. I really want to say thank you for what you did. It was jolly decent of you to attempt to help those poor, unfortunate students.'

Freddie had switched to perfect Oxford English. I stared at him, astonished.

'You didn't realise I spoke proper English, did you?' I felt my face flush red with embarrassment.

'I must admit I didn't think about it at all. I assumed your Pidgin English was the extent of it.'

He smiled like a mischievous schoolboy.

'So, you like gulling people, Mister Wang, is that it?'

'No more than you do, Mister Gallagher. The honest Irish cop. But I see the hunger for *cumshaw* in your eyes.'

I roared with laughter.

There was something hypnotic about listening to Freddie speak. He was perfectly fluent, indeed, more erudite than many native speakers were. He spoke like a man reading text from a great book, rather than someone engaging in social chitchat.

I began thinking of Freddie as 'the talking textbook.' His dry, academic conversational style was incongruent with the coiled strength of his supple, athletic frame.

I learned that he was from a relatively wealthy family that had now fallen on hard times. His father had been an imperial government official in Sichuan province before the 1911 revolution. Freddie's proper Chinese name was Wang Xiao Ming, but, like many Chinese working for the English, he had taken an anglicised name for ease of communication and to fit in. Freddie was well educated and had spent a year at university in Paris. He spoke Pidgin English because it was the norm for Chinese constables in the SMP and he chose not to draw attention to himself.

* * *

As Freddie and I talked over the dinner table, I began to get insights into the world through Chinese eyes.

'It is extraordinary,' said Freddie, 'that the West shows patronising benevolence towards the Chinese. You have no idea how deeply offensive it is. To your people, the East is outwardly subdued but you don't realise that the Chinese feel scorn towards the foreigner. Many young Chinese, such as myself, go to study in the West and get treated as equals while overseas, but then we come home and we are instantly relegated to an inferior position and the back door. It is the by-product of colonialism. The coloniser looks down on the colonised, because really they feel guilty for it.'

'You know what, Freddie? It reminds me of something that a man once said to my father years ago in Ireland. He said: "The British took away our language and our culture and then laughed at us for having no language and no culture." You see?'

Freddie sat up, rigid, his eyes wide. 'Damn it! That's it.'

'Do you really think so, Freddie?'

'Why, yes, Michael, that's exactly it. Anyway, who could understand the

British? Or anyone from the West, from our point of view. We find your demeanour towards life to be inexplicable. The West can rise heroically to a war or a natural disaster but show an unbearable temper when meeting small discomfort. The Chinese, on the other hand, have perfected the art of meeting small discomforts and inconveniences with a smile, in courtesy and consideration for other people's feelings. In short, Michael, we don't understand you.'

He sat back, silent and satisfied, having delivered his great speech. I pictured him as a priest delivering his sermon from the pulpit.

'Why did you join the SMP, Freddie?'

'I want to get on in life, just like everyone else. A career, a house, a nice girl. We're not so different from you, *gwailo*. That is why I was prepared to become a servant of the empire.'

'Do you really think of us as servants of the empire?'

'Of course. What else are we?'

'So you're political?'

'No! I hate politics. My younger brother dabbles, but I think it's for fools. You can't really change the world. I just want to get on in life, and the police looked like a decent career. For as long as you *gwailos* stay here, anyway!'

Freddie's sermonising made me feel compelled to reciprocate.

For the first time since getting on the ship to China I recounted the story of my life in Ireland, and of my father's dilemma—a good Irishman sworn to uphold a system of law now seen as alien by his friends and neighbours.

Freddie ordered Shanghai specialities: fried noodles, pork in dark sour plum sauce, steamed river fish with green onion, and Shanghai hairy crab. For the first time, I experienced the fire in my mouth of hot chilli and the piquant taste of spicy plum sauce. It made the food that I'd eaten all my life taste like pulped newspaper.

We sat contented, the table now scattered with bowls, napkins, chopsticks, chicken bones and grains of rice. 'I feel a certain responsibility for you, Michael,' said Freddie.

'Responsibility?'

'In China we believe that when you save a man's life you take responsibility for it. And I did save your life, Michael. Those policemen in the square would have chopped your head off.'

'I thought that the "life saving" story was just a myth for the tourists.'

'Oh, indeed no. Did you ever see how Chinese people flee from the sight of a burning building? Heaven forbid that they might be stuck with saving a life. It is a big commitment.'

'Well, thank you. I'm grateful. If ever I can do anything for you…'

'I understand that you have had some contact with our esteemed Mister Lu.'

My jaw dropped with astonishment, which I quickly turned into a cough. *How the hell did he know that?*

'I've met him.'

'Did he ask you to do something for him?'

'Well, yes, but it was only an enquiry of a personal nature.'

'Michael, be very careful with Lu. He is as dangerous as a snake. Please tread carefully. I don't want to think that when I saved your life, it was only putting off the inevitable. Mister Lu garrottes people who displease him.'

I didn't want to talk about Mister Lu. 'So, tell me about this rickshaw coolie business,' I said.

'The rickshaw coolies live as beasts of burden. I don't think you would find a more terrible job in the whole world. A newspaper article recently called it "the deadliest occupation in the East, the most degrading for the human to pursue." Can you imagine what it is like to spend your whole life running through traffic at top speed, pulling a carriage and passenger maybe twice as heavy as your own bodyweight in all weathers, for only enough coins to keep yourself from starvation?'

He paused then, staring out the window, and watched a greyhound-thin rickshaw boy toil past the restaurant.

'Why do they do it, then?'

'They have no choice. Most are tenant farmers who were forced off their land. They are not natives of Shanghai and the city is as strange to them as London or New York. But the work requires no special talent or ability beyond having the physical strength and stamina of a mule. And the work generates an immediate cash payment, small as it is.'

'Why did you go undercover, then, as a coolie?'

'They are organising. They have a union and, if they go on strike, it could be big.'

'How so?'

'There are eighty thousand of them in Shanghai. So, in number terms alone, they could be quite significant movers on the political scene. And they are pretty angry, I can tell you.'

'How much do they earn?'

'Practically nothing. They don't own their rickshaws. They hire them for a twenty-four-hour shift. Usually one rickshaw is shared by two coolies who work for twelve hours each. They make sixty or seventy cents per man. Just enough to hire a bed in a flophouse and buy a bowl of rice. The owner of the rickshaw typically has ten or twenty vehicles and does very well out of renting them to the coolies.'

'Jesus, that's rough.'

'If the coolies need a little extra money they borrow from the money-lenders who charge one hundred and twenty percent interest. They get trapped into a lifetime of bondage.'

'Christ, there is no way out for the poor bastards.'

'Exactly. The work is so physically demanding that they typically die by age forty. There are no old rickshaw coolies. The city is so filthy, and the coolies encounter the worst of it. Thirty thousand dead bodies are picked up off the streets in a typical year and are just thrown into unmarked paupers' graves.'

'It is a pretty rough city, right enough.'

'It certainly is. I find that, even though I was required to investigate their union organisation and write a file for Special Branch, I felt immense sympathy for them.'

'I can imagine.'

'They work like dogs, but they are no fools. They are smart, intelligent men. They have to negotiate fares with unscrupulous passengers who would refuse to pay them in the blink of an eye, and they navigate very complex traffic, weaving their way through cars, trams, bikes, pedestrians, lorries and everything the street throws at them.'

Just then a passing waiter stumbled and an empty wine glass went spinning off his tray, tumbling towards the ground. Almost without looking Freddie's hand shot forward, quick as a snakebite, and the glass landed with a heavy smack in his open hand. He handed the glass back to the waiter with a smile.

'Jesus, you're fast, Freddie.'

'Oh, I try to keep in shape,' he replied modestly.

'Anyway, the rickshaw boys. Is that why they always turn up in police reports?'

'Exactly. They pick up a passenger, a fare is negotiated and, when they get to their destination, the passenger changes his mind. The coolie was too slow, too rude, or whatever reason they can find. So there are fights. Coolies have been stabbed and beaten, and sometimes, in return, have beaten or killed the passenger. But they have no redress if they are cheated.

'Many of them prefer to convey a triad man, who might ask them to conceal a pistol under the seat, but will pay a very generous fare for the service. And can you blame them?'

'Yes, the Unit's always very careful with rickshaw coolies during stop-and-searches. Cops have been shot dead by rickshaw passengers.'

'A wise precaution.'

'I see many of them have that yellow colour of the opium smoker.'

'And who could blame them again? At the end of a day's shift their whole body is wracked in pain. Opium is the most wonderful painkiller and it guarantees a deep, undisturbed night's sleep. It is their only peace.'

'Amazing.'

'There is a verse written by a rickshaw coolie.' Freddie closed his eyes and began to recite:

> *"Pull your rickshaw like a beast of the field*
> *Back broken, blood to yield*
> *Life is hard, long for death*
> *Cough and spit*
> *End my days in an unmarked pit*
> *Bring me peace, bring me sleep*
> *Smoke opium my rest is deep*
> *I fly with the dragon*
> *To a far-away garden."'*

Freddie fell silent then, his expression thoughtful. 'Hmm, interesting what you said. "They took away our language and culture and then they laughed at us for having no language and no culture." I must remember that. This man who made such a profound statement to your father, he was no doubt a learned man, Michael?'

I laughed. 'He was a bank robber, Freddie, and my old man nabbed him redhanded.'

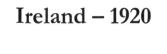

Ireland – 1920

Chapter 18

15 May 1920

PATRICK BONNER HAD BEEN BROUGHT into the barracks, a bloody bandage on his leg where the RIC bullet had lodged. The whole town knew him well. I'd watched him play hurling many times, wishing that I had his skill.

He and a group of men had held up the bank in the nearby village of Bruree. My father and Dan Ryan arrived on the scene just as they were escaping. Patrick took a flesh wound. He fell, couldn't run and my father apprehended him. The rest of the group made off in a creamery lorry after they held up the unfortunate driver at gunpoint.

Patrick was taken back to Kilmallock Barracks and locked in a cell. Late in the evening Father went to interrogate him. When I saw this I ran upstairs, on tiptoe, to my father's bedroom, which was above the cells, and lay down and pressed my ear to the floor. I heard the heavy metal door open and close.

'Jesus, Patrick, what do you think you're doing?'

'I am fighting for the freedom of our country.'

'And you with the fine education that you have!'

'This country has been enslaved for eight hundred years and I intend to set it free.'

'What have the British ever done to you?' said my father.

'Wake up to yourself, man. They have the country destroyed.'

'Destroyed?' said my father. 'Sure isn't Dublin the second city of the British Empire? Look at everything we have, roads, bridges, post offices, banking. None of this would be here otherwise.'

'You're just a Castle Catholic. They have you by the balls, Mister Gallagher.'

'I'm no *shoneen*, Patrick. I took an oath to uphold the law. You fellows are running wild, robbing banks and shooting innocent people.'

'I take my orders from Michael Collins, Mister Gallagher, while you obey a foreign power. I think that speaks for itself.'

'Well, they've never done you any harm, have they, Patrick, with your fine education.'

'The British took away our language and culture and then laughed at us for having no language and no culture.'

'All I know is this,' said my father, in the tone of someone passing final judgement, 'you fellows are causing chaos, and chaos ultimately means nobody can live a normal life. Including your own family, Patrick.'

'Temporary chaos is a small price to pay for our freedom, Sergeant.'

'Ah, but that's where you're wrong. You're riding a tiger. That tiger will eat you up in the end.'

'I have faith in the Republic, Sergeant.'

'I'll tell you this, Patrick; you can't put the genie back in the bottle. The chaos will destroy you. Mark my words. You could have died today of a gunshot wound. And I wouldn't have taken any pleasure in it, telling your mother, a decent woman that I know well.'

'You're the lucky one, Sergeant. There's many an RIC man left lying in a ditch with a bullet behind his ear. If you're not with us, you're against us, and that's the way it is.'

'Listen here now, Patrick. I have nothing against Home Rule. I joined the police twenty-five years ago, before you were even born. There was no trouble then. I took an oath to uphold the law of the land and that is what I am doing now. What do you expect me to do? Break my oath?'

'That's exactly what I expect, Sergeant. That oath was to a foreign power. You were relieved of any obligation the moment the leaders of 1916 declared our independent republic. When the British put the leaders of the 1916 Rising up against a wall and shot them like dogs you had even more cause to side with your countrymen.'

'I tried to talk sense into you,' said my father. Then I heard the rattle of keys as Patrick was locked up for the night. I quickly tiptoed back to my own room and got ready for bed.

I lay awake in my bed until dawn broke.

* * *

The following morning we were in the dayroom, my father sitting on a tall stool behind the public counter, slowly and carefully writing up his notes in the report book, his flowing, elegant copperplate writing a work of art on the finely lined page. I was cleaning the window with old newspaper and hot water with a dash of vinegar added. 'The only way to clean a window,' Father always said.

'Go back up, on your left, you missed a bit,' he commanded, without looking up.

'Father?'

'Yes, Michael, what is it?'

'What about Patrick Bonner?'

'The man is a criminal. He'll be dealt with.'

'Yes, Father. Are you worried?'

He placed his pen neatly on the page and sat up straight. 'I took an oath. That oath was to uphold the law of this land. If I hadn't joined, it would have been the immigrant boat for me. Sure I had nothin'. I would have been down a gold mine in Australia, or laying railroad tracks in America. It gave me a fine job, a good wage and a roof over our heads.'

I continued to vaguely wipe the window without really watching what I was doing.

'What about the Shinners? Do you not think they have a point? Isn't this our country?'

He stopped speaking for a moment, as a farmer driving a pony and cart loaded with milk tankards jangled and clanked past the station at a brisk clip.

'I don't dispute that. I voted for the Home Rule party. And we got Home Rule, despite the Orange Order threatening civil war. A fine way to show loyalty, by the way. And then wasn't Home Rule suspended because of the Great War in '14? How could we get Home Rule now with the country in anarchy? No government would agree to that.'

'Are you not afraid that you might get shot?'

He sighed wearily. 'God is good, Michael. You must never show fear to any man, or else you're finished, entirely. No, I'm loyal to the Force, and loyal to my comrades, and I have the code to live by. And that's that.'

'A boy at school said we were imperial lackeys. They called me a British spy and a peeler's brat. I didn't know what to say to him.'

'You tell him that you have a father who sticks to his oath. That's all there is to it.'

'Should we not go away, Father, somewhere safe?'

His face darkened. 'Go away?! Have you taken leave of your senses?'

'I'm just trying to be practical, Father.'

'What would your mother think of me, casting off my uniform and going away?'

'She's dead, Father.'

'Get on with your work.'

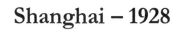

Shanghai – 1928

Chapter 19

I READ THE FILE THAT Lu gave me. The woman in question was Jade Kwan and the story she presented apparently stood up to all scrutiny. She worked as a nurse's assistant at the French Hospital. Miss Kwan had been born in Pudong, was sold as a young girl to be a domestic servant to a prosperous farming family near the lakeside town of Hong Zhou. She spent her childhood working as a domestic servant for them. She had claimed that when she was thirteen, the master of the house had attempted to rape her. She escaped rather than submit to his advances. She walked all the way back to Shanghai and found work as a maid for a French Catholic Missionary Priest. She had been greatly influenced by her employer and, in time, she was baptised a Catholic and apparently had felt a firm calling to help the destitute. She was a daily communicant and expressed a desire to join a French order, the Missionary Oblates of Mary Immaculate. Since arriving in Shanghai she trained as a nurse.

Big Ears Lu had a childhood memory of his baby sister having a burgundy birthmark just above her left knee. Consequently, Lu's medical doctors had examined Jade Kwan and established that she had a similar birthmark. All the physical indications were that she was of the correct age to be his baby sister. She was tall and slim, like Lu, and had strong, high-cheekboned features, so, from her appearance, it was entirely plausible that she might be his long-lost sister as she claimed.

* * *

I examined her photograph from the file. There was something compelling about her face. She had an expression of regal elegance and dark, soulful eyes, with the most extraordinarily fine high cheekbones. I was excited by the thought of meeting her and thought it was a pity that such a beautiful woman would choose to be locked away in a cloister.

From several days of observation, I knew what time her shift at the hospital ended. I had followed her home from work several times and asked discreet questions of her neighbours, aided by the donation of some small *cumshaw*. She appeared to live an entirely blameless life, not doing much more than working and going home to sleep.

On Thursday evening I waited across the street and, a few minutes after 8 p.m., she walked through the gates of the hospital. She was simply dressed in a plain and inexpensive overcoat, hair tied up in a clip, and her face free of makeup or lipstick.

I stepped in front of her. 'Miss Kwan. A word, if you please?'

She looked at me, eyes widened, the alarm evident on her beautiful face. I took an involuntary step back, stunned by her beauty.

'No need to worry, Miss,' I said, flashing my police identity card. 'I am with the Shanghai Municipal Police.'

'You don't have authority here, in the French Concession. Only the French Police can act here,' she said sharply.

'That's true indeed, Miss,' I said, taking note that she was smart and aware of the legal niceties of such things. 'Your brother asked me to have a word with you. Is there somewhere we could talk?'

'All right, then; there is a quiet café just around the corner.'

I walked with her and she took me to a small Russian café next door to a Siberian furrier's shop.

* * *

After some small talk over two cups of Russian tea, served piping hot in glass cups with elaborate silver handles, she said, 'My brother doesn't believe me, does he?'

'He wants to, but he must be extremely careful. A man in his position is a target for all sorts of people. I can understand that you would be weary of all the interviews.'

She nodded in agreement. 'It has been difficult,' she said, 'but I can't complain.'

'I must say, your English is excellent, Miss Kwan.'

'Oh, thank you. I seem to be a quick learner.'

'Please forgive me, Miss Kwan, but I need to ask you some further questions.'

Her beautiful lips turned down, a sad pouting expression. 'Oh, must you? I'm so tired.' Her shoulders rose as she inhaled deeply and sighed, the weight of the world on her shoulders. I wanted to go easy on her. Then I remembered Lu's sphinx-like face.

'I'm sorry, Miss, I must.'

'Very well then, go ahead,' she said wearily.

I began to question her systematically, going through all the biographical details of her childhood, growing up on the farm, escaping to the city, working for the missionaries, all of it.

There was something about the way she answered that made me uneasy. She knew all the answers. I thought that a genuine case would make more mistakes and be less sure of herself and maybe have the occasional false recollection. Miss Kwan was perfect. I decided on a new tack.

'I understand that you are a Catholic, Miss Kwan?'

'Yes, that is right. I was baptised, and my faith is the centre of my life,' she said with eyes slightly upturned. 'I go to Mass every day.'

'I was wondering, Miss Kwan, if you could tell me what do you hear when the priest elevates the host?'

'I beg your pardon?'

'I was referring to the bells, Miss Kwan. You will recall that as the priest elevates the host the altar boy rings the bells.'

'Oh, yes, the bells. I love the bells. You can hear them all over town.'

'I see. What is the fifth commandment?'

Startled, she replied, 'I can't remember all of them. But I know what they are.'

'Who made the world?' I noticed her face began to flush.

'I don't know what you mean. *Who made the world?*'

'Please explain the miracle of the loaves and the fishes.'

She shook her head. 'What are you talking about?'

'Last question, Miss Kwan. Please explain what the miracle of the wedding feast of Cana was?'

'You are talking in riddles.'

'Miss Kwan, any Catholic nine-year-old child could answer those questions by rote. If you are not a Catholic, I assume the rest of your story doesn't stand up, either.'

She reached her hand across the table and gripped my arm. 'Please. I am desperate.' Her eyes were wide, an animal caught in a snare.

'Why did you even attempt such a dangerous, crazy venture? You've entered a pit of snakes,' I said.

She shook her head in reply, no words. I took her hand. I held it for a moment and gazed into her dark eyes, intoxicated by her beauty. Her eyes moistened and she bit her lower lip. 'My story is very close to the truth. I *was* sold as a child, to a farming family. And I did run away when I was thirteen. I was almost raped. All of it happened. But I don't know whose sister I am. It might as well be Lu Sun Yu that I am related to.'

'Couldn't you be content with a normal job?' I asked.

'I've had nobody to protect me since I was thirteen. The farmer was planning to marry me off to a rich old man. They'd made a deal already. But to be a desirable wife, I needed to be foot-bound. But I would never allow that!' Her eyes flashed with anger and defiance.

'Foot binding?' I asked. 'I have seen it but I don't understand it.'

'Foot binding has been considered erotic since the Tang Dynasty. A little girl's feet are bound in such a way that the four little toes hook under the feet.

'The bandages are tightened a little bit more, each and every day. The entire process takes about two years. When it is complete, the girl walks on her heel and the knuckles of her toes.'

'But why? It sounds like insanity.'

'It causes the girl to walk in a mincing style that strengthens the buttocks and vaginal muscles.'

I felt my face flush hot. I wasn't used to discussing such matters so frankly, particularly with an attractive young woman.

'The mincing walk and the tight muscles are considered highly desirable by many Chinese men.'

'I find that extraordinary.'

'Many Chinese men frequent brothels where the girls are foot-bound. When he is ready, the man drinks wine from the girl's shoe. Her crippled foot is considered as arousing as the finest perfume.' I could hear the anger rising now, in her voice. Her knuckles whitened as she gripped the Russian teacup.

'This is horrible,' I replied.

'The man will devote much of his time over the poor girl's feet. Sniffing, licking, and even eating almonds from between her toes.'

Her body shuddered now, repulsed.

'The big toe, which has not been bound, is called "*the Gold Lotus.*" This will be dipped in the man's wineglass.'

I held up my hand. I'd heard enough. But she continued. She sat back, folded her arms and in tones one might use to describe a surgical procedure continued:

'When his passion is overwhelming, he will put the girl's feet on his shoulders, suck her *Gold Lotus* in his mouth, and then his *jade spear* will be driven into her *jade gate*. He will continue to suck her *Gold Lotus* until *the moment of clouds and rain.*'

'I have never heard anything like it,' I said.

'During the process of foot binding, the girl's foot bones will be repeatedly broken over two years. Frequently, there are shards of bone breaking through the skin, leading to rotting flesh and oozing pus. It is not uncommon for rotting toes to drop off. As a nurse I have seen it many times. And if the pain wasn't enough, then she must endure some filthy, sweaty pig of a man moaning and grunting on top of her night after night.'

'But how can any man like such mutilated feet?' I asked.

'When the girl's feet are crippled, she can't walk far. But she is mobile enough to carry out her duties in the kitchen and the bedroom. She is thus controlled and under the power of the man, which is, of course, the Confucian ideal for a woman.'

'Monstrous,' I said, shaking my head.

'I would have killed rather than submit. And they would have killed me if I had not submitted. I ran away from the only home I knew. So you see, Mister Gallagher, for me, risking the wrath of "brother" Lu is a small thing.' She tossed her head angrily.

'If you have any sense, you will leave this city tonight, before Lu's men catch up with you. I will give you a twenty-four-hour head start.'

'Didn't he tell you to detain me and take me to his house?'

'He did.'

'Then why let me go? You risk your own life for me? He'll kill you if you don't follow his orders.'

'There's enough brutality in this town, Miss Kwan, without me adding to it.'

I didn't tell her that I couldn't stand the thought of her beautiful face being slashed with a knife. I stood, put some cash on the table, and walked towards the exit as she began to cry softly. At the door of the café, I turned and looked at her, fighting an urge to go back and take her in my arms.

Chapter 20

I WAITED TWENTY-FOUR HOURS BEFORE I phoned Mister Lau, the comprador. I was told to come to the house at ten p.m. that evening. My nerves were on edge all day. I had heard too many stories about visitors to Lu's house who vanished off the face of the earth.

At the appointed time, I stepped out of a taxi at Rue Wagner. I noticed that now, in addition to Lu's Green Gang goons, there was an unmarked Citroen parked across the street with two Europeans sitting in the front seats. I assumed they were detectives from the French *Sûreté*. I had heard on the police grapevine that, since the White Terror, Lu was a major target of the communists and he had been given official protection by the French Concession government.

The house had a dark, eerie quality. Lu's men had set up spotlights on the sandbagged perimeter, but the house itself was mostly in darkness. The spotlights made the house itself hard to see. It remained a dark shadow, like Lu himself.

I walked through the sandbagged gate and was met by Mister Lau.

He led me inside the house and took me up two flights of stairs, then along a carpeted and wallpapered corridor. We stopped before a dark timber door. He knocked, opened the door and ushered me inside.

* * *

The room was very dark and the only light was from a softly lit oil lamp. As my eyes adjusted to the gloom, I could see that I was in a comfortably furnished sitting room with big overstuffed armchairs and windows covered by dark velvet curtains. Furthest from the door was a dark green Chesterfield couch.

Lu reclined on the couch. He wore only threadbare shorts and a singlet like a farmer or a fisherman just returned from his labour. A blanket was partly draped around his shoulders.

'Come close, Mister Gallagher, and tell me your news,' said Lu in a low voice, almost a whisper. He waved his hand to me and gestured to a footstool that was a few feet away. 'Pull up the stool and whisper me your tale.' He spoke so quietly I had to strain to hear his voice coming from the gloom.

In his right hand he held a long, silver opium pipe.

'Did you speak to my sister?'

'I saw Miss Kwan, yes.'

'Is she my sister?'

'I'm sorry, sir, she is not.'

'You are absolutely certain?'

'Yes, sir, her story does not check out.'

'You have no doubt at all?'

'No, sir, I am entirely convinced that she is a fraud.'

'I am very sorry to hear it.'

Lu's body sagged like that of a man who had suddenly taken on a great burden. The oil lamp flared brighter for a second, and I saw a tear glisten on his cheek.

'I have the comfort of my pipe,' he said mournfully.

'I am sorry, sir.'

'Don't be sorry, Mister Gallagher. You have brought me the truth.'

'I didn't want to give you false hope, sir.'

'Everyone is afraid of me, Mister Gallagher. They tell me what they think I want to hear. But nobody understands what I want to hear. The truth, I keep telling them, the truth. But do they listen? Fools—all of them.'

'I see, sir,' I said, wondering what was coming next.

'Why don't you come and work for me, Mister Gallagher? I will make you rich and powerful. In the maelstrom of this city a man can make his fortune. You could be a right hand to me, Mister Gallagher, I feel it. Use this opportunity while it lasts. I need Western men to help me understand the Western mind. I want to expand into America, Europe, and South America. You could do this with me.'

I sat silently for a moment, not wanting to offend him. 'Sir, I appreciate your confidence in me. But I have dedicated myself to police work. My father was also a policeman. I am not made for business.'

'That is not entirely true, is it, Mister Gallagher?'

'Sir?'

'I hear stories of your Mister Dell. I understand you assist him in his endeavours. I know you have a fondness for *cumshaw*.'

'We may occasionally do some minor favours for people. But it is on a very small and limited scale. I couldn't go beyond that.'

Lu placed the opium pipe on the couch and gripped the backrest. Using his right arm, he slowly and laboriously hauled himself upright and faced me.

'You dare to refuse Lu Sun Yu?' His eyes blazed in the lamplight. Was it the reflection of the lamp or was he the very devil?

'I mean no offence, sir. I am simply stating my position.'

'Nobody refuses Lu Sun Yu.'

'Sir, I mean no offence. I am just a humble policeman.'

He laughed then, his tight lips pulling back from his big teeth, a skeletal grin.

'All right, Mister Gallagher, I accept your reply.'

'Thank you, sir.'

'I appreciate your loyalty to your comrades, Mister Gallagher, and also the way you handled this matter.'

'It was nothing, sir.'

'I do not forget. I wish to give you a gift that is of great value to a man. You are to be my guest at the House of Multiple Joys.'

'Thank you, sir.'

'Just one thing, Mister Gallagher. Where is she?'

'Sir?'

'Where is she, this imposter woman?'

'She managed to slip away, sir.'

'From a member of Mister Fairlight's Emergency Unit? I doubt that very much.'

'I'm sorry, sir.'

'Don't take me for a fool, Mister Gallagher. Pretty, was she?'

'She was beautiful, sir.'

He laughed again, the same skeleton leer. 'You are too soft for Shanghai. But I will overlook it, because you told me the truth. Anyway, my men will find her.'

Slowly he reached forward to the coffee table by his couch and pulled open a small drawer concealed under the tabletop. His hand went into the drawer. I feared he would produce a pistol. But surely he wouldn't shoot me down after singing my praises? When he withdrew his hand, he was holding a small gold key, which he handed to me.

'Sixty-six Hardoon Road. Go to the house any night and present this key. You will experience great joy.'

'Thank you, sir.'

'Now, I must sleep. Please leave me, Mister Gallagher. Mister Lau will see you out and he will settle your account as I promised. The equivalent of two years' salary paid in American dollars. Two years, not three, because you failed to bring her to me as I asked. Mister Lau has an envelope already prepared.'

* * *

The following morning, I found a letter with Irish stamps waiting for me at the Gordon Road Depot. The letter was addressed to 'Constable Michael Gallagher' and the address was 'Care of the Shanghai Municipal Police, Shanghai, China.' It was a miracle it got to me at all. There was no sender's address, which told me that the writer wasn't used to sending letters internationally.

I opened the envelope to find a letter and newspaper cutting. A man named Jim Frost, a clerk like myself at Brown Thomas, had written to me.

His letter told me that Charlie Watkins had died. The newspaper cutting was from the *Irish Times*. It was only a small paragraph and it described how Charlie was on duty at the main door during the Christmas rush. He just collapsed and was dead before he hit the ground. He lay there in his uniform, medals on his chest, exactly as he would have wanted it. The article retold one story about Charlie that I had heard from the man's own lips. He stayed by his post at the main door throughout the 1916 rising, his peaked cap temporarily replaced by a British Army helmet scrounged from a passing Tommy.

I folded the letter carefully and slipped it into my pocket. I felt a numb, dulled sadness. Where did I stand in the world? Both of my parents dead and no siblings. My childhood sweetheart dead. Charlie was my last link with Ireland unless you counted a yearly Christmas card to Dan Ryan.

I had no home now, other than Shanghai.

Shanghai – 1929

Chapter 21

North China Daily News – January 15 1929
Editorial—City of Sin

Shanghai is known by many names, some of which we can be proud of. 'The Paris of the East' is a fine name that conveys the beauty and magnificence of the Bund's architecture, an array of some of the finest buildings East of Suez, the headquarters of this newspaper being one of them.

However, the city bears other names, which should make any decent citizen feel ashamed: 'The whore of the orient' and 'Babylon of the East' to name but two. And what is the reason for these shameful appendages?

Our city is awash with the blight of prostitution, in all its guises. The charade is played by so-called 'taxi dancers', 'tour guides', 'massage therapists' and 'sing-song girls.' Despite the intrigue and curiosity engendered in tourist and locals alike by these somewhat harmless sounding names, they are prostitutes all, each and every one of them.

The city of Shanghai has more prostitutes per head of population than any other city in the world and that is not to mention the gambling houses and opium dens.

How is a fine upstanding young Englishman arriving from home going to retain his purity in the face of this vice?

It is a great difficulty faced by many a young 'griffin' that comes out to work in the trading houses, banks and insurance companies of this city.

What does the Shanghai Municipal Council propose to do about it? For too long the Council has thrown up its hands helplessly. This newspaper calls for decisive action. Stamp out the sin and restore the God-fearing light of Western example that the men who founded our settlements in 1842 intended.

15 January 1929

IT WAS A LONG TIME before I plucked up the courage to visit the house that Lu urged me to visit. I was fairly certain, from what Lu said, that it was some kind of 'house of ill-repute' as the missionaries would have it. However, despite a couple of discreet enquiries, nobody I had spoken to in the Police admitted any knowledge of the House of Multiple Joys.

Before I resolved to visit, my nights were spent wrestling with my conscience. All the sermons of my childhood came back to me. 'Woe to the scandal-giver,' thundered the Jesuit missionaries from the pulpit of Kilmallock church. 'Beware of women of easy virtue,' intoned my father.

And yet, I could not wipe my mind clean of the beautiful young May at the Blue Lady nightclub. Making love with May was better than I ever imagined it could be. I wanted to have it again.

Finally, after the competing voices in my head had shouted at each other until I was half mad, I resolved to go to this house that Lu promised me. What harm was there in satisfying my curiosity? It was probably a dive, anyway.

When I arrived at the street I was taken by surprise. Sixty-six Hardoon Road was an impressive house. It was fronted by a well-tended English garden with a gravel pathway leading to a large, panelled red door. The house itself was of grey stone and had four levels. Individual balconies, decorated with lacy wrought-iron rails, fronted the windows of the building. It was a fine house, dignified and imposing.

I pushed open the gate and walked up the path, the gravel crunching under my leather shoes. The night was cool and pleasant and I had downed a couple of drinks at the Gordon Road canteen before setting out. I had come by rickshaw in order to have a slow journey. I reached the front door and used the lion's head doorknocker to announce my presence. As I stood back from the door, I noticed two Green Gang types standing at the corner of the house, cigarettes cupped in their hands, both of them eying me up and down, their shark eyes boring into me, an unsettling reminder of the house's ownership.

A tall thin Chinese man dressed like an English butler opened the door. His hair was oiled and slicked back from a bony face with high cheekbones.

'Good evening, sir, and do you have a key?'

I hurriedly searched through my pockets and found the small gold key. I displayed it to the butler who took it from my hand, held it close to his eyes and examined it carefully, turning it backwards and forwards before returning it to me with a polite bow.

'Thank you very much, sir. Any friend of Mister Lu is most welcome at the House of Multiple Joys. Please come in.'

The hall was illuminated with soft, golden light from lamps arranged around the walls. I heard music coming from somewhere off the hallway. A piano was being played. *Moonlight Sonata.*

'Won't you come through to the piano room, sir. Several other gentlemen are present.'

I followed the butler who opened a door leading off the hallway. It was a large and busy room. The predominant colour was red. The deep pile carpet was rose red, as was the thick, expensive wallpaper. Scattered around the room was an inviting array of comfortable, soft, well-upholstered couches and armchairs. In the far corner, a European man wearing an evening suit with white tie played a glistening rosewood baby-grand piano.

Men sat around the couches and armchairs, most wearing evening suits. Some sat together but most separately. They sipped from whiskey tumblers, champagne flutes or tall cocktail glasses. I heard a pleasant buzz of voices in conversation, interspersed with laughter.

There were many young women present. All with the fashionable *modeng* haircuts, perms and bobs, and bold makeup. Some moved around carrying trays of drinks. Several sat at tall stools arranged by a small bar in the far corner of the room. A neat, white-coated Chinese barman tended to the drink preparation. Many of the young women sat beside the men on the couches or on their laps.

Each of the young women was beautiful.

I took an armchair in a quiet corner of the room. Almost immediately a young woman was standing by my side. 'Sir, can I offer you a drink?'

I asked for a scotch and the girl brought this on a small silver tray. 'Would you like some company now?' she asked.

'Not just yet, perhaps later,' I said, as I needed to figure out the rules of this place before I acted with confidence.

'Certainly, sir,' she replied. 'Just call any one of us should you need anything at all.'

I sipped my drink, and the alcohol had its effect. The evening darkened and the room became an interplay of shadow and softly glowing light from the wall-lamps. I began to recognise the faces of various men. There were members of the Municipal Council and the French Council, diplomats, businessmen, journalists, and several military and naval officers from a variety of countries.

I began to feel more and more cheerful. This had to be the most high-quality bordello in the whole of Shanghai. Perhaps in the whole world. Was there another like it anywhere? Surely, for a man with an eye for a pretty girl, there couldn't be a finer house in the entire world.

The pianist shifted tempo from soft classical to popular jazz numbers. Couples got up and danced. As I watched, my glass was continually refreshed. The babble of voices became louder and more boisterous.

Many of the ladies slipped off their dresses and comfortably walked around the room in négligée, stockings and suspenders. Men made their selection by simply grabbing a young woman as she walked past.

The sounds of the room became louder. Laughter, shouts, clinking of glasses, and the music volume went up. Another group of young women arrived, also in a state of undress.

A girl wearing a red silk négligée came to me, her small pert breasts exposed above the silver tray. 'Would you like some refreshment, sir?' she enquired. I looked at the tray and saw balls of black opium, sprinkles of white powder, and an array of white pills. 'Nothing for me, thank you; I'll stick to the whiskey.' As I gazed at her breasts, I felt myself become very aroused.

I had a disturbing thought then. If the police raided this house my career was at an end. I quickly dismissed it when I remembered that the most powerful men in Shanghai were here.

I observed many of the black-suited men and near-naked women locked in embrace, the men's hands greedily roving over the women's breasts and buttocks. This elicited shrieks of laughter and mock protest from the women. The pace of activity quickened and more than one couple was just about engaged in full congress on their couches.

One man, portly and red-faced, threw off his jacket, ripped open his white tie and waistcoat, fumbled with his fly buttons, and mounted the girl who lay on the couch under him. He began to move rhythmically on her and shortly a small crowd gathered around them. As the man moved, the crowd chanted, 'Faster, faster, faster' and, as he cried out in orgasm, the crowd cheered, whooped and applauded.

Chapter 22

A YOUNG WOMAN ENTERED THE room carrying a tray of drinks and stood by the far wall. She was tall and slim, and wore only pale cream-coloured French knickers, suspenders, silk stockings and a pair of black stiletto shoes. Her face was beautiful and framed by black bobbed hair, the classic *modeng* girl haircut. She looked stunning. It was Jade Kwan.

I felt my skin tingle in a strange mix of lust, guilt and embarrassment to see her in this place. Dare I talk to her? I felt fear, thoughts of what might happen if I earned Lu's displeasure. But here, of all places…

She's here because you exposed her to Lu, my inner voice screamed.

I waved for her to join me. She quickly finished serving the drinks on her tray and I moved to a two-seater couch by the French windows looking on to the front garden, so that we could sit together side-by-side.

I rose just as she came and gave me the faintest kiss on the cheek. 'Another drink,' she said theatrically, the enthusiasm in her voice counteracted by a deadpan face. She picked up the decanter from the side table and poured the drink into the cut-crystal tumbler I held.

She held out her hand and said, 'My name is Miriam Tsai.' I shook hands with her as if we were in the most respectable drawing room in Shanghai.

'I remember you having a different name,' I said.

'No, you don't,' she replied firmly. 'You don't remember anything of the sort.' She placed her hand on my arm and squeezed, as she looked in my eyes in silent appeal. *Don't talk about my past now.*

'All right then,' I said, with a slight bow of my head. I was aware of the butler hovering nearby.

I took a moment to observe her as she filled her glass and sat down. Made-up and rouged and expensively dressed, she was barely recognisable as the simple young hospital worker I had questioned at the Russian café.

I picked up my glass and took a sip. 'It is very nice to talk to you, Miss Tsai.'

'Call me Miriam, please,' she said. 'Have you been in Shanghai long?'

She obviously wanted to maintain a façade of friendly conversation, as we would if we had never met before. I made my mind up to oblige.

As we began to talk, it continually ran through my mind that Miriam was forced to work here at the House of Multiple Joys because of me; it was I who exposed her deception to Lu.

However, despite my discomfort, as time passed our contrived conversation became real. We relaxed. An hour passed as we chatted about inconsequential things. She was entertained by my poor jokes and I liked her smile and the tinkling sound of her laughter. My stories of the ridiculous rules of police bureaucracy amused her greatly.

Finally, I said, 'I wonder if you would like to come upstairs with me. It's just that I'd really like to continue our conversation in private. There's so much I want to ask you and I don't expect anything…'

'Oh, I would love to, truly I would. But I have an appointment with a gentleman already. Such appointments are unbreakable.'

With perfect timing the butler arrived. 'Miss Tsai, your gentleman guest is ready for you.'

Miriam looked at me and I could tell that she really didn't want to go. 'Sorry,' she said. 'It has been lovely chatting with you, Mister Gallagher.'

'Call me Michael, please. And I wonder…'

'Yes, Michael?'

'How can I see you?'

She smiled and briefly touched my arm. 'I am here every evening. You could make an appointment, which means I am guaranteed to be yours for a time.'

I stepped through the French doors into the garden. I didn't want to see the man she was meeting.

I left the House of Multiple Joys that evening without picking a companion. Before I left I had a word with the butler. I slipped him a generous tip in American dollars and asked him to ensure that Miriam Tsai was free and available for me tomorrow night.

* * *

I returned the following evening. I wore a new evening suit, bought in the morning from a tailor in Frenchtown. It didn't do to look out of place. Miriam was even more stunning than I remembered. She was dressed like the finest fashion model on the catwalk at the Wing On Department Store. I felt intoxicated to be sitting close enough to merely inhale her perfume.

We sat and chatted and drank for a little while.

Finally I decided to ask for some privacy, away from the buzz of activity in the room, where we could have a real conversation, and somewhere Lu's butler wouldn't watch her. I needed to understand her circumstances and my contribution to them.

'Miriam, could we go to a private room? We don't need to do anything. We need only talk.'

As we stood, Miriam glanced quickly around the room and said, 'May I see your key?' I reached into my pocket and again produced the small gold key. She took it, examined it as the butler had on the previous evening, and handed it back to me as she said, 'Wonderful.'

As she stepped ahead on the elegant, lushly carpeted staircase, I watched her perfect, silk-encased buttocks wiggle suggestively, and her long, shapely legs. We climbed two flights of stairs and went down a carpeted corridor. She opened a door and we stepped inside to a comfortably appointed bedroom with a large four-poster bed covered in a red silk quilt.

We sat together on the side of the bed. Suddenly I was lost for words.

She took my hand and pressed it to her breast.

'Michael, do you like me?'

'Of course I do, Miriam.'

'No, I don't just mean "like". Every man here likes me. I mean do you like *me*?'

I looked into her eyes. 'I like you, Miriam. I liked you even when I was interrogating you in the café.'

'It would be nice to make love for once, instead of...' Her voice trailed off.

'Is this real, or did Lu put you up to it?'

Suddenly she recoiled from me, her arms folded, her face turned away.

'You know nothing about women,' she said sharply.

'What do you mean? Lu is forcing you to work here, isn't he? Perhaps he wanted you to get close to me?'

'Oh, you are such a little boy,' she said.

'Miriam, I'm trying to understand.'

'You think I'm a prisoner here. Nothing in Shanghai is so simple.'

'I don't understand. Didn't Lu force you to work here? Aren't you a prisoner?'

'I was for a while. But things relaxed. Prisoners don't give good service to the guests, so in time I was allowed some measure of freedom.'

'Don't you still want to get away?'

'Where would I go—back to a life of starvation?'

'You are a nurse.'

'Stroking a man's *jade spear* isn't much different to sponge-bathing some old man on his sickbed. And here I get well paid, sleep in a nice room, and I make love with rich and powerful men. Some of them are nice to me.'

'Is that enough for you?'

'No, Michael, it isn't enough for me. That's what you don't understand. Sometimes a woman needs to be loved rather than bought.'

'I'm sorry, Miriam, for being so dense,' I said as I turned her face to me and kissed her lips softly. She returned my kisses passionately.

She said, 'Let's blot out this crazy city for a couple of hours.'

Our kisses became more intense and in a moment we were on the big, fluffy bed. Our desire was urgent and we clawed at each other like two starving people. I realised then that she was as lonely as I was.

Afterwards, we lay in each other's arms, overcome by the sudden and unexpected passion of our lovemaking.

'Welcome to the House of Multiple Joys,' she said.

* * *

We lay side by side and I was conscious that our breathing had synchronised.

'Miriam,' I said, 'placing you in this house, this is how Lu took his revenge?'

'I suppose so,' she said. 'Perhaps he sent you here to put us together, in some strange experiment. I don't know.'

'So what is the real story? Where are you really from?'

'It's almost exactly as I described it, apart from being Lu's sister. And I'm not a Catholic—that was a flourish I added merely to make my story appear more sympathetic.'

'But why did you even attempt such a crazy venture? You were playing with fire.'

'I just wanted to make more of my life than squandering my youth working in a hospital. I came to Shanghai hoping for something more and had done some modelling for the cigarette calendars, but the income was horribly irregular.'

'Yeah, it's hard to make ends meet in Shanghai. And then what?'

She sat up then, suddenly, and said, 'Oh God, I need a drink. I hate even thinking about this now.'

She picked up an elaborate white and gold telephone receiver from the bedside table. 'Room service? This is Miriam. Please send us up some champagne... That's right, champagne. Something expensive.'

'I see you have luxurious tastes now,' I remarked.

'Well, when you're surrounded by wealth...' she replied.

'So, what happened after the cigarette modelling?'

'I met a man, an apparently rich Chinese businessman, but aren't they all?'

'What was wrong with him?'

'Typical. He was a gambler and opium smoker who had lost everything. He was out of money but he wasn't out of ideas. Lu's story was well known and over the years many people had suggested to me that I might be Lu's sister. When I saw his photograph in the mosquito press, I agreed that it could be so. The rest you know.'

We were interrupted then by a knocking on the door. After a pause the door opened and a young Chinese woman wearing a maid's uniform entered carrying a tray laden with a champagne bottle in a silver ice bucket, a bowl of bright red strawberries and two delicate champagne glasses.

The maid placed the tray by the bed and discreetly withdrew, eyes averted. At Miriam's urging I had to open the bottle and pour the drinks before she would continue with her story. She quaffed her first glass in one gulp and presented the flute to me for a refill. We both sipped in silence for a moment.

Then I said, 'Miriam, there is still something troubling me. What happened after I told you to get away?'

'Well, I perhaps wasn't as quick as I should have been. I was picked up by some Green Gang gunmen at North Station and was taken to see Lu. During the time I was impersonating his sister, Lu hadn't actually met me. When he saw me, he decided that he could make more use of me here at the House of Multiple Joys than having me garrotted and slipping my body into Soochow Creek.'

I sipped my drink, contemplating the implications of Miriam's story.

'So my attempt to help you achieved nothing?'

'Don't worry, you saved my life. I was told that if you had handed me over to Lu's people as you were supposed to, I would have been disposed of on the spot by one of his goons. Lu himself would never have laid eyes on me. My attempt to escape made Lu angry but it also aroused his curiosity. I think he wanted to meet the girl who had tempted you to let me go. He demanded that I be brought to him.'

'So then what happened?'

'He liked the look of me and sent me here.'

'So I saved your life but condemned you to work here?'

'Better than feeding the fish in Soochow Creek, Michael. Don't feel bad. Anyway, I played a dangerous game.'

'Even so, I'm supposed to be protecting people.' As I said this, I wondered what my father would make of me and the kind of policeman I had become.

Her eyelids began to close over her very dark brown eyes. 'Great guy,' she murmured in a half-asleep voice. I kissed her gently on the lips, her eyes closed again and her breathing deepened.

I looked at Miriam, taking in the beauty of her black hair spilled over the pillow, eyelashes fluttering slightly. I reached over and touched her shoulder very lightly, marvelling again at its golden, healthy tan. How unusual for a Chinese girl in Shanghai, where the fashion was to favour a pale, cold climate pallor. In China, pale skin was upper class.

I adjusted the pillow as I sat up and looked around the cosy, tasteful bedroom. Miriam reached for me and I held her, my nose pressed into the sweet, clean scent of her hair. I had a sudden thought then. With Miriam by my side, I could rekindle my simpler self, the man I was before Shanghai.

I sensed that, in Shanghai, I was sliding into an abyss. War, terrorism, brothels, and Jack Dell's *'ramblin' boys of pleasure.'*

Where would we go, so that an interracial marriage would not be a problem? Certainly, in Shanghai it was not unheard of, but was regarded as career suicide for anybody working for the authorities in the International Settlement. Perhaps French Indo-China? I'd heard that many Frenchmen took up with local women there, and French society, in its way, responded with casual indifference. Or maybe America. Plenty of work for an experienced cop. Just as I was about to sleep I was suddenly alert. Did Lu's tentacles extend so far that he could have us killed even in America?

* * *

Sometime during the night I woke up and saw that the room was in darkness. I felt her body beside me and I was overcome by an urgent excitement. I reached for her and we made love, fast and urgent. Afterwards, she reached for the bedside table and turned on a soft pink bedside lamp.

To my astonishment, it was a different girl.

'Who are you?' I demanded. 'Where is Miriam?'

'Oh, she was called to an appointment. But you were sleeping so deeply she didn't want to wake you and so she asked me to stay with you. It is all right; at the House of Multiple Joys we are all friends. There is no jealousy here.'

'I don't even know your name,' I said.

'It doesn't matter.'

'But we made love.'

'And we may do it again. There are many nice girls for you here. It doesn't do for a man to become too attached to any one girl.'

'I know you,' I said. 'Why do you look familiar to me?'

'I did a calendar for Pairbelles cigarettes,' she said. 'You might have seen it around town. Lots of the girls here are models or in the movies.'

As I felt the soft, downy bed under me, my eyes began to grow heavy. I lay back, eyes looking at the ceiling lamp, trying to understand the House of Multiple Joys, a world without normal rules. Sleep overcame me and when my eyes opened again, the soft light of morning was coming in through a crack in the thick velvet curtains. I was alone in the room.

I recalled the shock when I realised the young woman in my bed had been a replacement for Miriam. The shock, and yes, the excitement that made my stomach lurch at the thought of the endless possibilities of the House of Multiple Joys.

Chapter 23

A<small>FTER MY FIRST NIGHT WITH</small> Miriam, I went back to the House of Multiple Joys many times.

Powerful men chose to conduct meetings at the House of Multiple Joys because of its neutrality. It was not uncommon to see communists and nationalists chatting, British and German naval officers sharing a bottle of rum and swapping notes on where they might have fought against each other in the sea-battles of the Great War. *Taipans* from rival trading houses got drunk together.

* * *

I became friendly with Jeremy Northbridge, who wrote for *The Times* of London. Jeremy was a grey-haired, red-faced, portly man with a relaxed, *hail-fellow-well-met* manner and one of the sharpest minds in Shanghai. I was surprised to discover that, despite his appearance, he was only ten years older than I was. We had struck up a conversation one night when sitting in side-by-side armchairs. He liked talking to me to pick up titbits of information on the crime situation in Shanghai. Jeremy was very 'public school' and I was secretly rather pleased and flattered with my easy, chatty, companionship with him.

The first night I met him he pointed towards two men sitting in a far corner of the piano room, heads together in whispered conversation.

'Take a look at those two chums—strange bedfellows.'

'Who are they, Jeremy?'

'Well,' he replied, 'the stiff chap in the dinner suit is Captain Karatovin, late of the Tsarist Imperial Navy, and now head of the All Russia Fascist Party. These days he earns his salt by conducting the orchestra at the Del Monte. The other fellow in the nasty rat-catcher's suit is the head of Soviet espionage here at the Embassy in Shanghai.'

I watched as the two men raised their whiskey tumblers and clinked them in toast to each other.

'There's a gathering of journalists and scribblers in a private room upstairs. Why not come up and join us? It could be a bit of a laugh.'

'All right, Jeremy, what room is it?'

'Oh, it's room fifteen, I think. Just knock on the door.'

I was happy then, feeling that I was gaining membership of the inner sanctums of the Shanghai International Settlement.

* * *

I finished my drink, had another, and then as the grandfather clock in the grand hallway chimed out ten o'clock I thought if I was going to bother, I should get myself along there. I walked up the carpeted staircase and approached room fifteen, knocked, opened the door and stepped inside to find a dimly lit smoking room, the tips of cigars glowing like fireflies.

A group of men in evening suits were engaged in murmured conversation, which petered out as they saw me.

I stood looking at them, feeling unsure of myself in the silence. A tall man stood by the window. A side lamp glowed and reflected off the glass and put his face in shadow. Where had I seen him before? I felt the hairs rise on the back of my neck and I quickly took a couple of steps backwards.

The man stepped into the lamplight and I could see that he was tall, lean and athletic, with a full head of grey hair. His glittering blue eyes shone against the lamplight. Apart from the grey hair and a few lines on his face, Major Jamie Flyte was exactly as I remembered him on the day my father died.

'Hello there,' he said to me as we vigorously shook hands. His grip had lost none of its strength and potency.

'Jamie, it's me, Michael Gallagher.'

'Michael, and in Shanghai of all places,' he said, his face lighting up with charm and delight, just as I remembered from so long ago.

'I didn't even know if you were alive,' I said.

'Let me give you my calling card, old chap. You must drop round.'

'Of course, that would be lovely,' I replied, trying to recover my composure. I released his hand and took the stiff white embossed calling card that he had smoothly slipped from his inner jacket pocket—a magician pulling a rabbit from a hat.

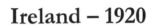

Ireland – 1920

Chapter 24

9 June 1920

THE OLIVE-GREEN TRUCK CAME ROARING through the main street of Kilmallock, its exhaust pumping black smoke into the air. The cabin's windscreens had been replaced with bomb-repelling chicken wire. Lashed to the front fender was a rough, timber cross-shaped structure. Hanging from it, tied with rope was the slumped body of a man in ragged, dirty clothing. They were using the man as a hostage, to discourage enemy gunfire. The truck braked sharply. The hostage's body jerked roughly in response.

Simultaneously, the doors of the cabin and the back flap of the covered truck crashed open. From the truck jumped groups of laughing, shouting men dressed in a variety of worn and faded unconventional khaki military uniforms, topped with dark green tam-o-shanter caps.

The prisoner on the crucifix groaned in pain, which elicited cheers and catcalls from the uniformed men. One of men spat at the prisoner as he walked by the unfortunate soul.

A man who exited the cabin of the truck approached me as I stood in the doorway of my father's police barracks. He walked swiftly, a man in a hurry. He was a tall, handsome man with startling blue eyes and blond hair. His uniform, unlike the others, was expensive and well-tailored and fitted his athletic body perfectly. His chest was crisscrossed with leather bandoliers full of bullets, which made him, I thought, look something like a pirate. He wore a dark brown leather belt around his waist and suspended from it was a holstered pistol and on his left hip a battered and scarred leather map case.

'Hello there,' he said briskly, with a friendly smile, hand extended. I shook his hand, feeling his strong and rapid handshake.

'I say, is the Sergeant about? I mean Sergeant James Francis Gallagher,' he said cheerfully.

'That would be my father, sir,' I replied.

'Are you the young Gallagher, then?' he said with a smile.

'Yes,' I replied. 'I'm Sergeant Gallagher's son. He's out on patrol at the moment.'

'All right then, we'll sort ourselves out.'

He turned back to the milling group of uniformed men and called for their attention. One word from him and their shouts and laughter stopped.

'Unload your gear, chaps, if you wouldn't mind.'

'I'm sorry, sir, but who are you?' I asked.

'I'm Major Flyte of the Royal Irish Constabulary Auxiliary Division. Correctly, my rank is now Special Cadet Flyte. Major was my army rank, but many of us ex-officers have come over and joined the Auxiliary branch of the RIC to give you Paddies a fighting chance against the Shinners. Great idea, the Auxiliaries. It was Winston's wheeze.'

I looked at the man on the homemade crucifix. He was in a bad way. His body had slumped; his wrists were chafed and bloody from his bonds.

I hesitated for a few seconds and then spoke up. 'Excuse me, sir, but why is that man tied to the front of the truck?'

'Well, you see, young fella, he's one of those Fenian blackguards who are ripping the country apart. You needn't feel sorry for him.'

'I see, sir.'

'We're going to be based here at your father's barracks so you and I might as well get used to each other. Please show me to the barracks dormitories like a good chap,' the Major said, with a punch to my shoulder.

'One moment, please, sir,' I replied. 'Your prisoner can't be kept like that. My father puts men he arrests in the cells.'

'But he's a terrorist, old chap,' replied Major Flyte, the smile gone from his face now. 'He'd leave your body in a ditch if he had the chance.'

'I'm sorry, sir, but my father would not allow a prisoner to be kept like that outside his very own barracks.'

'You cheeky young fucker,' said one of the other uniformed men.

There was a moment of dead silence.

'Well, young man,' the Major said, 'is he right? Are you a cheeky young fucker?' He stood straight and strong, his face serious, his laughing eyes suddenly narrowed.

I stood as tall as I could, pushing my chest out, as I had seen Father do, and said, 'This station follows the RIC Code, sir.'

I felt every eye looking at the standoff between the Major and me. The silence continued. It felt like a long time. In the background, several of the men unholstered revolvers. There was a metallic click, as someone released a weapon's safety catch.

A bird sang from the station rooftop.

Then the Major laughed and clapped his hands together. He turned to the man who had called me a cheeky young fucker and said, 'All right, Lacy, take the man down and put him in a cell. Oh, and give him some water too. Our host here would expect it.'

As he walked past me, Major Flyte slapped me on the shoulder and said, 'Stoutly done, lad.'

* * *

After I led the men to the barracks dormitory, I cast my mind back to the morning's conversation with my father, in the barracks kitchen.

My father was rigid as an iron bar, his immaculate Royal Irish Constabulary bottle green uniform starched and ironed like a suit of armour. The black leather belt, brass buckle, and black boots shone like mirrors. The sergeant stripes on his arm screamed his rank and authority. My father had a black bushy moustache, waxed and pointed. He'd grown it as a young man and never shaved it off thereafter.

Father held intense ambitions for me, and his expectations weighed heavily. Most RIC men, from poor farms, wanted respectability for themselves and even more for their children. The priesthood, civil service, teaching, any or all were acceptable, but nothing less.

Father had been angry in the morning. He had a way of showing it; he sat with an elbow on the table, his head resting in his hands, the burden of the entire world on his shoulders. There was a grim, oppressive silence, and the slow tick of the clock on the kitchen mantelpiece.

My left leg clenched with tension, as I sat anticipating the outburst.

It was important to look relaxed whilst my left leg clenched. To look tense was to invite criticism, the very thing that I was trying to avoid. Therefore, my left leg did all the work. The rest of me sat relaxed, with my face poised into an expression of ease and happiness, to eat a meal with my father.

'Now, listen,' Father said, in his slow, controlled, pontificating voice, like a judge handing down a sentence. 'Sometime today, while I'm on patrol, we're to be joined by a group of Auxiliaries. Dublin Castle in its wisdom is sending us a bunch of these gentleman hooligans. I don't want them here but we have no choice, so be polite, be welcoming, but don't make yourself too free with them, is that understood?'

'Yes, sir.'

'They're dangerous men, these so-called Auxiliaries. They fight like bandits, and they're supposed to be police. There are reports of them executing prisoners, and they've torched the town of Tuam in County Galway. That's a disgraceful way for apparent policemen to behave.'

'All right, Father.'

'Don't go out,' he admonished with a wagging finger, ticking left and right like a metronome. 'And, listen here to me now, I am warning you, don't go near the big house. I know you're up there all the time. The Burleighs don't want you hanging around. And, besides, it's too dangerous. You're a target as much as I am. You may be only sixteen, but you're a peeler's brat, and there's no getting around that. I'd send you up to your uncle in Dublin but it's as bad up there.'

* * *

Prior to the troubles, my father had ten constables under his command. All were young men, fit, athletic, and full of life and looking for ways to amuse themselves. They took me swimming and fishing, and taught me how to ride a bike. I'd even had a couple of furtive lessons in target shooting with their RIC carbines and revolvers when Father wasn't about. I loved visiting the constables' dormitory. I enjoyed the gramophone music they were forever playing. They had three wax recordings, all of them by John McCormack with songs like 'The Rose of Tralee', 'The Last Rose of Summer' and 'Believe me, if all those Endearing Young Charms.'

Now there were only three of the original constables left. Five had resigned in the face of anonymous letters and two had been shot in a ditch.

The Auxiliaries took over the constables' dormitory and Major Flyte, as the Auxiliary commander, was given his own room, the spare bedroom next to mine.

Sometimes I woke up during the night and heard him scream.

* * *

It was a nice sunny day and Jamie and I sat on the back steps of the barracks facing the vegetable garden that had originally been planted by my mother.

A few minutes earlier, I had arrived from the kitchen to see Jamie examining the contents of his brown leather map case.

'What's that, Jamie? Why do you always carry it?'

Jamie sipped his tea, laced with a dash of rum, from the chipped enamel mug. He leaned close to me, his voice soft and conspiratorial; I found the smell of rum on his breath pleasant.

'Michael, do you see that round mark in the middle of it? That's a bullet hole. When I was on the Somme I wore this hanging over my chest. We went over the top; it was one of the great pushes. Thousands of men died. This map case stopped a bullet and I'm alive today because of it.'

'Oh,' I gasped. 'What was it like to get shot?'

'Like a kick from a mule. But the map case became my lucky mascot. I keep only my most precious things in it, ever since that day.'

'What have you got?'

He glanced up at the sky for a moment, thinking, and then looked over his shoulder to see that nobody was behind us in the doorway. 'All right, I'll show you a few bits and pieces, as long as you don't go shouting to the world about it.'

'Of course, Jamie,' I replied in my most manly voice.

He unclasped the case and reached inside. He pulled out a bundle of letters and photographs tied in up with a thin twine, a torn and mud-stained map, and what looked like a dark green jewellery case. Unfurling the map, which was faded and almost unreadable thanks to age, stains, mud, blood and brown rings made by a coffee mug, he said, 'That's a map of the Somme, where I nearly died more times than I care to remember.'

He painstakingly answered my many questions about the battles.

'What are the letters, Jamie?'

'Oh, just sentimental things, mementos of family and so on.'

Then I said, 'What's in the case?'

He picked it up from the step and opened it. Inside the box was a ribboned medal inlaid in a velvet cushion indented to take its shape. It was a white enamel cross with a crown in its centre; its ribbon was deep red with narrow dark blue borders on both edges.

'It's beautiful. What is it, Jamie?'

'That's the DSO. The Distinguished Service Order. The king pinned that medal on my chest personally, at Buckingham Palace. The citation said "for distinguished services during active operations against the enemy."'

'What did you do?'

'I say,' he said in tones of mock admonishment, 'it isn't done for a gentleman to go on about such things.'

'I'd love to hear the story, Jamie.'

'Ah, maybe one day, when my memory is clearer.'

'All right, I'd like that.'

'Michael, did I ever tell you about the first time I went on leave to Paris, from the front?'

'No, Jamie, you didn't.'

'You must know of the *Moulin Rouge*, surely?'

'No, what is it?'

'Well, it is a theatre, I suppose you could say. With dancers. And what dancers they are!' He leaned back, eyes cast upwards as he pictured them. He sighed, a man inhaling the joys of life.

There was a sound from behind us. I turned, recognising the heavy tread of my father. He stood, gathered himself to his full height, stretched out his chest, and cleared his throat.

'I'm sorry to interrupt you, Major Flyte, but I need my son.'

'Of course, Sergeant,' Jamie replied cheerily. 'No harm done.'

'Michael, you have chores in the kitchen. Please go and complete them now.'

'Yes, Father.'

Then, as I stood, Father put his firm hand on my shoulder.

'I told you not to bother Major Flyte. His rank is major and you are to call him that. Do you hear me now, boy?'

'Yes, Father.'

He turned sharply and marched away towards the dayroom.

'Michael,' I heard Jamie call to me softly.

I turned back, wanting Jamie to tell me what a bastard my father was.

'Don't be upset by him, Michael. He wants the best for you.'

'We were only chatting, weren't we? What harm did I do?'

'Your father is under a lot of pressure, Michael. These are very difficult times. Don't be too hard on him. And you can call me 'Major' when he is around. I won't mind. You can call me 'Jamie' when you're off duty, if you know what I mean.'

'All right, Jamie, I'll see you later.'

In the evening I stood in front of the old mirror hanging on the wall of my bedroom. I practiced the raise of the single eyebrow, signalling quizzical amusement, like Jamie did.

* * *

Eventually, I undressed and went to bed. I read my library book '*One of the 28th—A Tale of Waterloo*' until my eyes became heavy. Just as I was nodding off, I was suddenly wide awake. The sound of men's voices, raised in anger, came through the floorboards from downstairs. I instantly recognised the voices as belonging to Jamie and Father.

I threw back the sheets and went to the floor. Pressing my ear to the floorboards, I was able to hear the argument taking place in the dayroom below.

Father was obviously enraged. 'Your men are abusing prisoners, Major. This isn't the bloody Western Front. I don't know what you did to your German captives, but I will not allow you to employ such methods here in my barracks.'

When Jamie replied, his voice was controlled but tight. 'We volunteered to come here and use tough methods because you fellows weren't cutting the mustard. This is a war, Sergeant, as you should know, with some of your own men lying dead in a ditch.'

'By God, Major, you won't get away with this! You're not a soldier now. You're a member of the Constabulary and it's your duty to uphold the law. I'll make a personal report straight to Dublin Castle. You'll be back in an English dole queue before you know it, war hero or not.'

'You're a fool, Sergeant. We were sent here to do exactly what we are doing. Do you really think Winston Churchill sent us here to take afternoon tea with the terrorists? We were sent to spill blood and that's what we'll do, whether you like it or not. If you make a report, Dublin Castle will only laugh at you.'

There was silence then for a moment. Finally my father shouted, 'You're a disgrace, Major.' Then the door slammed and I heard Father's footsteps come up the stairs. His bedroom door opened and closed.

I stood and walked over to the window, which overlooked the main street. I saw a dark figure pacing up and down the kerb. A flare of a match then, a lit cigarette and I saw Jamie's face illuminated for a second, tight with anger.

I lay awake trying to understand it all. My father was the straightest and most honest character I had ever met. But Jamie was a war hero, an officer and a gentleman. What's more, I liked the man. He was the kind of heroic character I wished to become. And now I could be sure my father would let me have nothing to do with him.

Shanghai – 1929

Chapter 25

North China Daily News – July 9 1929
Hollywood of the East

Among the many successful industries that have arisen in Shanghai one of the most exciting and glamorous is the film industry. Few could have imagined but a few short years ago that Shanghai would develop studios and film production companies that would rival Hollywood.

Most Chinese-language films viewed throughout Asia have been filmed at a Shanghai studio. The local film industry took off from 1916 and it was further strengthened in the early 1920s when businessmen brought technicians from the USA to train local personnel.

The local industry blossoms with an array of studios including Bright Star Pictures, Shaw Brothers, and Unique. The Shanghai industry now produces comedy, folklore dramas, and historical adventure, which have proved a huge success throughout East and South-East Asia. Less welcome fare has come from some leftist filmmakers making so-called 'progressive' films with a distinctive communistic message.

The growth of the local film industry has, of course, led to the ascendancy of a coterie of local film stars who are elevated by their fans to the same level of stardom as to be found in Hollywood.

One of the greatest success stories has been British-owned Albion Studios, which not only make local Chinese-language films for distribution throughout China, East Asia and the Chinatowns across the Western world but also imports American and British-made films for distribution to Asian audiences.

16 July 1929

A MIDNIGHT BLUE DAIMLER PULLED up at the kerb. It was a magnificent car, long-bodied, strong and elegant. The driver's door opened and out jumped a tall, hard-faced Russian wearing a chauffeur's uniform. He came to attention.

'Good afternoon, sir. I am Ivan. Mister Flyte asked me to convey you to the Flyte residence.'

'Thank you, Ivan,' I replied, as he opened the rear passenger door and stood aside for me to enter. I put my foot on the running board and stepped inside. My body sank into the deep leather seat. There was a hint of perfume, whiskey, and cigars in the air. With a soft click, Ivan closed the door, got back in the driver's seat, and started the engine, and the car pulled into the stream of traffic.

Despite the soft, enveloping leather seat, I shuffled and moved, trying to find a comfortable position. I was nervous and worried. What would we talk about? Jamie and I were not from the same world. The only common topic was Ireland. I didn't want to talk about it. Too many painful memories. Too many deaths. No, it was time to move on. Could I say I had seen his films? Yes, I could, and, yes, truthfully—I had seen some of them. But I didn't have the grasp of films for a proper discussion. The boy got the girl, I understood that. But artistic vision? So, what else then? Police work? I didn't know if a *Taipan* would be interested, despite his time in the Auxiliaries.

We turned right onto Nanking Road and drove the length of it, passed the racetrack and continued on to Bubbling Well Road. Within a few minutes, the vista changed from shops and department stores to private dwellings. All the houses on Bubbling Well Road were built in European styles such as English Tudor and Spanish villas, and surrounded by neat landscaped gardens. My eye was caught by a snow-white house, like one from a glossy American magazine, with rounded curves, porthole windows and a flat roof. The light glinted on the blue water of a kidney-shaped swimming pool.

In a few moments the car stopped in front of a pair of massive white pillars. The black heavy gates had a heraldic crest woven on a wrought iron shield. Two uniformed Chinese men came out of a gatehouse and swung the gates open. The Daimler proceeded up a gravel-covered driveway and pulled up in front of a magnificent house, built in the style of a French country chateau.

Ivan opened the car for me and I walked to the front door, which was opened by an English butler.

'Good afternoon,' I said, feeling overawed by the sheer scale of the house. 'Constable Gallagher, Shanghai Municipal Police.'

'Mister Flyte is expecting you in the drawing room, sir.'

The butler stood aside, holding the door open.

The hallway was beautiful. White pillars rose from a marble floor. A golden chandelier hung from the high, airy ceiling.

'Please come this way.' At the end of the vast hall he opened a door.

Above the mantelpiece, dominating the room was a painting. It was large, about four feet square, in a very narrow black frame, and the majority of it was white space. It consisted of a few simple lines of black ink, representing a young woman wearing a long robe, standing by a lake as she held a parasol. In the background was a weeping willow with its leaves trailing into the water, and in the far distance, a mountain peak enveloped in summer haze. It couldn't possibly be the same one I'd seen at Burleigh Castle, but must have been done by the same artist, surely.

Standing by the fireplace, elbow leaning gracefully on the mantelpiece, was Jamie Flyte. I stood silently for a moment.

Jamie strode towards me hand outstretched. I found myself enveloped in a warm and strong grip as he shook my hand vigorously. He slapped my shoulder manfully.

'Michael, wonderful to see you again.'

I found myself thrown off balance by the sight of the painting and I had to take a few seconds to gather my thoughts.

'Thank you, Jamie. And you too. Until the other night I had no idea you were in Shanghai.'

'I like to be discreet,' Jamie replied with an exaggerated wink. 'Quiet pigs eat the most.'

'How strange to find you here,' I replied, still feeling amazed at the coincidence.

'The city of last resort, old chap,' he said with a laugh. 'And now you're a copper like your old man.'

'That's right, the Emergency Unit.'

'The Emergency Unit—just like the Auxiliaries, a bunch of lunatics!'

'It's nothing special.'

'I understand what you chaps do. It's a tough wicket and believe me the people of this town appreciate it. Every businessman in this town is afraid of being kidnapped. And you chaps are a great reassurance.'

'Thank you, Jamie, it's nothing really,' I said, feeling pleased and flattered.

'Your dear old dad would be proud of you.'

'I hope he would.'

'He was a bit of a stuffed shirt, your old man, but a jolly good stick all the same.'

'He was. You know, Jamie, nobody ever told me exactly what happened to him.'

'Well, there's not a lot to tell. On that evening, we were inside the house and we were under fire from the Shinners. We were vastly outgunned and we returned fire as best we could. Your old man simply caught a bullet during the melee. It was a head wound and he died instantly. No pain. Then the Shinners chucked petrol bombs and, before you knew it, the house went up in flames. And, as you know, not everyone made it outside.'

'He was a good policeman, wasn't he, Jamie?'

'He was, and that's why he'd be proud of you if he could see you now. But you know what, though?' he said. 'There's one area where the SMP is barking up the wrong tree.'

'Oh, what's that, Jamie?'

'Well, you chaps are forever raiding opium dens and arresting operators and so on. Now, this might please those missionaries that seem to have so much pull with the Council, but you chaps are wasting your time.'

'Why do you say that?'

'Well, you close down one opium den, and the same operator opens one next door. There is an appetite for opium in this town and nothing that the SMP does is going to kill it. Trying to stamp out opium, and gambling for that matter, is like declaring war on rudeness, or nose picking. It will happen anyway, because it is simply human nature to indulge in these things. The Municipal Council would be better off to legalise it and tax it and let the people get some benefit from it.'

'I'm not so sure, Jamie. The powers-that-be do take a pretty dim view of these things.'

'But not in the French Concession, they don't. You should know that the French cooperate with the opium dealers. You must know about Pock-marked Fan.'

'I'm aware of him.'

'The French accommodation with the drug dealers is more sensible and pragmatic and real than the approach taken by the Municipal Council and the SMP, don't you think?'

I was about to reply but then I heard the door open behind me and I turned. As I moved, I heard Jamie's voice:

'You remember Fiona, of course.'

My heart missed a beat.

There, before me, stood a ghost—a grown-up version of the girl I once knew.

I could feel the colour drain from my face. My legs grew weak, and I struggled to maintain my composure.

She was an adult now, not the coquettish schoolgirl I once knew. She had fashionably bobbed blonde hair. Her skin was healthily tanned and she glowed with vibrant good health. I gazed into those dark brown eyes that still visited my dreams.

She smiled, a dimple appeared on her left cheek, and her whole face lit up. It was a radiant smile, even more so than I remembered. It was a smile that could make a man forget himself, do something crazy. Then, like an on-off neon sign, her face instantly turned serious. Fiona looked into my eyes, paused for a second, uncharacteristic uncertainty and confusion on her face, and then it was gone. 'Hello, Michael. How wonderful to see you.'

I didn't reply. I simply stood there, beyond thought. Finally, I blurted out, 'Fiona, for Christ's sake. I thought you were dead. In my own mind, I had a funeral for you a hundred times over.'

'Oh, Michael. I'm so sorry for just vanishing like that.' Her hand rested lightly on my arm. Squeezing slightly: *you understand, don't you?*

Out of the corner of my eye I saw Jamie take a step towards us, watching.

'I just didn't want to be in Ireland or anywhere near it after what happened to the castle. I had an aunt in London and I knew I would have been sent to join her. Or maybe I'd be sent back to school. I didn't want that either.'

'Damn it, Fiona! You could have saved me years of heartache!'

'I understand, Michael. I am sorry.'

I shook my head and struggled to pull my emotions under control. I felt embarrassed then to be so emotional. I didn't have ice in my veins, not like these *Taipans* who ran the city.

'So where did you go?' I demanded, aware that my voice sounded shrill.

She looked over my shoulder to Jamie and, with some apparent signalled assent from him, she continued, 'The truth is, Michael, that Jamie and I were in love. We became friends in those few weeks he was based at your father's barracks. He saved my life in the castle that night, when everyone was killed and the castle burned. I just wanted to get away. Jamie took me in the truck to Limerick, gave me some money for a hotel, put me on a train to Dublin and met up with me there. We have been together ever since, and I came out to Shanghai with him in 1922. I'm sorry I didn't write. You were always a good friend to me.'

I struggled to keep my voice calm. 'I would have liked to know you were all right.'

'I know, Michael. And I'm sorry. I just wanted to forget Ireland. I'm very sorry about what happened to your father; he was such a good man. I never want to think of that night again. Oh, when I remember the flames…'

She turned away to face the window.

Then Jamie was beside us. 'Enough of the sentimental stuff. Let's have a drink. What's your poison, Michael?'

Before I could answer he had marched purposefully to the drinks cabinet and begun to mix cocktails.

Fiona looked into my eyes and she smiled apologetically.

I excused myself and, encountering a maid in the hallway, requested directions to the bathroom. I entered the marble bathroom, bigger than my bedroom at Gordon Road. Standing before the vanity mirror, I gripped the washbasin and forced deep breaths into my lungs. I gradually felt my pulse settle and slow down.

Fiona was alive. I didn't know if I was happy or sad, pleased or angry. Of course, it was wonderful that she was alive. But was there a part of me that rather enjoyed the tragedy of my lost love? Now it seemed that she had simply gone off and not bothered to tell me. Was I angry? Yes. But how could I be angry that she was alive? Why did she not tell me? Was I so unimportant that I wasn't even worth a postcard? I squeezed the washbasin hard. I could almost imagine my fingers imprinting on the surface.

* * *

The alcohol took effect and I became more relaxed. The cocktail hour passed in light-hearted conversation and, despite my strange rush of mixed-up feelings, the evening was more than bearable. I enjoyed it. I found myself dreaming that Fiona didn't love Jamie, that, in fact, she really loved me. I studied her carefully to see if there was any sign.

As Jamie handed Fiona a drink, he lightly touched her arm. In response, her mouth turned up in that radiant smile, the one that could fill a room, and her eyes briefly held his. I felt my lips tighten, suppressing the bitterness I felt.

I asked about the painting.

'It's not the original, of course. I had this one commissioned. My grandfather bought the original in Hangzhou, and I found the grandson of the artist still living in his grandfather's house. He works in the same style. I couldn't resist having it done; I'd loved the original, as you know.'

Fiona wanted to know what I had done after 1920.

'Well, there's not much to tell,' I explained. 'I was looked after by the neighbours for a short time, then Father O'Brien sent me up to Dublin where I lived with my Uncle Jim. He owned a general grocery store and did well for himself.'

'But you didn't want to stay in Dublin?' asked Fiona.

'It wasn't too bad. I managed to avoid entanglement in their civil war after the treaty. Dublin was all right once the civil war was over. I became a city boy, did a commercial course. Uncle Jim had a nice house in Rathmines. My first job was junior sales clerk—Brown Thomas on Grafton Street.'

'But you came to Shanghai?' she said.

'I had a yearning for something different.' It took all my willpower not to stare at Fiona.

'A playground for adventurers is what Shanghai is,' said Jamie then. 'Busting heads for the Emergency Unit beats the hell out of selling drapery, what?'

Jamie began enthusing about his film studio and, despite my shock at meeting Fiona, I was fascinated.

After an hour or two of cocktails and chat, Jamie announced that they had to attend a function at *Le Cercle Sportif.*

I bid them goodnight and Fiona walked me to the door, her arm linked in mine. She stood close to me.

'It has been so good to talk to you. I haven't had a proper conversation in eons. Jamie is always working.' I felt her breath for just a second, against my cheek.

'Can I see you soon, Fiona?'

'I'd like that very much. We usually go to meet the gang at the Venus Café. Do you know it? It's on North Szechuan Road. They have dancing and cocktails; it's great fun. You must join us one evening. I'll send you a note.'

We both stood, she took my arm lightly and guided me towards the door, and gave me a feather-light kiss on the cheek. 'Well, goodbye then, until later.'

I stepped into the hallway and a young Chinese servant girl opened the front door for me.

Ivan stood by the Daimler. He bowed sharply, opened the passenger door and said, 'I will take you home, sir.'

I sank into the soft leather seat and closed my eyes. I could feel my heart thumping all the way down to my toes.

Chapter 26

A ROAR FROM FIVE THOUSAND throats. They marched shoulder to shoulder, moving down Nanking Road. A young student leader had died in a holding cell at Louza station. It was the same location as the 1925 riots and couldn't have been a worse spot for inflaming passions. They chanted, 'Burn Louza Station. Kill the foreign police. Burn Louza Station. Kill the foreign police.'

Sirens wailed and bells rang from the Red Marias.

The Big Chief motorcycles, as usual, zipped ahead through the traffic and pulled up at intersections, blocking traffic and giving the Red Marias smooth and speedy passage to their destination.

We arrived on Nanking Road about two blocks east of the protest march and debussed at high speed. Three Red Marias were positioned in a line across the street front towards the oncoming mob. Inside each vehicle was a narrow ladder leading up to a small platform opening to the roof. We had named this 'the turret' and it was used as a command and observation point for the senior officer.

The riot squad quickly grouped itself in the formation that we had drilled so many times.

Three foreign officers and two Chinese constables manned each Red Maria, while three rows of men formed up, fourteen men per line.

The first and second rows were made up of twelve Chinese constables with a foreign officer at the left and right. The third line consisted of twelve Sikh constables, also with a foreign officer at each end. I was in line one, on the extreme left.

We stood, in formation, standing straight with our batons held high, in a visible demonstration that we had weapons.

The mob marched on, coming closer and closer. The marchers armed themselves with rocks and cobblestones ripped up from the street. They began smashing the plate-glass department store windows.

They threw a hail of rocks. A Chinese constable reeled, his face bloody.

'Prepare to charge,' ordered Fairlight through his megaphone. Then, as the mob crossed a line that the Superintendent had marked out in his mind, he shouted, 'Charge!'

We moved at a fast-paced jog. Police and rioters collided. Batons swinging, we pounded our way into the first line of protesters. The task of line one was to break up and press back the mob as quickly as possible.

Instantly line two came running into the melee. The job of line two was to scatter the mob and to fill the empty spaces caused by the impact of line one.

We swung, and punched, and kicked until the street became a blur of moving bodies, shouts, curses, and screams. It was bloody, brutal work.

The mob began to weaken and fall back. As the vanguard of the protesters panicked and began to run back, colliding with their compatriots still pressing ahead, it caused more panic and mayhem. The mob became a disjointed, chaotic crush of people trying to get away from our batons.

Then line three began to move in, but going more slowly. This line consisted of twelve Sikhs and two foreign officers. The Sikhs were huge men, all over six feet tall, ex-Indian Army most of them, burly as grizzly bears and intimidating with their bushy beards and red turbans concealing most of their faces. The Sikhs all carried *lathis*—four-foot long bamboo poles, which were tipped at each end with small brass pointed knobs. These giant Sikhs wielded the *lathis* with murderous force. A hit by a *lathi* could break a man's arm. The job of the third line was to protect lines one and two, as well as break up the toughest elements of the mob who might be showing resistance to the first two lines of police. The Chinese hated the Sikh policemen and called them '*red-headed monkeys*' in Shanghainese.

When the line of Sikhs joined the melee, it was soon over. The mob ran for it, and within minutes they were a hundred yards from us. Fairlight shouted an order, his voice crackling in the megaphone: 'Disperse now and return to your homes.'

Within a matter of minutes, the mob of five thousand had vanished like morning dew. We stood by for two hours and when it was obvious that nothing further would happen, Fairlight gave the order to get back on the Red Marias. We drove back to Gordon Road sedately and without bells or sirens.

This was becoming more and more like a normal day's work for the Emergency Unit.

5 August 1929

The drops of condensation rolled down the side of the champagne glass, gathering in a little wet pool at the base of my glass.

The Charleston blared from the Filipino Jazz band on the tiny stage, as bodies crushed themselves together on the overflowing dance floor. You could cut the smoke with a knife. Sweaty Chinese waiters, trays magically balanced on upturned hands, weaved like ghosts through the throng.

Around me sat Fiona's crowd, well fed and scrubbed, happy young people in evening suits and colourful dresses. The mood was of gaiety and jokes; rebuttals bounced across the table.

Somebody got to the punch line of a story: 'Timmy Wharton fell off his bloody horse, drunk as a judge, if you please.' This was met with peals of laughter.

I picked up my champagne and sipped. What I wouldn't give for a beer.

I looked at Fiona, sitting across the table. She wore a sheer black dress, thin straps over her elegant shoulders and a headband with an outrageous peacock feather attached to it. On anybody else, it would have looked outlandish. On her, it looked like the crown jewels.

Fiona was talking with a young public-school chap, tall and skinny as a pipe cleaner, with a brown fuzz of moustache stretched across his almost pubescent face. He was telling some interminable story and she seemed captivated. She was looking at him as if he was the only man in the world. I ran through the entire training manual of killer blows Mister Fairlight had taught us at Mystery House.

I had arrived at the Venus Café, as promised, one hour before. Fiona was welcoming and friendly. She quickly introduced me to her friends sitting at the champagne-laden table.

From the start, I felt uncomfortable. I was hoping not to make an ass of myself and had actually enrolled in dancing classes at Miss Broadhurst's Academy on Bubbling Well Road so I wouldn't look like a total clod.

Henry, who had some big job with the Chartered Bank of India, America and China, started asking questions.

'Gallagher. Irish, eh?'

'Yes, that's right.'

'Are you anything to Colonel Gallagher, late of the Enniskillen Fusiliers?'

'No, I'm not, actually.'

'Maybe you know Roger Pakenham-Gallagher, chap read law at Trinity College?'

'Can't say I've met him.'

'And what do you do, then?'

'I'm with the Shanghai Municipal Police.'

His lip curled upward and his reply was delayed a heartbeat. 'Really, how splendid!'

He turned and began to speak with the man seated on his right and both began to laugh.

As the MC announced a short break, I stood up and began to leave.

As I pushed through the crowd towards the door, I felt a hand on my arm. I turned. It was Fiona. 'Michael, I hope you didn't feel left out. They're awfully nice people when you get to know them.'

'Fiona, can I see you somewhere quiet, not like this?'

'Yes,' she said, 'but I'm going with Jamie to Hong Kong and Singapore. We shall be travelling for several weeks. But I'll send you a note the minute I return.' With surprising strength, she pulled me close, gave me a kiss on the cheek, and with that, disappeared into the crowd.

I pushed through the exit of the Venus Café, the Sikh doorman said, 'Good night, sir.' Stepping into the street, I walked into the night. I didn't know where I was going but I needed a drink.

* * *

I couldn't get Fiona out of my head. She entered my dreams, even more now than when I thought she was dead.

Warding off my confusion, I began to spend more time at the House of Multiple Joys. My habit was to sit with a drink and observe the behaviour of my fellow club members. I grew accustomed to observing the most powerful men in Shanghai get drunk or drugged, fornicate on a couch, sniff cocaine off the breast of a young girl or dance and sing like a drunken sailor. I could have made a fortune as a gossip writer for the mosquito press.

Miriam made it clear to me that she did not object if I picked another girl when a client engaged her. I said I would not, and I didn't want to. But, if truth be told, I sometimes did, driven by a confused, stormy brew of lust, anger, jealousy and a strange and almost unacknowledged sexual excitement at the thought of her in a nearby room with another man, while I made love with her colleague.

1 September 1929

The rickshaw coolie ran, his shoulders bobbing up and down, his skin thin and stretched over his lean muscled body, like an anatomical model in a medical school. A sheen of sweat glistened on his body. I sat back in the rickshaw seat, my body pleasantly bobbing up and down with the rhythm of the coolie's run. I wondered about his life, thinking about what Freddie Wang had told me. I felt a bit guilty since Freddie had described their lives to me, and I had made it a habit to catch a taxi or ride the tram when I could. But there was a student demonstration on the Bund and the traffic was chaos. I was prepared to swallow my scruples in order to meet Fiona on time.

It brought my mind back to my forthcoming appointment. I'd phoned the Flyte house and hung up several times when it was answered by staff. I tried one last time and came close to hanging up when I heard Fiona's voice. I desperately wanted to talk to her, but was terrified too. I imagined myself leaping from a cliff. I asked to see her—alone, conscious that my voice sounded high-pitched and nervous. Fiona sounded relaxed and breezy. She suggested the Mayfair Hotel for morning tea.

I was scared, and exhilarated. I wanted to tell her I loved her and had never forgotten her. So many times I had caught her looking into my eyes while I was in conversation with Jamie or one of their friends. I tried to push thoughts of Miriam to the back of my mind.

At times like this, when I tried to figure out what I was feeling, I had an image of Doctor Peng's chest of herbs. Each drawer contained a separate item. There were many drawers from floor to ceiling. My feelings were like that. When I was inside one drawer, I was hardly aware of any of the others. When I moved to a different drawer the preceding one didn't seem to matter anymore. I spent my life in Shanghai jumping from drawer to drawer: good cop, corrupt cop, lover of Miriam, lover of Fiona, Irishman, exile, stateless. In the end I didn't know what I was.

I loved Miriam, but Fiona and I had such an extraordinary history. I'd known her since I was thirteen; it felt like a lifetime.

But maybe I was wrong. If I were wrong I would make a total fool of myself. I could never see her again—or Jamie. Would she laugh at me and call me 'a silly boy', as she used to?

The rickshaw arrived at the grand entrance of the Mayfair Hotel. The coolie lowered the handles and I stepped out of the seat and paused for a moment as the glare of the sun hit my eyes, raw from lack of sleep.

A Sikh doorman wearing an immaculate white military uniform with a scarlet turban stood at the mahogany and brass doors. A thick black beard cascaded down his chest, partly obscuring a row of medals. He snapped an immaculate salute. For a moment I thought fondly of Charlie Watkins at the door of Brown Thomas.

I walked through the lobby, and entered the tearooms. It was a carpeted room with comfortable Chesterfield couches, and low tables laden with the accoutrements of morning tea. I saw Fiona seated alone at a corner table. She was wearing a white dress, a white straw hat with a yellow flower, and was engrossed in a newspaper.

'Hello, Fiona,' I said with a smile, my pulse audible to my own ears.

She looked up; her beaming smile made my chest flutter.

'Hello, Michael.'

There was a moment of silence.

I sat opposite her and said, 'Fiona, I must talk to you. I have been thinking about you constantly since we met again in Shanghai.'

'Don't, Michael, please.'

'Fiona, you know where I come from. I am not some cricket-playing toff with the right school tie to open all the doors. But I have loved you since the first day I met you. I thought I'd lost you. I won't lose you again.'

'Michael, please… don't start something you can't finish.'

'Leave him, Fiona. Be with me.'

'I want to.'

'Then why not?'

'I can't explain. Jamie has… I can only say that you are playing with fire.'

'What is this special power he has over you?'

'I could never explain to you, Michael.'

'Is it his money?'

'Don't be a fool!'

'Are you still in love with him?'

'In a way I am. He can be cruel beyond belief, to me more than anyone. But just when I think he is the most horrible man in Shanghai, he does something that takes my breath away. He loves me.'

'So, if you're loved by the richest man in Shanghai, and loved by a lowly cop, there isn't much of a dilemma, is there?'

Fiona reached across the table and took my hand. 'Please take a room upstairs for us.'

* * *

A big bed dominated the hotel room. At the foot of the bed facing the window was a small two-seater couch. Fiona and I sat side by side, like two passengers on a train. I took her hand in mine, and she allowed me to hold it, her hand neither squeezing nor resisting me. I turned my face towards her, and with my other hand, I touched her chin, and gently brought her face in line with mine.

I looked into her eyes then. I felt tenuous and unsure of myself. My mouth was dry.

'Well, here we are,' she said, as if sensing my unease.

'Here we are.'

I leaned forward, my lips on hers, soft and warm, neither yielding nor unyielding. I began to kiss her now, stronger and stronger, and then, in a moment, I felt her tongue against mine.

Excitement building now, I wrapped my arms around her and crushed her close to me. She kissed me back passionately. I slipped the dress off her shoulder and began to kiss her skin, healthy and firm and perfumed.

Then I stood, pulled her by the hands, and led her to the bed. We stood together then, apart for a moment. I slipped the other strap of the summer dress off her shoulder, and it slid to her waist, revealing her tanned skin and breasts covered by a silky, delicate, creamy brassiere.

'Wait,' she said, and pushed me gently back so that I was sitting on the side of the bed. Slowly she began to undress. It was not a striptease, merely functional undressing, but I found it intensely arousing. Naked now, she walked around the bed and lay on the other side, her hands covering her breasts.

I quickly undressed and in a short time I was lying naked beside her. I didn't know what to do with her. This was Fiona Burleigh, daughter of the Big House. It was as if I had been presented with some complicated and strange mechanism, like a printing press or an iron lung that had been delivered without an instruction manual.

'Fiona, I wonder…'

'Don't speak,' she said then and kissed me hard. Instantly my body responded and then everything was all right. She and I were locked together, biting, kissing, touching, hands roving, bodies prepared for each other.

Suddenly she stiffened, every muscle rigid. Her arms pushed me back. I leaned on my elbow, looking into her eyes.

'Fiona, for God's sake! What's the matter?'

She stared at me, wild-eyed, the look of a mad creature.

'I can't make love with *you*!'

'I don't understand, Fiona. I thought you wanted to…'

'I simply cannot explain it to *you*.'

I slumped back on the pillow, my forearms covering my eyes. I was crushed. Her words rang through my head. She didn't say she couldn't make love with another man. She said that she couldn't make love with *me*. Poor Mikie Gallagher from the village, the sergeant's son.

I kept my eyes covered as I heard the sounds of her dressing speedily. Her stilettoed feet clicked on the floor. A pause then, the room door was opened, another pause. 'Goodbye, Michael. I hope you find someone nice.'

The door closed. She was gone. The smell of her perfume lingered on the pillow.

Chapter 27

1 December 1929

A GROUP OF STUDENTS FROM St John's University marched to the International Settlement, heading for the Bund, carrying placards displaying anti-Western and anti-imperial sentiments. We stopped them at the western end of Bubbling Well Road. I arrested a young ringleader and took him to the Red Maria. He was a skinny, studious-looking young man, wearing round-lens reading glasses and a scholar's robe. As I frogmarched him towards the Red Maria, he said to me in Shanghainese, '*You are a coward and an imperial lackey. You prop up a corrupt regime that exploits decent working people.*'

'*You little fucker!*' I replied. '*I put my life on the line for people like you. Next time your little sister is kidnapped by a triad gang you'll be a bit more pleased to see me.*'

I threw him into the Red Maria pretty roughly, and then landed a few punches on him. I think I might have given him a cracked rib.

That evening I got very drunk at the police canteen.

When I went to bed that night, I fell into a fitful sleep and after a vivid dream about my father I woke up. I got up, showered and dressed and, from the street, hailed a taxi and told the driver, 'Hardoon Road, chop chop.'

8 December 1929

I was only just back at Gordon Road from leading a stop-and-search patrol when the emergency alarm sounded.

The men gathered bulletproof vests and helmets and took their positions in the Red Marias. I took my place on the turret. We left the base, alarm and bells clanging, the motorcycles blocking side streets.

As we drove, Superintendent Felton, the senior officer who stood leaning against the steps to the turret, briefed us. As second-in-command, I stood beside him. The Unit had received a call from the manager of the Majestic Nightclub. There was a riot in progress between off-duty US

Marines and Italian sailors off the *Bartolomeo Colleoni*, an Italian Navy gun-boat, currently moored on the Whampoo River.

We were in front of the Majestic in minutes.

It was payday for the US Marines, and they had come to the club with money to spend. They drank and showered their earnings on the girls. Full of confidence and alcohol, they expected to gain the full benefit of the money they had spread around.

The Italians turned up at one a.m., just as the recently formed couples were leaving. The Italians were the movie stars of the military world. Their uniforms, nipped in at the waist and padded at the shoulders, with a white cap worn at a rakish angle, together with their Mediterranean charm, made them the men of choice for the nightclub girls. As soon as the Italians arrived, the girls began to desert the Americans in droves. Men on both sides threw wild punches and in no time every man in the room was fighting.

When we burst in the entire ballroom floor was a tangled mass of US Marine grey-green and Italian navy uniforms as men punched, kicked, head-butted, and eye-gouged their opponents. Lifeless men lay in pools of blood on the floor, and opponents thudded boots into their unprotected bodies. A giant US Marine picked up an Italian Petty Officer and hurled him through a glass window. An American king-hit an Italian but then he slipped on a pool of blood. Suddenly, he was surrounded by four Italian sailors who rained kicks upon his now defenceless body. Similar acts of brutality were happening all over the dance floor.

Screaming cabaret girls were knocked flying as they ran, scrambling for refuge in the powder room, behind the bar or in the kitchen. One girl collapsed across the orchestra bass drum and several girls fainted where they stood.

The famous glass columns of the club were shattered. Chairs were thrown through windows. Tables were thrashed to matchwood.

We swung our batons and gradually began to separate the fighting mobs.

An American plunged a flick knife at my belly but my bulletproof vest deflected it. I swung my baton at him and broke his collarbone. He slumped in a heap, face ashen with shock and pain.

It took a long time but eventually order was restored. The nightclub was left looking like a battlefield. A line of ambulances pulled up on Bubbling Well Road and men were carried out, many with extremely serious injuries.

As we assisted in carrying the wounded outside, we stepped gingerly to avoid pools of blood and broken glass. A line of curious onlookers had gathered across the street and was being marshalled by a group of SMP constables.

The owner of the Majestic, Mister Wong, ran around the street screaming at everybody in uniform. He shouted, 'I will sue the American government. I will sue the Italian government. Curse you long-nosed barbarians!'

It was many hours before we were able to go back to Gordon Road.

Later, in bed, I couldn't sleep. When I finally drifted off, I dreamed of the nightclub riot. The knife went through my bulletproof vest and I watched my blood gush on the floor.

Chapter 28

I WALKED UP THE DRIVEWAY of the House of Multiple Joys, impatient to see Miriam. I felt desire, but it was an angry lust, not loving desire. I wanted to blot out the world for a few hours, with vigorous drinking and love-making.

Warm golden light spilled out from the house and I could hear the tempo of a lively dance number coming from inside.

I asked myself again if I could persuade her to go away with me. She was determined, however, that her life now was at the House of Multiple Joys. Admittedly, I hadn't thought through the ramifications of such a rela-tionship. In Shanghai, to marry a Chinese woman was certainly considered, in the SMP, to be a career killer. A man who made such a choice had 'gone native' and certainly was not to be trusted. And of course the biggest question of all was if Lu would ever consider letting her go.

Then there was Fiona. I was crushed by the brutal way she had discard-ed me. Now I felt as much anger and bewilderment as love for her.

How strange that I should be attached to two women, at opposite ends of the social spectrum, who were both utterly unattainable.

As I reached the top of the driveway, I saw there was a convoy of black cars parked in the drive. I recognised Big Ears Lu's heavily fortified Dusen-berg and the Packards used by his bodyguards. *This can't be good*, I thought.

From the house came a group of Green Gang foot soldiers. They formed a protective cordon around the cars. Then Big Ears Lu emerged with Miriam on his arm.

I stopped dead, a cold rage gripping my heart. Miriam gripped his arm closely and smiled up coquettishly at him.

My stomach knotted in a nauseous pool of jealousy and possessiveness.

It was crazy; I knew Miriam was seeing other men. In fact, at times I had found the idea perversely exciting.

But this was different. The idea of Miriam sleeping with Lu was utterly repulsive. I imagined myself pulling my police pistol and launching myself at Lu, bodyguards and all.

They got in the cars and the convoy moved down the driveway. As Lu's car drove past, Miriam glanced through the passenger window, her face blank and expressionless, and her eyes looking past me.

The convoy reached the gates, drove quickly through and turned right on the street. I ran back down the drive, my hand inside my jacket, gripping the butt of my pistol. Squeezing hard, longing to kill.

* * *

Anyone who read the mosquito press could tell you that Lu's favourite restaurant was The Highwayman on Bubbling Well Road. He was frequently photographed there with the latest *modeng* girl at his table. Standing on Hardoon Road, I hailed a taxi and ordered the driver to take me to Bubbling Well Road 'chop chop.'

The taxi pulled up outside the Highwayman, which was a popular restaurant that had an English menu and was much favoured by the *Taipans*. It was a richly appointed place, all red carpets and silverware and white-jacketed Russian waiters.

I paid off the taxi and walked to the entrance of the restaurant. The heavy red-leather padded door was opened for me and I stepped into the restaurant, ignoring the *maitre d'hotel's* podium.

The room was a buzz of gay conversation. It was a large room, every white linen-covered table full to capacity with happy patrons, the men in black evening suits and the women in expensive dresses. All foreign, the exception being one table of evening-suited Chinese men.

Miriam was seated by Lu's side, together with his entourage, at a large corner table, strategically positioned so that he could observe and be seen by the entire room.

I walked towards Lu's table, not quite knowing what I would do when I reached them. My blood had boiled with sexual jealousy and possessiveness. But in the time that it has taken to travel to the restaurant, my anger had fallen back to a controllable level.

Lu made eye contact with me. He nodded silently, as I approached, my palm squeezing the butt of my pistol. Miriam saw me then, her eyes widening in shock and fear.

This was the moment. I could have pulled out my pistol and, in a second, snapped off two shots, and two more for Miriam if I'd felt like it. I looked in Lu's eyes, the blank, soulless evil of him. I could have done all of Shanghai a favour.

He stared at me, haughty, curious, and provocative. *What will Gallagher do now?*

It was at that moment, as I stared into Lu's dead eyes, I realised I could not shoot a man in cold blood—any man. In the heat of combat maybe, but not like this. I was, after all, my father's son.

Despite my focus on Lu, there was something that caught my eye about the table of black-clad Chinese men. They unsettled my policeman's instinct. This was a rich man's restaurant, a place for the foreigners to come and play. The only Chinese here were the menial workers, the kitchen hands who scrubbed pots. The waiters were White Russians, a job considered too refined for the despised Chinese coolie. The only Chinese who could walk in here were men like Big Ears Lu. Only those Chinese who exploit their countrymen could get on in the foreigner's world.

The group of Chinese men wore the appropriate eveningwear, but there was something about the way they sat, hunched and contracted, as if they couldn't quite allow their skins to touch the suit that was such a symbol of the upper-class foreigner. As if they didn't *deserve* to touch the suits they wore.

At that moment one of the Chinese men stood up so suddenly that his chair crashed to the floor behind him. From inside his jacket he pulled a sawn-off shotgun, both barrels and the stock cut down, the weapon almost pistol-sized. 'Die, you parasite! Revenge for the White Terror!' he screamed in English, the gun pointed towards Lu.

Long hours of training at Mystery House took over. On reflex, I whipped out my pistol and fired two rapid shots from the hip without aiming, and then as the man staggered backwards, I fired two more shots. The other men at the table then got up and, in a mad scramble, sprinted for the door. Diners threw themselves on the floor, waiters dropped trays laden with plates, glasses and cutlery, and people at every table screamed and shouted.

A bodyguard pushed Lu under the table and then his men were up and had their guns covering every corner of the room. I allowed my pistol to slip to the floor. I was surrounded by Lu's men, two of whom pinned me by the arms.

'Leave him,' ordered Lu.

He stood before me then. 'It appears that once again you have saved the day, Mister Gallagher. Miss Tsai and I are very grateful to you.'

I bent and picked up my pistol, conscious that it still contained two bullets. I imagined Lu with a bloody gunshot wound between his eyes.

'How generous you are to take responsibility for me. And Mister Fairlight will be very proud of you. All that training at Mystery House paid off,' said Lu. 'I shall take Miss Tsai home now, where I shall ensure her *protection*. Good night, Mister Gallagher.'

Lu snapped his fingers and the entourage surrounded him, guns still at the ready. A bodyguard held Miriam's arm. The group walked briskly towards the exit, all eyes scanning the room for further trouble. I had a sudden realisation. I wasn't angry about Miriam being with Lu. I was angry with Fiona for her cruelty, angry enough to consider killing.

I stood in the middle of the restaurant surrounded by pale-faced, shocked diners whilst in the distance I heard the bells of the Emergency Unit Red Marias. No doubt Mister Fairlight would congratulate me. An Emergency Unit man might be out of uniform, he'd say, but he was never off duty.

Shanghai – 1929–1930

Chapter 29

December 31 1929

NEW YEAR'S EVE, AND THE Cathay Hotel Ballroom was ablaze with party lights and balloons, ribbons and streamers hung from the ceiling. The white-uniformed hotel orchestra accompanied a sharp-suited vocalist singing '*I may be wrong, but I think you're wonderful*' into a silver radio microphone. The music was being broadcast live on Radio 2KA Shanghai and to the US Pacific Fleet. The dance floor was crowded with elegant dancers, the men in black or white-jacketed evening suits, the women in floor-length silk evening dresses, displaying every colour imaginable.

I stood by the bar, about to order a drink when I caught a glimpse of Jamie and Fiona waltzing through the dance floor crush.

'Yes, sir?' said the barman.

'Later, thanks,' I replied as I left the bar and pushed my way through the crowd. I tapped Jamie's shoulder and said, 'May I cut in?'

He smiled and said, 'How jolly American of you. I didn't know that custom had reached our fair city. But be my guest, old chap.' He stood aside with a bow and extended his arm towards Fiona, indicating that I should step into the place he had occupied.

I took Fiona's hand in mine, placed my other hand on the small of her back, and we began to dance through the crush of people.

'I didn't know you'd be here, Michael,' she said.

'I didn't know myself. I got some tickets through Jack Dell. He knows everybody.'

'How is that pretty young lady that I saw you with the other evening at the Venus Café?'

'Fiona, can we please cut the chitchat. I want to talk to you. This is driving me crazy. Don't you feel anything for me at all?'

'Michael, please,' she said, a strained look crossing her face. 'Don't make a scene. It isn't going to do any good.'

'Just tell me that you don't love me. Then I will leave you alone.'

Fiona furtively glanced over her shoulder, even though it would be impossible for anybody to hear our conversation.

'Michael, please stop. You know how people gossip in this town. The last thing I want is for idle talk to reach Jamie.'

'He doesn't love you more than I do.'

Our conversation stopped for a moment as we collided with another couple. After nods of apology we began moving in time to the music again.

'He's your friend, Michael. Haven't you thought of that?'

'Of course I have. But I've loved you for half my life. Doesn't that mean anything to you?'

'I'm protecting you, Michael. His jealousy is bottomless, despite his penchant for whores. But then, what man doesn't whore in this brothel of a city?'

'Fiona, please. Give me a chance.'

'I can't talk to you like this, Michael.'

'Let me meet you, even for just a cup of coffee.'

'Michael, there's a shadow over everything, something terrible. I can't explain.'

'Do you mean Shanghai?'

'The city gets more frenzied every day. They've all lost their connection to home,' she said, her hand gesturing to take in the entire room. 'But they understand less about China than those who stay at home and read a book about it.'

'Well, that's Shanghailanders for you,' I replied.

'Some force will make it all stop. I feel something terrible coming.'

'Then let's get away from here now.'

She moved away from me a little then and looked up into my eyes. 'I try to imagine what it would be like to simply take a ship with you, to sail away somewhere far away and to start again.'

'Well, let's go then,' I replied.

'Here's Jamie now. Meet me for coffee tomorrow morning, eleven o'clock at the café across the road from the Sincere.'

Then I felt a tap on my shoulder. 'May I cut in, old chap? What's sauce for the goose is sauce for the gander.'

'Of course, Jamie. Enjoy yourselves.'

I pushed my way back to the edge of the dance floor. As soon as Jamie and Fiona were out of sight, I walked to the lobby of the hotel, onto the Bund and flagged a taxi. I couldn't stay and watch them.

1 January 1930

I sat back in the wicker chair and felt my whole body soften for a moment as the winter sun shone on my face. I just wanted to take a moment to myself while Fiona completed her shopping at the Sincere Department Store. If I knew Fiona, she'd be in there for an hour or more.

I was so weary of constantly declaring my love and being rebuffed.

I knew she loved me. She had practically admitted it last night.

The white-coated waiter brought my coffee and croissant and I opened the newspaper. The hot, dark, bittersweet coffee tasted good and the delicate croissant melted on my lips.

I caught my reflection in the silver coffeepot and felt rather pleased with the look of my new tailor-made light grey suit worn under a charcoal wool overcoat, the ensemble topped off with a burgundy cashmere scarf. Surely Fiona couldn't keep ignoring me forever?

I scanned the busy street taking in its fast-paced energy. Streams of cars, bicycles, rickshaws, and pedestrians. Most cars were late model American or European.

Then, for no obvious reason, I felt a knot tightening in my stomach and a chill breeze on the back of my neck. I put down my coffee cup and started examining faces in the street. I sat up straight. Why did I feel like this?

The uniformed doorman of the Sincere Department Store held the door open and I saw Fiona come through. She wore a bright yellow dress with a fur stole. Fiona, I think, preferred feeling the winter chill to hiding her dramatic fashion sense under a bulky winter coat. A Chinese servant girl laden down with gift-wrapped boxes accompanied her. They both stepped towards the café.

A black model-T Ford pulled up with a screech of brakes. Three Chinese men jumped out and ran towards Fiona. I knew in an instant, from their appearance, they were triad kidnappers. I saw the doorman run to Fiona's side. The leader swung an evil-looking meat cleaver and the doorman slumped to the ground, blood gushing from his neck. The second man punched the servant girl in the face and she crumpled in a heap, gift boxes scattered round her.

The third man stood behind Fiona, wrapped his beefy arms round her, picked her up like a parcel, and stepped towards the Ford with the obvious intention of bundling her inside.

I ran to the car, standing between it and the man holding Fiona, cursing the fact that my .45 was in the Depot workshop. I hadn't felt much need to sign the paperwork for a replacement when the Russian technician could recalibrate mine in only a couple of hours.

The kidnapper stopped and looked at me in astonishment. I stared him in the eye as I softened my knees, *Defendu* style, and spoke slowly and firmly. '*Shanghai Municipal Police. Release the lady. We have you completely surrounded. We've been watching you for weeks. Release the girl I say.*'

Slowly he put Fiona down, maintaining uncertain eye contact with me. How I wished to be in uniform, bulletproof-jacketed and armed.

With an angry cry, his companion with the big cleaver rushed forward, slashing wildly. I ducked as the blade sliced only inches from my face. He raised his weapon to bring it crashing down on me. I stepped back and lost balance, my fall actually saving me from the blade.

The gangster who'd punched the servant came around to my side and kicked me hard in the ribs. I nearly blacked out with the pain.

Then the Russian chauffeurs from the luxury cars parked along Nanking Road were amongst us. Bodies pushed and shoved, and onlookers screamed and hurled abuse. Then I heard the sound of a police bell. I picked myself up, watching for the cleaver. I realised that there were several SMP constables in the melee and, between them and the chauffeurs, the kidnappers were outnumbered.

In a short time the three kidnappers were handcuffed. An ambulance arrived and, before I could talk to her, I saw Fiona and her servant being led towards it. They were guided inside, the doors closed, and it drove off, bell clanging.

Another doorman from the Sincere Department Store unfurled a white sheet and covered the body of his colleague. I walked back to my seat at the French coffee shop. I picked up my cup with hands trembling so badly that the black liquid slopped into the saucer. I suddenly had the urge to cry. I stifled the impulse as an SMP sergeant approached me. He paused and studied my face.

'That was good work there. Gallagher, isn't it? I know you from Gordon Road. You saved that girl, so you did.'

He tipped the peak of his cap in a half-salute and walked back towards the crime scene.

Chapter 30

I RECEIVED A LETTER FROM Jamie, written in the flowing copperplate so reminiscent of my father's hand. Jamie invited me to meet him for drinks at the Long Bar of the Shanghai Club. I was both nervous and intrigued.

The Shanghai Club was the most exclusive of its type in the whole city, its nearest rival being *Le Cercle Sportif* in Frenchtown. However, while the French sports club had extraordinary facilities like a heated swimming pool, gymnasium, dance floor, gardens and restaurants, nothing could compete with the Shanghai Club at Number Two the Bund for its sheer status and exclusivity.

Of course, I had never been there before. What lowly policeman had? But I had read breathless descriptions of it in the mosquito press.

* * *

I arrived in a taxi and stood at the kerb for a moment, taking in the sights of the Bund. It never failed to impress me, this striking row of European buildings facing the Whampoo River. From Garden Bridge running south was a line of buildings that practically controlled the economy of all Asia. I could pick out the *Banque d'Indochine*, the North China Daily News, Jardine Matheson, Yokohama Specie Bank, and the Cathay Hotel with Sir Victor Sassoon's green pyramid-shaped private penthouse on top, and the Customs House with its clock 'Big Ching'.

I turned and looked towards the brown muddy river crammed with vessels of all shapes and sizes from bedraggled fishing boats to gunmetal-grey battleships. The elegance of the Bund was marred by the smell from the river of sulphuric, smoky pollution, engine oil, raw sewage, and rotting fish.

I announced myself to the doorman as a guest of Mister Flyte, then I was led by a uniformed pageboy to find Jamie.

Inside the exclusive, blood-red door of the club we turned left at the marble hallway. There I saw a large room, hung with English landscapes, with stained-glass windows shining multicoloured sunbeams on a gleaming rosewood bar stretching a hundred yards—the length of the room.

Club members stood at the bar, polished shoe resting upon brass foot rail, careful to pick the correct spot, for, by some unspoken rule of the club, your position at the bar was determined by your power and status in Shanghai. A griffin stood close to the door if he was lucky enough to get an invitation at all. The middle management men stood further down the bar. The *Taipans*, the men who ruled Shanghai, stood at the end, a hundred yards from the door.

We walked right to the end of the bar, which was reputed to be the longest bar in the whole world, and maybe only three or four spots from the end was Jamie, standing with a glass of whiskey in his hand. A group of men was gathered around him, and he had his audience captivated with one of his amusing stories. It made me think of how he used to be at my father's barracks.

'Michael,' he cried when he saw me, 'welcome to the club, old chap.'

'This is Michael Gallagher of the Shanghai Municipal Police. One of Mister Fairlight's finest, in the Emergency Unit' is how Jamie introduced me to the group of men gathered round him.

'Oh, thank you, Jamie,' I said with a distinctly uneasy feeling.

'What's more,' Jamie added with great enthusiasm, 'this is the chap who saved my lovely wife from a triad kidnap.'

'It's just the sort of thing we trained for,' I deflected modestly.

'Not at all, old chap, it was positively heroic. And fancy you being in a café across the street *at just that moment*. We have a lot to be thankful for indeed.'

A fresh round of drinks was ordered and he introduced me to the various important men in his company. As the Chinese barman came with the drinks on a polished silver tray, I observed how the *Taipans* looked through him somehow, as if he was made of smoke.

A tall, well-built, balding man joined the group. He walked with a pronounced limp, a legacy of the Great War, I presumed. A hearty, loud, cheerful man, he was introduced to me as Sir Victor Sassoon. 'Call me Victor,' he said with a firm grip on my hand. When he'd moved on, Jamie murmured in my ear, 'Owns the Cathay. His cousin's Siegfried Sassoon. You know, the war poet.'

There was much talk of business and travel and social gossip that I was unfamiliar with.

I nodded and smiled along with the group as a portly, walrus-moustached *Taipan* told a story about some chap who '*steered the punt from the Cambridge end.*'

The conversation ranged over cricket, the Shanghai Jockey Club, and, inevitably, back to business—starting prices in Wall Street and London, the rather worrying volatility of the New York market, wool prices in Australia and gold prices in South Africa. I had nothing to add. What of my status as a humble policeman? A cop in Shanghai might well be foreign and white, but he was on the lowest possible rung of the Shanghai social totem pole. My inability to contribute made me feel ill at ease and I began to tug at my tight collar.

As the evening passed, the sunlight dimmed and the staff began to light the elaborate copper gas lanterns that dotted the walls, casting a golden glow over the room.

Suddenly it hit me that the club members were basically the same class of men who attended the House of Multiple Joys. I began to relax, just absorbing the atmosphere of wealth and sophistication. A waiter silently refreshed my drink as I gazed up at the beautiful stained-glass windows.

A tall, portly man with white hair and Edwardian mutton chops covering half his face, whose name I couldn't recall, was holding court on the international situation. Jamie whispered in my ear: 'He's a director of the Hong Kong and Shanghai Bank.' The man spoke in tones of great indignation, as if the international political situation was specifically set up to inconvenience him personally. 'I must say it makes me *quite annoyed.* American unemployment is over *twenty percent*, this fellah Gandhi, *wrapped in a bed sheet if you please*, stirring up India, German banks closing…' His voice trailed off, fading, like a typewriter with a used-up ribbon. His florid face took on a gloomy expression.

Jamie touched my arm and gently steered me apart from the group.

'Listen here, old chap, you can't be a copper all your life. It's all very well for a bit of adventure while you're young but it's about time you got yourself a paying job. Why don't you get involved in the commercial world? The studio could use a chap like you.'

'I don't know, Jamie. I'm not sure I'm cut out for it.'

'Don't let these snobs fool you, Michael. Their snobbery blinds them to appreciating genuine talent. They'll give the whole thing away if they're not careful.'

'What thing?' I asked.

'This,' he said, waving his arm to encapsulate the whole room. 'Shanghai. They'll fuck it up. It will all be gone if they are left to run the show.'

'What do you mean, "gone"?'

'Like the Roman Empire, old chap, here today, gone tomorrow.'

'Is it really that tenuous?'

'You'd better believe it. There's war and revolution in the wind. That banker chap had it right.'

'So shouldn't you be thinking about moving the business somewhere else?'

'Eventually, yes. But not now. Did you ever hear the saying: "In the valley of the blind the one-eyed man is king"?'

'Yes. How does it apply in Shanghai?'

'Shanghai is an artificial entity, grafted on to the edge of an alien country. It's surrounded by warlord armies and run by gangsters. Japan wants to take over. The KMT and the Reds are in a civil war. Squeeze money can buy anything. Joe Stalin is casting his eye over the country and he has his local man in China, that schoolteacher fellah Mao. It can't last. But, in the midst of that chaos, a strong man can make his fortune. Seize the moment, Michael. Use this time while you can.'

'Let me think about it, Jamie.'

'Good lad. It has been jolly good getting reacquainted with you. And Fiona is delighted to see you also. You are one of her more pleasant child-hood memories, you know. Practically family. Anyway, she'd want me to keep an eye out for you.'

'Thank you.'

'No bother at all. And we'll have to find a nice girl for you too. Shang-hai is full of temptation. But a young man at the start of his career mustn't be tempted in the wrong direction.'

'Do you mean the House of Multiple Joys?' I asked very softly, making sure my voice didn't carry.

'Oh, God no, old chap. That's just for fun. Oh no, I mean messing about with wives and all that. There's a lot of bed-hopping among Shanghai's leading lights, but it can get very... complicated.'

Chapter 31

FIVE DAYS AFTER THE ATTEMPTED kidnapping I was in the Emergency Unit office writing up intelligence reports, general observations gleaned from stop-and-search patrols.

I put my pen down, sat back in the stiff-backed office chair, and began to massage my neck. I looked around at the pea-green walls, covered in police notices. A pile of patrol reports waited in my in-tray. As I sighed and reached forward to take a sip of Chinese tea, I heard a soft knock on the office door.

'Come in,' I called. No response. Then, another timid knock.

I got up, stepped to the door, and opened it. In front of me stood a young Chinese girl wearing the standard black uniform of an amah.

'Hello,' I said. 'What can I do for you?'

She gazed at the ground as she extended two hands holding an envelope. 'Sorry, sir, for you, sir, sorry to disturb, sir.'

I took the envelope and she made a bobbing, genuflecting gesture from the knee, quickly turned, and left.

I sat at my desk and studied the envelope. It was a rich cream colour and felt heavy and expensive. Written on the front in neat schoolgirl handwriting was 'Mr. Gallagher.' I held the paper to my nose and breathed in the soft perfume.

I slit it with my steel letter opener. Inside was a single sheet of pale pink stationery. The note was in the same neat copperplate writing. I scanned it quickly.

It was from Fiona, thanking me for what I had done and asking to meet me for morning tea the following day at the Palace Hotel on the Bund.

* * *

The next morning I met Fiona in the hotel's tearoom. She looked well and apparently unharmed from her ordeal. However, her demeanour was serious and quiet. I sat beside her on a flower-print couch and began to make small talk. Suddenly, she gripped my hand and gazed intensely in my eyes.

'Oh, Michael,' she said. 'We could have both died at the hands of those men. And you were so brave. Nobody has ever done anything like that for me.'

'I love you, Fiona. I'd die for you,' I replied quietly.

'I'm tired of fighting, Michael,' she said. 'I want to love you.'

'Finally,' I said. 'Shall I take a room for us?' my voice awkward as my throat constricted nervously.

'That would be wonderful,' she replied, her voice sounding tense but determined.

* * *

I keyed open the door to our room. We stepped inside to semi-darkness, the curtains drawn.

'Don't turn on the lights,' she said, as I looked around to get my bearings. She took my hand and pulled me to the centre of the room.

'Wait here.' I heard the bathroom door open and close.

After a few moments, the door opened again and I sensed a movement behind me. I turned.

Fiona stood before me, smaller now, having stepped out of her stiletto shoes. She wore a white hotel bathrobe.

I put my hands on her shoulders and, pushing the soft white material aside, exposed her breasts. Then I pushed the bathrobe to the floor; it made a soft whooshing noise as it slid down her body.

She raised her lips to mine. We kissed then, passionately, and moved towards the bed. As we fell on the bed I pulled my clothing off like a madman.

We locked in embrace; our lovemaking frenzied and rough, like two starving people. I felt myself almost overcome. This was the girl of my dreams, the one who was dead and then alive, the one I couldn't have. We cried out in mutual orgasm, a sense of release now, something denied for close to fifteen years finally expressed.

After we made love, we moved under the quilt and she lay in my arms, her hair pressing in to my nose, the clean, cornsilk smell of her filling me up. I thought I would never be happier.

'Fiona, I love you.'

She kissed me. 'Don't talk now, Michael. It's all so complicated.'

Chapter 32

IT WAS AFTERNOON. I LAY on the futon with Fiona. She lay stiffly, not touching me. We had argued again. I wanted her to leave Jamie and yet again she refused. We lay back on our pillows, staring at the ceiling. A strange heaviness pervaded the air.

'Fiona, I love you.'

'But you see other women, don't you?'

'Yes, but only because I don't have you.'

'You sound just like Jamie.'

'Fiona, I told you I love you. For God's sake, come away with me. Let's go somewhere.'

'Where would we go?' she said in a flat, dull voice.

'Anywhere,' I replied. 'The world's our oyster. America, Australia, Mexico.'

'The trouble with going away, Michael, is that when one gets there, one still wakes up in the morning as the same person. It's like carrying a suitcase with contents that never change, wherever one goes.'

'Fiona, don't you believe in a fresh start?'

'Shanghai was a fresh start and now look at us.'

I turned, looking at her face, trying to fathom her mood.

'Where's that fun girl who used to play cowboys and Indians with me?'

'She died in a fire in a big house in Ireland.'

I lay back on the pillow, saying nothing. Minutes passed.

'Michael, you think that because I'm the wife of a *Taipan* and have an expense account, I can do anything. I'm more trapped than a rickshaw coolie.'

'Whatever do you mean?'

She remained silent for a time. Then: 'I want to show you something. Will you take a short journey with me now?'

'Yes, alright.'

We dressed, went to the street and hailed a rickshaw. Fiona directed the coolie to take us towards the river. When we arrived at the Whampoo River, we stopped at a small wharf where ferryboats were available to carry people across to Pudong. We boarded and the boat spluttered to life and laboriously started chugging across the brown, polluted, noxious river. Leaving a trail of oily smoke, we arrived at the opposite bank. Pudong was an industrial district and, apart from many factories, its only claim to fame was that it had been the childhood home of Big Ears Lu. Fiona paid the ferrymen and we jumped onto the bank. Pudong was not part of the International Settlement, although many European, British, American and Japanese firms had factories and cotton mills there.

'Come with me,' she said.

We walked through a dark and grimy industrial landscape. Redbrick factories with tall chimneys pumped black sulphuric smoke that made me gag. Emaciated men and women of all ages trudged heavily to or from their place of work. They looked undernourished and exhausted, tired and defeated.

We reached the main entrance of a factory with a name written in Chinese characters. I could read enough to recognise it as a silk factory.

'Come inside,' she said to me.

We entered the building and nobody asked us what our business was. Such was the power of a European face and an expensive suit.

The air in the factory was hot and humid, and the steam created a dense fog. As my eyes adjusted to the atmosphere, I could see workers, mostly children. Each one stood by the rim of large metallic cauldrons of bubbling, steaming water. Their little hands made darting movements as they plucked silk fibres from boiled cocoons. Nearly all of them had severely scalded hands with skin hanging off like threadbare pairs of gloves.

'That's how they make silk,' she said.

I watched in horrified fascination as those shredded hands nipped in and out of the bubbling water.

'Come this way. There's more.'

We walked to the far end of the factory; the same scene was repeated throughout. We moved with difficulty because the factory was poorly illuminated, and the walkways were strewn with rubbish. We came to a rear door—an emergency exit. The double-door handles were chained and pad-locked, the chain rusty with age.

'If there were a fire in here, everyone would die. Most have TB and won't last long, anyway. Those who don't die of TB will get infections in their hands. That's if the pain doesn't kill them first. And this is only the silk industry. You should see the accumulator factories. Did you ever see those children with the blue line in their gums? That's from the lead poisoning. They all die in less than two years.'

I grabbed her arm and said, 'Let's get the hell out of here.'

* * *

We sat at the bar of a small Japanese teahouse on Broadway. I ordered two cups of *sake*. I drank mine down in one hit and signalled for another. Fiona sipped her drink delicately.

'All right, Fiona, why did you take me there to that hellhole?' I asked her.

'An education,' she replied.

'What do you mean?'

'Michael, you are a strong man.'

'In your opinion, perhaps.'

'Have you heard of *Mien Shiang*?'

'Someone mentioned it to me once.'

'It means "face reading" and I have become a student of such esoteric arts since my arrival here. I have learned that there is much wisdom in China, much that we don't know in the West. Face reading allows one trained in the art to divine not just a man's state of health and prognosis, but his character, strengths and weaknesses. You are strong, Michael, and I am burdened. I want to share my burden with you.'

'What exactly do you mean?

'I wanted you to see another side of Shanghai. You should know that Jamie owns this factory.'

'But what about his film studio?'

'He has fingers in every pie. I don't know what to do. I am not sure I can ever take pleasure in the benefits of such earnings.'

I took her hand. 'Fiona, let's go away together. You don't need to live like this.'

'You don't know him like I do. He would never let me go. I am tied to him like a fly in a spider's web.'

'We can always go away. Go somewhere far away.'

'You still don't know him, do you, Michael? He would hunt us to the ends of the earth. He would kill me with his own hands rather than allow another man have me.'

* * *

Visions of the children's hands, scalded skin hanging like threads, stayed with me, waking and sleeping. What a curse poverty was on the city of Shanghai.

I felt guilty pangs when I contrasted their poverty with my briefcase stuffed with cash of half a dozen denominations, carefully concealed under the floorboards in my Hongkew apartment. The money came so easily to me, thanks to the *ramblin' boys*.

After several sleepless nights I determined to at least make some gesture to assuage my conscience. The following Tuesday, I was off duty and walking through Frenchtown, a bulky wad of cash packed in an envelope in my inner jacket pocket. I flagged down a rickshaw coolie. *'Where is the soup kitchen?'* I asked in Shanghainese.

'Ah, you want Zao Char Road,' he said. *'I will take you.'*

We set off and I was shortly in front of a redbrick European house located not far from Yu Gardens.

A large banner was stretched across the front of the building, black letters on white canvas. It said: *Christian Relief for the Poor of Shanghai.*

On the opposite side of the street, facing the soup kitchen there was a twenty-four-hour casino offering a crude version of roulette with a home-made wheel and numbers painted on a splintered wooden table. The sign proclaimed that the casino offered free wine, beer and cigarettes and even fresh milk for the little children. Upstairs was an opium den. Next door to the casino was a row of pawnshops. What bastard thought of that idea, I asked myself.

I stepped through the door of the soup kitchen. Inside, there was a large, rough, but cheerfully decorated dining room. Big trestle tables sided by rough wooden benches filled the space. People in various states of distress sat at the tables hunched over bowls of soup and rough lumps of bread. At one end of the room stood a tall, thin, elderly European man wearing a dark grey suit over a clerical collar. He stood behind a lectern reading from a bible. *'"And, lo, he came upon them and spake to them…"'*

A group of European women, prosperous and well groomed, stood behind a counter dispensing the food.

I joined the queue and, when I reached the counter, the lady serving looked at me oddly, as she scanned me up and down, taking in my well-cut suit.

'Can I help you, sir?' she said in a broad Highland accent. I reached inside my jacket and pulled out the thick brown envelope.

'Take this,' I said. 'It might help a bit.'

Before she could say another word, I walked briskly to the exit.

Chapter 33

North China Daily News – August 5 1930
Policeman Decorated for Valour

At a ceremony this morning at the offices of the Shanghai Municipal Council Sergeant Michael Gallagher of the Shanghai Municipal Police Emergency Unit was awarded the Distinguished Conduct Medal. Sir Edward Hilton-Mere, Chairman of the Council, presented the award.

The citation describes how Sergeant Gallagher single-handedly disarmed a gunman who was holding up the Golden Dragon Jewellery shop on Nanking Road. Sergeant Gallagher was responsible for saving the life of the proprietor of the shop, Mister Ho, and two American tourists, Mr. and Mrs. Barton of Sacramento, visiting Shanghai from the Dollar Line cruise ship SS Theodore Roosevelt. Mr. Barton commented, 'The police officer came storming in like a wild west gunslinger. He was ready to die for us. I've never seen anything like it.'

I HAD BEGUN TO NOTICE a few grey strands showing in my dark brown hair, and there was a subtle tremble in my fingers. A good night's sleep was proving difficult also. Duty with the Emergency Unit meant being on call at all hours. When I was off duty, even sleeping in my apartment, it was difficult for me to shift into a relaxed state. Many a night I paced my bedroom floor as the sun came up. I was drinking more and spending more time at the House of Multiple Joys.

I'd learned from Jack not to put any squeeze money in the bank but to keep it in a safe hiding place. By 1928, I'd been able to leave the police accommodation and rent myself a comfortable apartment in the Greycliffe building on Bubbling Well Road. It was described in the agent's brochure as the second tallest residential building in Asia.

It was understood by all members of the *ramblin' boys* that we were not to obviously flaunt the money we were making. But in the flashiness of

Shanghai we were able to live a great life—cabarets, restaurants, nightclubs, cinemas, taxi dances, and the girls. I began to buy good quality suits, shoes, hats, and haircuts. I became comfortable with hailing taxis and rickshaws, and employed a Chinese boy to take care of my laundry, cleaning, grocery shopping, and cooking.

Part Two

–

The Rokusan Gardens

Shanghai – 1931–1932

Chapter 34

14 July 1931

IT WAS DIFFICULT FOR FIONA and me to meet with any frequency. I was working very long hours with the Unit as the city was in a near-constant state of emergency. If we weren't dealing with political events like riots and strikes, it was criminal activity such as kidnapping and armed robbery. We ran almost constant stop-and-search patrols to weed out illicit arms.

Fiona was equally busy, playing the part of the dutiful wife of a rich *Taipan* and therefore serving on endless charitable committees, such as the anti-foot-binding society.

Hongkew became the place we met, because it was not the sort of area that would attract Jamie or his crowd. The district of Hongkew, which started just north of Garden Bridge, was nicknamed 'Little Tokyo.' At the turn of the century, it had been quite a wealthy area and Shanghai's first luxury hotel, the Astor, was built there. By now it had lost its upper class reputation; the rich had been replaced by a population of Japanese, Eurasians and Portuguese.

The nickname came from its population of fifty thousand Japanese and another five thousand or so Koreans. Its main street—Broadway—was a lively thoroughfare of Japanese shops, bars and geisha houses, cabarets, theatres and cafés. Hongkew was a refuge for jazz musicians, dancers, homosexuals, single mothers and members of the *avant-garde* who wished to avoid the clutches of Japan's military regime.

The district was substantially cheaper than the rest of the International Settlement. I found that its cheapness attracted a young and happy crowd and it didn't have the stuffiness of many of the posh clubs of Bubbling Well Road or the French Concession. For that reason, we never expected to be disturbed there by friends of Jamie.

Before Fiona and I had started our love affair I had already begun to rent a second apartment in Hongkew and, with the liberal spreading of a bit of *cumshaw* to the letting agent, the lease was not recorded in my name. He assumed I was a married man looking to set up a love nest. I didn't dissuade him of that idea. In fact, I wanted it as a place to hide my cash earned from the *ramblin' boys of pleasure*.

However, for Fiona and me it was the ideal place to be together. Away from prying eyes, discreet, and not even leased in my name.

We met when we could. When we were together it felt like the most natural thing in the world. But she would not, under any circumstances, consider leaving Jamie. It was clear to me that she no longer loved him, but she was unshakeable in her resolve.

* * *

Sometimes, when I was alone in the Hongkew apartment waiting for Fiona to arrive, I would suddenly be overcome with an urge to touch the money —to feel it, smell it, and allow the weight of it to sit in my hands.

Moving the bed aside, I would carefully prize up the floorboard. Underneath was a small cavity. I would put my hand inside and pick out the bundles of cash. I'd throw the cash onto the bed and run my hands through it. It was a rainbow of colours and denominations—Yankee dollars, English pounds, Philippine gold coins, Japanese Yen with its rising sun, and the strange and colourful Chinese money. Lovely. It was all lovely. What my mother wouldn't have given for a fraction of this.

* * *

When we felt like a stroll we would take a walk at the Rokusan Gardens, a complex of traditional Japanese guesthouses, restaurants and manicured gardens designed after old Imperial Kyoto. A Japanese Navy Marine Officer, Lieutenant Nakamoto, who was my occasional sparring partner at the Gordon Road gymnasium, had introduced me to it. The first time I took Fiona there she was captivated.

* * *

Fiona and I stepped through the sliding doorway that led to the gardens and entered a world utterly different from the streets of Hongkew. Narrow, neat gravel pathways wound their way through moist, green lawns. Standing rocks and stones were dotted around the gardens looking like miniature mountains. Little streams bubbled from the rocks.

There were many trees: weeping willows near the pond, their leaves hanging low towards the lily-covered surface of the water, pines and sycamores around the edges of the park.

In the middle was a large pond with a small, red wooden bridge crossing it. Although the bridge was fully functional in the sense that one could walk across it, it served no purpose other than decoration. I smiled as I imagined my father saying, 'Jasus, why did they build that thing? Sure, it goes nowhere.'

Close to the pond was a small gazebo and, sitting in the doorway, a young female classical Japanese musician, wearing an azure silk kimono, played a three-stringed shamisen. She was a famous instrumentalist from Kobe, invited to Shanghai for a two-month residency by the Rokusan Garden's owner Mister Ito, and her name was Aki-san. Fiona and I sat, hand in hand, on a stone bench under a willow tree and listened to her play. Aki-san's slim, elegant fingers plucked the instrument and created soothing, calming sounds. I watched her face, snow-white and a slash of crimson red lipstick.

'Close your eyes and listen,' said Fiona.

I allowed the sounds of the music, the rustle of the trees, and the scent of the pine to soothe me. We sat there for a long time.

'Fiona, I need to ask you something.'

'Oh, don't get all serious on me now, Michael,' she said with a sigh.

'I have to; this has been on my mind forever,' I said, determined to press on but wondering if it was wise to do so. As the Chinese would say, 'The shattered cup may be glued together but the cracks will show.'

'Go on, then.'

'Why didn't you tell me you were alive after the fire?'

'I was afraid.'

'What do you mean? Afraid of what?'

'Michael, it couldn't have worked out for us.'

'You mean our class differences?'

'Yes, that's right,' she said, a certain edginess creeping into her voice.

'So, I wasn't good enough for his Lordship's daughter?'

'No, I wasn't good enough for Sergeant Gallagher's son.'

'Whatever do you mean?' I was astonished to hear this.

'For you and I to be together, whether it was in an independent Ireland, or in Britain, we would have been an anomaly. A snooty, aristocratic girl and a working class boy. Everywhere we went, fingers would have been pointed.'

'I wouldn't have minded.'

'That's exactly my point, Michael. You're brave. I'm not. I didn't have the courage to sail against the wind.'

'But you ran away with Jamie all the way to Shanghai. Wasn't that scarier?'

'Not really. We were off to build the empire, just like my father and grandfather had done. And Jamie was an officer and a gentleman, a man of my own class. It was easy. I could do that with my eyes closed.' She said this in a matter-of-fact, businesslike tone as if her people explored new countries every day. Which, I suppose, they did.

'And now here I am in Shanghai. Not quite an officer and not quite a gentleman.'

'I'm sorry, Michael.'

I took her hand and kissed it.

* * *

Later, we were standing in the lobby of the Rokusan guesthouse while the owner, Mister Ito, tried to flag down a taxi for us. The sky was laden with storm clouds and we didn't want to chance a rickshaw. Across the street was a line of rickshaw coolies waiting for a fare. They huddled in a circle, noisily shouting as they threw dice. One coolie sat apart, still and quiet. He was looking towards me. As I returned his gaze, he looked downward, his conical straw hat hiding his face. I could have sworn it was Freddie Wang.

Chapter 35

North China Daily News – January 9 1932
Outrage in Japanese Community

A mob of Chinese hooligans today murdered five Japanese Buddhist monks who were peaceably going about their business. This latest outrage follows a series of riots and the Chinese boycotting of Japanese goods, which pile up on the docks untouched by dockside coolies. Many of the small trading houses of Hongkew's 'Little Tokyo' have been brought to the brink of ruin.

A group of Japanese citizens were provoked into burning a Chinese-owned factory in neighbouring Chapei. The Japanese government has expressed its outrage and it appears that the KMT government is in the mood for making concessions. Not so, however, the mayor of Greater Shanghai, General Wu Tiecheng, who has promised the Japanese nothing but an eye for an eye.

The Japanese government has landed five hundred Imperial Japanese Navy Marines to protect its citizenry in the Hongkew district. The Shanghai International Settlement is on alert and our Shanghai Volunteer Force has been mobilised.

Alarmingly, the Chinese 19th Route Army, commanded by General Cai, currently camped in the countryside outside the Shanghai metropolis, is making threatening noises. This threat is not to be taken lightly as General Cai has 31,000 men under his command. General Cai has already questioned the right of the Japanese to land their Marines. He has stated in no uncertain terms that should Japan attempt to seize the industrial area of Chapei—which is the Chinese territory located immediately next door to Hongkew—then his army will move against the Japanese forces.

Let us hope that sanity prevails and peace is maintained. Shanghai is a place of business; let us trust it remains so.

28 January 1932

I SAT AT THE DUTY officer's desk in a dream, thinking of my night ahead with Fiona, making love on a soft bed, hot sake in a stone jar on the side table. My thoughts were interrupted when the phone jangled, cutting through the silence of the afternoon.

'Gallagher, it's Fairlight. I want all personnel to stand by in barracks tonight and over the weekend—full alert, I'm afraid.'

'What's up, sir?' I felt my stomach sinking.

'I have a feeling that the balloon is going up today, or pretty soon.'

'Why's that, sir?'

'Well, as you know, I spar weekly in *ju-jitsu* with a group of Japanese naval officers. All of them have cancelled on me in the past forty-eight hours and now they're incommunicado. They're normally very reliable. I have a feeling that they are all under starter's orders.'

'All right, sir, I'll issue the order here among the Unit.' Damn it, I thought. I have to warn Fiona. If Fairlight is right, the streets around the apartment will be a battleground in the next few hours. I picked up the phone again and dialled the number for the Flytes' house on Bubbling Well Road. I did this with great reluctance. The phone was answered by a Chinese maid who told me that Mrs. Flyte was out and it was unknown when she would be returning. I quickly wrote a note telling Fiona not to cross Garden Bridge under any circumstances, and called my station servant to deliver it to the house. I instructed him that the note wasn't to be handed to anyone but Fiona personally. I tipped him extravagantly to ensure my orders were carried out. I felt very uneasy about committing such a note to paper but I didn't want Fiona to walk into potential danger. My other concern was the Hongkew apartment. If it was damaged, I ran the risk of losing my money hidden under the floorboards.

* * *

At 11 p.m. the phone rang. I picked up and said, 'Sergeant Gallagher, Emergency Unit.'

'Yes, Sergeant, glad you are there,' said an upper-class English voice that sounded tense and high-pitched, a man whose throat had constricted with fear but who was endeavouring to speak normally.

'This is Captain Ward of the Shanghai Volunteer Corps. The Japanese are on the attack. They have headed into Chapei. Now, Chapei is outside of our parish, of course, but they are going through Hongkew to get there.'

'How many of them, sir, do you know?'

'Five hundred of their blue-jackets. They have already taken North Station.'

'All right, sir, I will call out the Unit.'

As Captain Ward cut the call, I pressed the red button on the duty desk, which sounded the alarm. Immediately men roused themselves from their bunks or from seats in the canteen and began to button up their jackets and put on their body armour. Within three minutes we had mounted the Red Marias and, with bells clanging, drove towards Garden Bridge.

* * *

Across Soochow Creek the Hongkew and Chapei districts had been plunged into darkness and a battle raged. The International Settlement was a blaze of neon lights. The sounds of a jazz band wafted across the river to the Imperial Japanese Naval Marines encumbered in full battle dress.

In the shadows of Hongkew, they ran through the streets crouching at the sound of enemy fire. They were easily recognisable by their distinctive navy blue uniform with white webbing and white leggings. Each man was laden down with a helmet, ammunition pouches, rucksack and rifle. As they zigzagged down the streets, trying to stay in the shadows, they were harried and picked off by Chinese snipers hidden in the upper floors of the nearby buildings. Whatever advantage was given to the marines by the darkness of Hongkew was taken away by the blaze of neon from the International Settlement, which lit them up as effectively as searchlights. It was an unintended gift for the Chinese defenders.

Our squad took up position alongside a British Army unit and moved in to protect our side of Garden Bridge.

The night was freezing. There was a wind blowing down from Siberia that would have shaved your skin off.

By eleven-thirty, carloads of sightseers were driving from all over the International Settlement and Frenchtown to watch the entertainment. How could a cabaret show on Bubbling Well Road compete with a real war being fought only a stone's throw across the creek?

Men and women in their evening wear and fur coats stood around gossiping, exchanging comments and explanations, smoking cigarettes and swigging from silver hip flasks to ward off the bitter cold. Nearby cafés did a roaring trade in coffee and sandwiches while people settled in to watch the night's events unfold.

As the night went on, and more and more people arrived by car, taxi and rickshaw, it began to remind me of a race-day crowd. People stared through opera glasses and swapped them with friends, pointing and describing scenes of particular drama.

Across the creek, Japanese marines continued their crouching run through the streets, occasionally stopping in a doorway and returning fire when they saw the flash of a Chinese sniper's rifle. I saw a marine stop, fold over and gradually deflate, like a balloon loosing air, until he slowly crumpled flat on the kerb.

A British army motorcycle dispatch rider came careering towards us at breakneck speed. He stopped with a screech of brakes and handed me written orders from the Municipal Council. We were to make the crowd move away and take shelter.

We fanned out through the crowd and pushed the sightseers back. But our shouted orders: 'Move back, you may come under fire' were met with derision. I heard plummy public-school types running commentary on the battle, as if they were at school sports day.

A portly English fellow, his shirt buttons straining, chortled at me, 'Come on, old chap, how often do we get sport like this?' The man next to him clinked flasks in a toast and said, 'Spot on! Let's see the Japs give 'em a bit of what for.'

A tall, thin, balding man further along the line called, 'That's right! They're doing the white man's job for us.'

There was one man, pink-cheeked, young but balding, with the build of a rugby man. He had been bellowing encouragement at the Japanese marines as if he was watching his team play. My hand shot forward and I grabbed the collar of his shirt. I pulled his face close.

'If you take a bullet in the face, don't expect me to get you to the hospital, you plummy bastard,' I growled at him through gritted teeth. His eyes widened with fear.

'Steady on, old chap, we're just having a bit of fun,' said one of his companions.

'War isn't fun, *gentlemen*,' I said. 'You should try being in one sometime.'

* * *

After a full night on duty, we were ordered to stand down as the sun was rising and a truckload of Royal Marines arrived to take over our post.

As the British marines clambered down their trucks and took up their positions, I approached an SMP motorcyclist sitting astride his Big Chief motorcycle, its engine purring smoothly. The constable was a young man and not long out from England, judging by the wide-eyed expression on his acned face—a mix of fear and exhilaration.

I adjusted my posture into a rigid parade-ground stance. He sat up straight and said, 'Yes, Sergeant?'

'I need that machine—Mister Fairlight's orders.'

'I don't know, Sergeant. I'm not supposed to surrender it to anyone.'

'You are absolutely correct, Constable. But Mister Fairlight wants up-to-date intelligence from across the river. He has asked me to reconnoitre.'

'But you could get killed over there, Sergeant.'

'Hongkew is part of the International Settlement and I'm entitled to go. And anyway, orders are orders.'

'All right, Sergeant. I assume you know how to ride?'

'Of course. I've had training at the Depot.'

He dismounted from the motorcycle and I immediately took his place. I gunned the motor and took off.

I raced across Garden Bridge, the metal structure of the bridge seeming the shoot past me. I came off the bridge and accelerated north along Broadway with Japanese marines shouting at me, 'Go back! Go back!'

Well, to hell with them! I was wearing an SMP uniform and Hongkew was still part of the International Settlement. They could all piss off.

With a bit of luck I could park at the front of my Hongkew apartment, run upstairs, grab the briefcase of cash from under the floorboards and be back across the Creek within ten minutes.

During the night, the Japanese ships on the river had started shelling Chapei and I had been alarmed to see some shells fall short into Hongkew.

I speeded past the Astor Hotel heading up Broadway, then took a sharp turn left to Yuen Fong Road and then right again up East Seward Road. I sensed bullets fly by uncomfortably close. I turned down a narrow cul-de-sac off East Seward Road and stopped. The row of neat apartment buildings looked like a mouthful of gapped teeth. Most buildings had shattered windows and smoke stains. Several buildings had collapsed entirely.

My building was one of them. Where the neat European-style apart-ment building had stood there was a debris-filled pile of brown and grey rubble, a jumble of dust, bricks, timber beams, smashed furniture and shards of glass. Somewhere in there was my fortune, no doubt blown to dust.

I hadn't time to be upset now. I gunned the bike's engine, rode a few feet up the street, did a u-turn and raced back the way I came.

It took me only a few minutes to speed back to Garden Bridge. I was waved through the sandbagged and barbed-wire barrier and I pulled up where the young constable was sitting on a pile of sandbags, drinking a mug of tea.

I dismounted, returned the ignition keys and walked away heading towards the Bund, trying to hold myself together.

My head was dizzy and my legs weak. I leaned against the wall of the *Banque d'Indochine*, taking deep breaths until I had regained my composure.

* * *

That evening I changed clothes and went to the rooftop bar of the Cathay Hotel on the Bund. From here one could take in a magnificent view over the whole city.

I was devastated about the loss of all that money but tried to tell myself that it wouldn't take too long to build it up again. It was very unsettling after the feeling of security that the money had brought me. I'd gotten used to it.

My thinking didn't make sense but I felt that if I could observe the battle, safe on my perch high above the city, I had some kind of control over events.

Above the buzz of conversation a small jazz trio played and sang *'Dream a little dream of me.'*

Chapter 36

30 January 1932

ALL ACROSS THE INTERNATIONAL SETTLEMENT, affluent westerners sat on their balconies and rooftops, sipping cocktails as they watched the show.

The Japanese high command boasted that they would take Chapei in four hours. In fact, as we soon observed, they'd been driven right back to the Whampoo River and very nearly failed in the first hours of the assault. The fighting intensified and continued for long after anyone expected.

The *North China Daily News* had front-page photographs of twenty thousand Japanese infantry disembarking from troopships to join the battle of Shanghai.

The Japanese air force bombed and strafed Chapei while Japanese naval ships on the Whampoo shelled the area. Chapei burned.

I witnessed waves of refugees, many carrying their life's possessions in a pillowcase, as they pushed their way into the International Settlement. Over six hundred thousand refugees poured across the Garden Bridge.

* * *

At the end of another shift, I sat alone at the Cathay's rooftop bar staring towards Chapei. I heard someone call my name. I looked around and there was Jack Dell striding towards me, his powerful body clad in an elegant black evening suit. I hadn't seen him in a while, since Special Branch had snapped him up. I was very happy to see a friendly face. 'Well, young fella, enjoying the show?' He said this with a laugh, as if the war was purely for his own amusement.

'Jack, have a drink! How's life among the spooks?'

'Not too bad, Michael. Some great gossip in the files.'

He pulled up a cane chair and joined me near the railing. He waved to the white-jacketed Chinese waiter and ordered two scotches. When the drinks were brought on a silver tray we picked them up and clinked glasses.

'Cheers!'

'Cheers.'

'Jasus, Michael, this is one hell of a fucking crazy city,' said Jack with a harsh laugh.

'It is that, Jack.'

I continued looking towards Chapei. The clash of small arms fire intermingled with the heavy cough of artillery. Black smoke billowed over the skyline and buildings burned, flames shooting into the sky. There was a smell of burning meat coming towards us on the breeze.

'Poor bastards.' I said this as my eyes scanned the Garden Bridge. The Bridge was bottlenecked with a crush of people, heaving and pushing to get to the safety of the International Settlement. British soldiers manned the checkpoint at our end, and Japanese troops on the Hongkew side. Both were trying to contain the flow without success.

'Why the fuck should you care?' asked Jack.

I looked at him, for the first time seeing hardness in his dark brown eyes. I found his expression unsettling.

'Well, they're all people, aren't they, Jack? Like us.'

'Listen here to me, Michael. They are nothing like us. Don't you go getting soft on me now.'

I watched a Japanese bomber circling slowly over Chapei.

Jack signalled for another round of drinks. We picked up our glasses and once again clinked.

'Here's to the fucking craziest city in the world. Long may it continue,' said Jack.

'Cheers,' I replied.

Jack finished his drink in one big, noisy slug. He stood up and threw a bundle of notes on the table. 'This is on me.' He nodded to me, adjusted his black bow tie and said, 'Take care of yourself now, Michael.' Then he strode away, brisk as always, towards the hotel elevator.

31 January 1932

I didn't go home to Greycliffe during the emergency but slept at Gordon Road. The following morning I was woken by a station servant who handed me a white envelope from a silver tray.

'Sorry, sir, this came in several days ago but it was misplaced until now.'

'Why didn't someone get it to me?' I snapped, feeling a sudden unease as I recognised Fiona's handwriting.

---

28 January

Dear Michael

My darling, I have big news.

I cursed you when your note was delivered; it was so risky. But then something amazing happened. Jamie caught me reading the note and I was terrified of his anger and jealousy. We had a huge row.

But I stood my ground and I told him that I love you and that I was leaving to be with you.

Without so much as picking up more than my handbag I went off in a taxi. I am in the Hongkew apartment now, my darling, waiting for you tonight.

That's it. No more Mrs. Flyte for me. I have finished with him entirely.

Darling, there are things I must speak of, hard things to tell you. But I know that you love me and I can't wait to be in your arms tonight.

Please see if you can get away a bit early. I can't think of anything nicer than spending Friday night with my boy.

Your darling Fiona

PS. I know you mentioned that Hongkew might be getting dangerous now but at the moment the city seems settled. Let's talk tonight and we can decide where to go next. I don't want to go to Greycliffe because Jamie's people might find me there.

An old familiar dread settled over me. Fiona might have been caught in the battle. She could be injured, even dead. Is it possible that this could all happen again, just when I'd found her and made her mine?

I threw open the bedroom window and stood there, the chill wind freezing my body. I needed to feel something, anything, rather than the fear in my heart.

* * *

I dialled the number for Jamie's house. The last place I wanted to phone was the Flyte residence, but I didn't know how else to get some solid information. Was it possible that she *had* come home?

The phone rang for a long time and I was on the point of hanging up when finally someone picked up.

'Flyte residence.' An English accent, male, cultivated. *Not Jamie, thank God.*

'Good morning. Could I please speak to Mrs. Flyte?'

'I am afraid that is not possible.'

I paused for a heartbeat, the line crackling.

'This is the Shanghai Municipal Police. I must speak to Mrs. Flyte.'

'I regret to inform you, sir, that Mrs. Flyte is deceased.' A long pause. 'She was in Hongkew during the attack. Her body was retrieved by Mister Flyte's chauffeur.'

The telephone receiver slipped from my hand. The grief felt physical, like a knife blade in my chest. I gazed out the window towards Hongkew and watched the plumes of smoke and flames rising from the ruins.

Chapter 37

MY TAXI PULLED UP OUTSIDE the Shanghai Club. The sky was heavy and grey, clouds low, almost touching the rooftops of the Bund. The rumble of artillery fire drifted down from Hongkew.

I was met at the door by a pageboy and, as I had no appointment and wasn't in uniform, I flashed my police badge. 'I need to see Mister Flyte.' The voice in my head cried out, Fool! *Fool!* But even though Jamie was my rival for Fiona, he was the only person in Shanghai who had known her almost as long as I did. Our very rivalry was the thing that also joined us— our love for the same woman.

I felt an overwhelming compulsion to face him. What was it that drove me? Maybe I wanted his forgiveness, or did I want to blame him? Was it my fault that she was in caught in the Japanese attack?

'Yes, sir, please follow me.'

I was led into the bar, walking along its familiar length until we arrived at Jamie's usual spot. He was there. As I arrived, the low conversation in his group came to a sudden stop, leaving a pregnant silence in the air. Jamie turned and looked at me, his face dark and grim.

'Jamie,' I said.

'So you have the nerve to turn up here,' he said slowly, almost under his breath.

'Jamie, I'm sorry about Fiona.'

He stepped closer to me. His fist flashed and I reeled back as it crunched into my face. I staggered and nearly fell. I tasted blood in my mouth. Jamie moved close and I put up a hand to defend my face. Behind me someone said, 'That man is a bloody cad.'

'Jamie, I don't know what to say. I loved her.'

'And you dare to assume that I didn't! You'll pay for this.'

He gripped my jacket and pulled me close, speaking softly only to me, almost a lover's voice.

'At least you didn't cry. Your father cried like a little girl before I put a bullet between his eyes.'

Someone behind me said, 'Get that bounder out of our club.'

I was frogmarched by two club members who half-pulled, half-lifted me to the door of the club. I was unceremoniously thrown to the ground, my knee scraping on the kerb as I fell.

'Never come back here again, if you know what's good for you. This is a club for gentlemen.'

* * *

I took a taxi home, my mind in such a swirl that I didn't even realise when the car pulled up at the front of Greycliffe. I sat in the car until the driver said, 'We're here, sir.'

Jamie killed my father. But why? I knew there had been some tension between them about mistreatment of prisoners, but to kill him? To shoot him down as they fought side-by-side? Damn him to hell. Jamie was a ruthless bastard, a cold-hearted killer. I would make Jamie pay for my father's murder and for Fiona's death.

As I put the key in the door of the apartment I heard the phone ringing. I struggled to open the door. I was so distraught I could hardly think. There was no sign of my houseboy so I ran to the phone and picked it up.

'Gallagher,' I said, aware of the quiver in my voice.

'Oh, Michael, it's Miriam. Can you come and see me at the House?' Her voice sounded tight and strained.

'Something has happened, Miriam. I can't do anything now.'

'Michael, I need you to come. Please. I must see you.' The fear in her voice was contagious. Every instinct told me not to go.

'All right, Miriam, I will be there shortly.'

I quickly showered, shaved and changed into an evening suit. It helped clear my head and I knew that I wouldn't do myself any favours by turning up at the House looking out of place. Especially now. I left the apartment and hailed a taxi to sixty-six Hardoon Road.

I walked up the driveway; the guards looked me over without comment. When I knocked at the door, the butler greeted me as normal. I asked to see Miriam.

'She will be available shortly. Please go through to the piano room and enjoy a drink.'

I sat in the corner with a double scotch, my hands shaking. The pianist played '*Night and Day.*' I held the glass with both hands and brought it to my lips, drank deeply and finished the drink in one gulp. I signalled for another. 'Double, please,' I said to the girl. The butler approached me and said, 'You may see Miss Tsai in room twenty-seven.'

* * *

I knocked softly. I did not hear a reply and, after waiting for a few seconds, I opened the door and stepped inside. The room was dark. I swept the wall with my open hand and found a switch. I flicked the switch but the light didn't come on. As my eyes adjusted, I was able to make out the room well enough.

Then there was a flame of a lit match. Sitting on the bed, his head leaning against the padded headboard was Lu. He reached to the sideboard and switched on a dimly illuminated bedside lamp.

Lu smoked a thin Philippino cigar held in a long ebony cigar holder. He inhaled contentedly and blew out a neat cloud of blue smoke.

'Where's Miriam?' I demanded.

'Take a look outside,' he replied.

The window presented a view of the driveway and I could see two men marching briskly towards the gates, a young woman held between them. Her head turned up towards the window and I saw her face. It was Miriam. She saw me and through the windowpane I heard her scream, 'Help me, Michael, please! Help me!' The men dragged her through the gates and pushed her into a black Packard. As soon as the rear door slammed on her, the engine revved and the car sped away.

'What are you doing to her?' I demanded, as I turned back to face Lu.

'Relax, Mister Gallagher. She will live. And so will you, I am pleased to say.'

'I don't believe you. You'll attempt to kill us both, won't you?'

'Mister Gallagher, I am not rash enough to challenge the wisdom of the Gods. I believe that to kill a man who once saved my life would be to defy the heavens. Anyway, I try to avoid killing policemen whenever possible. I find it not conducive to the smooth running of my business affairs and it causes me great irritation.'

'If you harm Miriam, I'll kill you with my bare hands,' I said.

'Do not push your luck. I am giving you one chance only.' He inhaled again, and rounding his lips, blew another perfectly circular smoke ring.

'Do not worry, Mister Gallagher. Miss Tsai will be fine. We will send her away to one of my overseas establishments. I have many houses. She will be well taken care of and she shall work. But be aware, if you make trouble for Mister Flyte or myself, the young lady will die a painful and lingering death. Of that you have my word.'

Then the door opened and the butler stepped through. Lu snapped his fingers.

From downstairs the piano tinkled cheerfully, '*I Found a Million Dollar Baby.*'

The butler addressed me. 'Mister Lu wishes for you to return the gold key,' he said softly. I reached in my pocket, picked out the key and handed it to him.

'He also commands that you do not patronise our House any further.'

'Very well.'

'You must refrain from bothering his friend Mister Flyte.'

I nodded slowly. As I walked downstairs, my steps muffled by the thick carpet, I heard Lu's voice behind me. 'You must be very careful from now on, Mister Gallagher. Do not tread on any toes. The fate of Miss Tsai is in your hands and yours alone.'

* * *

I went home to the apartment and lay awake in my bed all night.

Next morning, as I arrived at the main entrance at Gordon Road, a fast car pulled up sharply. It was a black Special Branch Pierce Arrow. Jack Dell was at the wheel. He approached me, his face black as thunder. I offered a handshake; he ignored it.

'Hello, Jack.'

'I've had a very disturbing phone call,' he answered.

I just nodded in reply.

'For fuck sake, Michael, what sort of game are you playing?'

'I'm sorry, Jack. It's a long story.'

'Jasus, it had better be. Don't you know that in our business we can't afford to upset powerful people? The boys are all very disappointed. They don't want you in the gang anymore.'

'I didn't mean to make trouble for you or the boys, Jack.'

'You'd fucken-well better not. It wouldn't be at all hard to arrange for you to die in the line of duty. There'd be a queue of people lining up to do it if the money was right. You couldn't go out on a job ever again without wondering when you were going to cop a bullet in the back of the head.'

'What do you want, Jack? I've had enough trouble already.'

'Keep your mouth shut about the *ramblin' boys*, that's all.'

'I'm sorry, Jack,' I said again. 'I have to go.'

I turned and walked away down the street. Count the steps. Anything rather than think. I could have sobbed like a child. Jack dismissed me like a fishmonger chopping the head off a fish and gutting it. Chop, slice, gut. Throw the entrails into a bucket. Move on. Years of friendship dismissed in a second. My life threatened. I should have seen it, since the night at the Cathay, or long, long before, if I had been honest with myself. Jack was a ruthless, brutal man.

* * *

I walked the streets of Nantao. I passed through the doorway of the Temple of the Jade Buddha.

The smell of incense. The alien statues. The burgundy red ceiling darkened to the point of blackness by the burning of incense and candles. A bald monk in grey robes chanted rhythmically in an ancient language I didn't recognise. There were no pews to sit on, just an open, black-tiled floor where people kneeled, squatted, bowed, and chatted like people on a picnic.

By the back wall there was a timber stool and I walked there and sat. I stared at the altar, a big statue of a human figure, a Buddha, reclining on his side, his head propped up by his hand, elbow on the carved base beneath him. He was smiling, looked content, not like the suffering and crucified saints. There was something comforting about his relaxed smile.

I breathed deeply, in through my nostrils and out through my mouth. As I began to slow my breathing, I felt calm. The monk's chanting took on a soothing quality. The smiling Buddha was smiling at me.

I felt calm but infinitely sad.

I stood up and walked towards the altar. I slipped a coin in a box and lit a stick of incense. As I watched the grey smoke curl towards the black ceiling I resolved to never lose sight of Jamie Flyte. I didn't know how, but I would pay him back for all of it.

* * *

The loss of Fiona perversely made me more, rather than less, interested in the war's developments. I read every newspaper and police report I could lay my hands on. It was strange and crazy thinking—the idea that I could somehow control events.

I followed the battles, dreading the deaths they caused. The Chinese soldiers, just boys in faded cotton uniforms and torn tennis shoes, carrying only rifles, fought off a modern Japanese army equipped with heavy artillery and backed by air and naval support. It was tragic to see their thin, child-like bodies piled in trenches only yards from the gilded hotel lobbies of the International Settlement.

To my relief, and indeed to the relief of the entire city, a ceasefire was signed at the League of Nations in Switzerland, and by early March the Chinese forces withdrew to beyond a twenty-kilometre exclusion zone while eight thousand more Japanese troops arrived in Shanghai. On March 8, the Japanese flag was finally raised over North Station after fourteen thousand had died on both sides.

Before the withdrawal, the fighting had spread beyond the city into the farmland around greater Shanghai. After the ceasefire, carloads of sightseers —the same class of idiots I'd seen on the first night at Soochow Creek— many with picnic baskets and bottles of chilled champagne—drove out of the city to view the battlefields.

Under orders from the Municipal Government, the Emergency Unit organised stop-and-search parties to prevent souvenir hunters from taking unexploded bombs to their homes. We confiscated shells, grenades, and ammunition boxes from their cars, over the sound of their whining complaints. I marvelled at the stupidity of the rich.

Then, a permanent peace agreement was signed in May. Instantly, Shanghai was doing a roaring trade again. The parties grew louder and crazier than ever. I suspected that people who had observed battles as an entertainment were, in the dark of their dreams, disturbed. They drank and screwed to forget.

The Japanese insisted on taking over policing in Hongkew. Nobody objected. It was hard to imagine that the Japanese would ever do anything further to encroach on European possessions.

Shanghai – 1932–1937

Chapter 38

MIRIAM'S SAFETY WEIGHED HEAVILY ON my conscience whilst I seethed with anger towards Jamie. Not a day went by that I wasn't worried about her. I tortured myself with impotent rage towards Jamie. He'd murdered my father and took delight in it. If it wasn't for Jamie's mysterious hold over Fiona, she'd still be alive and we'd be together. Every night I had night-mares about Fiona waiting for me in the Hongkew apartment while the battle raged around her. And in the dark of the night, I dreaded that Jamie was right, that I had caused Fiona's death.

In the years since the battle of 1932, I observed that I had become an angry and brutal man who was rough with prisoners, merciless in riots, and quick to draw my gun if there was even the least sense of danger.

My life in many ways had changed entirely since the days of the *ramblin' boys*. My fortune had been destroyed in the battle for Chapei. Since Jack Dell had dismissed me from the gang, I had no means other than the meagre wage paid by the Shanghai Municipal Council.

During the heyday of my time with Jack's gang, I had lived the high life. New suits, handmade shoes, nightclubs, cabarets, and so on. Now I was financially back where I started as a walloper on the beat in 1924. Admit-tedly, the Unit paid a little bit extra but it didn't make that much difference. I struggled to hold on to the apartment at Greycliffe. I dismissed my servant boy but I managed to pay the rent. I was damned if I was going to live back at the police dormitories at Gordon Road like some little boy in a boarding school.

The years since the battle of 1932 were a kind of hell on earth. I obsessively followed the doings of Jamie, mainly through the mosquito press. I'd allowed myself to sink into a life of cheap drink and debauchery. Meanwhile the danger of my job was unabated. I needed to find release from the nervous energy generated by my frustrated anger and bitterness. I craved to have some kind of facsimile of the old life and so I had become a regular at Blood Alley, the last port of call for the desperate and the broke. I took refuge there, among the hopeless people. It was only the intense physical training demanded by Mister Fairlight of all Emergency Unit members that kept me in any kind of decent shape.

From time to time Freddie would phone up and insist that I join him for a healthy Chinese dinner. During the meal he would lecture me on Confucian ideas of good health and morality and the importance of balancing one's yin and yang. He meant well, but at times I wanted to scream at him. I often accused him of being a mother hen but I don't know where I'd be without him. He kept me in contact with the human race.

1 July 1936

As I rounded the corner into Blood Alley, that infamous street, the lights, noise and chaos assailed my senses. The street was a kaleidoscope of neon signs, jazz music, hustlers, doormen, street girls, food hawkers and drunken sailors. It was wild and dangerous and suited my mood.

I walked through the flashing lights passing by the Palais Cabaret. The club names were spelled out in garish neon in a dozen colours—The Crystal, George's Bar, Monk's Brass Rail, the New Ritz, and a host of others. Blaring saxophones and trumpets screamed from each doorway, loud and clashing, a discordant din.

The Alley—real name Rue Chao Pau-San—was on the north side of Frenchtown, close to Avenue Edward VII. It was a small but busy street, only a hundred yards long, of low-class dives, bars, cabaret clubs and brothels.

* * *

Earlier in the afternoon, I had sat at a French pavement café on Rue Mercier. I slowly nursed a cold coffee and ignored the glares of the French waiters. I'd been reading the newspaper and the headlines did nothing to cheer me up. Mad Hitler corrupting Germany. Strikes in Europe. Civil war breaking out in Spain. Tension in China between the Communists and the KMT. The world economy depressed.

Then turning to the social pages, I saw a photo of Jamie with a starlet on his arm. I felt the bile of hate in my stomach. God, how I wanted to kill that man. And then, as always, I remembered Miriam and felt fear for her.

A Chinese man walked towards me. A small, skinny man, wearing a western-style black suit and waistcoat with ill-matching brown shoes, topped off with a white fedora a size too big for him, the brim of it slipping down over his face. There was something furtive and rat-like about him, the impression caused by both his buckteeth and the way he shifted nervously and looked over his shoulder. He reached my table, his hand went inside his jacket and I braced, my hand on the butt of my pistol. He smiled, an oily, shifty, ingratiating leer. 'Hello, sir. Something for your entertainment, sir.' He pushed a small white advertising flier into my hand. Then he scurried away. The paper read:

The Sister Flowers Dancing Service
Telephone number 95831 and 90020
Room 38 Rue Chao Pau-San

Dancing Companion, Tourist Guide, Massage and SingSong.
We have more than forty members, all well educated in English, French and Chinese. Skilled in dance and familiar with social affairs.
Miss Kiang Man Li, a well-known social star in dancing and singing, has now become one of our guides. Once upon a time she sang more than 20 recordings for the Pathe Company. She will attend you when a call is received, or you may visit our premises.

Excellent rates for the frugal gentleman.

I knocked at the door of 'The Sister Flowers Dancing Service' and I was shown into a drawing room cheaply furnished in a mix of second-hand European and Chinese styles. I sat on a low couch, badly sprung and lumpy. The darkness almost concealed the stains on the couch, the origin of which I would not wish to speculate upon. There was a stale, sweaty smell in the air. I told the maid to bring me a cold beer. I was hot and sweaty, having taken a detour to avoid trouble with a student protest march on Avenue Joffre.

After a moment, a woman entered the room. She was Chinese, tall and thin, with dramatically heavy makeup, a red slash of lipstick and black-painted, feline eyebrows, hiding a face of indeterminate age. Her thin body was shown off by an impossibly tight black silk cheongsam. She smoked from a long black cigarette holder. I felt her dark eyes study me closely, assessing and categorising me. *How much will he spend?*

'Oh, such a handsome young gentleman. I will summon the girls for you.'

She clapped her hands twice and almost immediately a curtain was opened and a line of women filed into the room. They stood along the wall and I could not but help think of a police line-up.

There were seven of them in total. Each one wore a silk cheongsam in a different colour. Each dress was skin-tight, with a dramatic slit from ankle to thigh. The women were a mixed bunch—some attractive, some rather plain. Several looked like they were past the first bloom of youth. They smiled flirtatiously and all tried to catch my eye. Their smiles were a pleading, humourless leer.

'You may choose any one that pleases you,' said the lady in black. 'You may choose two if you wish. Whatever is your pleasure.'

I sat silently looking at the girls. The girls of Blood Alley were the lowest caste of the floating world of Shanghai. 'I'll have the one in blue.'

'Oh, an excellent choice, sir.'

As I pulled the money out of my suit pocket, my hands were shaking. I hadn't quite settled in my conscience the fact that I was frequenting bordellos while poor Miriam was most likely a prisoner in some similar establishment somewhere in Lu's kingdom stretching across the Asian coastline from Manchuria to Calcutta.

The mama-san said, 'Tonight you will have our finest room. Shall I bring you a pipe?'

The girl in blue came forward and took my hand in hers. It felt delicate, like holding a small bird.

I was led upstairs and into a bedroom that was softly lit by warm yellow glowing gaslight. The soft light could not disguise a smell of mustiness and sweat; a room slept in by a thousand desperate and lonely men.

I undressed and lay back on the bed as the young woman slipped off her silk dress. She moved to the bed and lay beside me.

A vein on her neck was fluttering nervously.

I was aroused by her beauty and wanted to have her but her obvious fear made me simultaneously want to protect her.

'Why are you working here?'

'*I have five dollars and one small suitcase. That is my whole life.*'

I thought then of Miriam and how it must feel to be trapped in a place like this.

'*How long have you been here?*'

'*You are my first client.*'

I sat up then, shocked and ashamed.

'*Do you mean you have never done this before?*'

She turned her face away from me. '*In the past I worked in a restaurant. Now I must work here.*'

'*How did you come to be here?*'

'*I got off the train at North Station. I had no place to stay. I was sitting and waiting. I don't know for what. The mama-san came to me, there on the platform, and offered me work and a place to sleep. Here I am.*'

I put my arms on her thin shoulders and turned her face towards mine. I looked into her eyes and said, '*I want you to listen to me now, very carefully. You can't start working here now, just like this. If you stay here you will never leave.*' She looked alarmed and I saw her eyes well up with tears.

Then I bounded out of the bed and reached for my pants. I took out a bundle of notes, about fifteen dollars. Everything left in my pocket.

'*Take this. Leave here now, tonight. Use this to pay for a room until you get a proper job. This house is a prison. You must flee for your life. Run from this place as if the house was on fire.*'

Chapter 39

I WALKED HOME SLOWLY AND thoughtfully, my mind on the events that transpired at the Sister Flowers. I had come to detest such places but going to them had taken a grip on me, a furtive pleasure that I seemed unable to simply give up. The very sordidness of such places both repelled me and drove me on to further debauchery. Perhaps it was a way to lose myself for a few hours, a contrast to the constant dangers I faced on the lethal streets of Shanghai. And it was a way to forget for a little while, forget the tragedy of losing Fiona for a second time, and seeing Miriam a slave or worse.

As I reached the front of the Greycliffe Building, a dark figure of a man stepped from the doorway.

'Hey, buddy, you Mikie Gallagher?' he asked. I heard a strong American accent, working class.

I stopped, my hand automatically reaching for the pistol concealed under my jacket.

'That depends upon who's asking,' I replied.

'OK, buddy, I'm a pal. I just want a word.'

His voice was firm but not aggressive and my instinct told me that he wasn't a threat.

'Step forward and let's have a look at you,' I said then.

The man moved out of the shadows and I saw a short, bulky man, maybe eight or ten years older than me, Slavic face, high cheekbones, wearing the dark double-breasted uniform and white peaked cap of a US Naval Petty Officer.

He offered a handshake, and when I took it, I was gripped in a powerful clench.

'Steve Grabowski, Mike, very pleased to meet you.'

'Likewise, Steve, but what's this about?'

'I have news of Miriam Tsai,' he said.

A dart of fear ran through my stomach. 'Is she all right?' I asked.

'She's fine, buddy. Miriam asked me to give you a message.'

'Come on up. We'll have a drink and you can tell me about it.'

We took the elevator to my floor and I brought him inside the apartment. He slipped off his jacket and white peaked cap and threw them over the arm of the couch. His crisply ironed white shirt was short sleeved, and I noticed his strong, hairy forearms were covered in tattoos. I saw blue-inked images of mermaids, anchors and chains. He took a seat on my couch while I poured two neat scotches.

I handed him his drink, we clinked glasses and began to sip.

'All right, Steve, tell me,' I said then, beginning to feel anxious that he would tell me that she was already dead.

'All right, Mikie. You don't mind if I call you Mikie, do you?

I waved him on.

'She told me you'd saved her life once and taken care of her pretty good. Said I could trust you.'

'Well, I hope so. So what have you got to tell me?'

'I'll give it to you straight, Mikie. I'm Miriam's husband.'

'Husband? Last I heard she was a prisoner of a Chinese triad.'

'She's fine, buddy.'

'How did this come about?' I asked, hardly daring to believe his story.

'Now you and me are both men of the world, I guess. So I don't mind telling you I met her in a brothel in Singapore. Well, it was a bad place, and she and the other girls was treated pretty bad. The place was run by pretty lousy bastards. I fell for her on the spot, and I wised up pretty quick that she was a prisoner.'

'What did you do, Steve?

'Well, in the US Navy we don't goof off. I guess you SMP guys don't either. I got a bunch'a the guys together and we went round there in a truck, about ten of us, all armed with baseball bats. We beat the place up pretty bad, gave 'em a scare and got her and the other girls out of there.'

'That's extraordinary, Steve, the best news I've had in about five years. So where is she now?'

'We got married and I took her home to Hawaii. Well, I'm from Chicago but I'm serving in the Pacific Fleet and we're based in Pearl Harbour.'

I went to the sideboard, got the bottle and refilled our glasses, not taking too much care of the measurement.

'Is she all right? Is she happy?' My sense of relief was huge and I felt a weight lift and my spirits soar.

'She's swell, buddy. I brought ya a letter, Mikie, from Miriam herself. You can read it. She told me she wanted you to know she was doin' fine.'

He handed me an envelope. I opened it to find a single sheet of white notepaper covered in neat black writing.

After I read the letter, Steve and I got blind drunk on my scotch and he spent the night snoring like a grizzly bear on my couch. By the time the dawn had come up we had sworn eternal brotherhood to each other with a drunken, slurred embrace.

United States Naval Base
Pearl Harbour
Hawaii

3 June 1936

Dear Michael

I am safe and well.

Lu told you that I would be killed if ever you made trouble for him. But I don't want you to do anything at all; I just wish you to be safe. But I need you to be assured that I have a new life. I am happy and you should not be in the least bit concerned about me.

After that horrible night at the House of Multiple Joys I was shipped away to Singapore. Lu's men made me work in a terribly low class brothel in a part of Chinatown called Tanjong Pagar that attracted many rough customers. It was nothing like the House of Multiple Joys and I am sure that I was sent there as a punishment. All the girls were treated brutally and beatings were an everyday occurrence. Our customers were the roughest sailors, soldiers and gangsters. There were nights I thought of killing myself.

Then a most wonderful thing happened. An American sailor, Steve, chose me and we fell in love. What happened next he will tell you himself.

You may be surprised to hear it, Michael, I am a boring old housewife now. I have a son that I named Michael because of you, who also saved my life. Now I shop for groceries and change nappies and cook. But we are happy here. Hawaii is paradise and as I read about all the trouble in every quarter of the world I think how lucky we are to be so far away from war here in our jewel of the Pacific.

With love
Miriam

Chapter 40

13 September 1936

FREED OF THE RESPONSIBILITY OF worrying about Miriam's safety, I renewed my active interest in the doings of Jamie.

I checked the newspaper every day to keep track of his comings and goings. Since Fiona's death, Jamie had become much less reclusive. The social pages of the *North China Daily News* were always a useful source. One morning a photograph caught my instant attention. It was Jamie, morning-suited and with a gorgeous young starlet on his arm. According to the caption, Jamie was snapped, on Saturday, emerging from Sir Victor Sassoon's private box at Shanghai Racecourse.

Jamie looked unchanged in appearance from our last meeting. In fact, he looked pretty pleased with himself, not a care in the world. There was something that caught my eye about the photo. I had to squint and bring the page close to my eyes, the black, white and grey dots almost distorting the picture as I examined it closely. There was an object in Jamie's hand. It looked like his brown leather map case. His lucky map case, where he kept his most important and precious treasures.

I put the newspaper down, remembering, thinking.

* * *

I phoned Freddie at the Special Branch office, ready to hang up if I heard Jack Dell's voice. We made an arrangement to meet at Jimmy's American Diner. It was always busy, which was very helpful for a discreet conversation.

I was already sitting at the red and white chequered table, when Freddie arrived. A smell of grilling hamburgers and fried onions permeated the air. He came to the table, shook hands and sat down. I signalled the waiter for two coffees.

'You look well, Freddie.'

'You look terrible, Michael. What are you doing to yourself?'

'I'm all right, Freddie. The Unit is forever on call. Maybe I just need a bit more sleep.'

He nodded, looking unconvinced.

'So, Michael, it sounded like you had something in particular you wanted to ask me?'

'I'm working on something at the moment, Freddie. Can you tell me anything about Jamie Flyte? Is he up to anything fishy?'

'Isn't everyone in Shanghai?'

'That's true enough.'

'It doesn't sound like an Emergency Unit type of job. What are you up to?'

'It is more for my own curiosity rather than an SMP business, Freddie.'

He sat up straight and adjusted his posture, ready to deliver his sermon.

'Personally, I'd advise great caution with Mister Flyte.'

'What can you tell me?'

'Why do you want to know this?'

'Freddie, I can't explain this now. Just do me this favour, all right?'

'Very well, then. I can give you some information.'

He picked up his coffee, took a sip and leaned forward. He began to whisper conspiratorially, his voice barely audible over the lunchtime hum.

'Jamie Flyte is up to his neck in it with Big Ears Lu. They say they have known each other for years but I don't know the exact connection. Lu runs the opium in this town. Opium is an expensive product to deliver. It has to be grown in poppy fields, harvested, packed, delivered, and then there is the way people consume it. You've seen what an opium den looks like.'

I sipped my coffee, my eyes scanning the room.

'Yes, I understand. Is there a simpler way?'

'A fortune could be made by the drug dealer who could dispense with all the fuss and simply pack it all into a little white pill that is easy to manu-facture, distribute, sell and consume like a headache pill.'

'That makes sense.'

'Lu and Pockmarked Fan came up with the idea of the "anti-opium" pill. The Green Gang grow the opium in Szechwan province, ship it in and process the raw material in small labs hidden in everyday-looking family homes around Shanghai. The pill is a very simple combination of heroin and strychnine, easy and cheap to make. They advertise it in the Chinese language newspapers saying, "*Give up opium with the help of our anti-opium pill.*"'

'You're saying that they sell opium in the guise of an opium cure?'

'Exactly,' he said, looking as satisfied as if he had thought of the idea himself.

'So, Freddie, what's the connection with Jamie Flyte?'

'Among Chinese immigrants to America, there is a huge demand for their own films.'

'Films?'

'Lu sends the pills to Flyte's studios. They're concealed in film canisters, and then shipped to American Chinatown cinemas where the pills are sold on the streets.'

'Doesn't Flyte make enough money in his legitimate business?' I asked.

'I believe Flyte simply needs the nervous arousal associated with such risk-taking. There are some men who fall in love with war and when hostilities cease they cannot resume an ordinary life. They require constant danger and excitement. Jamie Flyte is one of those men.'

'But it must pay him well also, mustn't it, Freddie?'

'Oh, indeed. The Branch knows that Mister Flyte has numbered Swiss bank accounts where he keeps his income from his projects with Lu.'

'Why doesn't the Branch arrest him?'

Freddie raised his eyebrows in surprise. 'You can't be serious, Michael. He's totally protected. The Municipal Council wouldn't dream of such a thing happening. Flyte and his type keep this city in business.'

'What if solid evidence was presented, Freddie?'

'Well, I suppose if it was really solid, they'd have no choice.'

I thought for a moment and then asked him, 'What about those Swiss numbered accounts? Does that mean that anyone who gets hold of the details could get access to the money?'

Freddie reached across the table, his hands sliding the salt and pepper shakers around the tablecloth like a chess master moving the pieces.

'Yes, Michael, that's exactly what it means. But I hope you aren't thinking of robbing Mister Flyte. That would indeed be too dangerous.'

'I'm just thinking aloud, Freddie. Now are you sure I can't tempt you with some *gwailo* food?'

'No, thank you, Michael.'

'Any chance of a look at the Branch file on Mister Flyte, is there, Freddie?'

His face formed into an expression of astonishment.

'Michael, you can't be serious. Do you want me to lose my job?'

'Ah, come on, Freddie, I'm only pulling your leg.'

20 September 1936

At the end of my shift, I went to the Central Police Station records room. It was a massive room in the basement, harshly lit by naked white bulbs suspended from the ceiling. It was a virtual forest of yellowing, dusty paper. The system was organised into various topics, like traffic offences, household registration files, and all sorts of minor and major crimes.

I walked to the far corner of the room where there was a heavy locked door. A stencilled sign announced, 'Special Branch Only. Authorisation Required to Enter.' I carried a universal key, borrowed from the Emergency Unit. Handy but illegal, it could open just about any lock.

The Special Branch was, in fact, an espionage organisation located within the police service and maintained extraordinarily detailed files on every important person in Shanghai.

The Special Branch room has a system of file index cards, each card guiding the searcher to a numbered file. I searched for the name 'Flyte', checked the file number, and went straight to the cabinet that bore the matching number. In a moment, I found the file I wanted. It took only seconds, a tribute to the efficiency of the Special Branch.

I opened my jacket, slipped the file under my left arm, pressed it to my chest, and then buttoned up the jacket. I turned off the light and stepped through the door, closing it softly behind me.

'Hello, Michael.' I heard a voice at my shoulder.

I turned towards the sound. It was Jack Dell. He smiled, except for his eyes.

'Hello, Jack.'

He extended his hand to shake mine. 'Long time no see, Michael. I hope you don't hold any grudges.'

I shook his hand, clenching my left arm to hold the files in place.

'And how are you, Michael—getting enough rest?'

'Fine, Jack, fine.'

'You look a bit tired, Michael. Maybe it's just the dim light here?'

'I'm fine, thanks.'

'Have you injured yourself, Michael?'

'Why is that, Jack?' I said trying to keep my voice steady.

'Your left shoulder seems unnaturally stiff. Have you injured yourself?'

There was something menacing in his voice, an unspoken threat in his solicitous questioning.

'It might be a bit tight from the gymnasium. I might have gone too heavy with the dumbbells.'

'Give me the file, Michael, there's a good lad. You don't want to go falling over a filing cabinet or experience any other nasty accident, do you?'

I opened my jacket and handed the file to him.

'Good man. Look after yourself now. And go straight home, won't you?' he said with a friendly pat on my shoulder.

Chapter 41

No matter how experienced an Emergency Unit member was, Mister Fairlight insisted that each man, irrespective of rank, go through Mystery House once every six months and be timed on his performance. Any man that didn't make it inside the requisite time was sent back for further training. To be canned by Mister Fairlight was considered to be highly embarrassing and every man did his best to cut the mustard.

On Tuesday morning, bright and early at 6 a.m., it was my turn to enter Mystery House.

I stood at a white starting line with a police instructor behind me. He was from Birmingham, of Irish extraction, Sergeant O'Farrell, a big barrel-chested man with dark eyes and a booming voice. The instructor carried an athletics starting pistol and a stopwatch. I was wearing full uniform, police hat, Sam Browne belt, boots and my pistol and holster in the cross-draw position. It was a requirement of the course that we be dressed exactly as we would on a normal street patrol.

'Ready, get set...... go,' said O'Farrell as he fired the starting pistol.

I ran at full tilt towards the beginning of the obstacle course. First came a four-foot high fence. I jumped over it easily enough and sprinted on to the next post. There was a deep trench full of water, with a narrow plank bridging it. I had to step across, one foot in front of the other, like a circus tightrope walker. Once I crossed that, there was a barrel hanging suspended from a high wooden frame. I jumped headfirst into the barrel, crawled through it as fast as I could, while the movement of my body made it spin around in a circle. At the end of the barrel I tumbled out headfirst, stood up, grabbed my police hat, found my orientation and ran on. Twenty feet further on was a knotted rope suspended from a fifteen-foot high frame. I cursed when I was halfway up and I slipped back to the ground, painful friction burns on my palms.

'Shit!' I exclaimed.

'Come on now, Mister Gallagher, no slacking,' shouted the burly American Instructor Sergeant who was stationed by the rope obstacle.

I grabbed the rope again and hauled myself up. This time I made it. I clanged the brass bell at the top of the rope. I went down the rope as fast as I could, trying to protect my smarting hands. When I hit the ground I ran on.

Next obstacle was a narrow plank at a 45-degree angle going up to a six-foot wall. I ran up the plank to another plank going down the other side of the wall to the ground.

Running on again, I found that the following obstacle was a six-foot brick wall with no obvious way of getting over it. I attacked it with a running jump and hauled myself up and over, dropping down on the other side, my friction-burned hands in agony.

After the final obstacle there was a final hundred-yard dash to the house. As I ran, I heard an instructor shout, 'Faster! Faster! Faster!'

As I drew near the house, another instructor shouted, 'Draw your gun. The Mystery House is next.'

Pistol ready, I made my way to the house in a semi-crouch, gun held by my hip, as we had been taught.

I opened the door, stepped inside and found myself in a dark corridor. I stood for a few seconds, allowing my eyes to adjust. My breath was heavy, and my legs were shaking. I felt my pistol weigh a ton in my trembling hands.

I took a few steps inside. A shower of confetti rained from the ceiling, momentarily confusing me. I stepped around a broken chair on the floor. Then I kicked a broken cup. I heard a voice shout, 'Who's there?' I didn't respond.

Suddenly, I heard a panel in the wall slide open and a string of Chinese firecrackers was thrown into the corridor. They were alight, crackling and fizzing.

I felt every muscle in my body freeze. My heart raced and my head lightened. I began to breathe rapidly and out of control.

Every cell in my body screamed at me, 'Get out of here, get out of here before they kill you.'

I stood unmoving. Paralysed.

With a deep breath I took a step, then another. My body felt heavy, my feet encased in concrete.

Then, suddenly, from above, the noise of a door crashing open, a target, a human-shaped mannequin dropped from the ceiling.

I fired, two rounds quickly, bang, bang! Fairlight's instructions were uppermost in my mind. *Don't aim, just use your senses and fire off two ultra-fast rounds. Speed will save your life. Always shoot in rapid bursts of two shots. This will overcome the problem of convulsive gripping. It will give you a greater chance of hitting the criminal.*

I moved on, quicker now. Through a door and into a bigger room. A man-shaped target ran across the room propelled by some hidden mechanism. I snapped off two quick shots, and then as I was still firing, another target popped up on my left. I swivelled round and fired off two more shots. That was six.

I ejected the magazine and quickly slid in a fresh one from my belt pouch. As I did so, a smoke bomb landed at my feet. There was a soft explosion and then the room was full of bitter, stinging smoke, making my eyes water. Another target ran quickly across the room. It bobbed up and down, and I fired off two more shots.

I continued through the smoke, coughing and blinking my eyes, and came to a narrow staircase. I stepped softly but my boots crunched on broken glass. A target swung from the ceiling. I fired again.

A broken kitchen chair was wedged awkwardly half way up the stairs. I stepped over it and another string of lighted firecrackers was thrown at me.

I kicked at the firecrackers with my boot and nudged them down the stairs. Behind me there was gunfire. I fell to a lying position on the steps. A figure appeared at the top of the stairs and I fired off two shots from a lying position. Quickly I reached for another magazine and reloaded.

Someone shouted, 'Keep going, Gallagher, keep going!'

I stood and went to the top of the stairs. There was a long corridor with mirrors on the walls. My multiple reflections created a confusing image. At the end of the corridor was a closed red wooden door. I opened it and stepped through. The room was a mock-up of an opium den.

I stepped inside. One of the figures on the bed sat up and pointed a pistol at me. I snapped off two shots at the target and it fell back on the bed.

Then from the ceiling came a cloud of confetti, showering me and distracting me. A voice shouted in my ear, 'Give up now, man. You haven't a hope.'

Someone loosed off three pistol-shots in the staircase behind me. I pressed on. The door at the other end of the room burst open and a human-shaped target came flying through. I rapidly fired off two more shots at the target, and from the sound of the gunfire, the target was shooting back. I snapped off two more shots. The target fell to the ground.

As far as I could recall from my last training, this was the final stage. As I stood, chest heaving, feeling satisfied with my overall performance, my neck went cold and I could feel my hairs stand up. Some instinct made me dive for the floor as I heard the loud boom of a pistol-shot and felt a blow like my shoulder was kicked by a mule.

I fell to the ground, rolling, shouting, 'Live fire, live fire, I'm hit!'

The door plunged open and Mister Fairlight and several training officers came running through. 'Hold your fire!' shouted Fairlight.

As one of the men checked my shoulder, I heard the sound of running footsteps.

'Get a medical orderly. He's hit,' someone shouted.

I was carried outside to the open air. The bullet had almost missed me so my shoulder wound was merely a graze. I was able to stand although I felt pale and shaky.

Fairlight paced up and down, agitated, his face white with fury. 'What bloody fool used live ammunition in a training exercise? I'll have his job, see if I don't.'

A quick search was mounted through Mystery House and its surrounds but nobody was found other than the Chinese staff who operated the automatic targets. When questioned, they merely looked puzzled and confused. As a medical orderly applied a bandage to my grazed shoulder, Fairlight approached me.

'Not a bad effort, Gallagher, one of the best in your group actually, but you'll need to be at least sixty seconds faster next time.'

I nodded, not trusting my voice to sound steady. I didn't know who shot me but I was certain that I knew who had a hand in it.

Chapter 42

13 February 1937

AFTER THE ATTEMPT ON MY life at Mystery House I became very cautious. It was clear that I was a watched man. I went to ground for a couple of months, not calling attention to myself. It took several weeks for my shoulder to return to full function and in the meantime I didn't want to get into a lethal fight whilst I was still wounded.

Over Christmas and the New Year I started following a delivery van that made regular trips between Albion Film Studios, Lu's house in French-town and various other private houses around the city.

* * *

I couldn't borrow a police motorcycle for my unofficial detective work, so I rented a small BSA motorcycle from a car and motorcycle showroom owned by an Armenian on the Great Western Road.

On the evening that I was ready to make my move I went to the same café from where I had recently staked-out Lu's house. I saw the van drive out at its usual time. I put some money on the table for my coffee, went out to the motorcycle, pulled on a leather aviator's helmet and goggles, then leather jacket and gloves over my suit, mounted the bike and kick-started it. I moved into the traffic and began to trail the van, not too close and not too far. It drove without incident and after a time arrived in front of Flyte's house on Bubbling Well Road.

I saw the gates opened by Flyte's Russian bodyguards and the van drove up to the house. I parked the bike down the street and waited. After about twenty minutes, the van pulled out again. Once more I followed behind and this time it headed in a westerly direction until it arrived at the gates of Albion Film Studios. The gates were opened by security and the van drove inside. At that point I turned the bike around and rode home. I had at least established a link between Lu, Flyte and his film studios.

* * *

Later that night I took the motorcycle and rode out to the studios again. It was around 11 p.m., and the night was dark. I drove past the studio entrance and rode around the perimeter of the complex. It was surrounded by a high wall, about six feet, and topped with strands of barbed wire.

I parked the motorcycle very close to the wall and, making sure the bike was in a stable position, stood on the seat.

I took a wire cutter out of my leather jacket pocket and, from my vantage point, snipped the strands of wire. I pulled myself to the top of the wall; after the obstacle course at Gordon Road this was easy.

I rolled myself over the wall, hung there for a few seconds, and with knees bent, I dropped silently to the ground.

Using the shadows of the buildings I walked slowly and carefully towards the car park not far from the main entrance. I had to stand back in the shadows as a night watchman bearing a torch walked slowly by on his night patrol.

I reached the car park and saw the grey delivery van. I was grateful the car park was not brightly lit, as I was able to approach the van and, using a bunch of common car keys borrowed from the Unit, had no trouble opening the back door of the van.

I entered and found a box of about a dozen film canisters. I picked one up and shook it. It made a sound like a box of candy and I assumed that it must be the pills inside. I tested each canister and each one made the same noise.

Using a penknife I prized one of the canisters open, careful not to drop any of its contents on the floor of the van. As I expected, the canister was full of white pills, with some soft tissue paper to provide cushioning.

I picked up a pill, licked it and found the taste I expected. I dropped it in my pocket, closed the box, put it back in its place and squeezed into the driver's seat.

On my fifth attempt a key fitted in the van's ignition. The engine started and I released the handbrake, feather-touched the accelerator and began moving at low speed.

Just as the van began to move, the night watchman approached me, torch in his hand. He pointed the beam through the windscreen. I accelerated, heading for the main gateway.

I heard a car behind me. Up ahead a long red and white security barrier was down and blocking the exit. Standing in front of the barrier were two guards. I pressed the accelerator to maximum speed.

The security guards jumped out of the way. The van crashed through the barrier and I was on the street. I curved sharply, almost overturning the van as my foot kicked the accelerator.

Looking in the rear-view mirror, I saw that two black cars were in pursuit. Men stood on the running boards of the leading automobile with Thompson submachine guns. They opened fire and the rear windows of the van shattered. Bullets whizzed past my head. I raced along Brennan Road and swung left into Robinson Road heading towards the city.

I raced past the cotton mills. I reached Macau Road and continued heading east at high speed, the two automobiles still in pursuit. I reached Soochow Creek and sped across the bridge, past the Cantonese cemetery and on to Kwang Tsao Road. I continued east, the driving becoming more difficult now, as the streets became narrower and busier. I had to swerve sharply to avoid a small sports car that emerged from a side road, its horn blaring behind me as I sped onward. Every time I glanced over my shoulder, I saw that the pursuing automobiles were still close behind.

I crossed the Shanghai-Nanking Railway line and I continued heading east, desperately trying to maintain high-speed without losing control of my vehicle. By now I had reached Jukung Road with the pursuers still just behind. Whenever we reached a straight road the Thompson submachine guns would open fire. At the sound of their guns I crouched as low as I could, feeling increasingly panicked at the sound of bullets thudding into the body of the delivery van. If I couldn't shake these guys then it was all over for me.

I sped along Juking Road and then, just as I again crossed the Shanghai-Nanking railway line, I lost control of the van. It spun across the road and sideswiped a telegraph pole. It came to a sudden stop, the engine cutting out, steam hissing from the radiator, and tinkling glass from the windscreen scattering around me.

I sat there for a moment feeling stunned and then I heard rough male voices speaking Chinese, from all around my vehicle. The driver's door was wrenched open and I felt strong hands pulling me out of the van. I collapsed on the ground. Guns were pointed towards my face and I heard a voice say in Chinese-accented English, 'You are a dead man.'

They picked me up unceremoniously and bundled me to one of the cars. The passenger door of the nearest car was opened and I was manhandled inside onto the back seat, my captors crushing in beside me. I heard a man say in Shanghainese: '*Put the contents of the van in the other car and drive back to the studio. Dispose of the van carefully. Leave nothing behind.*'

Then the car moved off. We appeared to be heading in an easterly direction. I couldn't see where we were going because the men seated to my left and right pushed me to the floor.

I could tell that we were heading towards the river because in a short time its pungent, distinctive smell hit my nostrils. I could hear the mournful hooting of ships' foghorns. We drove on for a little while and then the car stopped.

I was pulled out of the car and dragged towards the river. I realised that we were on one of the river wharves south of Broadway Road. I could see the factories of Pudong on the other side of the river. The men hustled me right to the river's edge. They positioned me so that I was standing with my heels right on the edge of the stone-flagged wharf.

One of my captors stood before me, a long-barrelled Mauser pointed steadily into my face.

'Drop the gun!' shouted a voice. 'Drop your weapons or every man will die.' Then, out of the shadows stepped a group of Japanese Imperial Navy marines.

A man stepped into the faint glow of light from across the river. He carried a long-barrelled handgun and pointed it steadily at my potential executor.

'Drop the gun now if you want to live.' My captor released the pistol and it hit the ground with a metallic clatter. The Japanese officer stepped forward and with his booted foot kicked the gun into the river. The patrol of Japanese naval marines, brandishing long rifles with fixed bayonets, began disarming the rest of my captors.

'Well, Mister Gallagher, I'm surprised to see you out here tonight.'

I recognised him then. He was Lieutenant Nakamoto who I'd sparred with at *ju-jitsu* practice at Gordon Road Depot. 'It's lucky that I recognised you, Mister Gallagher. I would have assumed that you were some White Russian criminal who had fallen out with his Chinese compatriots.'

'Mister Nakamoto, I'm grateful to you. I wonder if you could organise a lift home for me.'

'Certainly, my friend.'

'What will you do with these men?'

'I assumed they are criminals. We will deal with them in our own way. Do not concern yourself any further with these people.'

Lieutenant Nakamoto issued the command in Japanese and one of the marines immediately left, jogging towards the street. Within a few moments, a car with Japanese navy markings had pulled up driven by the same marine. 'This man will take you anywhere you want to go,' said Mister Nakamoto.

I shook his hand and said, 'I cannot thank you enough.' Then I got in the back seat of the car and asked the driver to take me to Bubbling Well Road. I lay down and tried to get some sleep, feeling utterly exhausted by my close shave with death. As my eyes closed, I realised that my case against Jamie had been destroyed. They'd never give me an opportunity to make such a case again.

Chapter 43

I BEGAN TO DESPISE SHANGHAI, but I couldn't leave. This city with all its horrors and delights had seeped into my blood, gripped me like a fever and wouldn't let me go. My vendetta against Jamie had reached a stalemate. Miriam was safe in Hawaii with her sailor, but my attempts to get Jamie had only cost me two close brushes with death.

Nevertheless, my obsession with him continued. Just as I had searched the shipping lists for Fiona when I arrived in 1924, I now read every police report, every newspaper article and every hint of gossip that had any vague connection to Jamie or his various businesses. I began to take an interest in his top managers and researched their activities also. I was looking for any hint of opportunity to get Jamie by fair means or foul.

I was unable to find any incriminating information that could make a police case against Jamie or his companies. I began to consider simply killing him. He was well protected but I thought I could succeed. But I dreaded being caught. It wasn't so much a long prison sentence I feared; Shanghai was prison enough. It was the shame I would feel were I to be arrested for murder. The shame of a decorated police officer, the son of an RIC sergeant.

I was aware also that my interest in Jamie might not be a one-way street. I lived with one eye over my shoulder waiting for a bullet or a stiletto in the ribs. I nursed my anger, biding my time until some opportunity presented itself.

I continually experienced nightmares involving Fiona. In one frequently recurring dream, Fiona and I walked through the corridor of Burleigh Castle and met Lord Burleigh with his yellow cravat and folded *Irish Times*. We stopped to talk to him just as we had in reality. He looked at me sadly and said, 'Why did you kill my little girl?' I tried to speak, to reply, to explain that she was alive and well and standing beside me. But when I turned to where Fiona stood there was nothing but empty space.

* * *

I began to frequent the Great World. I was initially drawn to it simply to check out the Savoy cinema located in the building, which was owned by Jamie. The Great World was located not far from the racecourse, just on the border of Frenchtown, on the corner of Tibet and Edward VII Roads. The building itself was a strange architectural mish-mash. A Florentine palace crowned by a wedding cake tower, the large complex consisted of six floors, occupying most of a city block. I quickly realised that the Savoy cinema could tell me nothing useful about Jamie. It was just a cinema. However, once I had seen the inside of the Great World, I was seduced by it.

The Great World comprised every human delight and misery one could imagine. Its six floors had restaurants, teahouses, gambling parlours, dancing, first-class cinemas showing both Chinese and Western films, massage, fortune telling, circus acrobats, theatres, cabarets, casinos, and Singsong girls. A patron could eat and drink to his fill, get massaged and have his ears cleaned, be entertained at the theatres by western cabaret or Chinese opera and make love with a Singsong girl. Afterwards, he could go on to gamble his fortune at the fan-tan tables, and end his despair by plunging from the sixth floor, all in the one visit to the Great World. It was said that the gang of corner boys throwing dice and smoking on the street outside made bets on who was going to jump that day.

Their casual cynicism fascinated me. Such men, just loafers and wastrels, had the measure of Shanghai. They turned the city's tragedy into their entertainment.

The Great World was a circus, a nightclub, a bordello, a market and a funfair all under one roof. It was an ever-changing kaleidoscope of the bizarre.

* * *

I went to my favourite cabaret on the fifth floor and ignored a variety performance of dancers and comedians reproducing the latest hits from Britain and America while I finished a bottle of cheap Italian wine.

I drained the last of my glass, paid my bill and left the cabaret. In the corridor, an old man wearing black pyjamas approached me. He stopped and reached for my hand.

'You come!' he said. 'You need to chase the dragon.' I hesitated for a moment and then allowed myself to be led away. I was past caring what happened to me.

He led me through a door into a dark room where the air was sweet and smoky.

The room was almost in complete darkness, with little flickers of light here and there. Weak oil lamps positioned on the floor threw out a faint light that barely illuminated a foot in diameter around them, creating little islands of light in the gloom.

As my eyes adjusted I could make out people lying on low cots arranged in two facing rows, configured like a hospital ward. The room was silent apart from occasional bouts of coughing.

We stopped by a low couch and the man slipped the jacket off my shoulders. 'You lie down now. Soon feel better.'

I was tired enough to collapse onto the cot. I hardly noticed the stale smell of other men's sweat as I adjusted myself to get comfortable on the mattress. He held my hand and said, 'Chase dragon make you happy.'

Then an old woman was kneeling beside me. She made the preparations and extended the mouthpiece of the long silver pipe to me.

I took the pipe in my mouth and breathed in the sweet smoke. I puffed again, impatient for the hit. When my mouth was full of the smoke and I felt it circulating through my throat and nasal passages and billowing down into my chest, I lay back with a sigh. I closed my eyes, feeling peaceful at last.

I reached into my pocket and took out the photograph Fiona had given me when we were both fifteen. The picture was worn and dog-eared now from too much handling. I observed the way she stared wistfully into the middle distance and wondered if she could somehow see her tragic future.

As the opium did its work, I slipped away from the dark and musty room into another realm, a world where Fiona was alive.

Part Three
—
The Great World

Shanghai – 1937

Chapter 44

North China Daily News – August 10 1937
Alarming Developments in Sino-Japanese Situation

Since shots were exchanged on July 7, at the Marco Polo Bridge outside Peking, between the armed forces of Japan and China, the state of affairs has escalated alarmingly.

The Marco Polo incident was shortly followed by a declaration of war by Japan.

Once again the Shanghai International Settlement has mobilised. The 88th Division of the Nationalist army has appeared outside the city. Meanwhile, the International Settlement is swamped with refugees. Rents have quadrupled in a matter of days and every available space is snapped up. People continue to rush into the Settlement from Chapei, Hongkew and Pudong.

Memories of the battle of 1932 are fresh. During that battle, readers will recall, Chapei and Hongkew were razed to the ground and have only just recently recovered from that unfortunate period.

Yesterday, a Japanese army lieutenant and his military driver were stopped, captured and executed by forces unknown, whilst on their way to inspect the Chinese airdrome at Lunghua.

Ten thousand Chinese Nationalist soldiers have arrived by train at North Station. Meanwhile, 21 Japanese warships are anchored on the Whampoo River including the 'Izumo', which also saw action in the trouble of 1932.

12 August 1937

ON AUGUST 12, THE WAR BEGAN. Once again I observed, with perverse fascination, as the bright young things of the Shanghai social scene made entertainment of the battle. They watched, cocktails in hand, from the roofs and balconies of the International Settlement and the French Concession.

I dreaded the thought of another war. But surely, I told myself, it would finally bring the whole edifice of Shanghai crashing down. Another war in Shanghai had to hurt the *Taipans*, and that included Jamie. I began to wonder if I could use the war as a cover to get him.

Mister Fairlight asked Sergeant Kirlov and myself to change into civvies and drive down through Frenchtown, in an unmarked car, to the border with Nantao. He wanted us to get a feel for developments over the line.

Twenty thousand Chinese troops had taken up positions in the old city of Nantao where they met stiff fighting from the Japanese. Frenchtown was only a stroll away from intense house-to-house combat.

While the two forces engaged in a house-by-house fight to the death, only two hundred yards away people queued up in the safety of Frenchtown to watch Marlene Dietrich in '*Desire.*' I saw it with my own eyes as couples stood in line for tickets. A second group, chiefly made up of children and nannies, waited impatiently to see Shirley Temple in '*Poor Little Rich Girl.*' They squabbled over the eating of popcorn and chocolate as the ugly rat-tat-tat sound of two armies raking each other with machine gun fire wafted over the babble of conversation.

When I drove up Avenue Foch, heading back to Gordon Road, I witnessed another disturbing scene. I saw that not all the violence was outside of the borders of Island Shanghai.

A group of about thirty drunk, red-faced Germans, unmilitary-looking butchers and bakers, rolls of fat showing through their brown-shirt uniforms, were creating a scene. They strutted around, singing German marching songs, shouting, and abusing anybody that looked foreign. Which, of course, in a city like Shanghai was like going into the sea and abusing the fish.

The Gendarmes stood around watching, but did not intervene.

* * *

The following day I read accounts by foreign journalists marvelling that one could book a table for dinner at the Park Hotel across from Shanghai racecourse and, between soup and main course, watch Japanese shells fly harmlessly over the air space of the International Settlement and the French Concession in a four-mile arc from Chapei to Nantao.

The KMT air force, flying American Northrop aircraft and manned by poorly trained and inexperienced crew, began flying bombing missions against the Japanese and the sound of their aircraft became another background noise of this insane city.

13 August 1937

Some morbid force brought me to the rooftop bar of the Cathay Hotel. I hadn't been up there since the 1932 battle but the desire to observe events drew me back.

I sat in a cane chair, my scotch on a glass-topped cane garden table, and a small crystal bowl of shelled and salted peanuts beside it.

Crowds of partygoers in eveningwear occupied every table. Busy, harassed-looking white-coated waiters wove their way from table to table dispensing Scotch, pink gin, and glasses of champagne.

A tall, red-faced grizzly bear of a man, with cropped grey hair and wearing an evening suit a size too small for him, turned to me from the next table with hand outstretched. 'Jim Robertson, *New York Times*.'

I shook his hand and we began to talk. I told him I was a cop.

'You're a Mulligan! That's great, buddy.'

He began picking my brains about the war and what would happen.

According to Robertson, the battle for Shanghai was the perfect newsman's story.

'You know what, Mike, this is a better than a Broadway show. Both sides have already allowed us to observe the battlefront. So, it was Chinese lines this morning, a good lunch with wine in Frenchtown, the Japanese lines in the afternoon, and from five to seven p.m., both sides gave press conferences. After cabling a report, it's on to drinks at the Cathay.'

'That must be quite an experience,' I said.

'Best war I ever covered. In Abyssinia I lived in a goatskin tent among flies and cowshit. This is the life.'

'Amazing,' I replied, shaking my head. I didn't know whether to laugh or cry.

'It sure is, buddy. We have to make the most of it while we can.'

'What do you mean?'

'Well, consider this. We saw Mussolini grab Abyssinia last year, then there's Franco kicking out an elected government in Spain. They all kiss ass with Hitler, and now an invasion here, sponsored by a rather scary military government in Japan. The world is heading for something big, I tell you. I've been around a few wars and I feel it in my bones.'

He drained the last of his scotch and, with a friendly pat on my shoulder, said, 'Anyway, enough of the doom and gloom. Must fly now, buddy. Gotta date with a Russian princess.'

I sat there alone, sipping my drink. I wondered was this the war that would finish the *Taipans* in Shanghai? Would it be the finish of Jamie?

About every two minutes, a large artillery shell fired from Chapei flew overhead to Nantao. As each shell went over the hotel, one could actually feel the displaced air. Seconds later, there was a corresponding loud flash, followed by the 'crump' of the explosion. Many of the partygoers cheered. I imagined going over there to kill one of those smug, self-satisfied bastards with my bare hands.

* * *

The battle raging on the doorstep of the International Settlement put me in a strange, restless mood. On the street the parade of Settlement life continued. But there was a disturbing murmur drifting over from Chinese Shanghai, like a summer storm that wouldn't move away: the steady rumble of heavy artillery, the clash of rifle and machine gun fire, the lazy drone of military aircraft flying over Chapei. It created a mood of impending doom.

On impulse, I decided to visit the 'Casanova.' It was my favourite taxi dance where a ticket could buy a dance with a girl—'dime-a-dance-girls' the Americans called them. For such a girl, the more tickets she had at the end of the evening the higher her income. The girl also made commission on drinks bought by customers. Many of the women, who were generally in dire financial straits, were pleased to make further more intimate arrangements.

Although many of the girls were Chinese, quite a few came from Japan, the Philippines, Siam, Formosa and Korea as well as the White Russian refugees. This year I'd noticed a new influx of German Jewish girls.

When I walked inside the Casanova, dance tickets purchased, I found the place was full to the point of being a fire hazard. A Filipino Jazz band was enthusiastically belting out the popular tunes—'*The One O'clock Jump*', '*Slap that Bass*', '*On the Sunny Side of the Street*.' People gyrated on the dance floor. The music and voices mercifully drowned out the sounds of battle. The dance floor was a heaving movement of human bodies holding on to each other and bobbing up and down in time to the music.

I pushed to the bar and managed to find a single unoccupied barstool. I had just sat and ordered a drink when I felt a tap on my shoulder. It was a thin, fair-haired young man wearing black tie and evening suit, a weak, shadow-thin moustache across his bony face.

'I say, old chap, terribly sorry to bother you, but I'm afraid you have taken my stool.'

I stared him in the eye without speaking for a very long twenty seconds. His Adam's apple bobbed nervously.

Finally I spoke. 'How would you like me to bash your skull open?'

His jaw dropped. 'I say, there's no need for that.' He looked around nervously, saw that no one had overheard, then turned and walked away through the crowd, his shoulders slumped.

I would have been happy to start a fight. With anyone. I just wanted to smash a face in, feel the pain in my hand as it crunched into flesh and bone. Self-satisfied bastards. What right did they have to chortle like fools while young men died in trenches not a mile away?

The band played on. Their music got hotter and jazzier as they played. Their ecstatic faces were slick with sweat. They removed their jackets, their shirts wet. Ties were unknotted and thrown aside. The crowd matched their energy. The louder and hotter the music, the more frenzied the dancing of the people. Bodies crushed closer and closer. Couples locked their arms around each other and exchanged passionate kisses. I leaned back on the bar and continued to drink.

My head buzzed and my stomach was a pool of acid but I didn't care. The music got to me. Foot tapping, my fingers drummed a rhythm on my knee. My drinking pace intensified.

The muscles around my shoulders and neck finally relaxed and I began to stop thinking of anything but the music.

The hits blared from the Filipino Jazz band as bodies crushed themselves together. A haze of cigarette smoke hung over the room like a fog.

At a nearby table sat a crowd of young upper-class English kids, out for the night, slumming it, seeing how the other half lived, well fed and scrubbed, happy young people in evening suits and colourful dresses. The mood was gaiety, and jokes and rebuttals bounced across the table. I thought of Fiona and her posh friends at the Venus Café.

They began to sing *Happy Birthday*. Balloons were burst and I heard the popping of champagne corks. I had a sudden vivid picture of Fiona, our bodies coiled together in lovemaking. The memory as fresh as if I'd seen her yesterday. But it was five-and-a-half years ago.

I felt very alone.

Chapter 45

I CONTINUED DRINKING, BUT TRY as I might, I couldn't reach intoxication.

I raised my glass and spoke aloud: 'Here's to the last days of the Roman Empire.'

Then I saw her. She was small, slim, and dark-haired. Although she was European she looked exotic, almost Oriental. A mix, perhaps Slavic. Her hair was dark, almost black, and cut in a short and fashionable bob. Her eyes were sparkling blue. She had high cheekbones and a delicate facial structure. She carried her lithe body with the fluid movement of a ballet dancer.

My eyes followed her. She had a feline, sexual quality, and a loose-limbed easy movement. Her face had a noble cast—someone who had seen a lot at a young age.

She was dancing with a big blond-haired man in a dark evening suit that I figured was American. He made loud conversation with her, and laughed at his own jokes. She nodded and smiled, but did not laugh. He was a clumsy dancer but her graceful movements somehow guided him into an approximation of smooth movement. When he spoke, she tilted her head to one side, as if to say she was deeply interested in everything he had to say.

She was so light, and gliding, and pure. I longed for my innocence. What had I turned into? A hard, violent man, as tough as the city itself. Young Mikie Gallagher, the Sergeant's son.

The song ended. The MC, a Spaniard in a white dinner jacket with a red carnation, who sported a sharp moustache, announced the beginning of a new set. I didn't even hear the names of the songs he announced. The girl bowed her head slightly and walked away from the American, who looked crestfallen.

I left my seat and pushed my way into the crush. At the far end of the room she stood talking to a pretty, brown-skinned Siamese girl with a long mane of silky black hair.

'May I please have this dance?' I asked as I offered her my hand. Her bright, intense blue eyes held mine. Then she scanned me from head to toe.

'Yes, I will dance with you. May I please have your dance ticket?'

I handed her half a dozen tickets. She took the tickets, fanned them like a deck of cards, extracted one and then handed me back the others.

I took her hand in mine and placed my other hand on the small of her back. The music started and we began to move. Her body was slim but strong, like an athlete. Her hand, although small and refined, gripped mine strongly.

For the first time that I could remember, I felt shy.

'My name is Michael,' I said.

'I am Katya.' Her accent, I thought, was Germanic, but softly spoken, not harsh. Her voice had an attractive, clear quality.

Each of my questions was met with a polite but non-committal answer. When I asked where she was from she replied, 'Frenchtown, off Avenue Petain.'

* * *

When the music stopped she bowed her head slightly, just as she had done for the American, said, 'Thank you,' and began to walk away. I followed, catching her by the arm. She turned around, her eyes blazing.

'I'm not for sale!'

'I don't want to buy you,' I said. 'I want to know you. Who are you? Where are you from?'

'I am a refugee.'

Then she walked away and was lost in the crowd.

I caught a glimpse of her dancing with clients several times.

* * *

Four German Brownshirts sat at a table. Probably from the Shanghai German Club, I assumed. All big men, loud, obnoxious, and intoxicated. Each man wore polished leather riding boots, dark brown jodhpurs, and light brown shirt with the red, white and black swastika armband. Four brown peaked caps lay on their table. They drank beer and sang German marching songs, in competition with the music.

One of the Germans approached Katya. Tall, blond-haired, blue-eyed, and athletic, he was a poster boy for Hitler's master race.

They stepped onto the dance floor together. As they danced, she took on a trance-like expression. She was essentially freezing him out, perhaps a worse insult than refusing his offer to dance.

He began to wrap his thick arms around her slim body and pulled her closer. She put her arms on his shoulders and tried to push him back. He was double her size and must have been double her strength. He forced her closer to the table by the edge of the dance floor where his comrades sat. Then they stood and formed a circle around Katya, laughing, jeering and catcalling.

She looked alarmed. They began pushing her towards the door.

As the uniformed men moved with her, I had a memory of standing in the driveway of Burleigh Castle. The empty shell of a building. Dread in my heart. My stomach sinking like a stone. The priest muttering in my ear:

'It's your father, Michael, and also Lord Burleigh, and Miss Fiona Burleigh is missing, nowhere to be found. And the castle destroyed.'

I failed. That's the truth of it. I failed her.

And again. God gave me a second chance. Fiona had been alive in Shanghai, against all the odds. And I let her die a second time.

I scanned the room, hoping to see someone I knew, who could help me save Katya. All I saw was a roomful of grinning, desperate, drunken strangers.

Nobody interfered with the Germans; nobody even took any notice. In a few seconds they had disappeared through the door into the night.

* * *

I ran outside. At the side of the building there was a long dark alleyway. The Germans had pushed her up against the wall. Meaty hands roved over her body. The blond Brownshirt crouched low, his hand under Katya's skirt.

Silently, I came behind them. With a quick, sharp kick, my leather-shod foot slammed into the face of the man who was bent forward. He shot up and staggered backwards, his nose broken into a bloody pulp, blood flowing down over his mouth and chin. The man at Katya's left shoulder turned round in surprise. I met him with a sharp jab of the heel of my hand into his nose, followed by a punch into his solar plexus.

The other two moved into an attack position. One of them grabbed me from behind. I threw him using a *ju-jitsu* move. He sprawled on the ground. Now only the fourth man was without injury. He crouched into a fighting stance and I heard a 'click' and saw a flick knife open. In the dim alleyway the blade glinted from the reflection of a street lamp, evil and sharp. We circled around each other. He lunged forward, slashing the knife. I dodged backwards, and as I did so I slipped off my jacket. I continued to step backwards as I wrapped my jacket around my right forearm.

I moved forward as he slashed with the knife, and met it with my padded arm. The knife made contact with the jacket and I punched him in the face with my left fist. He reeled backward, dropping the knife. He stumbled backwards against a dustbin, lost balance and staggered. I quickly jumped forward, and punched his stomach. He doubled up and I crunched my knee into his nose. He collapsed holding his face. The three other men had regrouped and were forming to attack.

I grabbed Katya's arm and said, 'Run for your life.' We took off at top speed, ran from the alley to the busy street, full of neon lights, cars, and pedestrians. I stepped off the kerb, extended my arm and hailed a taxi.

The driver stopped his car and I pushed her in, and then got in the back seat beside her. 'Drive! Now!' I shouted.

As the car took off, she was holding herself together, but her pupils were dilated in shock and her lower lip was trembling.

'It is okay to cry,' I said.

'I know that, but in the privacy of my own home. I refuse to collapse in public.'

'Let me take you home,' I said. 'What is your address?' She gave me the address just off the Avenue Petain near the Cathedral. 'I will get you home safely.'

'I am all right.'

'I'm a policeman and I'm taking you home.'

* * *

As we drove through the streets, the sound of the battle from Chapei became louder. She wrapped her arms around herself and shivered. 'This dreadful war. They are as bad as the Germans.'

The taxi driver turned on his windscreen wipers as a sudden downpour of rain began.

We arrived at the front of a small but rather run-down apartment building. I paid off the driver and ran with her to the front door. We stood under the building's awning to avoid the rain. She turned to me and said, 'This is not necessary,' but her voice was trembling. I took the keys from her shaking hands and opened the front door.

'Which apartment?' I asked her gently. She indicated the top floor.

We walked up the dark, creaking stairs. I opened the door and we stepped inside. She lit a small desk lamp and I placed her key on the chipped coffee table.

The room was small and neat, without much furniture but I could tell a great effort had been made to create a pleasant living space.

'This is nice,' I said. She nodded and quietly whispered, 'Thank you.' Then her whole body was shaking and she began to sob.

'I was so scared. I thought I had left them in Europe. Why are they here?'

I put my arms around her.

'Don't hold me too tight. I need to discharge.'

I didn't understand what she meant but I relaxed my arms and held her loosely.

I felt the vibrations in her body become more and more intense. I felt anxious, not knowing what to do. I tightened my arms around her again, and she shook her head and said, 'Don't do that.' After several minutes her movements slowed and became less intense. Eventually, she stopped moving completely.

'Now I must sleep,' she said.

She curled up on her narrow, single bed and I draped a quilt over her. She closed her eyes and fell into a deep sleep. I pulled up the only armchair near the bed and made myself as comfortable as I could manage. I watched the rise and fall of her breathing while I listened to the sound of the heavy rain.

At the sound of the tropical rain pounding on the roof I began to relax. In Ireland I'd always found rain drab and depressing—low, slate-coloured cloud, driving and constant, swirling sideways, driven by the wind, relentless, for hours and days. In Shanghai, the summer rain was sudden, dramatic, and intensely heavy, but was clear in an hour. Afterwards the air always felt crisp and clean.

In a little while I fell asleep myself, on the armchair, sitting by Katya's bed.

Chapter 46

I AWOKE EARLY, FEELING STIFF and sore from sleeping on the old chair, a dream about my mother still lingering. I was startled by the details of the dream, which came back to me with cinematic clarity.

My mother had often spoken of the handsome young policeman who swept her off her feet and took her crossroads dancing around the *boreens* of County Clare. She had been riding a bicycle without a lamp and my father had pulled her up for the offence. Instead of issuing her a court summons, he asked her to come with him to a crossroads dance. She agreed and within weeks they were engaged. RIC rules forbade a policeman from serving in either his home area or the home area of his wife. They had been transferred to County Limerick.

I was only nine when my mother became ill. It was wintertime. A bitterly cold wind, the ground hard with frost. She'd been at the market selling eggs from the hens kept in the police station's back garden, a little extra to supplement my father's police wage. She came home and took to her bed with a chill. The chill turned to a cold, the cold to pneumonia, and within a frighteningly short time she was fighting to breathe. Within days we had her funeral, my father rigid as a ship's mast by the graveside, in the November wind, resplendent in his best uniform. For an RIC man was never allowed out of uniform, on duty or off.

* * *

I watched Katya sleep. Her face had an innocent, child-like quality as she lay there on the bed. Eventually she woke. She asked me to wait for her outside while she bathed and I felt strangely shy to be in such intimate circumstances with her in the small apartment.

I went downstairs and waited for her on the street. In a short time she joined me. She smiled and said, 'I'll take you to my favourite café.' We began to walk towards the café, and, after a few steps, I felt her take my hand. My heart jumped. For a while at least, we could ignore the rumble of battle.

* * *

We took a table at the small café in the French style, run by an old Russian couple. Katya looked different now, without makeup and just woken. Smaller and younger. Vulnerable. Even so, Katya had not lost her aristocratic grace—a quality not bred by title or high birth, but by her self-possession.

We ordered strong, black coffee and sweet, soft, crumbly croissants served with cuts of cold ham and slices of cheese. We ate greedily and quietly. After the meal, I signalled for more coffee.

We sat in silence, staring at our cups. Finally I said, 'Tell me about yourself.'

Katya sighed. After a moment of silent thought she began.

'I was born in Munich, an only child.'

'I was wondering where you were from. So, you're German.'

'Well, that really depends upon who you ask. If you ask me, I'm as German as a beer stein. If you ask Herr Hitler, I'm the spawn of the devil, just like my family and my entire race. To him, we are not German and he has passed laws to that effect.'

I stopped for a moment as the old Russian lady brought fresh cups of coffee, the cups rattling slightly in their saucers, her hands trembling with age.

'But that's crazy,' I replied. 'I read about it in the papers, but is it really as bad as they say?'

'Yes, it is bad. In fact, worse than anything you can imagine. My father is a German Jew and my mother a Jew of Russian parents. Apparently, there is some Gypsy blood on my mother's side. Both of them are medical doctors.'

'Both doctors, eh? I would have thought they would be assets to their community.'

Katya smiled bitterly. 'In any other country they would. But not in Germany. The crazy thing is that my father served in the German army in the Great War. He was a medical officer, a captain. He had an Iron Cross pinned to his chest by the Kaiser himself. Now he's an enemy alien.'

I thought for a moment, my mind going back over the Troubles in Ireland.

'So how did Hitler engineer this situation?' I asked.

'It was remarkably simple, really. Last year, he passed the racial purity laws, and Jewish people lost their citizenship, could not work in their professions, and lost their rights to property. Everyone went along with it. At the stroke of a pen, my parents were no longer doctors and didn't own the house that they bought with their own money thirty years ago.'

'Jesus! But where are they now? Did they come with you?'

'If only they could,' she replied. Her voice began to tremble and her eyes moistened.

'My parents were in more danger than most.'

'Oh, how's that?'

'My mother was a member of the German Communist Party. That is practically a death sentence in itself, but there's more.'

I shook my head at the sheer evil of it. 'What else could there be?'

'Well, both of my parents were very progressive. They strayed into areas of research that were anathema to the Nazis. Have you heard of Dr. Reich, Wilhelm Reich—a former student of Sigmund Freud?'

I shook my head. 'No, go on.'

'Dr. Reich and his students believe that the neurosis caused by early childhood trauma show up in physical constrictions in the human body. These blocks can be weakened and removed by deep breathing, exercises and physical massage. Breaking the blocks led to the free flow of vital energy in the body. This vitality is primarily sexual.'

'So you mean that someone with some kind of disturbance can be cured through physical treatment?'

'Exactly,' she said.

'But why is that objectionable to Hitler?'

'You remember my body vibrations you saw last night? That is actually nature's way of releasing trauma. It was an entirely natural process, but one, which was typically stifled by adult humans, the logic of the brain over-coming the innate wisdom of their bodies. All I did was allow my body's instinct to disregard my thoughts. My muscles and tissues trembled as animals do, and now the trauma is fully released. I feel fine today, despite what happened last night.'

'Why would the Nazis object to that?'

'Dr. Reich enraged Hitler by suggesting that the Nazis' desire to conquer the world was a symptom of their sexual repression. This was illustrated, Dr. Reich believed, by the stiff goose-stepping march of the SS.'

'I'm not sure I follow you.'

She smiled. 'Hitler and the Nazis are in need of a good fuck!'

'All right, I understand.'

'Because of these theories,' Katya explained, 'the Nazis look upon the Reichians as perverts and degenerates. Both of my parents have disappeared into a Nazi prison. I turned Germany upside down and I still don't know if they are even still alive.'

'Oh God, Katya, that's horrible.'

'And what's more, some Nazi pig is now living in our house and legally owns it.' Her fists squeezed with fury.

'So what about you? What did you do in Germany?'

'I had just graduated as a physician from Berlin University. But can you believe what the pigs did? Despite being a gold medal student, I was unable to collect my diploma, owing to Hitler's new laws.'

'I'm so sorry, Katya,' I said, reaching across the table to take her hand.

'You see, I had just spent a year privately studying the techniques of Doctor Reich when my parents were arrested. Having narrowly escaped arrest myself, I managed to sell a small Klimt painting that had been a prized possession of my parents—a wedding present, in fact. With the proceeds of the sale, I packed one suitcase and bought a train ticket to Italy. From Genoa I spent most of the money on a first-class ticket on a cruise liner to Shanghai. Spending big was the only way to jump the queue, and it cost me every cent. I voyaged in luxury to arrive to a life of grinding poverty in Shanghai. And now I taxi-dance while former German professors of literature sell pots and pans on the streets of Hongkew.'

I shook my head in disgust. 'Well, they call Shanghai the city of last resort. It's the only port in the world that you can enter without so much as a passport or visa.'

'Thank God for Shanghai,' Katya said with passion. 'Without it I might be dead.'

'If there is anything I can do to help you...'

'I often wonder if I should have stayed. Perhaps I could have done something more for them. Was I a coward to run away and leave them?'

'You did the right thing, Katya. You're better off alive in Shanghai than dead in Munich. Your parents would want you to live. You can't help them if you're dead.'

'I suppose so,' she replied uncertainly.

She picked up her cup and sipped, her eyes lingering on the street scene through the window. 'It's funny, isn't it?' she said. 'From where we sit right now it could be Paris or Vienna.'

'I don't know if there is a city with more contrasts in the whole world,' I replied as I watched a neat little red Jaguar two-seater sports roadster come by, driven by a young European man with one hand on the steering wheel, his free arm draped over the shoulder of his pretty blonde girlfriend.

'So what happened when you arrived in Shanghai?' I asked.

'Well, when I landed at the docks in Frenchtown a Jewish family from Munich took me in. I began life here with those kind people in a shared room in a cramped laneway and a communal toilet used by more than a hundred people. That family helped me get on my feet, and find a job and a place to live.'

'You see!' I said. 'You're a survivor.'

'I hope I am. Now, as you can see, I make a living as a taxi dancer while I wait for the result of a visa application to the United States. The response to the application, I am informed by the embassy, could take several years. For now, I'm stuck in Shanghai.'

* * *

We talked for hours. I learned that she had had a happy childhood, although she had early memories of the Great War and its aftermath as a grim shadow.

She asked me, 'How does an Irishman find himself policing the British Empire?' I told her my story, a limited version of it, anyway.

After a time the conversation petered out. We sat, playing with our coffee cups. Then Katya took my hand and said, 'Come back to my room.' I paid the bill, and we walked along the street back to her building.

As we entered, a door leading off the lobby opened and a small, bird-like, very regal old lady appeared.

Katya and the lady exchanged kisses and greetings in Russian.

'Michael,' said Katya, 'may I introduce you to Countess Olga, late of St. Petersburg, my very kind landlady and guardian angel.'

The old lady kissed me on both cheeks and I said, 'I am delighted to make the acquaintance of Katya's guardian angel.'

* * *

When we reached Katya's room I stood awkwardly, feeling unsure of myself.

Katya slipped the jacket off my shoulders, undid my tie, and unbuttoned my shirt. She continued undressing me, gently, as one would with an infant. I stood naked and shy.

She put her hands on my shoulders and guided me onto the bed. 'Lie down,' she said. 'Face down.' I did as she asked and I felt her begin to massage my neck and shoulders. Gradually I felt the tension in my muscles relax. I felt a shock of cold as massage oil was applied to my body. Katya worked through my whole body from head to toe. I was in a deep state of relaxation and almost asleep. She whispered in my ear to turn over.

When I turned she began to massage my scalp, forehead and temples. Then she put her hands on my chest and diaphragm and began to deeply push and manipulate my muscles.

'Breathe deeply, in time with my hand movements,' she said.

I felt my chest gradually go soft.

Then she began to massage my chest in a circular fashion. I was strangely emotional, and without knowing exactly why, a tear ran from my eye.

Katya continued to work on my chest, pushing hard and rhythmically, until I thought my sternum would crack. Then I felt something move in my chest. It was physical: a release, an unknotting of muscles and tissue, but it was more than that. My chest became hot and somehow—I couldn't explain it—free. My breathing deepened.

I began to experience waves of sadness and see images from my past.

A picture of my mother. A black and white photo of my parents' wedding from the mantelpiece of my parents' bedroom. Fiona's face appeared in my mind's eye. I saw Miriam in her shimmering dress one night at the House of Multiple Joys.

Katya pushed on my chest, harder and harder, in deep circular motions. 'Breathe!' she commanded. 'Breathe! Breathe!' My body shook as I sobbed like a broken man. Hot tears spilled down my cheeks as my aching heart poured out its sorrow. I was beyond words, incoherent with all that had happened.

Katya wrapped her arms around me, squeezing tighter with each sob that racked me from head to toe.

I don't know how long we stayed locked in embrace.

Finally, my tears subsided, and we moved apart. Then my face flushed with shame. A man doesn't cry. Katya slipped her hand into mine but I didn't move. *What must she think of me, breaking down like a baby?*

Katya left me and disappeared into the small bathroom. A few moments later, she reappeared wearing a dark blue Japanese silk dressing gown. The colour matched her eyes. I sat up on the side of the bed and then rose to my feet.

Katya stood a little apart from me. Her blue eyes looked into mine and she smiled. Her hands began to slowly untie the blue cord that held her silk dressing gown closed. Slowly she slipped it off, until she revealed her naked body.

I stepped towards her and put my arms around her, pulling her close, feeling her slender athletic form. We kissed, and then I took her hand and led her to the bed. We lay down side-by-side, staring into each other's eyes.

Slowly, we began to make love.

Afterwards, we lay together, Katya enfolded in my arms.

* * *

I fell into a deep, dreamless sleep, the deepest I'd had in years. Sometime later, we awoke and made love again. She lay in my arms on that narrow single bed and we began to talk. For the first time since my arrival thirteen years ago, I began to realistically conceive of a life outside of Shanghai. I spoke to Katya of the possibility of going somewhere and taking her with me. If she were with me, she would not have to worry about passports or visas.

She looked at me with a quizzical expression. 'Are you proposing to me?' she said.

I thought for a moment and, to my own surprise, replied, 'Yes, I suppose I am.'

She squeezed me with her strong arms and said, 'What a good man you are!'

'Is that a "yes"?' I asked.

'Yes,' she said, 'I suppose it is.'

At that, she fell asleep again.

I lay awake for some time, thinking. Was I finally prepared to give up my vendetta with Jamie? The thought of being free of my obsession was strangely disturbing, as if my hatred for him brought me some odd, peculiar comfort.

Later, Katya phoned her employers from the French Post Office on Avenue Petain and told them she could not come to the 'Casanova' tonight. We walked streets of the French Concession pretending it was Paris. We went to see '*King Solomon's Mines*' at the Cathay Cinema on Avenue Joffre.

Chapter 47

15 August 1937

I WAS ON STANDBY AT Gordon Road in the officer's day room, lying on a couch and reading the *North China Daily News*. I was barely concentrating on the page, my thoughts continually returning to Katya. *What's she doing now*, I wondered.

The front page was full of reports of the war. It was a strange experience to be reading about the war in a comfortable room, lying on a couch, while the sounds of the battle were audible in the background. Side-by-side with the war news, the newspaper displayed the everyday advertising of automobiles, gramophones, stationery, and a sale starting at the Wing On Department Store.

I turned the page, eager to find something that wasn't about the situation in Shanghai. I read that Eamon de Valera had won the general election in Ireland. Not too bad, I thought. The leader of the losing side of Ireland's civil war goes on to achieve power by democratic election. Maybe the country wasn't so lost after all.

I flicked through the pages until I got to the social gossip section. In the midst of the war, the paper still wrote of affairs, divorces, movie releases and the parties attended by the great and good.

A heading over a short paragraph caught my eye: 'Philanthropist moves to Hong Kong.' It described how Big Ears Lu had closed his house on Rue Wagner and put his entire entourage of wives, concubines and servants on a liner to Hong Kong. Mr. Lau was put in charge of operations in Shanghai. A family spokesman released a statement to the effect that the milder climate of Hong Kong was of greater benefit to Mr. Lu's health. I knew then that Shanghai was finished.

A station servant approached me and said, 'Visitor for you, sir.' I sat up, pulled on my jacket and went to the door. Standing there was Freddie Wang, wearing the uniform of an SMP Sergeant. We stood facing each other, a moment of wary silence.

'Freddie, I haven't seen you in quite a while, and I don't think I've ever once seen you in uniform,' I said, as I shook his hand coolly. We hadn't been particularly close since our meeting at Jimmy's Diner and Jack Dell's convenient appearance soon after when I tried to take Jamie's file.

'How are you, Michael?' he replied. 'I had a meeting here at the depot and I thought I'd drop in and see how you are. And, with all the fighting around these days, it's safer to be in uniform when I can. I'm still with the Branch, of course.'

'Come in, why don't you?'

We had only just settled down in the day room when I heard the alarm go off. I jumped up, buttoned my tunic and ran to the office. I sensed Freddie coming in behind me. The duty-officer, Sergeant Kirlov, sat at the desk, his face tight with anxiety.

'What is it, Kirlov?' I asked.

'We just had an emergency phone call from the Outside Roads.'

'What's going on?' I asked.

'The call was from Albion Film Studios,' said Kirlov. 'Mister Flyte put in the call himself. The Chinese and Japanese are waging a pitched battle throughout the grounds and Mister Flyte is pinned under heavy fire.'

Trying to keep my voice calm and businesslike, I said, 'Let's have a look at the map.'

I unfolded the paper, spread it on the desk and gave the impression of concentrating deeply on it. Kirlov stood at my left shoulder.

Assistant Commissioner Fairlight came striding in, accompanied by Superintendent Desmond, our new boss. Mister Desmond was the head of the Emergency Unit since Fairlight had been promoted to Assistant Commissioner. Strictly speaking, Fairlight should have been at Central HQ but he couldn't be kept away from the Unit. He still went out on raids with us regularly.

Fairlight spoke: 'Gentlemen, I have just been relayed the news by the switchboard operator.'

I introduced Fairlight and Desmond to Freddie.

After brisk handshakes, Freddie asked, 'Do you mind if I sit in on this? The Branch likes to keep an eye on sensitive situations.'

'Can't refuse the Branch, I suppose,' said Fairlight distractedly as he cast his eyes over the map.

'Hmm, tricky,' said Fairlight. 'The studio is, of course, located in the Outside Roads Area.'

I traced the location with my finger on the map. The studio was a mile or so beyond the International Settlement near Jessfield Park and St John's University.

Mister Fairlight said, 'The International Settlement claims the municipal roads as ours on the grounds that we built, funded and maintained them.'

He took off his spectacles and immediately put them on again, a sign I had long recognised as irritation on his part.

'A bloody mess,' he went on. 'Houses directly on the roads pay taxes to the Settlement and are under SMP protection. But houses off the roads fall under Chinese jurisdiction. How one judges what is on or off the road remains without clear definition.'

'Yes, it's crazy. I've seen Westerners held up at gunpoint and the damned Chinese police only yards away, refusing to intervene.'

He took off his glasses again and rubbed his eyes. He looked more tired than I'd ever seen him. He sighed heavily. 'It would be easiest to take no action. We have orders from the Municipal Council not to go outside the Settlement borders. And with this wretched war on, anyone who goes out there could wind up under attack from either side.'

I could feel my pulse race despite my outwardly calm demeanour.

'We have to do something, sir,' I said. I tried to keep my voice calm and steady. I didn't want to give the impression I had any unusual emotional involvement in this situation.

'Yes, we have to do something, Mister Gallagher, I'm aware of it. Mister Flyte is one of the most influential businessmen in the entire Shanghai settlement. We cannot simply leave him to his fate.'

'Let's go and get him then,' said I.

'I cannot ask policemen to expose themselves to a full-scale war. This isn't a bar room brawl we're dealing with.'

'I'm volunteering, sir,' I said.

Surely this was the chance I'd been longing for. Years of obsessing and plotting and now Jamie could be in my hands. I thought of the possibility of killing him in the heat of battle, just as he had killed my father. Nice poetic justice. Or could I find an opportunity to seize the leather map case? What did he keep in it? Was it his Swiss account details? I would have to see what could be done. And what the devil was Freddie doing here?

Fairlight hesitated for a moment and glanced again at the map. Kirlov cleared his throat and spoke, his voice strained. 'There is something you should know, sir. Mister Flyte specifically said not to send Mister Gallagher.'

'*Not send Gallagher?*' said Fairlight incredulously. 'Don't be ridiculous;

he's one of my most experienced officers. What's this about, Gallagher?' he said, turning to me.

'I knew him in Ireland, sir. I think he didn't like my father much.'

'We haven't time for ancient history now, gentlemen. This is urgent. Are you sure you're prepared to go, Gallagher?'

'Yes, sir, I'm certain.'

'All right then, if you're willing to lead a team, I will call for volunteers. But we had better make it hasty.'

'I'd like to come,' said Freddie. 'I speak Japanese, and, luckily, I'm in uniform.'

'What a fortuitous coincidence that you're here, Freddie,' I said, wondering if my sarcasm was obvious to the senior officers.

Freddie smiled modestly.

* * *

Two Red Marias raced out of Gordon Road depot with sirens and bells blaring. Freddie and I occupied the turret of the leading vehicle, my second-in-command sitting on the benches with the men. The Big Chief motor-cycles, machine guns mounted on their sidecars, roared ahead, blocking side roads and clearing traffic. They would stay with us until we came to the edge of the Outside Roads Area and would then turn back, leaving the two Red Marias proceed, with all haste, to Albion Film Studios.

As we drove westward, the sounds of battle became louder. The streetscape transformed from busy, commercial rows of shops, cafés, and nightclubs to a suburban vista of elegant family residences surrounded by manicured gardens, swimming pools and tennis courts.

When we crossed the line taking us outside the International Settlement, the long streets of elegant houses looked exactly the same, except for unmistakable signs of battle. Dotted along the suburban streets were burned-out cars, walls with bullet and shell holes, houses on fire, black smoke rising from their damaged interiors.

Groups of Japanese soldiers dug trenches in gardens and tennis courts. A dead horse lay in the driveway of a house, its body almost obscured by a black cloud of flies.

At a roadblock manned by Japanese soldiers we were flagged down. A young Japanese lieutenant shouted, 'You cannot pass. Return to the International Settlement.'

I shouted back, 'We are on a humanitarian mission. Open the barrier.'

Then Freddie began to speak in rapid-fire Japanese, entirely different to the way he spoke English. The conversation was punctuated with rapid and staccato polite bows from both parties, but I sensed that the politeness barely masked a dangerous level of aggression.

'No good,' said Freddie, 'they won't let us pass.'

At a command from the lieutenant, the soldiers began to bring their long rifles up to aim at us. Freddie swung the turret-mounted Thompson sub-machine gun towards them. There was a loud click as he cocked the weapon ready to open fire. It was clear that we outgunned them and could have cut them down in a second. For a time the guns were ranged against each other. The young lieutenant, who was only about nineteen, blinked rapidly as a bead of sweat ran down his face. Then his jaw clenched with humiliation. He shouted a command in Japanese and two soldiers pulled back the barrier.

* * *

Within minutes we were at the main entrance of the studio. The tall metal gates had been closed but were now hanging off their hinges. Above the gates was the film studio's logo, a large black letter 'A' with two white wings. The red and white security barrier inside the gates was fully raised, pointing to the sky like a giant barber's pole. We drove fast, the Red Marias bashing their way through the gates and bringing them crashing to the ground. Our vehicles raced up the driveway, engines roaring, heading towards the centre of the complex. As I scanned the area for signs of danger, I was struck by the astonishing vastness of the studio grounds. It was a miniature city, a world of its own.

Each building had a large sign, black letters on a white background, identifying the building's purpose. I saw executive offices, cutting rooms, a fire department, casting offices, and the enormous sound stages—vast, corrugated iron buildings with rounded roofs, and many storeys tall that looked like giant aircraft hangars. Most were on fire or damaged by shellfire.

Jamie's phone call had said that he was in the main administrative building, holed up in his office on the top floor. We knew from our map that our destination was a large house, originally a suburban residence predating the recently expanded studio, located in the very centre of the complex.

As we came nearer to the centre of the grounds we saw further signs of battle. There was a loud crackling sound of multiple small arms fire. Many Chinese soldiers huddled by a low stone wall, their rifles pointed towards their enemy. Directly behind them a sound stage smouldered. Bullets pinged off the body of the Red Maria.

We accelerated down the main drive and arrived at a film lot. It was a medieval European street. Further along there was a small lake with a timber 19th century sailing ship surrounded by canoes. As we raced further through the lot I saw a small area of jungle. We rounded a curve and the street looked like a small village from rural China, the setting for a folk-tale. Beyond the 'village' main street, the film lot took on the appearance of an ancient Chinese Palace. As we whizzed past, I saw a body on the ground, a film extra, I assumed, dressed as an armoured warrior from medieval China.

Chapter 48

UP AHEAD WE SAW THE office complex. I shouted for our driver to stop and simultaneously raised my hand to signal the other Red Maria to pull up beside us. It was a large house with curved walls and rounded balconies, oval porthole windows and a flat roof with a retaining wall. The building was painted pale cream with blue touches to window frames, doors and decorative motif.

The facade of the building was peppered with bullet holes and the windows were shattered. The garden erupted in a shower of earth as a mortar bomb exploded. The west wing of the house billowed black smoke and flames.

In the immediate vicinity, two opposing forces faced each other: the Japanese occupied a small warehouse a hundred yards to the left of the house, and the Chinese forces were entrenched in a building that had 'Editing Room' stencilled on the wall. They were engaging each other with rifle and small arms fire.

From a porthole window upstairs, a hand extended, waving a white handkerchief.

I ordered the two Thompson gunners to fire at both forces. 'Fire over their heads. Make them duck for cover. Try not to kill anyone,' I said.

Freddie aimed towards the Japanese and the other gunner, Kirlov, opened fire towards the Chinese. The sound of the gunfire from the Thompsons was loud, rapid and terrifying. Soldiers on both sides quickly dived for cover.

I jumped out of the Maria and took off at a fast sprint towards the house. I zigzagged to throw off the aim of anyone trying to shoot at me. I felt bullets zing past.

The door opened and I rushed inside. Leaning heavily against a wall was Jamie. His tie was loosened and shirt buttons undone, his business suit was smoke-stained and grimy, his face marked by several small cuts and abrasions. His left pants leg was soaked with blood.

'What the bloody hell are you doing here?' he said, his face distorted in a grimace.

'I just wanted to see you with your empire falling around you,' I replied.

He reached inside his jacket and his hand reappeared pointing a small Beretta pistol at me.

'I can do you just like I did your old man,' he said.

'You can try. But you won't get out of here alive. None of those fellas on the trucks care enough to come under enemy fire for you. If you want to get out of here alive, you'll have to work with me. But then, you did once offer me a job.'

I saw him hesitate, calculating. Part of me longed for him to shoot. I didn't know if I wanted to die or if I wanted a justification to break his neck with a *ju-jitsu* chop. I knew my bulletproof jacket would stop a shot from the Beretta. I was close enough to disarm him, a move I'd practiced a thousand times. I was pretty confident, given his weakened state.

'Leave the pistol here, or you won't get out alive,' I said.

He considered for a moment and said, 'All right, then. A truce, for the moment.' He dropped the weapon behind him on the ground.

He opened the door a crack and peered out. 'Well, this takes me back,' he said.

'You're wounded. Can you run?' I asked.

'I have a bullet in my thigh. But I can do it.'

'Take my shoulder.'

'Wait!' he commanded as he opened a drawer in the big reception desk. I saw him remove his brown leather map case.

He wrapped his free arm round my shoulder. I wanted to recoil.

I pulled the door open. The Thompson sub-machine guns were firing, disciplined short, accurate bursts. Then, with Jamie hanging on to my shoulder and holding the leather map case in his left hand, we moved towards the safety of the Red Marias.

We moved at a shuffling jog, much too slow for my liking but he couldn't move any faster.

A mortar bomb exploded on the lawn, hurling up a cloud of earth, and we were thrown flat on the ground. We picked ourselves up and started to move again. We hobbled towards the Red Marias. Progress was painfully slow.

Freddie came out from the Red Maria, crouching low, running towards us. Another man had taken over the machine gun on the turret. Freddie reached us and I shouted, 'Take Mister Flyte!'

Freddie picked Jamie up with a sharp exhalation and put him in a fireman's lift. He ran effortlessly and they quickly reached the safety of the Red Maria. I ran and dived through the back door. Before the door was even closed, I heard the engines rev up and quickly the trucks reversed and began to race towards the studio gate.

I sat on the hard bench-seat beside Jamie.

'How are you?' I asked, concerned that if I didn't show reassurance to the *Taipan* the other constables might think it suspicious.

He glared at me. 'I'll live.'

'We'll have you at the hospital in no time,' I said in tones of mock concern. As I spoke, Freddie was applying a tourniquet to Jamie's leg. He caught my eye. His expression was blank but I knew he was reading the unspoken hostility between Jamie and I perfectly.

With his face pale and jaw clenched with the effort of suppressing his pain, Jamie moaned softly and said, 'When I was in the Great War, I lapped up that sort of business. Don't think a few scratches will stop me in my tracks.'

* * *

We drove flat out with bells and sirens sounding and now had no trouble passing through the lines of combatants. Roadblocks were opened for us without question, both by Japanese and Chinese forces. Within a short time, we were back safely inside the International Settlement.

I shouted out to our driver, trying to keep my voice businesslike and normal. 'Mister Flyte needs medical attention. Drive immediately to the General Hospital on North Soochow Road.'

Jamie sat slumped on a seat, the leather map case clutched to his chest. He looked pale and weak.

As we pulled up at the front gate of the hospital, I grabbed the leather map case and pulled it from his grasp. I felt his arms resist but he was weakened by blood loss and it was no contest. 'I will keep this safely for you, Mister Flyte.'

'I wouldn't do that, old boy. Our friend from Rue Wagner might be upset,' he gasped, his face wracked with pain.

'He's gone, Jamie. You're on your own.'

I shouted to my Sergeant, 'See that Mister Flyte gets medical attention and have one of the men to stay with him. Make sure he doesn't leave the hospital. I will see you all back at the depot shortly.'

As I stepped towards the street, Freddie Wang stared at me intensely. I stepped off the kerb and crossed the busy traffic.

* * *

A rickshaw coolie ran past me fast, pulling his vehicle unoccupied. He halted in front of me on the kerb, dropping the handles of his rickshaw, creating a barrier in my path.

He reached inside his shirt and pulled out a meat cleaver. 'Give me the map case,' he shouted in English. I stepped back and sensed movement behind me. I glanced over my shoulder; there was another rickshaw coolie brandishing a knife.

I pulled my gun fast from the holster and fired off two shots from the hip. The coolie fell backwards, the cleaver falling noisily on the concrete. I turned, pointing my pistol at the second man. He dropped his knife and held up his hands.

'*Run away now!*' I shouted in Shanghainese. '*If I see you again, I'll kill you.*'

He turned and ran, leaving his rickshaw on the kerb.

I walked rapidly away as on-lookers began to point and shout, and a crowd gathered by the fallen man.

* * *

I jumped on the Bubbling Well Road tram and got off at the stop near the Greycliffe Building. I went to my apartment, phoned Gordon Road and told them I would be at home for a few hours, then slipped off my helmet and bulletproof vest, jacket, and boots.

Quickly swallowing a mug of tepid water I sat and opened the map case. The leather map case contained a small black notebook with pages lined in the style of a ledger. The heading 'Zurich' was handwritten in bold letters at the top of the first page. The pages were covered in neat rows of small black letters and numbers; I presumed they were bank account numbers and each piece of information, combinations of up to twenty letters and numbers, were too numerous for any man to remember them all.

On the last page I found neatly written instructions. It was clear that the notebook contained a list of numbered Swiss bank accounts with the relevant numbers and passwords to withdraw cash.

A surge of excitement gripped me. Here, I had access to Jamie's vast wealth. No proof of identity necessary apart from the numbers.

I put the notebook back in the map case and fell asleep where I sat.

Chapter 49

WHEN I AWOKE, I SHOWERED and shaved to clean off the grime and smut of battle. I changed into a civilian suit and caught a taxi to Katya's place in Frenchtown.

As I approached the front door of the building, I saw signs of damage to the door and noted a glistening new lock. I knocked and got no reply. I knocked again, feeling a mounting sense of impending disaster.

After an age, I heard a faint voice from inside: 'Who is it?'

I called out, 'It is Michael, Countess, and I am here to see Katya.'

I heard the sound of bolts being pulled, then the door opened a single inch and she peered out warily. When she saw it was I, she opened the door fully and let me into the tiled hallway.

She looked smaller and frailer than last time I had seen her and had a haunted expression, her eyes wide with shock.

'Countess, what is it?' I asked.

'Oh, Michael,' she said. 'They have taken her.'

'Who did?' I demanded.

'The police,' she replied timorously.

I could see that she was close to collapse. Her hand, fluttering like a small bird, went to her chest. Her breathing was laboured.

'What police—the French?'

'Yes, I think so. Yes, in fact I am sure of it. There was a French officer in uniform, and *gendarmes*, you know the ones in the conical hats, the Indo-Chinese.'

'Yes, I understand,' I replied.

'There was another man with them. I listened at the door. His accent was like yours. A big man in a black suit, red tie.'

A cold hand spread itself through my guts. Jack Dell. I was certain of it.

I rushed upstairs to Katya's small apartment. Furniture was overturned, the mattress slashed, bedding scattered and ripped, books piled on the floor.

* * *

I approached the French Central Police Station at the corner of Route Stanislaus and Route Pere Robert. The street was bustling, shoppers going about their business, apparently not bothered by the war. I watched a pair of pretty French girls alight from a tram, and skip lightly to the kerb, both of them laden with pink-coloured shopping bags from a boutique on Avenue Joffre.

I went to the front desk and showed my Municipal Police identity card. I asked the French desk sergeant to see the senior man. After what seemed like a very long wait, I was shown into the office of a Senior French Officer. The nameplate on his desk said 'Captain Lavelle.'

He stood and shook my hand and offered me a cigarette.

The French officer had slicked-back, oiled hair and a pencil-thin moustache on a pale, thin face.

'Yes, Mister Gallagher, what can I do for you? We seem to be inundated with visitors from our dear friends in the SMP these days.'

I asked him if he knew anything of the arrest of Katya.

'We had a visit from Mister Dell of your Special Branch. He identified the lady as a communist agent, a German Jew. He had a warrant for her, issued in the International Settlement, but of course she is a non-citizen and not subject to extra-territoriality. Naturally, she would be handed to our Chinese colleagues. Such a shame, really. A pretty little thing to have her head sliced off by one of their brutes, but *c'est la vie*, eh, my friend?'

As he said this, a memory of the head in the birdcage suspended over the Nantao marketplace came back to me. My blood ran cold.

* * *

I took a taxi to the Cathay Hotel where they had private telephone kiosks. I alighted near the corner of Nanking Road. I rounded the corner to the Bund and looked at 'Big Ching', the clock on the Customs House building. It was 11 a.m. I walked to the Cathay Hotel.

A pianist played a cheerful Strauss waltz. The clatter of cups and cutlery and a buzz of female conversation hummed from the tearooms.

I took a seat on a soft, enveloping armchair in the lobby. For a moment I dreamed of falling asleep where I sat, to simply drown out the war and my fear. I shook my head, angry with myself for my weakness.

A Chinese waiter approached me, bowed obsequiously, and asked me if he could bring me a coffee. I took out my Shanghai Municipal Police identity card and impatiently waved it towards him. 'Police business. Call me as soon as a private telephone booth is available.'

I became aware that people in the lobby were looking at me strangely. I picked up a copy of the *North China Daily News* and began to scan the headlines in a parody of normalcy. There was something about the Spanish Civil War—Franco's troops conquered the Atlantic port of Santander. *Fucking war everywhere.*

* * *

When I was called to an available phone booth I first telephoned the Public Safety Bureau.

After several false leads, frustrating waits and long silences, I managed to speak to a senior officer by the name of Zhong that I had once spoken to at a police conference. He was very guarded at first and then, apparently feeling sorry for me and recognising the desperation in my voice, he decided to be frank.

'As I'm sure you are aware,' he began, and the sound of shuffling paper told me he was reading directly from a document, 'since September 1935, Germany has passed legislation—the *Reich Citizenship Law*, and *the Law for the Protection of German Blood and German Honour.* Anybody of Jewish blood has been stripped of his or her German citizenship. Your lady friend is not legally German. Without a passport, the lady falls under our jurisdiction. If she is a spy, she will face the death penalty.'

'Mister Zhong, what can I *do* about this?' I asked struggling to keep my voice measured.

'You may have to find yourself a new lady friend.'

* * *

I dialled Jamie's number. I still remembered it from my days with Fiona.

'Michael, hello, old chap.' His tone of voice was cheerful, the joy of a man who had the enemy right where he wanted him.

'Jamie?' I said again. 'You're out of the hospital.'

'Feeling right as rain. Just a superficial wound. Very lucky, bit of blood loss, shock, that sort of thing,' he said breezily.

'You took Katya.'

'Well, you know what I want, Michael. I really don't have to spell it out for you, now do I?'

'All right. I will return the map case and its contents to you, and in exchange you will release the girl into my custody. She is not to be harmed or I will kill you with my bare hands.'

'Jolly good. I'll tell you what, let's make it easy for you. The studio is out of bounds, as you know. I will meet you with the lovely young lady, at noon, in my cinema at the Great World. Make your way to the Savoy Cinema and find the manager's office.'

'All right. I'll be there.'

'Don't forget the map case.'

I hung up.

* * *

I left the Cathay Hotel and began to pace nervously along the Bund. I stopped in front of the Hong Kong and Shanghai Bank and rubbed the paw of the bronze lion for good luck, as the locals did.

I was scared.

I thought of Katya. I had only been with her for a matter of hours. Really, I barely knew her. The leather map case felt heavy with the wealth it represented. I could walk for ten minutes and be on at ship at the docks in Frenchtown. Since the war started I'd been carrying my Irish Free State passport along with my wallet, a sign of some primitive survival instinct. I had in my hands the account numbers to make a life of wealth. Everything I'd dreamed of since the day I'd sat in Fiona's drawing room at the age of thirteen.

Streams of refugees were pushing their way across the Garden Bridge and walking south along the Bund.

The Hongkew end of the bridge had a barrier manned by a group of Japanese infantrymen. They pointed their bayoneted rifles menacingly into the faces of the desperate people streaming through the barrier. They hammered their rifle butts at people seemingly at random. There was a flurry of pushing and beating as the soldiers spotted a European couple in the middle of the stream of people. They wore good quality overcoats and carried polished tan leather suitcases. The Japanese punched and kicked an opening in the sea of bodies and the couple was ushered onto the bridge with a courteous bow. An officer, Samurai sword in hand, took the woman by the arm and walked with them across the length of the bridge. When they reached the south end, the officer saluted and bowed. A British Army officer approached the couple and saluted before ushering them through the Settlement barrier.

Many refugees had set up camps in the Public Gardens, among the magnolias, while many others filed on down along the Bund towards the city, trying to find some corner or doorway to huddle in, where they could set up a cooking fire. The clouds of black smoke from Hongkew cast an oppressive, gloomy pall over the park.

Through the open window of the Cathay Hotel's tearoom came the tinkling sound of piano music–'*It Looks Like Rain in Cherry Blossom Lane.*'

The refugees were, in the main, peasants from the countryside, dressed plainly in typical pyjamas and padded jackets. They looked hungry, dirty and exhausted.

Most were burdened with sacks, bags and baskets of household goods, bedding, pots and pans, framed black and white photos of ancestors, and brass candle-sticks and statuettes of household gods. Many were barefoot; some wore homemade sandals; only a few had decent boots.

An old man collapsed with exhaustion, and his wife, equally old, picked him up and, wrapping her arm around his waist, the two stumbled along like two wounded soldiers on a battlefield.

A little girl, not more than five years old, came running out of the mass of bodies shuffling along the street. She wore padded pants and jacket, her hair in two pigtails, tied with little red ribbons. Her eyes wide with fear, she stared around her, head swivelling this way and that, panicked and obviously separated from her family.

She began to wail. It was a wail of piteous despair, a soul abandoned, swimming in a sea of danger.

She came running towards me. Her little arms wrapped around my legs and she shook and sobbed and howled. She squeezed my legs tight. I remained unmoving for a time and then, as I felt her grip relax a little, I bent down, and put my arms around her, and just held her, firmly but not too tightly. She cried piteously, her eyes wide with fear, and her whole body trembled. After some time, her cries subsided.

I spoke to her in Shanghainese. '*It is all right, little girl; you are safe now.*' I repeated this until it got through and I saw some understanding in her eyes. Still, she did not speak.

Then there was a flurry of movement in the crowd and an elderly, grey-haired lady, dressed like a farmer, pushed her way through the crush of bodies. The grandmother cried, '*Aaliyah*' and the little girl screamed back, '*Poi poi.*'

The woman ran to us and scooped the little girl up in her arms. They hugged each other tightly and then the old lady looked at me and said, '*Thank you, sir*' in Shanghainese.

I slipped my watch off my wrist and offered it to the old lady. It was a gold watch, expensive, a present from Fiona. Her eyes widened and she quickly grabbed the watch and in a second it had disappeared inside her quilted jacket. '*Grandmother, please sell it and buy some food for yourself and the little girl,*' I said.

Within seconds they had disappeared into the mass of people walking towards the city.

I was determined that Katya would live, even if it cost my own life.

Chapter 50

I WAS ABOUT TO MOVE off when a single aeroplane with Chinese Nationalist markings flew over the river. It flew low and slow, towards the *Izumo*,
the Japanese cruiser anchored in the middle of the Whampoo, more or less
in a straight line from the Japanese Consulate on the north side of Garden
Bridge.

The *Izumo* was using its anti-aircraft weaponry. I heard loud flat bangs
and saw puffs of black smoke appear around the plane. They looked like
black flowers instantly opening and fading away. The plane rocked violently
from side to side, and the pilot pulled up, a dark shape dislodging itself
from his aircraft's undercarriage. I watched the bomb fall in a straight line
into the river, splashing harmlessly as it landed a hundred yards or more
from its target.

The pilot banked and flew in a slow circle and gradually began its
approach to the ship again. Although I knew next to nothing about aircraft,
I could sense that the pilot was inexperienced. He flew so unhurriedly that
his engine shuddered and came close to stalling. The aircraft, I could see,
was sluggish and wobbly and I would not have been surprised if it had
plunged like a rock into the river.

As the aeroplane approached the ship for its second bombing run, the
air was again peppered with anti-aircraft fire and the black flowers of smoke
surrounded the plane.

Then, suddenly, one puff of black exploded so close that the aircraft
jerked like a wounded animal. The aircraft decelerated alarmingly and the
pilot pulled up and banked in a struggling, ponderous circle, its engine
spluttering and labouring to keep aloft.

As the plane swung around it flew slowly towards the Bund, gaining
altitude as in went. Then the craft was above the perpendicular junction of
Nanking Road and the Bund, where the Cathay Hotel and Palace Hotel
occupy the opposite corners of the junction. The plane was even now so

low in the sky that I could make out the pilot's leather-clad head and aviator's goggles.

A dark object detached itself from the undercarriage of the craft.

I threw myself to the ground. Then came a violent explosion, a gout of flame and black smoke. A wave of hot air rushed over me like a desert wind. My ears fell momentarily deaf. As they cleared I could hear, above the screams, the sound of the aircraft slowly and laboriously lumbering away, engine spluttering, flying towards the west.

I stood up and looked towards the Cathay. I froze for a moment simply trying to gather my wits.

There was a huge crater in the road, and I saw human bodies thrown around like toys scattered by an angry giant. Cars were squashed like tin cans. The facades of the two hotels were blackened by smoke; every window was shattered, the glass littering the ground like hailstones. People slowly began to stand up and I saw men, women and children, covered in blood, stunned and moving like sleepwalkers.

In the background the incessant murmur of the war from Nantao and Chapei continued, like a summer thunderstorm that would not go away. Dull rumbling, high pitched whines, and plumes of smoke rising in the air from north and south.

My instinct was to run to the bombsite and help. But I had Katya to think of. I stood for a moment, paralysed with indecision.

A black car, a Ruxton, pulled up at the curb. The front passenger door swung open. Sitting behind the wheel was Sergeant Freddie Wang, now wearing a smart navy pinstripe suit.

'Michael, get in.'

'I'm sorry, Freddie, I can't come with you now.'

'Get in the car.'

'I told you I don't have time.'

'Listen to me. I know about Katya, and Jamie Flyte and all that.'

I jumped in the passenger seat and slammed the door. My mind was spinning. I was in shock from the bombing, scared for Katya and I didn't know what to make of Freddie any more. He'd offered me his friendship, I'd learned more about China from him than any other person, but he seemed to be forever turning up when my life was in danger. I didn't know if he was friend or foe, or both.

'You better take me somewhere and tell me what you know. I hope it's important. There are people back there who need all the help they can get,'

I said sharply, as the car pulled into the traffic. 'So, I think you had better tell me exactly what you know and how you know it, Freddie, and the truth this time.'

'Michael, I am a member of the Chinese Communist Party.'

'You're kidding me!'

'No, I'm dead serious.'

'But SMP men, your own comrades, have been killed by the Communists!'

'That is regrettable.'

'For God's sake, Freddie, your own comrades! Men you trained with. Men you sat down and ate meals with.' I was angry now. Freddie was the enemy. I could have shot him on the spot and been congratulated for it by my comrades.

'I have been a member of the Party for many years, since my undercover work with the rickshaw coolies. What I encountered in the world of rickshaw coolies would turn any man communist.'

'Even so, Freddie. The Reds, for God's sake!'

'Sometimes a man finds that he must live with ambiguity for the sake of his country. As your father experienced in Ireland.'

'It's not the same!' I was furious now. How dare he compare this with my father's dilemma?

'It's exactly the same, Michael. My country is in a poor state and is occupied by foreign powers. Naturally, a man begins to think of his priorities.'

'Jesus Christ, Freddie!'

'Do you know what finally decided it for me, Michael? One night, it must have been ten years ago, I was working undercover as a rickshaw coolie and I saw two SMP constables beat up a rickshaw man. They did it for entertainment. They beat him to a pulp and then threw him into Soochow Creek. I intervened, and identified myself as an undercover SMP man.'

'Jesus! Did you stop them?'

'They laughed at me and punched my face. They pulled their service pistols on me and threatened to kill me.'

'What did you do?'

'I lost my self-respect. I bowed and *kowtowed* and begged for my life. They laughed and called me a "dirty little Chink." But they let me go. Well, Michael, no communist ever called me a "dirty little Chink." From that moment, I was a dedicated Party man.'

'I see.' Despite everything, I could understand how he felt. Humiliation is a terrible thing and a powerful motivator for revenge.

'I have never done anything that would compromise any member of the SMP. I believe in good police work in this cesspit of a city.'

'All right then. I haven't time to argue about it. Now what did you want to tell me?'

'The Party is very interested in Jamie Flyte. He is a significant source of funding and intelligence for the KMT. He's also tied up with Lu Sun Yu. My people want to acquire the contents of that map case that you took from Mister Flyte. We intend to access his numbered Swiss bank accounts. Revolutions don't come cheap.'

'And how come you are so well informed?'

'Special Branch files.'

'Of course!' I replied.

'But I also have my own private Special Branch.'

'What do you mean?'

'Every rickshaw coolie in this city works for me. I can find out when and where any man in this city breaks wind. It's a shame you shot my man yesterday. He is alive, I'm pleased to report.'

'So, where do we go from here?'

'We have a common interest, Michael. You wish to save your girl. My people wish to put Mister Flyte out of action and get hold of his accounts. We haven't much time.'

'Very well, Freddie.' I could see the benefit in an alliance of convenience.

'Oh, one more thing, Michael. I no longer use that name. My Chinese name, my only name, is Wang Xiao Ming.'

* * *

We parked across the street from the Great World.

In the distance, I heard the sound of the battle. High up in the clear blue sky a couple of Chinese Air Force Northrops flew in slow circles, still attempting to land a bomb on the Japanese ships on the river. I felt a cold chill run down my back when I thought of the carnage I'd seen on the Bund. But no time for that now. I had Katya to think about.

I took the leather map case out of the car and we crossed the busy corner of Tibet Road and Avenue Edward VII and made our way to the main entrance of the Great World.

The building had become a refugee centre. Whole families had camped out in the corridors and stairways. The chatter of voices was deafening. In corners, families had piled up mounds of the possessions they had travelled with. Tables, chairs, mattresses, pots and pans, and bundles of clothing tied up in sheets. A few traders remained open but most shopkeepers had closed their doors under this onslaught of unwashed farmers who, a week ago, probably had never even heard of the Great World.

We took the stairs to the fifth floor. The throngs of refugees were on every floor, all the way to the top of the building. Finally we arrived at the entrance of the Savoy Cinema. The door was locked, and a big, burly White Russian bodyguard, with an obvious bulge under the tightly fitting jacket of his dark suit, prevented refugees from getting inside.

Wang and I approached him, flashed our police badges and demanded that he gives us entry.

We stepped inside to find ourselves in a plush, softly lit, but completely empty, cinema.

The deep crimson seats looked soft and inviting. The carpet was thick with an attractive pattern of multicoloured swirls—it muffled our footsteps. Red theatrical curtains, tied off at the bottom by thick golden cords, covered the screen. An overhead balcony faced the large cinema screen. We walked to the rear of the cinema and found the door that led to the projectionist's room. At the top of the stairs were two doors: one marked 'Projection' and the other 'Manager.'

I leaned close to the manager's door and heard a very soft murmur of voices.

I put my hand on the door handle, hesitated for a moment and looked at Wang. He met my eye and nodded. I opened the door and stepped inside.

The office was plush and expensively appointed with soft lighting. Heavy, polished wood bookshelves dominated the room. On another occasion it would have been a very pleasant room indeed, but I didn't have time for such thoughts now. Behind a large desk sat Jamie Flyte. He wore a sharp business suit, charcoal grey, and a red carnation in his buttonhole. Sitting in front of him was Katya. She looked thin and exhausted.

Standing behind her was a uniformed senior Public Safety Bureau officer and three KMT soldiers with rifles slung on their shoulders. Standing off to one side was Jack Dell. Jack raised his hand to his forehead in a lazy approximation of a salute, an amused twinkle in his eyes.

'Ah, Michael,' said Jamie as if he was delighted to see us. 'I was just handing this young communist insurgent over to the authorities. Now, please return my property.'

'We have an arrangement.'

'Well now, Michael, I might be tempted to renege on the man who caused the death of my wife.'

I looked to Katya. She was pale and drained with fear. Her eyes pleaded with me. I moved towards her and put a hand on her shoulder.

I placed the leather map case on Jamie's desk. He reached for it and put it in his desk drawer.

'It will be all right,' I said to Katya.

Jack raised his arm, his pistol pointing square into my chest. 'I think I'll just kill the lot of you right now.'

'Relax, Jack, all in good time,' said Jamie. 'Why don't you disarm them first?'

Jack smiled menacingly and said, 'Put your weapons on the table now like good lads.' I reached for my pistol and signalled for Freddie to do the same. As I glanced towards Freddie, I saw him nod to me, almost imperceptibly.

I held my pistol by its barrel and placed it on the polished desktop and slowly positioned myself as close to Jamie as I could.

I spoke, my voice high and strained. 'Please, Jack, Jamie, for old times' sake don't end it like this. For God's sake, we're all old friends.' As I spoke I relaxed my muscles and allowed myself to feel the shock of the bombing; I let the stress and trauma and exhaustion flow through my muscles. I began to shake and slowly sank into a crouch. My body trembled like a leaf; I allowed the shock of the bombing to express itself, as I moaned, 'Oh please, no, no.'

'You're a right fucken girl, Michael,' Jack growled. But he relaxed his guard and lowered his weapon. I slowly moved my right hand inch-by-inch until I could touch the stiletto knife strapped to my ankle. I inhaled deeply all the way down to my stomach. In one sudden explosive movement I sprang up, launching myself at Jamie. We went crashing to the ground behind the desk, a tangle of arms and legs. But then I had him in a headlock, knife pressed to his throat.

From the other side of the desk I heard grunts and the sound of fists connecting to flesh.

'Hold your fire, hold your fire,' Jamie shouted in his best Sandhurst voice.

I stood, pulling Jamie up with me, the blade never leaving his throat, Freddie stood in the middle of the room, his feet wide, his knees bent and fists clenched, elbows by his chest, a classic Chinese martial arts stance. Bodies lay scattered on the floor.

'Just tell them to let us out of here alive, Jamie, that's all we want.'

'Everybody drop your weapons,' said Jamie.

Since we'd arrived, I had been peripherally aware of the buzzing aircraft, circling overhead.

Suddenly there was silence. In my mind I saw a sudden picture of this morning's broken bodies on the Bund.

'I think everyone should take cover, immediately,' I said calmly but firmly, addressing the whole room.

'Ah, don't be such a gobshite, Michael,' sneered Jack, as he picked himself off the ground, sounding angry enough to kill me with his bare hands.

I let go of Jamie, rushed to Katya, pushed her from the chair and dived on top of her.

* * *

The world exploded. A wave of powerful energy swept the room and threw us like chess pieces. My ears rang, a high-pitched shriek. My nostrils, eyes and throat burned with smoke.

When I opened my eyes, Katya was lying beside me. Her face was smudged. A bookshelf had fallen over and rested at an angle against the desk. It had acted as a shelter for Katya and me. I wiped my eyes and found my hand wet with blood.

I staggered to my feet. Through the thick, acrid smoke I saw a tangle of broken furniture, scattered books and broken bodies. The occupants of the room lay on the ground, some thrown on top of each other, mingled with books thrown from the shelves and the paraphernalia of Jamie's office. One of the soldiers lay nearby with his head almost detached from his shoulders. Jack Dell's lifeless eyes were open wide in surprise.

Katya gripped the leather map case. I took her hand and led her to the door. We shakily picked our steps down the stairs to the cinema. Most of the seats were smouldering and the air was thick with black, oily smoke. Visibility was very poor and the room was intensely hot. I stopped Katya and said, 'You must get out of the building. I have to find Wang.'

I ran back up the stairs to the ruined office and immediately saw that Wang was lying on the ground, the lower half of his body trapped under piles of debris. A part of the ceiling had collapsed on him. I started pulling at the pieces and then Katya was beside me. We worked furiously and within a minute or so Wang was free. Katya ran her hands over his legs and hips. 'Nothing broken,' she said. Wang stood, put his arm round my shoulders and tested his legs. 'I'm fine,' he said. The three of us went down the stairs and through the smouldering cinema.

We pulled the door open and stepped into the public corridor of the Great World.

Chapter 51

A SCENE FROM HELL AWAITED us. The floors were strewn with the bodies of the dead and dying. A black Bakelite telephone receiver lay on the floor with a bloodless, white hand clenching it.

We stumbled through the dark, down each flight of stairs until we reached street level. I don't know how long it took, but it felt like hours, stumbling down the bloody, corpse-laden stairs.

On the street, bodies were everywhere. A row of cars that had stopped at the traffic lights were scorched and burned, never to move again under their own power.

I looked up at the Great World. The middle of the building had collapsed like a wedding cake smashed by a giant fist. Flames and smoke plumed out of the top windows.

In the middle of the street was a huge crater, ten feet deep, rapidly filling with sandy-coloured water from a burst pipe. A man in the uniform of a French police captain ran up to me. It was Captain Lavelle. My thoughts became unemotional, robotic. '*What's he doing here? Of course, the French Concession starts on the other side of this street.*' He shouted at me and I realised that my hearing had come back.

'Inspector! We were bombed! We must organise help!'

'What happened?' I shouted back.

'It was the goddamn KMT air force,' he screamed back at me, flecks of spittle on his lips. 'They're still trying to bomb the Japanese cruisers on the river. They hit the Bund a while ago, and Nanking Road.'

'Yes, I was at the Bund. I saw it.'

'Boy-scouts trying to be war pilots. Stupid boys, they bomb their own people.'

I turned to Katya and said, 'Wait for me.'

I ran across Tibet Road to a small café. As I opened the door, a bell rang its welcome, but when I stepped onto the black and white tiles, my boots crunched on broken glass. A European man lay on the floor. He wore a white linen suit. Both his legs were gone from the knees down. Numbed from the carnage outside, the sight of this maimed man almost appeared normal by comparison.

I went to the public call box and opened the door, and, as I searched my pockets, I realised that I needed a five-cent coin to make the call. I desperately searched my pockets and found nothing. I left the phone box and went to the injured man, who looked at me, his face animated and comprehending.

I said, 'I'm sorry to trouble you, but I need a coin to make the call.'

He smiled ironically, *isn't life strange*, and with his hand reached into his suit pocket and pulled out a fistful of change.

I went back to the phone and dialled the number for Gordon Road.

I recognised the voice of Sergeant Kirlov.

'This is Inspector Gallagher. The Great World has been bombed from the air. There are casualties in the hundreds. Send all the help you have—phone the Chinese and the French too.'

'Yes, sir, immediately.'

I hung up and stepped out of the phone booth. My friend with the smart white suit was dead. I leaned down and closed his eyes. I hoped that the shock he felt would have blocked any pain.

* * *

Fire brigade, ambulances, doctors, nurses, and civilian volunteers came from all over the International Settlement, the French Concession and the Chinese area. An emergency centre was set up in a small hotel, the Duke of York, across the street from the Great World. The walking wounded were sent home. The emergency cases were packed, a dozen at the time, into ambulances and driven to hospitals all over the city. The dead and the severed limbs of the dead and dying were packed into furniture removalists' trucks and taken to the racecourse.

Katya worked with the wounded, using her medical skills. With the help of a Sikh SMP Sergeant, I coordinated the rescue teams that went into the ruins of the Great World building to bring out those still living. I wasn't in uniform but an SMP constable who recognised me loaned me his police cap as a temporary badge of office.

We worked for hours. French, SMP, and Chinese forces worked side by side, borders and uniforms forgotten in the extremity of the situation.

* * *

Uniformed men went in and out of the Great World carrying out the injured and maimed. Many had very serious injuries. The lucky ones were merely in shock, walking mechanically with glazed looks in their eyes.

Many adults walked out carrying dead children in their arms. I felt nothing. I was numb. However, my body appeared to have its own wisdom. Two tracks of tears slipped down my face, the salt lingering on my lips, as I wiped them away with the back of my hand.

Those who could walk did so, some with the assistance of rescue workers. It was a miracle that the entire building did not burn down, killing everyone who did not immediately escape.

I saw a French gendarme walking out of the ruins, guiding a man by the arm. He was a tall man and I could see that he had been very seriously burned. He walked with shoulders hunched, and eyes cast down towards the ground. He was completely bald, and without eyebrows. His ears appeared to have melted into the side of his head and his face was a shiny, glazed mass of scorched meat.

He looked towards me and the startling blue eyes of Jamie Flyte met mine. As the policeman led him towards the temporary hospital set up in the hotel lobby, Jamie continued to watch me until he was inside the building.

I spoke to the Sikh SMP Sergeant in my parade-ground voice. 'Sergeant, take over for ten minutes.'

I walked inside the hotel lobby and searched through the faces of the casualties lying on the mattresses that had been brought down from the hotel rooms. The entire lobby had been turned into an emergency hospital. Broken bodies lay on the mattresses, on couches, and even on tabletops. Doctors, including Katya, performed surgery with lights augmented with mirrors taken off the dining room wall.

Finally, I found Jamie lying on a mattress on a floor of a corridor leading off the lobby to the phone booths. A white sheet with the hotel's monogram covered him to chest level. A European doctor wearing a white coat, blood-soaked like a butcher, was just moving away from where Jamie lay. I caught the doctor's arm.

'Doctor, what is this man's condition?'

'He is in enormous pain, but I have given him a shot of morphine. It is helping him, now. Soon he will be asleep.

'Thank you, Doctor,' I said, then went on my knees and bent over Jamie.

Up close, his face was even worse than it had appeared on the street. If he lived, it was obvious that he would never be a normal man. In that moment, despite everything, I found that I felt compassion for him in this terrible state of injury.

'Michael, I wanted you to come,' he rasped, his voice like sandpaper.

I crouched down beside him and looked at him lying there.

His hand shot out from under the hotel blanket and he gripped my wrist with an amazing strength.

And then I thought the bastard was going to get away with everything, simply by dying before facing any retribution. I had no hope of revenge now.

His grip on my wrist grew stronger. He croaked again: 'For Christ's sake, Michael. Kill me, I beg of you.'

'Major James Flyte, I arrest you…'

He groaned and lifted his hand weakly as if to cut me off. But I persisted. This was so important to me. Otherwise, who would speak for my poor dead father? 'I arrest you on the charge of murder of Sergeant James Francis Gallagher of the Royal Irish Constabulary on the night of 20 August 1920.'

He gasped for breath, his breathing a struggle.

I felt his grip weaken and I just watched him for a moment. Then his strength rallied as the morphine took effect.

'I didn't shoot your father. It was Fiona. Just a stupid accident.'

'Jamie, for Christ sake, what are you saying?'

'Don't blame her, Michael. Everything was crazy, bullets flying in all directions, petrol bombs through the windows. In the confusion, she shot him with her father's revolver.'

'What?'

'It's the truth, no point in lies now. I'm dead.'

'But why, Jamie, it doesn't make sense? How come nobody told me?'

'It's my fault,' he gasped. 'That was my power over her. She was desperate to keep the truth from you.'

'I don't understand any of this.'

'Fiona didn't love me. She loved you. She chose a schoolboy over a war hero. It ate me up. I blackmailed her to keep her.'

'Why did you tell me that *you* did it?'

He pulled his ravaged face into a semblance of a smile. 'Revenge. I just wanted to hurt you...'

He slumped back into the mattress. The confession had taken the last of his strength. I watched Jamie's face. He was unrecognisable from the golden boy I had seen in 1920, the hero that I had worshipped, the brave and dashing servant of the empire. His body writhed in pain.

I knew then what I needed to do. I think what Fiona would have expected it of me, and my father as well. I leaned close to what was left of his ear and whispered, 'This is not revenge, Jamie. It's mercy.'

He nodded his head; speaking was now beyond his strength. His hand gripped my forearm again and he squeezed once, an agreement to my plan.

I gripped his throat in my right hand and pressed against his windpipe. He stopped breathing and within seconds he was dead. It was as easy as drowning a kitten. I pulled the sheet up over his face.

Then I went back to the street to the Sikh policeman, and said, 'All right, Sergeant, I'm back now.'

Chapter 52

WE WORKED LATE INTO THE night and into the following morning. As the sun came up, we were tired beyond words.

Finally, Katya and I had a chance to talk. We sat on the kerb, both holding mugs of strong sweetened tea given out by the Red Cross.

'Where's Wang?' I asked.

'He was following us out of the cinema. Then I didn't see him anymore.'

'I didn't see him either.'

I glanced upward. High up above the street was a billboard advertising 'The Awful Truth' starring Cary Grant and Irene Dunne. The poster was broadly spattered with blood and bits of human flesh.

'Let's go home,' I said to her.

Only a block from the Great World, the city continued as normal. Bars were busy, drivers honked their horns as they wove through the traffic, food vendors rang bells, and Singsong girls called out to customers. I flagged a taxi and we travelled to my apartment.

As our taxi edged through the busy streets I spoke to the driver and asked him to make a detour. The car stopped in front of a small shopfront on Canton Road.

'What's this?' asked Katya.

'Insurance,' I replied as I gripped the leather map case, and stepped out of the car. I walked through the door, a bell tinkling musically as I entered. Behind the counter stood Doctor Peng. For safety, he had moved his clinic inside the International Settlement after the battle of 1932.

'Ah, Michael, are you hurt? Isn't it terrible, the bombing?'

'I'm fine, Doctor. I just need a small favour.'

'Of course, happy to help.'

'Could you please hold this map case for me, just for a short time?'

'It is my pleasure,' he said, as I handed it across the dark wood counter.

* * *

We arrived at the front of the Greycliffe Building. I had to go upstairs for some coins, for I still didn't have any money in my pockets. When the driver was gone, we went to my rooms, threw off our bloody, smoke-blackened clothes and fell into bed without even so much as washing our faces. We slept the sleep of the dead.

17 August 1937

I awoke to hear a heavy and repeated knocking at the door. I struggled awake, got out of bed, pulled on a robe and went to the door.

'Who is it?' I called out.

'A friend,' was the reply. I recognised Wang's voice.

I opened the door, and there he stood, wearing a dark suit, a summer overcoat draped over his shoulders like a cape. Behind him stood three men, hard-faced and alert, radiating menace. They reminded me of Green Gang foot soldiers. I stepped aside and gestured for them to enter. This was a different Freddie Wang. He radiated authority and something more... now he was a dangerous man. I led them to the sitting room and Wang sat on an armchair facing the couch upon which I sat.

'I have come to discuss your future,' he said slowly, his textbook voice, at least, unchanged.

I nodded. I had seen enough bloodshed to last for the rest of my life.

A movement caught my eye; Katya was standing by the bedroom door, watching.

Numb from the carnage of the Great World bombing, I was saddened to think Shanghai would never be the same.

'Well, Wang, what happens now?'

'That depends upon you, Michael.'

'What do you want from me?' I asked.

'We can assist you in leaving this place. As I said to you a long time ago, you have no future here. There are many refugees leaving Shanghai now.'

'Why would you want to help me?'

'The Party requires you to surrender the information that you acquired from Mister Flyte.'

'It isn't here. I took a precaution and put them in a safe place.'

'I see. Well, we will not torture you. It's rather undignified for all concerned. What do you want, Michael?'

'Just guarantee to get us out of here, Freddie, and the map case and its contents are all yours.' I noticed a flash of irritation at my use of his English name.

Chapter 53

THE SMALL FRENCH-REGISTERED STEAMER WAS moored at the French-town docks. The dock itself was a scene of chaos as whole families lined up to walk up the gangplank. Babies screamed, children ran here and there, trying to make a game of it, adults clutched their hand luggage tightly to themselves.

This section of the dock was only two hundred yards from the old Chinese City of Nantao, and within its walls, a battle raged. The sounds of small arms fire, the crump of grenades, and the heavy thud of artillery was constant. Shells screamed overhead fired from the Japanese artillery located four miles north in Chapei and fell with deadly accuracy into Nantao.

Katya and I stood by the entrance of the dock, its watchman's hut unmanned, the glass shattered. We stood, two people without money or safe travel documents. For certain, the KMT would arrest and kill both of us if we travelled on my legitimate passport. To them, Katya was a communist spy and I was the helpmate of communist spymaster Wang Xiao Ming. No SMP rank would protect me from their vengeance.

I held Jamie's map case tightly.

Freddie's black car pulled up at the entrance of the dock. He and his bodyguards got out and approached us. He reached inside his jacket and extracted a thick yellow envelope.

He held it up and said, 'French passports for both of you. Money and tickets and a bit extra to begin a new life. Not a fortune but more than most have. I only require the leather map case.'

'I'm just wondering, Freddie,' I said. 'As a good intelligence officer, shouldn't you have killed us to cover the theft of Jamie's money by the party?'

'Well, we could. But it is not quite that simple. I owe you a debt.'

'You surprise me, Freddie.' Wang was silent for a moment, gathering his thoughts, unruffled by the sound of nearby battle.

'During the White Terror, you were involved in a raid on a boarding house on Museum Road.'

'I remember.'

'There was a young couple. You allowed them to escape through a roof skylight. Why did you do that?'

'I knew the girl. But mainly, I realised that if we handed them over to the KMT they would have been shot or beheaded. I'd had more than enough of beheadings already.'

'That young man was my brother. He and his fiancée survived the White Terror and are still alive and well. They live in Peking now. My family owes you a personal debt, Michael.'

'Very well then, I accept your repayment with thanks,' I said. 'I cannot imagine us staying here now.'

I handed the map case to Freddie. He turned and handed it to one of his young gunmen. Then he passed me the yellow envelope.

We shook hands and he said, 'Good luck to you. The Party will not forget.'

* * *

The French officer standing at the gangplank with clipboard in hand urged people to walk calmly but briskly onto the ship.

We both showed him the French passports bearing our photographs. The plan was to sail directly from Shanghai to Hanoi, and there we could choose one of the French liners sailing to all points of the globe. We had enough cash for two second-class tickets. From Hanoi, I would send a telegram to the Shanghai Municipal Police, giving my resignation.

* * *

The French steamer sailed down the Whampoo River, nudging past the Japanese naval ships, the sampans, sailboats, sand barges and the detritus of the river. Katya and I stood at the railing. Around us, passengers scanned the sky warily, expecting an aircraft to peel off and bomb or strafe our ship at any moment.

The Bund looked the same as ever, but a cloud of black smoke haloed the entire city. The fire of war and the smog of industrial pollution merged into a filthy soup that hung lifeless over the city.

'I will not miss it,' she said to me.

I held her in my arms and turned towards the river mouth and away from the city. Looking east, towards the sea, the sky was fine and sunny. A crisp breeze blew with just a hint of rain.

A note from the author

Growing up in Limerick City in Ireland, I spent every summer holiday at my maternal grandmother's dairy farm in County Limerick. On the wall of the farmhouse was an old black-and-white studio photograph of a serious young man in a formal suit, accompanied by four young Chinese men in silk robes. This was my great-uncle, I was told, my grandmother's brother, who along with a second brother, served as Sub-Inspectors in the Municipal Police in Shanghai, China in the 1920s.

As a child I spent many hours staring at this photograph and imagining the adventures my granduncles must have had. Thirty years later, I found myself living in Sydney, Australia, working in the international education sector and teaching students from Shanghai. I began taking frequent trips to Asia, and grew to love the exciting energy of the major cities such as Shanghai, Hong Kong, Tokyo, Kobe and Singapore.

To research the novel I travelled to Brandeis University, Boston where the top secret files of the Shanghai Municipal Police Special Branch are kept on microfilm since they were smuggled out of Shanghai by the CIA in 1949.

All characters appearing in 'Gangsters of Shanghai' are fictitious. Any resemblance to real persons, living or dead, is purely coincidental. Burleigh Castle and its occupants exist only in my imagination.

The major background events in the novel are entirely accurate, no matter how outlandish they may appear to the reader. Shanghai between the wars was a strange, exciting and dangerous place.

Omnia Juncta In Uno (All joined as one)
Motto of the Shanghai Municipal Police

Gerry O'Sullivan

Special Thanks

I would like to thank the following people for their help and encouragement. My wife Yumi and daughter Sophia who kept me smiling throughout, and to whom the book is dedicated, my brother Jim O'Sullivan, Patrick Moloney, Colette and Sam Moloney, Robert Johnston, David Moore, Julie Thoms, Holly Riva, Amanda Thoms, my long-time friends and business partners Ray Rose, Arthur Treibs and Kiaran Green. Rowland Fishman and his team at the Writers Studio, Sydney, helped get me started. Michael Domeyko Rowland, creator of the Screen Storywriter Course kept me on track. The Peng family introduced me to the city of Shanghai. My friend Robert Kirby is the foremost expert on Reichian psychotherapy in Australia. Thanks to Liam Kirby for the cool movie recommendations. Jim Parsons provided great advice on story structure. Nic Karandonis gave me much needed encouragement and professional validation, and Jason Fisher and David Yip gave me very helpful encouragement and feedback. Michael Alvear had very insightful advice on the new world of e-books and book marketing. Claude Lambert and Damien Peters expertly edited the second edition. Thanks to Kenny Chew and Eunice Ong for their hospitality during our stay in Singapore while writing the book.

I would like to thank the following institutions:

The Australian Society of Authors
Sydney Writers Room
The University of Limerick, Ireland
Brandeis University, Boston, USA
The Shanghai Library, China
The Shanghai Police Museum, China
The Hong Kong Police Museum, Hong Kong
City of Sydney Public Library
State Library of NSW
National Library of Singapore
National Museum of Singapore
Asian Civilisations Museum Singapore

Background and Further Reading

There are several excellent books available that tell the story of the city of Shanghai from the 1840s to the 1940s.

My stories' protagonist (an entirely invented character) is the son of a Royal Irish Constabulary sergeant. To research the RIC and life during Ireland's War of Independence (1919 to 1921) I referred to various books, listed below.

For a description of family life in an RIC Barracks I am grateful for 'The Irish Policeman 1822 – 1922: A Life' by Elizabeth Malcolm. I was given a copy of the book by the author's brother, Robert Johnston, my friend and neighbour in Sydney.

The following books are recommended for further reading:

Shanghai between the wars

Shanghai, Harriet Sergeant, John Murray, 1991
Shanghai, 1842 – 1949: The Rise and Fall of a Decadent City, Stella Dong,
    William Morrow, 2000
Secret War in Shanghai, Bernard Wasserstein, Profile Books, 1998
Old Shanghai: A Lost Age, Wu Liang, Foreign Language Press, 2001
Madame Chiang Kai-Shek, Laura Tyson Li, Atlantic Monthly Press, 2006
In Search of Old Shanghai, Lynn Pan, Joint Publishing Co., 1982
Old Shanghai, Gangsters in Paradise, Lynn Pan, Cultured Lotus, 1984

The Shanghai Municipal Police

Empire Made Me, Robert Bickers, Alan Lane, 2003
The Legend of W. E. Fairbairn Gentleman & Warrior, Peter Robins &
    Nicholas Tyler, CQB, 2005
Policing Shanghai 1927–1937, Frederic Wakeman Jr, University of
    California Press, 1995

The Shanghai Badlands: Wartime Terrorism and Urban Crime, 1937–1941, Frederic Wakeman Jr, Cambridge University Press, 1996

Shanghai Municipal Police Files 1894–1949 (Microfilm) Brandeis University Library

Social, cultural and art history of Shanghai

Shanghai Style, Art and Design Between the Wars, Lynn Pan, Long River Press, 2008

Shanghai A Century of Change in Photographs 1843–1949, Lynn Pan, Hai Feng Publishing Co, 1993

Assignment Shanghai Photographs on the Eve of Revolution, Jack Birns Ed, Carolyn Wakeman & Ken Light, University of California Press, 2003

Shanghai Girl Gets All Dressed Up, Beverley Jackson, Ten Speed Press, 2005

Selling Happiness, Calendar Posters and Visual Culture in Early Twentieth Century Shanghai, Ellen Johnston Laing, University of Hawaii Press, 2004

Changing Clothes in China, Antonia Finnane, Colombia University Press, 2008

Shanghai The Growth of the City, Joan Waller, Compendium, 2008

Tales of old Shanghai – webpage reproduction of 1930s Shanghai guide-book: http://www.earnshaw.com/shanghai-ed-india/tales/tales.htm

Jewish refugees in Shanghai

Shanghai Diary, A Young Girl's War: From Hitler's Hate to War-Torn China, Ursula Bacon, Milwaukie Press, 2002

British Colonial Life

Plain Tales from the British Empire, Charles Allen, Abacus, 1975, 1979, 1984, 2008

The Royal Irish Constabulary and Ireland's War of Independence

The Irish Policeman, 1822-1922: A Life, Elizabeth Malcolm, Four Courts Press, 2002

The Royal Irish Constabulary – a Short History and Genealogical Guide, Jim Herlihy, Four Courts Press, Dublin, 1997

The Black and Tans, Richard Bennett, Spellmount Staplehurst, 1959, 2001

British Voices from the Irish War of Independence 1918–1921, William Sheehan, The Collins Press, 2005

Guerrilla Days in Ireland, Tom Barry, Anvil Books, 1949, 1981

Michael Collins, Tim Pat Coogan, Arrow, 1991

Wilhelm Reich and Reichian Psychotherapy

Character Analysis, Wilhelm Reich, Farrar, Strauss and Giroux, 1933, 1980

The Mass Psychology of Fascism, Wilhelm Reich, Farrar, Strauss and Giroux, 1933, 1970

Filling Your Cup, Robert Kirby, Self Empowerment Pty Ltd, 1997

Made in United States
Troutdale, OR
10/12/2023